MW01631854

SAINT CATHERINE OF SIENA

EFFIGIES S. CATHARINÆ SENENSIS, QVAM PICTOR
IN PARIETE ECCLESIÆ S. DOMINICI DE SENIS,
DVM VIRGO EXTASIM PATIEBATVR, COLORIBVS
EXPRESSIT ANN. MCCCLXVII.

From the "Opere Della Serafica Santa Caterina da Siena, 1707.

SAINT CATHERINE OF SIENA

A STUDY IN THE RELIGION, LITERATURE AND HISTORY OF THE FOURTEENTH CENTURY IN ITALY

EDMUND G. GARDNER, M.A.

Author of 'Dante's Ten Heavens,' [illegible]
'Dukes and Poets in Ferrara,' [illegible]

[illegible] mirano nella luce del cognoscimento [illegible]

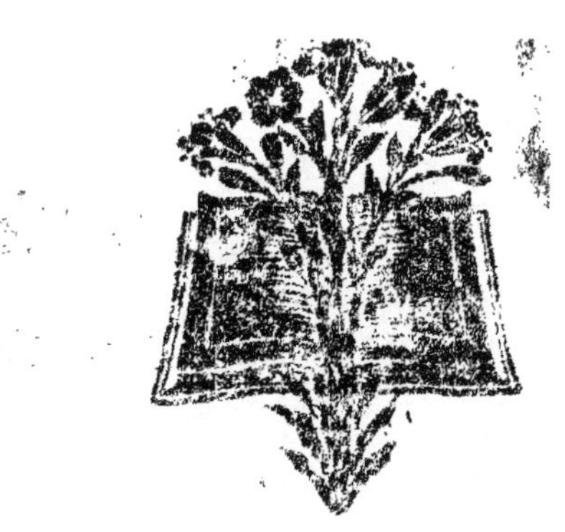

[illegible]

LONDON: J. M. DENT & CO.
NEW YORK: E. P. DUTTON & CO.

SAINT CATHERINE OF SIENA

A STUDY IN THE RELIGION, LITERATURE AND HISTORY OF THE FOURTEENTH CENTURY IN ITALY

BY

EDMUND G. GARDNER, M.A.

Author of 'Dante's Ten Heavens,' 'The Story of Florence,'
'Dukes and Poets in Ferrara,' 'The King of Court Poets,' etc.

"*Entriamo nella casa del cognoscimento di noi.*"

MCMVII

LONDON: J. M. DENT & CO.
NEW YORK: E. P. DUTTON & CO.

RICHARD CLAY & SONS, LIMITED,
BREAD STREET HILL, E.C., AND
BUNGAY, SUFFOLK.

Henry W Sage

To

MY FRIEND

MAUD F. JERROLD

PREFACE

In this book I have not attempted to write the conventional biography of a canonized saint, but a study in Italian history centred in the work and personality of one of the most wonderful women that have ever lived—the successor of Dante in the literature and religious thought of Italy, the connecting link between St. Francis of Assisi and Fra Girolamo Savonarola in the strange pageant of the progress of the mystical chariot of the Spouse, which the divine poet saw in part on the banks of Lethe in the Earthly Paradise. While devoting my attention mainly to Catherine's own work and her influence upon the Italian politics of her age, I have endeavoured at the same time to make my book a picture of certain aspects, religious and political, of the fourteenth century in Italy—the epoch that immediately followed the times of Dante, the stormy period in the history of the Church of which Petrarca and Boccaccio witnessed the beginnings. It may, indeed, be said that so much attention has been paid to Italian history of late years, and so many fresh sources of original information made accessible in every direction, that a new life of the woman who was the truest and most single-hearted patriot of her age seems not only permissible, but even—from the scientific point of view—necessary. In this undertaking, I have been greatly aided by the manuscripts still preserved of Catherine's letters, manuscripts full of unpublished matter which has hitherto been unaccountably neglected, having apparently escaped the notice of all her biographers and editors : matter which throws light upon every aspect of the Saint's genius, and has enabled me, at many points, to correct the hitherto accepted chronological order of her writings and the events in her life to which they refer.

Our contemporary materials for the life of Catherine of Siena, apart from isolated documents and the general history of her times, are derived from five principal sources: the *Vita* or *Legenda* (known as the *Legenda prolixa*, or, in Italian, *Leggenda maggiore*); the *Processus*; the *Supplementum*; the *Legenda abbreviata* (*Leggenda minore*, in Italian); and Catherine's own *Letters*.

(1) In 1384, four years after the Saint's death, Fra Raimondo delle Vigne of Capua, who had been her third confessor and chief director, and was then master-general of the Dominicans, began his admirable history of her, the *Vita* by excellence, which, in one of his letters, he calls: *Sanctae Matris Catharinae eximia Legenda*. This was finished in 1395. Raimondo's Latin text was first published in 1553 at Cologne (an edition now of the utmost rarity), and has been re-edited by the Bollandists in the third volume of the *Acta Sanctorum* for April. An Italian version, begun by one of the Saint's secretaries, Neri di Landoccio Pagliaresi, and finished by a native of Piacenza, whose name is unknown, was printed at the Dominican convent of San Jacopo di Ripoli near Florence, by Fra Domenico da Pistoia and Fra Piero da Pisa, in 1477. Another edition, in which the second half of the translation is identical with that of the *editio princeps*, while the first half (up to the middle of Part II. cap. x. par. 5 in Pecci's version, or § 283 in the *Acta Sanctorum*) differs considerably, was printed at Milan in 1489; it is evidently the complete translation made by the anonymous scholar of Piacenza, at the bidding of Don Stefano Maconi.[1] Instead, however, of these, a comparatively modern translation by the Canonico Bernardino Pecci, first published by Girolamo Gigli at Siena in 1707, may be said to hold the field. While relying mainly on the Latin text of the *Legenda*, I have consulted the convenience of readers by giving references to the divisions of part, chapter, and paragraph in Pecci's version, the corresponding paragraphs in the *Acta Sanctorum* being indicated in brackets. Although French, German, and Spanish translations appeared in the sixteenth century, Raimondo's

[1] Cf. F. Grottanelli, Introduction to the *Leggenda minore*, pp. ix.–xiv., where, however, it has escaped his notice that these two editions do not contain the same translation. I have not been able to see the intermediate editions, Naples, 1478, and Milan, 1488, respectively.

complete work has never been translated into English. *The lyf of saint Katherin of Senis the blessid virgin*, which Caxton printed, contains only certain portions of it, freely rendered, with considerable omissions. Says the translator in his preface : "I leve of also poyntes of divynyte whiche passeth your understondyng and touche only maters that longeth to your lernying." The version by John Fenn, confessor to the English Augustinian nuns at Louvain, first published in 1609, is translated from the abridged Italian edition composed by the famous Dominican controversialist, Fra Ambrogio Catarino Politi of Siena, in the middle of the sixteenth century.

(2) Second in date and in importance to the *Legenda* comes the *Processus.* The fact that, although she had not yet been canonized by the Church, the feast of "a certain person called and named the blessed Catherine of Siena" was being annually celebrated in the Dominican convents and churches of Venice and elsewhere, and pictures of her were being painted for veneration in many places, led to complaints being made to Francesco Bembo, the Castello bishop of Venice. A sermon preached in SS. Giovanni e Paolo by a certain Fra Bartolommeo da Ferrara on the first Sunday of May, 1411, led to him and Fra Tommaso di Antonio Nacci Caffarini, one of Catherine's earliest followers and most intimate associates, who was then a friar in that convent, being summoned before the Bishop ; and the famous *Processus contestationum super sanctitate et doctrina beatae Catharinae de Senis* was the result. This is a collection of testimonies and letters by Catherine's surviving followers, and others who had come under her influence, edited (so to speak) by Fra Tommaso Caffarini between 1411 and 1413, with a few later additions. Complete manuscripts of this Process are preserved in the Biblioteca Comunale of Siena (MS. T. i. 3) and the Biblioteca Casanatense of Rome (MS. 2668, or XX. v. 10) ; the former dates from the fifteenth century (but is not, as sometimes stated, the original), while the latter is a copy of it made in 1710. Several of the more important contestations, including those of Fra Tommaso Caffarini himself, Fra Bartolommeo di Domenico, Don

Bartolommeo da Ravenna, and Don Stefano di Corrado Maconi, were published by Martène and Durand (from a manuscript in the Grande Chartreuse), in the sixth volume of their *Veterum Scriptorum et Monumentorum amplissima Collectio.* Three others of the least important had already been given in Mansi's Appendix to the fourth volume of Baluze's *Miscellanea.* The contestation of Stefano Maconi is practically the *Epistola Domni Stephani de gestis et virtutibus S. Catharinae*, to Fra Tommaso, given in its original by the Bollandists in the volume cited of the *Acta Sanctorum*, of which an Italian version is prefixed to Aldo's edition of Catherine's Letters and another appended to Pecci's translation of the *Legenda.* But several contestations of the very first importance, including those of Don Francesco di Vanni Malavolti, Pietro di Giovanni Ventura, and Fra Simone da Cortona—all of whom had been of the inner circle of Catherine's friends and associates—have never been printed in the original, and have only been made use of, to any considerable extent, by Augusta Drane, who had copies specially made for the library of the Dominican nuns at Stone. In the present volume, I refer to Martène and Durand as *Processus* simply, while quoting the unpublished contestations direct from the Casanatense manuscript, with occasional reference to the codex of Siena.

(3) The public cult of Catherine being now, as the result of the Process, firmly established and recognized by authority, the indefatigable Fra Tommaso Caffarini, about the year 1414, while prior of San Domenico at Venice, composed a kind of appendix or supplement to Fra Raimondo's great *Legenda:* the *Libellus de Supplemento legendae prolixae beatae Catharinae de Senis.* This work, which has never been published in its entirety, exists in a fifteenth century manuscript in the Biblioteca Comunale of Siena (MS. T. i. 2), and a copy, made in 1706 from the original MS. (then in the Archivio di San Domenico), is preserved in the Biblioteca Casanatense, the codex numbered 2360 (XX. vi. 36). The professed translation by Padre Ambrogio Ansano Tantucci, published at Lucca in 1754, is merely a paraphrase of certain portions of the work, with the translator's own comments and

explanations inserted as though they were a portion of the original. In the present volume, I refer to the Latin text in the Casanatense manuscript as *Supplementum*, and to Tantucci's version simply as "Tantucci."

(4) Shortly after he compiled the *Supplementum* (to which he refers), Fra Tommaso Caffarini wrote an abridgement in Latin of Fra Raimondo's *Legenda*, with a few slight additions and modifications based upon his own personal knowledge of Catherine's life and acquaintance with Sienese matters. This was known as the *Legenda abbreviata*, and was printed (still further curtailed) as the *Epitome vitae beatae Caterinae* [*sic*] *de Senis*, in the first volume of the collection of the lives of the Saints known as the *Sanctuarium* of Boninus Mombritius, at Milan, in 1479. The *Leggenda minore* is a beautiful Italian translation of the whole of Fra Tommaso's Latin abridgement by Catherine's beloved disciple, Don Stefano di Corrado Maconi, when prior of the Certosa of Pavia, a manifest labour of love which brings the list of contemporary lives of the Saint to an appropriate close. Don Stefano's work was published by Grottanelli at Bologna in 1868, together with a most precious collection of letters of Catherine's disciples and associates. It appears to have escaped the notice of Grottanelli, and of every one else as far as my knowledge extends, that (with the exception of the prologue and first two chapters, for which free translations of the second prologue and corresponding chapters of the *Legenda prolixa* are substituted) it had already been printed in the fifteenth century. A copy of this edition, without date or place of publication, is in the British Museum, and it is worth noting that the "Sermone a laude della venerabile vergine," given at the end of Grottanelli's work, appears in the older edition as the sixth chapter of the third part, as a recapitulation, by way of conclusion, of the contents of the book.

Besides these works, Fra Tommaso wrote, in collaboration with Fra Bartolommeo di Domenico, a little-known treatise on the Dominican third order of penance, and began a history of that reformation of the Dominican rule in Venice, with which these two friars, together with Fra Raimondo, were associated. These appear to have been composed shortly before 1408, and were first printed by Flaminio Cornaro, in vol. vii. of his *Ecclesiae Venetae antiquis monumentis illustratae*, Venice, 1749. The latter, especially, is full of most interesting documents and letters concerning the lives of Catherine's disciples in the years immediately following her death.

(5) Of St. Catherine's Letters, the originals of only six have been preserved—none of them being in her own hand, but all written at her dictation by one or other of her secretaries. Four of these (two in a merely fragmentary condition) are in the Biblioteca Comunale of Siena, in the famous manuscript numbered T. iii. 3. ; they are the letters to Stefano Maconi and Pietro di Giovanni Ventura, numbered 255, 258, 262, 264, in Gigli's edition, and 319, 320, 329, 332 in that of Tommaseo. A fifth, also addressed to Stefano Maconi (numbered 256 in Gigli and 365 in Tommaseo), belongs to the Confraternity of Santa Lucia in Siena. The sixth, addressed to Jacomo di Viva, is among the treasures left by the late Mr. Hartwell de la Garde Grissell to the Jesuit church at Oxford, and was first published by Messrs. Frank Rooke Ley and Arthur Francis Spender in an article contributed by the latter to *St. Peter's* in 1899. It had not previously been included in any printed edition of Catherine's works, nor have I ever met with a copy of it in the manuscript collections.

In addition to these, there are a certain number of manuscripts containing copies of Catherine's letters, of which I have personally studied eighteen. Nine of these contain hitherto unpublished matter : in the Biblioteca Casanatense at Rome, MSS. 292 and 2422 ; in the Biblioteca Riccardiana at Florence, MS. 1303 ; in the Biblioteca Nazionale at Florence, MSS. xxxv. 199, xxxviii. 130, Palat. 57, Palat. 58, Palat. 60 ; in the British Museum, Harleian MS. 3480. The three Palatine MSS. and the Harleian MS. are fifteenth century copies, in one case complete, of the famous manuscript of the Saint's letters compiled by Stefano Maconi, now lost, which was once preserved in the Certosa of Pavia.

The first edition of Catherine's letters, published at Bologna in 1492, contains only thirty-one. Aldo Manuzio brought out what is regarded as the *editio princeps* at Venice in 1500, containing ostensibly 368 letters, but, in reality, allowing for repetitions, 350. This was the basis of three other editions printed at Venice in the sixteenth century; in 1548 (Toresano), 1562 ("al segno della Speranza"), and 1584 (Domenico Farri), respectively. In Girolamo Gigli's monumental *Opere della Serafica Santa Caterina da Siena*, the letters, illustrated by the learning of Padre Federigo Burlamacchi, occupy volumes ii. and iii. (Siena, 1713, Lucca, 1721); in this edition, which still remains the standard one, the number is brought up to 373. Niccolò Tommaseo's convenient edition in four volumes, published at Florence in 1860, is practically a reprint of Gigli and Burlamacchi, the letters being differently arranged, with a somewhat modernized and not always judiciously amended text.[1] A new and critical edition of Catherine's letters is greatly needed. In the following pages, for convenience of reference, I give the numbers in Tommaseo's edition, with those of Gigli in brackets, but, as far as possible, have revised the text of my quotations by collation with the manuscripts.

From the very outset, the biographical and historical value of Catherine's letters has been, to a considerable extent, impaired by the copyists (and the editors who followed them) omitting or suppressing passages which appeared to them of merely temporary interest, or not tending immediately to edification. A certain number appear to have been deliberately expurgated, in cases where the writer's burning words seemed likely to startle the susceptibilities of the faithful. This process seems to date back to the generation that immediately followed that of Catherine's original disciples. A striking instance is seen in a certain letter, of which the subject is sufficiently obvious, which Aldo introduces with the rubric: "To one whose name it is better not to write, because of certain words used in the letter. Let not whoso reads, or hears it read, wonder if the sense seems to him broken; for,

[1] An excellent selection from the letters, based on Gigli's text, has been published in English by Miss Vida D. Scudder (London, 1905).

where *et cetera* is written, many words are passed over, which it is not meet that every one should know, nor even the name of him to whom it went."[1] Neither these words nor the omissions are due to Aldo himself; the same heading occurs in every manuscript containing this letter which I have examined, and evidently dates back to the end of the fourteenth century. Other letters, though for different reasons, have been subjected to a similar process, with the general result that, even in the editions of Gigli and Tommaseo, the text is still sadly corrupt and too often mutilated. The printed versions of several apparently short letters are little more than the devout exhortations with which Catherine usually opened her correspondence, the real substance of what she had to say being in these cases still unpublished. Of peculiar interest and importance in this connection are two manuscripts which have hitherto strangely escaped the notice of students: the Casanatense MS. 292, and the MS. numbered xxxviii. 130 in the Biblioteca Nazionale di Firenze; both of which were evidently copied direct from Catherine's original letters. The former contains the full text of a number of those written in her name from Rome by Barduccio Canigiani; the latter the authentic and complete version of her correspondence with the Florentine tailor, Francesco di Pippino, and his wife, Monna Agnese, after the Saint's final departure from Florence. In an appendix to the present volume, besides six entirely new letters of St. Catherine, I print two of these latter in full, by comparison of which with the previously published versions, the reader may estimate the amount of work still to be done by whoso would restore to the world the true and complete correspondence of the seraphic virgin. I am not without hope of myself ultimately undertaking this task, unless some scholar in Italy should, in the meanwhile, accomplish it.

Catherine's great literary work, the *Dialogo*, was published at Bologna in 1472, at Naples in 1478, and at Venice in 1494. A number of editions were printed at Venice in the course of the sixteenth century. It was translated into Latin by Ser

[1] Letter 21 (306). Cf. *Dialogo*, cap. 124.

Cristofano di Gano Guidini and by Fra Raimondo ; the former's version remains in manuscript at Siena; that of Fra Raimondo was printed at Brescia in 1496, and at Cologne in 1553 and 1601. An English rendering of Fra Raimondo's Latin version, entitled *The Orcharde of Syon*, by Brother Dane James, was printed by Wynkyn de Worde in 1519. The vernacular text was reprinted by Gigli as the fourth volume of the *Opere*, in 1707, from a contemporary, but curiously inaccurate and incomplete manuscript, which he somewhat too readily accepted as the work of Stefano Maconi. In all these editions the Italian text is unsatisfactory ; but, though there have been alterations and some serious omissions made (amounting in one place, in every edition later than that published at Venice in 1517, to the greater part of two chapters), there has been no deliberate attempt at expurgation even in the most outspoken of its passages.[1] In making my quotations from the *Dialogo*, I have occasionally adopted a somewhat eclectic text, but have derived great assistance from the beautiful manuscript of Catherine's vernacular from the Biblioteca Barberini, now in the Vatican (*Cod. Barb. Lat.* 4063), which gives in many respects a much better reading than the printed versions, and one which is in more general accordance with Fra Raimondo's Latin interpretation of the work.

There is also ascribed to Catherine a short treatise on " Consummate Perfection," in somewhat the same form as the *Dialogo* ; a kind of spiritual conversation between the soul and her Creator upon the complete abnegation of self and the perfect fulfilling of the will of God. It was printed in Latin at Lyons in 1552, under the title: *Dialogus brevis Sanctae Catharinae Senensis, consummatam continens perfectionem.*[2] The Italian original has never been discovered, and only one manuscript of the Latin version appears to be known. An Italian translation, by Alessandro Piccolomini,

1 The *Dialogo* was well translated by Mr. Algar Thorold (London, 1896) ; but his new and abridged edition (London, 1907), which has the ecclesiastical *imprimatur*, omits the greater part of the terrible *Trattato delle Lagrime*.

2 Alphonsus Rodriguez, the Jesuit mystic, refers to it as St. Catherine's in his *Christian Perfection*, Pt. viii. cap. 12.

was published by Gigli as an appendix to his edition of the *Dialogo*, and was freely rendered into English by Augusta Drane. None of the Saint's early biographers or contemporaries make any mention of this work, which adds nothing to our knowledge of the thought and doctrine of the seraphic virgin. In the absence of any external evidence in its favour, I am disposed to regard its authenticity as highly questionable.

In dealing with the two great political struggles in which Catherine was engaged, I am much indebted to Alessandro Gherardi, *La Guerra dei Fiorentini con Papa Gregorio XI*, as also to his edition of the *Diario d'Anonimo Fiorentino*, and to the masterly work of M. Noël Valois, *La France et le Grand Schisme d'Occident*. The *pièces justificatives* published by the Abbé Gayet have often proved most useful. I have, however, in many cases preferred to go directly to the original documents bearing upon the Great Schism, still existing in the *Archivio Segreto* of the Vatican, by the aid of which I am able to give a somewhat full account of the origin of that extraordinary event.

My grateful thanks are due to the authorities and officials of the Vatican Archives and Vatican Library, of the Biblioteca Casanatense and Biblioteca Vittorio Emanuele at Rome, of the Biblioteca Nazionale and Biblioteca Riccardiana of Florence, and of the Biblioteca Comunale of Siena, for their kind assistance and never-failing courtesy; as also to the Canonico Vittorio Lusini of the Duomo of Siena, whose works on the churches of his native city are so highly valued by all students of Sienese matters, for his kindness in enabling me to have the opportunity of a more intimate study of the original letter of Saint Catherine to Stefano Maconi, now a treasured possession of the Confraternity of Santa Lucia in Siena.

E. G. G.

Siena,
In festo Nativitatis B. M. V.

CONTENTS

LIST OF ILLUSTRATIONS

SAINT CATHERINE OF SIENA

CHAPTER I

CATHERINE'S HIDDEN LIFE

"Soprastare alle passioni ed atti di tanta gioventudine pare alcuno parlare fabuloso."
—Dante, *Vita Nuova*, § 2.

"O stupor! O admiratio! O inaudita a seculis nostris familiaritatis ostensio!"—
Raimondo da Capua, *Legenda*, § 112.

CATERINA BENINCASA, whom we now call Saint Catherine of Siena, was born on March 25, 1347—the Feast of the Annunciation, which, according to Florentine and Sienese reckoning, was the first day of the new year. It was one hundred and twenty years since Saint Francis had died at Assisi in the arms of Lady Poverty, his mystical bride, and a quarter of a century since Dante had passed away in exile at Ravenna, again to behold Beatrice in the empyrean heaven of which he sang. These two men are Catherine's elder brothers in the spirit; the seraphic Father of Assisi, Standard-bearer of the Crucified, as the voice in the high vision on La Verna had hailed him, is her predecessor in the mystical life; she is the successor of the poet of the *Divina Commedia* in the history of religious thought in Italy.

Of her contemporaries, Francesco Petrarca was then nearly forty-three years old. Crowned six years before as poet laureate on the Capitol, he was now the literary dictator of Italy, but, in the year of Catherine's birth, was back in his Provençal home at Vaucluse, fighting with the Naiads (as he poetically puts it) who had destroyed his garden on the bank of the Sorgue during his long absence across the Alps. It was probably in this very year that he finished the first part of his *Canzoniere* for Madonna Laura with the sonnet "Arbor vittoriosa, triunfale," and he was about to open the second, nobler and more spiritual series of lyrics with the sublime canzone, "I' vo pensando": "For, with death at my side, I seek a new rule for my life, and I see the better but cling to the worse." Giovanni Boccaccio was thirty-four years old, and not yet the author of the *Decameron*. He had written his early prose romance and poems, had deserted or been deserted by his Fiammetta, and was now either at Florence or (as seems more likely) in Romagna at Forlì, under the protection of Francesco degli Ordelaffi. Geoffrey Chaucer, according to the most recent theories of the date of his birth, was a little boy of seven. Edward III of England had won the battle of Crécy in the previous year. Charles of Luxemburg, King of Bohemia, unworthy grandson of Dante's adored Henry, and son of the heroic blind King John who had fallen at Crécy, had been elected Holy Roman Emperor as Charles IV. From Avignon, Pierre Roger de Beaufort misruled the Church of Christ and profaned the throne of the Fisherman, under the title of Pope Clement VI.

The condition of Italy had altered but little since Dante had written his famous lament in the sixth canto of the *Purgatorio*. She was still "hostelry of sorrow," and not yet again "lady of provinces." "O wonderful poet," writes Catherine's contemporary, Benvenuto da Imola, "would that thou couldst come to life again now! Where is peace, where is liberty, where is tranquillity in Italy? Thou wouldst readily see, O Dante, that in thy time certain particular evils oppressed her; but these, indeed, were small and few; for thou dost enumerate among the woes of Italy the lack of a monarch and the discord of certain families; whereas now worse things oppress us, so that I can say of all Italy what thy Virgil said of one city: *Crudelis ubique luctus, ubique pavor, et plurima mortis imago.*[1] Assuredly, Italy suffered not such things in the time of Hannibal, nor in that of Pyrrhus, nor in that of the Goths or the Lombards. For Attila did not cross the Apennines, nor did Totila cross the Po, but only wasted Apulia and Rome. With how much greater excuse then, if it were lawful, could I cry out to the Almighty, than thou, whose lot was cast in happy times which all we now living in wretched Italy may well envy? Let Him then, who can, now

[1] *Aeneid*, II. 368, 369.

send the *Veltro* whom thou didst see in vision, if he is ever to come."[1] Although "Guelf" and "Ghibelline" had long lost all significance, the factions continued. The Italian cities either groaned beneath the heavy yoke of sanguinary tyrants, or, if they still ruled themselves as free republics, were torn by internal dissensions and harassed by fratricidal wars with their neighbours. And the anarchy of the country was intensified by the presence of the wandering companies of mercenary soldiers—Germans, Bretons, English, Hungarians—now in the pay of some despot, now in that of a republic, but always fighting for their own hands, levying large ransoms from cities as the condition of not devastating their territory and exposing the country-people to the horrors of famine.

The moral state of the land matched the political. The absence of the Popes, the example of the evil lives of the ministers of the Church, the growing immorality of high and low, were bringing religious life to a standstill in Italy. The Franciscan revival was utterly a thing of the past, while the encyclical letters of the Generals of the Dominicans testify to the deplorable degeneration of the Friars Preachers.[2] There is abundant evidence in the *Revelations* of Birgitta, and in the *Dialogue* of Catherine herself, that moral corruption was rampant in the convents and monasteries, amongst men and women alike. Many of the secular priests openly kept concubines; others were usurers; not a few followed the example of that bishop recorded by Dante, who was *trasmutato d'Arno in Bacchiglione*, "translated from Florence to Vicenza," and did worse.[3] The spirit of worldliness, of wickedness in high places, stalked unabashed through the Church, while the three Beasts of Dante's allegory made their dens in the Papal Court.

In the year after Catherine's birth, 1348, the great Pestilence, brought, it was said, in two Genoese galleys from the East, swept over Italy, Provence, France, and Spain, and in the following year spread to England and the rest of Europe. Giovanni Villani, the

[1] *Comentum super Dantis Aldigherii Comoediam*, iii. p. 181.

[2] Cf. especially the encyclicals of Simon Lingonensis (1359) and Elias Raimundi (1368), *Monumenta ordinis Fratrum Praedicatorum historica*, tom. v. pp. 299, 306.

[3] Cf. *Inf.* xv. 106–114 with the *Dialogo*, cap. 124.

chronicler who could speak of Dante Alighieri as "our neighbour," was among the victims at Florence; the Laura of Petrarca's poetical homage at Avignon; Ambrogio Lorenzetti, the supreme painter of allegory, at Siena. In Italy, the scourge did not rage everywhere with equal violence; Milan and other cities near the Alps suffered comparatively little; Florence and Siena endured its worst horrors. For the five months during which it devastated these two cities, from April or May till the beginning or end of September, all civic life was suspended, and about four-fifths of the population perished. Peculiarly appalling is the account given by the Sienese chronicler, Agnolo di Tura. Men and women felt the fatal swelling, and suddenly, while they spoke, fell dead. All natural and religious bonds seemed annihilated. Without any ecclesiastical ceremony, the abandoned dead were thrown indiscriminately into great trenches hastily dug in different parts of the city, and roughly covered up with a little earth to keep them from the dogs. "And I, Agnolo di Tura, called Grasso, buried five of my sons in one trench with my own hands." Men said that the end of the world had come. Bernardo Tolomei, the founder of the Olivetani, came down with his white-robed monks from the security of secluded Monte Oliveto, to labour among the sufferers in the streets of Siena and the other Tuscan cities, and, with many of his brethren, died in the work. He had fewer imitators in his own city than among the Florentines. Matteo Villani, who took up his brother's pen, tells us that at Florence many who devoted their lives to the service of the plague-stricken either escaped entirely, or, if they took the infection, recovered, and their example encouraged others to similar charitable effort. To him it seemed like a second universal deluge, sent as a divine punishment for the sins of men.[1] It is, indeed, in some

[1] Matteo Villani, i. 1, 2; *Cronica Sanese*, coll. 123, 124; *Il Polistore* (*Rer. It. Script.*, xxiv.), cap. 32; *Cronica di Pisa*, coll. 1020, 1021. The statements of contemporaries that 80,000 persons died in Siena, and 96,000 in Florence—incredibly appalling though they seem—are probably more or less accurate. During the decade preceding the pestilence, the population of Florence was between 120,000 and 125,000. The survivors numbered not more than 30,000. In 1351, the population of Florence was still under 50,000. Cf. N. Rodolico,

sort, a black flood across the ages, severing the Italy that had been Dante's from the Italy that was to be Catherine's.

Petrarca, as we know from the famous note on the margin of his Virgil, was at Parma when the news of Laura's death reached him; his *Trionfo della Morte* idealizes this fearful time into an impassioned homily on the transitoriness of all earthly greatness. Boccaccio was apparently at Naples, where, in the following year, he began his *Decameron* with the rhetorical description of the pestilence at Florence, the details of which he had not personally witnessed. The passed horrors had no permanent effect for good on men's minds, and those who believed that a great renovation of the world would ensue were speedily disillusioned. Restraint and convention had been cast off; riot and excess of every kind followed among the survivors. The deserted streets rang with the shouts of revellers or echoed to the fierce cries of brawlers. Lust, pride, and avarice tightened their grasp on men's souls. "Without any restraint," writes Matteo Villani, "almost all our city plunged into evil living, and the same and worse did the other cities of the world. And, according to the tidings that we could hear, there was no part in which those who had escaped from the divine anger lived in continence, but as though they deemed the hand of God was weary." Scarcity and famine followed in many places; work kept for long at a standstill; everywhere dissensions and quarrels arose over questions of heritage and succession. Not even the characteristic gaiety of the Sienese could hide the appalling desolation of their city: *per Siena non pareva che fusse persona.*[1] The cynical and shameless stories of the *Decameron* paint the corruption of the following years with the master's hand. Exaggeration, doubtless, there is, and the writer's hatred of the priests and their allies has coloured his pen; but the reader of certain terrible chapters of Catherine's *Dialogue*, written not quite thirty years later, will find only too striking confirmation of Boccaccio's testimony.

La Democrazia Fiorentina nel suo tramonto, pp. 29–39. These figures do not include the contado.

[1] Cf. M. Villani, i. 4, 5; *Cronica Sanese*, coll. 124, 125.

SAINT CATHERINE OF SIENA

The house in which Catherine was born still stands, albeit transfigured—not irreverently nor impiously—by generations of worshippers, on the side of that third of Siena's hills that rises opposite the Duomo over the deep and fragrant Vallepiatta, the hill which is crowned by the great red-brick church of the Friars Preachers, San Domenico. A little further down towards one of the city gates, a gate famous in the annals of Siena's wars, is "her deep green spring," Fonte Branda, from which we can still, with the poet of the *Songs before Sunrise*, gaze "up the sheer street":—

> "And the house midway hanging see
> That saw Saint Catherine bodily,
> Felt on its floors her sweet feet move,
> And the live light of fiery love
> Burn from her beautiful strange face."

Catherine's family belonged to the class and faction known as the *Dodicini*, or *popolo minore*, "to wit, of that rank of people that then ruled and governed the city of Siena." Her father, Jacomo di Benincasa, was a dyer, a simple and God-fearing citizen, pure in heart and gentle in speech, such a one as Giotto or Simone Martini might have painted for one of the first followers of Him whom men reputed the carpenter's son of Nazareth. Her mother, Lapa di Puccio di Piagente, was the daughter of a citizen of the same class of life, who seems to have been also a poet—as many a *popolano* of that time in Tuscany was: "a woman," writes Fra Raimondo, "utterly alien from the corruption of our times, albeit she was exceedingly careful and busy over the affairs of her household and family, as all those who know her are aware, for she is still alive." At the time of the Saint's childhood, her father was a fairly rich man, and the family all lived together in the house where his workshop was. All that part of Siena is still redolent with the aroma of the dyers' and tanners' labours, and the strange, pleasant smell links the past and present of the people of the city, whose maiden daughter, in Raimondo's phrase, "was made the bride of the King of Heaven."

Lapa bore Jacomo a very large family of children. The names are known of five sons: Benincasa, Bartolommeo, Sandro, Niccolò, and Stefano ; and five daughters older than Catherine : Niccoluccia, Maddalena, Bonaventura, Lisa, and Nera. Bartolommeo, the second son, married Lisa di Golio (or, according to others, di Chimento) Colombini, who appears to have been a first cousin of Giovanni Colombini (the founder of the *Gesuati*), and who was destined to be very closely associated with Catherine in her life and work.[1] Of the daughters, Niccoluccia and Maddalena married Palmiero di Nese della Fonte and Bartolo di Vannino, respectively. Such was the refined purity of the atmosphere of the dyer's house that when Bonaventura, the third daughter, married a certain Niccolò di Giovanni Tegliacci, she was so appalled by the licentiousness of the conversation of her husband and his young friends that she fell seriously ill, and was only restored to health by her husband's conversion. This Bonaventura was Catherine's favourite sister. A twin-sister, christened Giovanna, was born at the same time as Catherine, but died shortly after. From her birth, the Saint, who was the only one of her younger children that Lapa was able herself to nourish, was the chief darling and best beloved of her mother out of all the family. She is usually stated to have been the youngest, but Raimondo says : "After Lapa had brought forth Catherine, she gave birth to another girl, who was called Giovanna, to renew the memory of the departed sister of Catherine ; and this was the last, after she had given birth to twenty-five children."[2] This second Giovanna, or Nanna, died when Catherine was sixteen years old ; the entry in the *Libro de' Morti* of San Domenico runs : "Nanna filia Jacobi Tinctoris sepulta est die xviii Aprilis, 1363."

As she grew up in childhood, Catherine became the darling of all the district round. "Verily," writes Fra Raimondo, "the

[1] Cf. G. Pardi, *Della Vita e degli Scritti di Giovanni Colombini.* Giovanni sends a message to Lisa in one of his letters (addressed to their cousin, Caterina di Tommaso Colombini, who founded the Gesuate nuns). Lisa's twin-sister Francesca, like her, became a Dominican tertiary.

[2] *Legenda*, I. ii. 1 (§ 26). The *Leggenda minore* (p. 10) makes Catherine Lapa's youngest child. Cf. Grottanelli, *Albero della Famiglia Benincasa*, in vol. i. of Tommaseo's edition of the Letters.

wisdom and the prudence of her talk, the sweetness of her holy conversation, nor tongue nor pen could easily describe. Those alone know it who experienced it. Not only her speech, but also her whole bearing had a strange power, whereby the minds of men were in such wise drawn to good and to delight in God, that all sadness was excluded from the hearts of those who conversed with her, and every mental weariness was driven out; nay, even the memory of all troubles departed, and so unwonted and so great a tranquillity of soul took its place, that each one, marvelling at himself, rejoiced with a new sort of joy, saying in his mind: It is good for us to be here, let us make here three tabernacles." We are surely back in the atmosphere of the *Vita Nuova*; not otherwise had Dante sung of his Beatrice in those golden sonnets of his youth; and even as the glorious lady of his mind "was called by many *Beatrice* who knew not what they were calling her," so many in Siena felt such delight in Catherine's childish wisdom and in her company "that, by a certain excess of joy, they took from her her proper name, calling her not Catherine but *Eufrosina*, nor know I by what instinct."[1] And even as "the name of that blessed queen Mary was in very great reverence in the words of this blessed Beatrice," so from her fifth year Catherine practised the most complete devotion to the Blessed Virgin, kneeling to salute her on every step as she passed up or down the staircase of her father's house.

To such a child, in such an age, visions began to come as a matter of course. She was in her sixth year when, as she returned with her brother Stefano from the house of their sister Bonaventura, and passed down the steep Vallepiatta towards the valley of Fontebranda, she looked up and saw, over the summit of the church of San Domenico, Christ seated on an imperial throne, clad in the papal robes, and wearing the tiara, attended by Sts. Peter and Paul, and the beloved disciple, John. He smiled upon her and blessed her, and the girl was absorbed in ecstasy, knew not where she was or what she did, until her brother, calling and pulling her by the hand, brought her back to the sounds of earth.

[1] *Legenda*, I. ii. 2 (§ 27). Cf. *Vita Nuova*, § § 2, 21.

Then she grew silent, began to abstain from food and cruelly to afflict her flesh, wandered to woods and caves to imitate the ancient anchorites of the desert, dreamed of entering the Dominican order in the disguise of a boy, or gathered other little girls of the same age around her, to join in her prayers and discipline themselves together with her. Burning every day more and more with the fire of divine love, she consecrated her virginity to Christ. This, in after years, she told her confessors, was when she was seven years old—which we should, perhaps, interpret as we do Dante's statement of the beginning of his love for Beatrice: "It was about the beginning of her ninth year when she appeared to me, and I saw her about the end of my ninth year."

But, when she had passed the age of twelve and was considered marriageable according to the customs of Siena, her sister Bonaventura, whom she loved exceedingly, and to whom she could refuse nothing, at their mother's instigation persuaded her to change for a while her mode of life, to dye her hair and adorn her person, dress becomingly, and conform with the fashions of their little world. She bewailed this bitterly in after times as a grievous sin, and did heavy penance for it, accusing herself of having loved her sister more than God; nor could all the comfortable exhortations of Fra Raimondo make her see it in any other light. Bonaventura died in August, 1362, and Catherine at once returned to her former mode of life. This, however, her father and brothers would not permit, especially after the death of the elder sister, whose husband had been a man of some importance among the adherents of the faction in Siena to which they belonged. They were resolved upon finding a husband for Catherine whose alliance would strengthen the position of their family in the city. Finding her, as they deemed, obstinate and undutiful, they had recourse to a certain Fra Tommaso della Fonte, one of the friars of San Domenico, who had been brought up in their house and was probably a relation of the husband of Catherine's sister Niccoluccia.

This Fra Tommaso is the first of those sons of St. Dominic with whom Catherine was brought into contact—a group of worthy men who, in the midst of all the ecclesiastical corruption that surrounded them, maintained their single-hearted faith and religious fervour unimpaired, and found in the scholasticism of the Angelical Doctor a sufficient answer for all the problems of the time. Fra Tommaso was Catherine's first confessor, and seems to have written some account of her life, as far as it came under his observation, which was incorporated into Fra Raimondo's great *Legenda.* Finding her resolute, he bade her follow her inspiration, and counselled her to cut off her beautiful hair, as a sign to her family that her intention was fixed. The inevitable domestic persecution followed. Catherine's room was taken from her, and she was compelled to do all the menial drudgery of the house, the servant being sent away, in order that she might have neither time nor place for prayer and devotion. Abuse and reproaches were heaped upon her, and every unkindness shown her, in order to break down this seeming obstinacy. But all in vain. Thrown back upon herself, the girl invented the refuge that she was ever to urge upon her disciples that they, too, should find, and which could never be taken from them : the cell of self-knowledge. "She made herself in her mind, by inspiration of the Holy Spirit, a secret cell, out of which she resolved never to go by reason of any external occupation. So it befell that she who, when formerly she had her exterior cell, sometimes stayed within and sometimes issued forth, now that she had made this inner cell that could not be taken from her, never left it." All unkindness, all reproaches, she bore sweetly and cheerfully. "She told me that she firmly pictured to herself that her father represented Our Lord and Saviour Jesus Christ ; her mother the most glorious Mother of God ; and that her brothers and the rest of the household figured the holy Apostles and Disciples. And, because of this imagination, she served them all with such great gladness and diligence, that every one marvelled." [1] Nor did her visions desert her. In a dream she thought she saw St. Dominic holding in one hand a white lily, which, like the bush seen by Moses, burned and was not consumed, and with the other offering her the black and white habit of the Dominican tertiaries, the Sisters of

[1] *Legenda*, I. iv. 5, 6 (§ § 49, 50).

Penance, promising that she should be vested in it as she desired.

Jacomo di Benincasa had by this time been convinced that his daughter's conduct had a higher sanction, and was not prompted by any childish caprice. He had come upon her unawares, as she prayed in the room of her brother Stefano (the only brother who was still unmarried), and had seen a snow-white dove hovering over her head. And, so, when the girl, ordinarily bashful and silent, suddenly revealed to all the family her vow and her unalterable resolution of having Christ alone for her Spouse, he bade her follow the inspiration of the Holy Spirit, for she would meet with no more opposition from him, and enjoined on all the household to leave her in perfect liberty to serve her Divine Bridegroom as she thought fit.

"Then, having obtained this full and long-desired liberty of serving God, the virgin, already entirely dedicated to Him, began zealously and wonderfully to order all her life in the divine service. She asked and obtained a small room separate from the others, in which, as though in the solitude, she could devote herself to God, and afflict her body according to her desire. Here no tongue could narrate with what rigour of penitence she afflicted her body, and with what eagerness of love she sought the countenance of her Spouse. In this little chamber were renewed the olden time works of the holy fathers of Egypt, and all the more wondrously, inasmuch as they were done in her father's house, without any human teaching, example, or guidance."[1]

In order to make this liberty still more secure, Catherine shortly after took the habit of the Sisters of Penance of St. Dominic, called in Siena the *Mantellate*—the white robe of innocence and the black mantle of humility in which we still see her clad in the pictures. These *Mantellate* were not nuns, strictly speaking, but devoted themselves to the service of God in their own homes. At first the sisters refused to receive a maiden into their number, as their order was then composed only of widows; but at length, when Catherine lay ill and assured her mother that,

[1] *Ibid.*, I. vi. 1 (§ 57).

if her desire was not fulfilled, God and St. Dominic would take her from the world, they told Lapa they would grant her daughter's request, provided the girl was not too beautiful. Their representatives being reassured upon this point (for she was temporarily, but completely, disfigured by her illness), and immensely edified by her conversation, they accepted her as a sister; and, on her recovery to health, she received the habit from one of the Dominican friars who acted as director of the sisterhood at San Domenico in the Cappella delle Volte—that little chapel still so fragrant with her spirit. There is some small difference of opinion as to the date of her thus taking the habit, but I think it was most probably about the beginning of 1363.

Then began that wonderful life of almost incredible austerity and of mystical communings with the unseen, that made the whole existence of this young maiden of the people seem a new, unheard-of miracle. As far as the austerities were concerned, however, she was only continuing what she had already begun as soon as her family had granted her her liberty.

Gradually abstaining from one thing after another, Catherine freed herself from all dependence on food or sleep. In a short while, she could easily restrict herself to raw herbs, a little bread, and water. Then the bread was left out, and she ate only the herbs. Soon even that became a torment to her, and she seems often for a long time to have lived upon the Blessed Sacrament of the Altar alone. "In the time during which I was allowed to be the witness of her life," writes Fra Raimondo, "she lived without any nourishment of food or drink; aided by no natural power, she ever sustained, with a joyous countenance, pains and labours that would have been insupportable to others." In these later years she would usually, to avoid scandal (for while these things seemed miracles to Fra Raimondo and his friends, others, of no less repute in the spiritual life, cried out against them), sip a little water and force herself to chew some coarse food, but always with great physical suffering.[1] She slept on a bare board. At first

[1] On one occasion, to avoid singularity, she appears to have asked the Pope to impose a rigid fast of bread and water upon her, as a condition of gaining an

she wore a hair-shirt, but, characteristically dreading the least trace of uncleanliness, she changed it for a chain of steel, which she fastened so tightly round her sides that it pierced the skin and lacerated her tender flesh. Towards the end of her life, Fra Raimondo compelled her, in virtue of holy obedience, to lay it aside, which she did, albeit unwillingly. Gradually she overcame the need of sleep, until at times she would only have half-an-hour in the space of two days and two nights—and this she told her confessor was the hardest of all her victories in this kind. Especially, she loved to keep watch in prayer continuously while the friars of San Domenico, whom she called her brothers, slept, and then rest a little on her hard board when they rose to matins. Not content with this, she would scourge herself with a little steel discipline until the blood ran down from her shoulders to her feet. "Three times a day, she shed the blood from her body to render to her Redeemer blood for blood." Thus she, who had been an exceptionally robust and healthy child (as her mother told Fra Raimondo), became so attenuated and wasted that it seemed a wonder that the ardent spirit could still be confined in so immaterial a prison. In vain Lapa implored her to mitigate her austerities. When once, shortly before her taking the Dominican habit, she prevailed upon her daughter to accompany her to the Bagni of Vignone, one of the famous hot baths of the contado, Catherine waited till she was unobserved, and then exposed herself to the flow of the boiling water, meditating the while on the torments of Hell and Purgatory, beseeching the Creator to accept these pains which she thus voluntarily endured, instead of those others which (she said) her sins merited.

Thus Catherine became one of those saints, horrible and repulsive to the eyes of many in an age that worships material gain and physical comfort, who have offered themselves as a sacrifice to the Eternal Justice for the sins of the world.

There have been other women who have borne the same

indulgence. Cf. Letter 228 (278), and the notes of Gigli and Tommaseo, respectively, thereon. A detailed account, differing somewhat from Raimondo's, is given by Stefano Maconi, *Epistola Domni Stephani*, § 18.

burden at different epochs in the Church's history—especially in times of her greatest corruption—more frequently in the seclusion of the cloister or in the poor hovels of the peasantry. Catherine differs from such saints as Fina of San Gimignano and Lydwine of Schiedam, almost her contemporaries, or Rose of Lima in later times, inasmuch as this "existence of expiation" was only a small portion of her life's work; but the spirit that animated them in their sufferings was the same. This has been admirably expressed by a modern French writer, in the case of the young Dutch woman who was born in the very year that Catherine died: "She made expiation, even as the other saints of her age, for the souls in Purgatory, for the abomination of the schism, for the debauchery of the clergy and the monks, for the wickedness of the peoples and the kings; but, in addition to that obligation which she accepted of repairing the sins committed from one end of the Universe to the other, she had also the office laid upon her of being the scapegoat of her own country." Such an existence of expiation would be incomprehensible without a knowledge of the causes, the number, and the nature of the offences, to make reparation for which here on earth was, in some sort, her *raison d'être*.[1] For the salvation of others, Catherine was prepared to endure the very pains of Hell. "'How could I be content, Lord,' she prayed, 'if any one of those who have been created to Thy image and likeness, even as I, should perish and be taken out of my hands? I would not in any wise that even one should be lost of my brethren, who are bound to me by nature and by grace; I am fain that the old enemy should lose them all, and Thou gain them, to the greater praise and glory of Thy name. Better were it for me that all should be saved, and I alone (saving ever Thy charity) should sustain the pains of Hell, than that I should be in Paradise and all they perish damned; for greater honour and glory of Thy name would it be.' And she was answered by the Lord, as she secretly confessed to me: 'Charity cannot be in Hell, for it would destroy it utterly; it were easier for Hell to be destroyed than for Charity

[1] J. K. Huysmans, *Sainte Lydwine de Schiedam*, pp. 61–65.

to exist with it.' Then she: 'If Thy truth and Thy justice permitted it, I would that Hell were utterly destroyed, or at least that no soul ever more should descend thither, and if (so I were still united to Thy charity) I were put over the mouth of Hell to close it, in such wise that none should ever more enter it, much would I rejoice, so that all my neighbours might thus be saved.'"[1] And, on another occasion, she prayed: "Lord, give me all the pains and all the infirmities that there are in the world, to bear in my body; I am fain to offer Thee my body in sacrifice, and to bear all for the world's sins, that Thou mayest spare it and change its life to another." "And when she said these words, she was abstracted from her senses and rapt in ecstasy. But, when she returned to herself, she was white as snow, and began to laugh loudly and to say: 'Love, Love, I have conquered Thee with Thyself. For Thou dost wish to be besought for what Thou canst do of Thine own accord.'"[2]

Catherine's first step, after receiving the Dominican habit, was to enter upon a prolonged retreat. For three years continuously, she kept a complete silence, speaking only with her confessor, Fra Tommaso della Fonte, when she confessed to him, and occasionally with other persons at his bidding. She dwelt continually within the religious enclosure of her little cell, nor ever left it save when she went to hear Mass. In Fra Raimondo's poetical phrase, "She found the desert within her own house and solitude in the midst of people."

Now began the continuous series of her visions. In her narrow cell she smelt the fragrance of celestial lilies, and heard the ineffable melodies of Paradise, sweetest of all on the lips of those who had loved Christ on earth with the most ardent love. "Father," she said to Fra Tommaso, "do you not hear the Magdalene, how she sings with a high voice and with grace of singular sweetness, in company of all the choir of the blessed?" Christ Himself appeared to her spiritual eyes, instructed her in the secret mysteries of the Divinity, conversed continually with

[1] *Legenda*, Prologue I. (§ 15).

[2] *Supplementum* (Casanatense MS.), f. 30. Cf. Dante, *Par*. xx. 94–99.

her and familiarly as friend with friend, and kissed her with "the mysterious kiss that infused into her spirit the sweetness of ineffable delight."[1] And, at the very beginning of these visions and revelations, the Lord delivered to her the simple doctrine which became the basis of her whole conception of God and man: "Knowest thou, O daughter, who thou art and who am I? Thou art she who art not, and I am He who am. If thou hast this knowledge in thy soul, the enemy will never be able to deceive thee, and thou wilt escape from all his snares; never wilt thou consent to anything against My commandments, and every grace, every truth, every clearness, thou wilt acquire without difficulty." "The soul," said Catherine, in illustration of this, "that already sees her own nothingness and knows that all her good is in her Creator, entirely abandons herself with all her powers and all creatures, and immerges herself utterly in her Creator, in such wise that she directs all her operations primarily and entirely towards Him; nor would she in any wise go out of Him, in whom she perceives she has found every good and all perfection of felicity; and from the vision of love, which daily increases in her, she is in a manner so transformed into God that she cannot think, nor understand, nor love, nor remember aught save God, and what concerns God. She sees not other creatures or herself, save only in God, neither does she remember herself or them, save simply in God; even as one who dives down into the sea, and is swimming under its waters, neither sees nor touches aught save the waters of the sea and the things that are in those waters; he sees nothing outside those waters, touches nothing, feels nothing. If the likeness of those things that are without reflect themselves in the water, he can, indeed, see them; but only in the water and as they are in the water; not otherwise. And this is the ordered and right love of self and of all creatures, in which we cannot go wrong, because of necessity it is governed by divine rule, neither by it is anything desired outside God, because it is ever exercised in God and is ever in Him."

[1] Tantucci, pp. 36, 45.

And from this, too, she drew her doctrine of holy hate. The more a soul so conjoined with God loves Him, so much the more does she hate the offence she commits against Him, and, seeing the origin of every sin has its roots in her own sensual part, she is inspired to a holy hate of this and wages a relentless war of the spirit against it. "Woe to that soul," said Catherine, "in whom this holy hatred is not; for needs must be that, where it is not, self-love will reign, which is the sink of all sins and the root and cause of every evil greed."[1]

This doctrine, upon which her whole spiritual teaching may be said to depend, Catherine explained in detail, some nine or ten years later, to an Englishman, whom we shall meet in her circle, William Flete, one of the Augustinian friars of Lecceto. "The holy mother," he wrote, at the beginning of 1376, "speaking of herself in the third person, said that at the beginning of her illumination she set as the foundation of all her life, against self-love, the stone of self-knowledge, which she distinguished into three small stones. The first was the consideration of Creation; that is, that she had no being of herself, but dependent only upon the Creator, both in production and in conservation, and that the Creator had done and was doing all this through His grace and mercy. The second was the consideration of Redemption, that is, how the Redeemer with His blood had restored the life of grace which had until then been destroyed; and this through His pure and fervent love, which man had done nought to deserve. The third was the consideration of her own sins, committed after baptism and the grace received in it, for which she had deserved eternal damnation, and was stupefied at the eternal goodness of God because He had not commanded the earth to swallow her up. From these three considerations, there was born in her so great a hatred of herself, that she desired nought according to her own will, but only according to the will of God, who, she knew, willed nought save her good. From this it followed that she was content and glad at every tribulation and temptation; not only because it came to her by the will of

[1] *Legenda*, I. x. 1, 8, 9 (§§ 92, 100, 101).

God, but also to see herself punished and chastised. She began, therefore, to have the greatest displeasure from those things in which she at first delighted, and a great delight in what at first displeased her."

"She also said that self-love is the cause of every evil and the ruin of every good, and that it is of two kinds, to wit, sensitive self-love and spiritual self-love. The first is the cause of all sensual sins, and of all others that are open and manifest, and are committed through affection for earthly things and creatures; that is, when, for love of them, the commandments of the Creator are scorned and disobeyed. The second self-love, called spiritual, is that which, after despising earthly things, all creatures, and even his own senses, nevertheless makes man keep so tenaciously attached to his own spiritual appetite and to his own opinion, that he will not serve God nor walk in His ways unless in accordance with his own desire and feeling. Therefore, since God wants man without a will of his own, such a one cannot possibly stand firm nor persevere in his way; needs must he fall, because he adheres more to his own will than to the divine. Such are all those who would fain choose state and exercise according to their own liking, and not according as they are called by God and judged by the counsel of prudent and discreet persons. Such also are those who are too much wedded to some spiritual work or exercise, such as fasting or the like, as though it were an end in itself; for it then happens that, if they cannot practise it, they at once yield to despair and abandon everything. Among these should also be included those who love spiritual consolations and sweetnesses too much, and, when these fail them, soon despair. True spiritual love loves God alone and the salvation of the soul for God's sake. It makes use of all other things in due order for this end, and recks not what the means may be, provided that the end is the honour of God and the salvation of our neighbours. Whoso, then, possesses true spiritual love must judge and take all things according to the will of God, and not according to that of men; and when he remains deprived of any spiritual consolation, he must at once think and say: This befalls me through the divine disposition, by the permission of God, who, in all the adversities that He sends me, seeks and wills nought save my justification and salvation. And with this thought all bitter things will be rendered sweet."[1]

But, as the conversations with her divine Lover grew more frequent and familiar, and the revelations of the divine Beauty more full and overwhelming, so did the manifestations of the evil of the world the more insistently press themselves upon her. And, as ever with men and women of the Middle Ages, they took a personal and anthropomorphic form in the shape of temptations of the devil. At first, indeed, Catherine had doubted whether the visitation that seemed celestial might not, in reality, have some such diabolical source. "But I will teach thee," said the Voice in her heart, "how to distinguish My visions from the visions of the enemy. My vision begins with terror, but always, as it grows, gives greater confidence; it begins with some bitterness, but always groweth more sweet. In the vision of the enemy the contrary happens, for in the beginning it seems to bring some gladness, confidence, or sweetness, but, as it proceeds, fear and bitterness grow continuously in the soul of whoso beholds it. Even so are My ways different from his ways. The way of penance and of My commandments seemeth harsh and difficult in the beginning; but, the more one walks therein, the more does it become easy and sweet; whereas the way of the vices appears in the beginning right delightful, but in its course becomes ever more bitter and more ruinous. But I will give thee another sign, more infallible and more certain. Be assured that, since I am Truth, there ever results from My visions a greater knowledge of truth in the soul; and, because the knowledge of truth is most necessary to her about Me and about herself, that is, that she should know Me and know herself, from which knowledge it ever follows that she despises herself and honours Me, which is the proper office of humility, it is inevitable that from

[1] *Relatione d'una dottrina, o documento spirituale, scritta nell' anno del Signore* 1376, *il giorno settimo del mese di Gennaio, da Fra Guglielmo Flete inglese.* Published by Gigli as an appendix to the *Dialogo.* Cf. Letters 64 (124), 71 (358), 213 (163).

My visions the soul becomes more humble, knowing herself better and despising her own vileness. In the visions of the enemy the opposite happens ; for, since he is the father of lies, and the king over all the children of pride, and cannot give save what he has, from his visions there ever results in the soul a certain self-esteem or presumption on herself, which is the proper office of pride, and she remains swollen and puffed up. Thou, then, by ever examining thyself diligently, wilt be able to consider whence the vision has come, whether from the truth or from the lie ; for truth always makes the soul humble, but the lie makes her proud." [1] And again, when she prayed for strength against these assaults : "Daughter, if thou wouldst acquire the virtue of fortitude, thou must needs imitate Me. Albeit I could by My divine virtue annihilate all the power of the enemy, and take another way to conquer him, nevertheless, because I wished with My human actions to give an example to you, I would not conquer save by the way of the Cross, in order to teach you by deed as well as word. If you would become strong, to overcome every power of the enemy, take the Cross for your consolation, even as I did, *who* (as My Apostle says) *having joy set before Me endured the Cross*, in order that you may choose not only patiently to bear pains and afflictions, but even to embrace them as consolations. And, verily, they are consolations ; for the more you bear such things for My sake, the more do you make yourselves like to Me ; for *as you are partakers of the sufferings*, it follows, according to the teaching of My Apostle, that *so shall you be also of the consolation.* Receive then, My daughter, the sweet things as bitter, and the bitter things as sweet, for My sake ; and fear nothing henceforth, for certainly for all things thou shalt be strong." [2]

There came a time, towards the end of these three years, when these assaults and temptations became horrible and unbearable. Aerial men and women, with obscene words and still more obscene gestures, seemed to invade her little cell, sweeping round her like the souls of the damned in Dante's Hell, inviting

[1] *Legenda*, I. ix. 4 (§ 85). [2] *Ibid.*, I. xi. 1 (§ 104).

her simple and chaste soul to the banquet of lust. Their suggestions grew so hideous and persistent, that she fled in terror from the cell that had become like a circle of the infernal regions, and took refuge in the church; but they pursued her thither, though there their power seemed checked. And her Christ seemed far from her. At last she cried out, remembering the words in the vision: "I have chosen suffering for my consolation, and will gladly bear these and all other torments, in the name of the Saviour, for as long as shall please His Majesty." "When she said this, immediately all that assemblage of demons departed in confusion, and a great light from above appeared that illumined all the room, and in the light the Lord Jesus Christ Himself, nailed to the Cross and stained with blood, as He was when by His own blood He entered into the holy place; and from the Cross He called the holy virgin, saying: 'My daughter Catherine, seest thou how much I have suffered for thee? Let it not then be hard to thee to endure for Me.' Then, in another guise, He approached her to console her, and spoke sweetly to her of the triumph that she had already won in that battle. But she, imitating Antony, said: 'And where wast Thou, my Lord, whilst my heart was tormented with so much foulness?' To which the Lord answered: 'I was in thy heart. Thou, My daughter, who, with My and not with thine own virtue, hast so faithfully battled, hast merited still greater favour from Me; and therefore, henceforth, I will reveal Myself to thee more often and in more familiar wise.'"

This was the first time that the divine Voice had called her by her name, and it gave her such rapture of delight that she prayed her confessor, Fra Tommaso, that he would always address her in this way: *My daughter Catherine;* in order that the sweetness might be ever renewed. Her colloquies with the Saviour grew more frequent, more prolonged, more intimate. Sometimes He appeared to her with His Virgin Mother, sometimes with St. Dominic, St. Mary Magdalene, St. John the Evangelist, St. Paul, or other saints; "but most times He came unattended, and conversed with her as a friend with a most intimate friend ; in such wise that (as she herself secretly and bashfully sometimes confessed to me) ofttimes the Lord and she recited the Psalms, walking up and down in her room, as two religious or clerics are wont to say the office together. O wondrous, marvellous, and unheard of in our ages, demonstration of the divine familiarity ! "[1]

During this time of seclusion, Catherine learned to read, though it does not appear that she attempted to study anything more than the Psalms and the offices of the Church. Fra Raimondo tells us that she had originally got the alphabet from a companion of hers, but found it so hard to get further that, fearing that she was losing time, she prayed to God and was miraculously instructed. When he knew her, she could read any writing, rapidly and with ease, though unlike other people and as if she knew the meaning of the words without being able to spell out the syllables. Reading, however, was not her only recreation. She took great delight in flowers of all kinds, and would weave them into crosses and garlands in her spare time, singing mystical songs of divine praise the while. These she would send or give as presents, either directly or through Fra Tommaso della Fonte, in token of the love of Christ. A young Dominican friar, Tommaso di Antonio Caffarini, soon to be very closely associated with her spiritual life, tells us that, before he knew her, he had received some of these mystical gifts through her confessor.[2]

At the same time, perhaps inevitably, her ecstasies were growing upon her. After Communion, or at other times when meditating upon the mysteries hidden in God, she would be rapt out of her senses for a while, and her body left rigid and seemingly lifeless, insensible to touch or wound. This increased with years, and lasted all through her life. It is a not unusual feature in the legends of women saints and mystics, nor would it be hard to find a purely natural and scientific explanation.

There are, doubtless, many who will regard this simply as a form of catalepsy, and who will see in much of these visionary

[1] *Legenda*, I. xi. 5, 6 (§ § 109–112).

[2] *Contestatio Fr. Thomae Caffarini*, *Processus*, col. 1260.

experiences little more than hysterical phenomena; nor need the faithful followers of St. Catherine to-day deny this as a possible, or even probable, element in her life. In the record of her revelations, we are confronted with things that are incapable of literal acceptance, that, perhaps, at times even offend our religious sensibilities, occurring side by side with profound truths, expressed with wonderful precision and startling inspiration, shedding light upon every step of the believer's difficult path from the human to the divine. That phenomena not unconnected with organic hysteria existed side by side with the possession of a suprasensible revelation in the lives of many of the greatest mystical saints, may well be granted. It has even been urged, in the case of St. Teresa, that, while suffering in a sense from organic hysteria, her knowledge of the workings of her own soul was so clear and exact that she could distinguish perfectly between these two classes of experiences, the natural and the supernatural, and that this fact is the strongest guarantee for the truth of her account of the latter.[1] Catherine, like Teresa, with her unwavering fortitude and calm resolution, her firm will which was to impose itself upon the rulers and powers of the world, her practical sense and angelic wisdom, is poles asunder from a hysterical subject; yet, perhaps, with all her celestial endowments, this thing was given her as the Pauline "thorn in the flesh, the messenger of Satan to buffet me." She had learned early to discriminate between the two kinds of vision—those that proceeded from her divine Teacher and those that were the work of the father of lies. But I do not think that she could distinguish between the natural and the supernatural in the way that has been claimed for St. Teresa; at times, in her visions, we cannot but detect apparent hallucinations, to which a physician would probably assign a hysterical origin. Yet the "abundance of the revelations" is more surely there.

[1] For all this delicate question, see especially G. Hahn, *Les phénomènes hystériques et les révélations de Sainte Thérèse* (Revue des Questions Scientifiques, xiii. pp. 553–569, xiv. pp. 39–84), and cf. H. Joly, *Psychologie des Saints*, pp. 110, 111, and W. James, *The Varieties of Religious Experience*, pp. 14–18.

The mystical revelations and divine colloquies of these three years culminated in the "spiritual espousals" of Catherine with Christ on the last day of the carnival, most probably, I think, in the year 1366.

By this term, "spiritual espousals," the great mystics clearly mean something different, not in degree but in kind, from what every nun may be said to experience when she consecrates her virginity to Christ. They evidently hold that some chosen souls, after passing through the ways of purgation and illumination, having been tried in much tribulation and mortification, and enlightened by profound meditation upon spiritual things, attain to a state of mystical perfection which they call the "spiritual marriage," in which, by an intellectual vision of Christ in the centre of the soul, they become united to Him in some special and peculiarly absorbing manner, and become, in some sort, one thing with Him. The mystical poets of Spain, St. Teresa and St. John of the Cross, draw a distinction between "spiritual espousals" and the "spiritual marriage," for which the former is but a preparation. "That which God here communicates to the soul in an instant," says St. Teresa, "is so great a secret and so sublime a grace, and what she feels is such an excessive delight, that I know nothing with which to compare it, except that Our Lord is pleased at that moment to manifest to her the glory which is in Heaven ; and this He does in a more sublime way than by any vision or spiritual delight. More cannot be said (as far as can be understood) than that this soul becomes one with God ; for as He Himself is a spirit, His Majesty is pleased to discover the love He has for us, by making certain persons understand how it extends, in order that we may praise His greatness, because He has vouchsafed to unite Himself to a creature in such a way that, as in the marriage-state husband and wife can no more be separated, so He will never be separated from her." [1]

It would seem that Catherine does not regard the "spiritual marriage," as St. Teresa and St. John of the Cross understand it,

[1] *El Castillo Interior*, *Moradas sétimas*, cap. ii. (Dalton's translation).

as attainable in this world—at least for one who, like her, though ever walking with Christ and ever talking with Him even while in the midst of men, was, nevertheless, called to a life of active labour for His name rather than to sheer contemplation. Her "spiritual espousals" were to have their mystical consummation in the eternal nuptials of Paradise. "It would be foolishness," writes St. John of the Cross, "to think that the language of love and the mystical intelligence can be at all explained in words of any kind." The loving souls, in whom the Spirit dwells, "use figures of special comparisons and similitudes; they hide somewhat of that which they feel, and, in the abundance of the Spirit, utter secret mysteries rather than express themselves in clear words." "It is better to leave the outpourings of love in their own fulness, that every one may apply them according to the measure of his spirit and power, than to pare them down to one particular sense which is not suited to the taste of every one." [1] A mystic must express his vision in the symbolic terms of his own day, and it is, therefore, not wonderful that Catherine should describe her spiritual betrothal with imagery suggestive of the Italian painting of the fourteenth century.

She had prayed again and again, Fra Raimondo tells us, for the gift of the perfection of the virtue of faith, such that it should never be shaken or beaten down by any assault of the enemy, and ever had she heard the same answer made: *I will espouse thee to Myself in Faith.* At length, on the last day of the carnival, while all Siena was given up to the usual festivities of the season, the Voice told her that the time had come: "I will this day celebrate solemnly with thee the festival of the betrothal of thy soul, and, even as I promised, I will espouse thee to Myself in Faith." "Whilst the Lord was yet speaking, there appeared the most glorious Virgin, His Mother, the most blessed John Evangelist, the glorious apostle Paul, and the most holy Dominic, the father of her order; and with these the prophet David, who had the psaltery set to music in his hands; and,

[1] *Cántico Espiritual entre el Alma y Cristo, su Esposo,* prólogo (D. Lewis's translation).

while he played with most sweet melody, the Virgin Mother of God took the right hand of Catherine with her most sacred hand, and, holding out her fingers towards the Son, besought Him to deign to espouse her to Himself in Faith. To which graciously consenting, the Only Begotten of God drew out a ring of gold, which had in its circle four pearls enclosing a most beauteous diamond; and, placing this ring upon the ring-finger of Catherine's right hand, He said: 'Lo, I espouse thee to Myself, thy Creator and Saviour, in the Faith, which, until thou celebratest thy eternal nuptials with Me in Heaven, thou wilt preserve ever without stain. Henceforth, My daughter, do manfully and without hesitation those things which, by the ordering of My providence, will be put into thy hands; for, being now armed with the fortitude of the Faith, thou wilt happily overcome all thy adversaries.' Then the vision disappeared, but that ring ever remained on her finger, not indeed to the sight of others, but only to the sight of the virgin herself; for she often, albeit with bashfulness, confessed to me that she always saw that ring on her finger, nor was there any time when she did not see it."[1]

[1] *Legenda*, I. xii. 1, 2 (§ 115).

CHAPTER II

FROM DANTE TO SAINT CATHERINE

"Ha, mater piissima, sponsa Christi! quos in aqua et spiritu generas tibi filios ad ruborem! Non Charitas, non Astraea, sed filiae sanguisugae factae sunt tibi nurus."—Dante, *Epist.* viii. 7.

FULLY to understand Catherine's political work and mission, we must turn to the states and rulers with which and with whom she was to be brought into direct contact.

The "Babylonian Captivity" of the Popes at Avignon, which had begun with Clement V in 1305, was still, to some extent, the dominant feature in the situation. It was on Clement's death, in 1314, that the voice had been heard of "a man who was a prophet," and Dante, in his letter to the Italian cardinals at Carpentras, had renewed for Rome the lamentation of Jeremiah for Jerusalem.[1] Things had grown worse under Clement's successor, the Cahorsine John XXII (1316–1334). "The gold which is the holiness of virtues has grown dim in the Church," wrote Alvarus Pelagius, "for all covet material gold. Ordinations and the sacraments are bought and sold for gold. Whenever I entered the apartment of the chamberlain of our Lord the Pope, I saw brokers, and tables full of gold, and clerics counting and weighing florins."[2] Petrarca had written two poetical epistles to Benedict XII (1334–1342), exhorting him to return to Italy, and he duly offered a similar appeal in the name of Rome to the man who now sat on the papal throne, Clement VI (1342–1352).[3] In Clement, the typical Limousin pope, the corruption of this epoch of the Papacy was personified. Learned and eloquent, not without a certain magnanimity, his private life, both as archbishop and as pope, was scandalous, and such was the

[1] *Epist.* viii. 4.

[2] *De Planctu Ecclesiae*, II. 7. Cf. Dante, *Par.* xviii. 130–136; G. Villani, xi. 20.

[3] *Epist. metr.*, Lib. I. 2, 5; Lib. II. 5.

luxury and prodigality of his court that he would have taxed all Christendom, had he been able, to supply the funds. He wasted the treasures of the Church in lending money to the French kings to aid them in their wars with England, and in the advancement of his kindred, filling the Sacred College with men of his own stamp and country, godless and worldly, many of them of evil and dissolute life. If Petrarca is to be believed, the riotous licentiousness of these younger cardinals was but too well matched in the senile debauchery of their elders who wore that hat, in Dante's phrase, *che pur di male in peggio si travasa,* "which doth but pass from bad vessel to worse." "Our two Clements," said a French prelate of the Curia (probably the Patriarch of Jerusalem, Philippe de Cabassole) to Petrarca, "have destroyed more of the Church in a few years than seven of your Gregories could restore in many centuries."[1]

In his three terrible sonnets against Avignon, Petrarca has painted for all time the state of the society that gathered round Clement's throne. But in one of his Latin poems, the sixth eclogue entitled *Pastorum pathos,* St. Peter, in the guise of the old shepherd Pamphilus, rebukes his hireling successor Mitio, who is Clement himself, for the desolation of the pastures and the destruction of the flocks, only to find him brazen-faced and exulting in his shame.[2] Even more frightful is the picture of the corruption of the papal court which the poet has left us in his *Epistolae sine titulo*, albeit the note of exaggeration and rhetorical inflation is manifest. "What difference is there," he asks, "between those enemies of Christ, who betrayed Him with a kiss and bent the knee before Him in mockery, and the Pharisees of our time? That same Christ, whose name they exalt night and day with hymns of praise, whom they robe in purple and gold, whom they load with jewels, whom they salute and adore prostrate—that very same do they not buy and sell on earth like merchandise? As it were blindfold that He may not

[1] *Epist. sine titulo,* XIX. Cf. M. Villani, iii. 43; Benvenuto da Imola, *Comentum,* v. p. 289.

[2] *Egloga* VI.

see, they crown Him with the thorns of their impious wealth; they defile Him with most impure spittal, and assail Him with viperous hissing; they strike Him with the spear of their poisonous deeds; and, so far as in them lies, mocked, naked, poor, and scourged, they drag Him again to Calvary, and nail Him again to the Cross." Avignon is the Babylon of the West, the home of all vices and misery, the same that the Evangelist saw in spirit; little, indeed, according to the circuit of its walls, but immense in its accumulation of wickedness.[1]

On December 2, 1352, the campanile of St. Peter's was struck by lightning. All the bells were dashed to the ground and fused together as though they had been melted in a furnace. At once the report spread through Rome that Pope Clement was dead. "Lo now," it seemed to a Swedish widow that Christ said in her heart, "the bells are burning, and men are crying out: Our lord is dead, our lord the Pope has departed; blessed be this day, but not blessed that lord. How strange, for where all should cry: May that lord live long and live happily; there they cry and say with joy: Down with him and may he not rise up again! But it is no wonder, for he himself, who should have cried: *Come, and ye shall find rest for your souls;* he cried: *Come, and behold me in pomp and ambition more than Solomon. Come to my Court, and empty your purses, and ye shall find perdition for your souls.* For thus did he cry by example and in deed. Therefore the time of My wrath is now approaching, and I shall judge him as one that has scattered the flock of Peter. O what a judgment awaits him! But, nevertheless, if he will yet be converted to Me, I will run to meet him half-way like a tender father."[2]

Clement's successor, Etienne d'Albret, who took the title of Innocent VI (1352–1362), was a simple man, "of good life and not much knowledge;" he made an earnest, but ineffectual attempt to reform the papal court. The confusion of French politics and the presence of bands of mercenaries in Provence

1 *Epist. sine titulo*, XVI., XIX., XX.

2 *Revelationes S. Birgittae*, VI. 96. Cf. M. Villani, iii. 42. Clement actually died at Avignon on December 6.

were making Avignon a less desirable residence. Innocent spoke of returning to, or at least visiting, Rome. In 1353, he sent the great Spanish cardinal, Egidio (or Gil) de Albornoz, as legate to Italy, to re-establish the power of the Holy See in the States of the Church.

The two great powers of the peninsula (leaving Venice out of the question, as, indeed, she did not yet concern herself much with the politics of the mainland) were Milan in the north, where the Visconti—the typical Italian tyrants of the age—were absorbing a great part of Lombardy, and Naples in the south, under the sway of sovereigns of the house of Anjou, the descendants of the great Charles whom Dante saw in the Valley of the Princes outside the gate of Purgatory. The one state was an absolute despotism, under a family traditionally hostile to the Church ; the other a feudal kingdom, normally a staunch supporter of the Holy See.

On the death of Luchino Visconti in 1349, his brother, the Archbishop Giovanni—an able and astute ruler, one of the least atrocious of his cruel house—united the spiritual and temporal sovereignty of its dominions in his own person. Bologna, though nominally subject to the Church, had been the most powerful city in Romagna, and one of the chief free republics of central Italy. But the factions, raging there as elsewhere, had led to its falling in 1321, the year of Dante's death, under the sway of a single man, Romeo de' Pepoli, whose grandsons sold it in 1350 to the Archbishop of Milan. Clement VI shamelessly confirmed this transaction by granting him the investiture of Bologna for twelve years. On the death of Giovanni in 1354, he was succeeded in his temporal sovereignty by his three nephews: Matteo, Bernabo, and Galeazzo ; but in 1356, either consumed by his own lusts or poisoned by his brothers, Matteo died, and the other two divided the dominions of their house. Bernabo made Milan his capital, while Galeazzo, after the capture of Pavia in 1359, set his headquarters in the latter city. A Visconti of uncertain parentage, Giovanni da Oleggio (possibly an unacknowledged bastard of the late Archbishop), made himself independent master of Bologna, with aid from the Marquis of Ferrara, and ruled it with the usual brutal tyranny of his family.

Bernabo Visconti was now the head of the Ghibelline party in Italy. A man of fierce passions, subject to paroxysms of bestial fury, he was a cruel and sanguinary tyrant, but a prudent and subtle politician. A mighty hunter, he enforced his game-laws by wholesale blinding, torturing, and hanging of his unhappy contadini. On one occasion, he burned alive two friars who had rebuked him for these proceedings. He ground down his people with taxation, and quartered his five thousand hunting-dogs upon the citizens and convents ; their keepers were more dreaded than the magistrates of the towns. Bernabo married Regina Beatrice della Scala, the ambitious and able daughter of the despot of Verona. " This woman," writes Corio, " ruled in great part her husband's dominion ; she was of an imperious nature, proud and daring, insatiable of wealth." [1]

The ruler of the south, the head of what would, under normal circumstances, have been the Guelf party, was that mysterious and unhappy woman, Giovanna of Anjou : " the great harlot that sitteth upon many waters and was called the Queen of Naples." [2] Readers of Dante's *Paradiso* need not be reminded that Charles Robert, son of the poet's beloved Charles Martel and Clemence of Hapsburg, had been excluded from the throne of Naples by his uncle, Charles Martel's younger brother, Robert the Wise. Charles Robert became King of Hungary in 1308, and ruled till 1342. In 1333, a reconciliation of the rival claims of the two branches of the House of Anjou had been effected by the marriage of Andrew, second son of Charles Robert of Hungary, with Giovanna, the granddaughter and heiress of Robert of Naples—both being seven years old. But there were a number of princes of the royal blood of Naples who might have expected the old King's choice to have fallen

[1] *Storia di Milano*, III. 6. " Regina " appears to have been one of Beatrice's real names, not merely an assumed title.

[2] Walsingham, *Historia Anglicana* (ed. Riley), II. p. 49.

upon them, and the Hungarians were detested. The marriage was an unhappy one. Robert of Naples died in 1343. On September 18, 1345, Andrew was strangled as he left the Queen's chamber at Aversa; it seems probable that Giovanna was at least privy to the deed, and others of the royal family were implicated.

Such, at least, was the view of the avenger—the dead man's brother, Louis of Hungary—by strict descent the head of the house of Anjou. A young king, strong and terrible, he assembled a Hungarian army, and, in 1347, invaded Italy. Giovanna, who had married her cousin, Luigi of Taranto, fled to Provence (of which she was Countess), where she convinced the Pope of her innocence, and sold Avignon to him for a nominal sum. With his black standard of vengeance floating before him, the King of Hungary entered the kingdom of Naples. At Aversa, he executed his cousin, Charles of Durazzo, on the spot of Andrew's murder, as an accomplice in the crime; the rest of the royal family were sent prisoners into Hungary, with the little child, Carobert, Giovanna's son (ostensibly by her late husband), who died almost immediately. Naples surrendered in terror. But, in the next year, Giovanna and Luigi returned; and a long war was brought to an end by the Pope's intervention in April, 1352, leaving the kingdom to Giovanna and her husband, and to Louis what he professed alone to desire—the satisfaction of having avenged his brother's death.

Giovanna's second husband died in 1362, and, in 1366, she married a third, James of Aragon, son of the King of Majorca. The house of Anjou had now three chief representatives: Giovanna at Naples, still of surpassing beauty, luxurious and splendid, not devoid of enlightenment, presiding over the gayest and most gorgeous court of Italy; King Louis of Hungary, who was making his kingdom the most potent state in Europe, conquering Moldavia in 1352 and Bulgaria in 1365; and the younger Charles of Durazzo ("Carlo della Pace"), nephew of the Duke whom Louis had slain, and husband of Giovanna's niece, Margherita, in the service of his Hungarian cousin, and himself uniting the claims of two branches of the royal house. In 1370, Louis succeeded his maternal uncle, Casimir III, as King of Poland. To the Italians, who had seen the vengeance he had taken for his brother, and the stern justice with which he repressed the excesses of his own troops in Naples, he seemed a possible arbiter of the nation's destinies, more formidable than the Emperor himself. In their eyes, he was hardly more a foreigner than Queen Giovanna or the Visconti of Milan. It will seem perfectly natural to the Republic of Florence to appeal to him against the Pope, and to Catherine of Siena herself to look to him as the champion and defender of the Church.

Between despot-ridden north and feudal south lay the Republics of Tuscany and the nominal States of the Church.

And here the great Guelf Republic of Florence was still the dominant power. Excluded from the government by the famous Ordinances of Justice in 1293, the nobles (magnates or *grandi*) had been finally broken in the tremendous street battles of 1343. The power was mainly in the hands of the wealthy burghers, *popolani grassi*, members of the greater Guilds; but the smaller tradesmen and artisans, forming the minor Guilds, were gradually coming to the front, and sharing in the administration. And rumblings of social discontent, sounds from a still lower stratum of society, were being heard in the background. The supreme magistracy of the Republic, the Signoria, consisted of the Gonfaloniere of Justice and eight Priors of the Arts (instead of the six in Dante's days), two from each quarter of the city. These *Signori* held office for two months; their nomination was by lot, and was controlled by a complicated process of scrutiny. Next came the two "Colleges," that is, the twelve *Buonuomini*, who were the counsellors of the Signoria, and the sixteen *Gonfalonieri* of the city companies, four from each quarter. All magnates, whether by birth or declared so as penalty, were excluded from the Signoria and the Colleges, whose members were all *popolani*, Florentine burghers and artisans, ascribed to the greater or minor Arts or Guilds.

The executive, as in almost all Italian States of the epoch, was represented by three alien magistrates: the Captain and the Podestà, both foreign (that is, from some other Italian state) nobles, and the Executor of Justice, who was normally a foreign burgher. There were two great Councils of the State: the Council of the People, over which the Captain presided, and the Council of the Commune presided over by the Podestà. In the former, only *popolani* could sit, but *grandi* were also admitted to the latter. Measures proposed by the Signoria had first to be carried in the Colleges; if they passed there, they were then submitted successively to the Council of the People and to the Council of the Commune, after which they became law. Temporary measures could, however, be concerted between the Signoria and a special meeting of *richiesti*, citizens summoned for the purpose, without an appeal to these councils; and in theory, and now and then in practice, a general Parliament, open to all the citizens of Florence, was assembled.

There was, however, in addition, another organization within the Republic, one which we shall find very closely associated with Catherine in her dealings with the Florentines. This was the *Parte Guelfa*, with its six captains and two councils, originally founded in the latter part of the thirteenth century, to maintain Guelf principles in the State. And in this the magnates were predominant, three of the captains being elected from their number. Their power of "admonishing" persons obnoxious to them, as suspected "Ghibellines," thereby excluding them from office under heavy penalties, made them greatly dreaded—all the more as, now that nothing of Ghibellinism remained but the name, this power was for the most part used to gratify personal feuds and to fan the flames of faction.

In Siena, from the middle of the thirteenth century, there had been a more or less similar constitution of the Commune and of the People—but with the striking difference that the organization of the latter was not based upon the Arts or Guilds, which (with the exception of the two Merchant Guilds, the *Arti di Mercanzia*, and the Guild of Wool) were of little political importance, but upon the *Societates armorum*, the armed militia or train-bands of the *contrade*, or wards, into which the three terzi of the city were divided.[1] The *Concilium Campanae*, or Council of the Bell, elected the executive officials of the State, as usual from out of the lesser nobles of other Italian cities: the Podestà, the chief judicial officer, and the *Conservatore*, or *Capitano di Guerra*, later called the Senator, who led the forces of the Republic in time of war. But the Captain of the People, in the fourteenth century, was always a Sienese plebeian.

After the exclusion of the nobles or *gentiluomini (milites)* from the administration, in the third quarter of the thirteenth century, Siena had enjoyed a period of considerable prosperity under the oligarchical rule of the "good merchants of the Guelf party," the chief council or magistracy of the Nine. The Nine held office for two months, lived at the expense of the State, and (to the complete exclusion of the lower orders no less than of the nobles) were elected from the rich and enlightened burgher class, corresponding, more or less, to the *popolani grassi* of Florence. In Siena the orders that held sway successively were known as *Monti*. The adherents and families of this *Monte dei Nove* are famous in Sienese history as the Noveschi. The epoch of their rule, when Siena gained the title of *amorosa madre di dolcezza*, is that pictured to us in those vivid little masterpieces, the sonnets of Folgore da San Gimignano. Early in the fourteenth century, they had purchased the port of Talamone, by which they hoped to make the Republic a great maritime power, even as Pisa in the past; but the unhealthiness of the situation, and the impossibility of keeping the harbour clear, soon damped their ardour. The sanguinary feuds of the nobles—the Tolomei against the Salimbeni, the Malavolti against the Piccolomini, the Saracini against the Scotti—kept the State in chronic disturbance; plots and tumults against the burgher oligarchy, usually hatched by a combination of nobles

[1] Cf. R. L. Douglas, *History of Siena*, pp. 108–114; E. Armstrong, *The Sienese Statutes of 1262* (on L. Zdekauer's great work, *Il Constituto del Comune di Siena dell' anno 1262*, Milan, 1897), in the *English Historical Review*, vol. xv., London, 1900; G. Canestrini, *Della Milizia Italiana dal secolo XIII. al XVI.*, pp. xviii., xix.

and *popolo minuto*, threatened the administration ; while, in the contado, the Salimbeni were almost independent of the Republic, made their own alliances, and not unfrequently were united with the enemies of their fatherland.

The once mighty Republic of Pisa had sunk to a secondary position among the powers of Tuscany. To its destinies during the fourteenth century were united those of its neighbour, Lucca, which had been subjected to Pisan rule in 1342. Pisa was divided by the factions of the Bergolini and Raspanti ; the latter being expelled, the family of the Gambacorti swayed the Republic. Andrea di Gherardo Gambacorti held the chief authority until his death in 1351, when he was succeeded by his nephews, Francesco and Lotto. We shall find Andrea's son, Piero, among the friends and correspondents of Catherine. The rule of the Gambacorti was just, pacific, and beneficent—they were men of upright life and loyal to the Republic.

With these four communes, Florence, Siena, Pisa, and Lucca, Catherine was to be closely connected. The remaining Tuscan republic, that of Arezzo, hardly touched her life at all. It had already been subject to Florence from 1336 until 1343, and the days of its independence were numbered.

To the south and east of Tuscany lay what were nominally the Papal States, in which, however, the always vague authority of the Church had sunk to a minimum. Of the cities included in them, some, such as Perugia, governed themselves as virtually independent republics ; others, such as Rimini and Forlì, were in the hands of despots like the Malatesta and Ordelaffi, who ruled them either under the title of papal vicars or with no title but that conferred by the power of the sword and mercenary troops. The state of the Eternal City itself was peculiar, and was destined to affect all Christendom in the great struggle with which Catherine's closing days are associated.

Overshadowed by the Popes and Emperors, the Roman Republic had still existed throughout the centuries, always in name and at intervals in fact, when, in Giovanni Villani's telling phrase, *e' Romani si levarono a romore e feciono popolo*—"the

Romans rose in tumult and established a popular government." "The ancient people and government of Rome," writes Matteo, "was to all the world a mirror of constancy and incredible firmness, of upright and regulated living, and of every moral virtue. But those who at present possess the ruins of that famous city are, on the contrary, utterly fickle and inconstant, and without any shadow of moral virtues. With eager and excessive lightness, they often overturn their state, and, seeking liberty, they have found it, but have not known how to set it in order nor how to keep it."[1] The absence of the Popes, while weakening the power of the nobles, gave a fresh impulse of life to the Republic, whose rights had been formally recognized by Clement V in 1310. Revolution after revolution followed, until in May, 1347, the humanist Cola di Rienzo, full of poetical and unpractical dreams of Rome's past, established "the Good Estate," declaring the cause of Rome that of the whole of Italy, and calling upon the Italian States to free themselves from their tyrants and to send representatives to a national parliament. The scheme fell to nothing, through the disposition of the times and the unworthiness of the man who proposed it. Rienzi fled in December, and passed more than two years of mystical contemplation among the Fraticelli in the Abruzzi. An epoch of anarchy followed—scarcely abating during the Jubilee of 1350, when, finding themselves insulted and threatened, the papal legates put the city under an interdict. Sent by the Emperor as a prisoner to Avignon, Rienzi was reconciled to Innocent VI, and returned to Italy in the autumn of 1353, as the Pope's representative, to collaborate with the great Spanish cardinal in building up the fabric of the Church's temporal power—only to meet a shameful death on the steps of the Capitol.

"The Capitol was yet stained with the blood of Rienzi," writes Gibbon, "when Charles the Fourth descended from the Alps to obtain the Italian and Imperial crowns." For a while,

[1] M. Villani, ix. 87. For these changes and counter-changes, see the admirable essay by Pasquale Villari, *Il comune di Roma nel medio evo*, in *Saggi storici e critici*, Bologna, 1890.

Petrarca believed in him as Dante had believed in his grandfather —but was bitterly disillusioned. Crowned at Rome by the Cardinal of Ostia, on Easter Day, 1355, he returned to Prague: "with the crown which he had received without stroke of sword; with the purse full of money, which he had brought empty; but with little glory for virtuous deeds, and with great disgrace for the debasement of the Imperial Majesty."[1] "Oh," exclaimed Petrarca, "if thy grandfather and father met thee in the passage of the Alps, what thinkest thou they would say? Emperor of the Romans in name, thou art in truth only the King of Bohemia."[2]

At Siena and at Pisa, the imperial passage was marked by a revolutionary outbreak and the overthrow of the oligarchical government.

While on his way to Rome, the Sienese ambassadors, headed by Guccio Tolomei and Giovanni di Agnolino Salimbeni, had sworn fidelity to the Emperor at Pisa on behalf of the Nine, and he had sworn in return to preserve the liberties of Siena, and to make the Nine his vicars. But when, on his arrival at the city in March, the nobles and populace rose together, clamouring "Long life to the Emperor, and death to the Nine," the utmost that Charles would do for the unlucky magistrates was to refuse to surrender their persons to the fury of the mob. He received their abdication, forced them to renounce all the privileges he had granted them, and to annul the oath he had sworn to their ambassadors, while the populace were led by the younger nobles to sack their houses and drag their official chest through the city at the tail of an ass. The relations and adherents of the Nine hid themselves as best they could. No one would receive or speak with them. Their servants deserted them. The very priests and religious shrank from them as though they had the plague.

The government was entirely reformed in the interests of the lower middle classes. A new supreme magistracy of twelve *popolani*, henceforth known as the Twelve, the *Signori Dodici*,

[1] M. Villani, v. 54.

[2] *De Rebus Familiaribus*, Lib. XIX. ep. 12 (Fracassetti).

four from each terzo of the city, was appointed, holding office for two months, one of them to serve as Captain of the People and Gonfaloniere of Justice. There was at first a subsidiary council of six nobles, to be known as the Collegio, who were not to reside with the Signoria in the Palace, but without whom the Twelve could undertake nothing of importance nor open letters that concerned the State. But at the beginning of June, after the Emperor had passed again through Siena on his return journey, Giovanni di Agnolino Salimbeni (the most weighty in counsel of all the Sienese nobles, and a man most loyal to the Republic, with whose family Catherine was to be so closely associated), himself a member of the College, finding that this arrangement would not work, agreed with the Twelve to summon a general council in the Sala Grande of the Palace, at which the six nobles laid down their office and the College was abolished.[1] The government thus remained entirely in the hands of the Twelve and their adherents, known as the *Dodicini*, afterwards called the People of the Middle Number. The members of this new Monte (called, by Matteo Villani, of the "minuti mestieri") came from the class of the petty tradesmen and small notaries. It "formed a class intermediate between the order of the Noveschi and the lowest populace, and was composed for the most part of families which had become well-to-do by attending to trade and commerce, during that long period of prosperity that the Republic enjoyed under the oligarchical government of the Nine."[2] Their rule, however, proved the most corrupt and incompetent that Siena had ever endured, though they carried on an ultimately successful war against Perugia, and made attempts, partly by money, partly by hiring other mercenaries, to deal with the ever increasing scourge of the foreign companies that at intervals threatened the Sienese contado.

In the meanwhile, at Pisa, an alarm that the Emperor intended to liberate Lucca, and an attempt to reconcile the rival factions of the Raspanti and Bergolini, had led to a popular rising against

[1] *Cronica Sanese*, coll. 148–152.

[2] Grottanelli, notes to the *Leggenda minore*, p. 190.

him, in which his Germans suffered heavily. Both factions were equally implicated ; but the Raspanti had gained the ear of the Emperor, and obtained the support of the imperial troops in executing vengeance upon their enemies. The houses of the Gambacorti were destroyed, and the heads of the family put on their trial for treason. Their innocence was manifest, but the imperial judges wrung a confession by torture. On May 28, the three brothers, Francesco, Lotto, and Bartolommeo Gambacorti, with four of their principal adherents, were beheaded in the Piazza degli Anziani of Pisa, solemnly protesting their innocence to the last, and for three days, at the Emperor's orders, their bodies were ignominiously exposed in the mingled blood and filth of the piazza.[1] Piero Gambacorti, with his friends and kindred, was banished from the city ; while Caesar went on his way, leaving an imperial vicar behind him, and the State of Pisa in the hands of the treacherous Raspanti, who, in 1365, with the aid of foreign mercenaries, made Giovanni dell' Agnello, an unscrupulous and worthless upstart, lord of the city, with the title of Doge, to which he added that of captain-general of Lucca.

Cardinal Albornoz had come to Italy in the latter part of 1353. Temporizing with the Visconti, received enthusiastically by the Florentines and Sienese, welcomed even by the Perugians, he had begun by making war upon Giovanni di Vico, titular Prefect of Rome, the tyrant of Viterbo, Orvieto, Cività Vecchia, and other places in the Patrimony. Viterbo (henceforth the capital of the Patrimony), Orvieto, Assisi, Spoleto, and other Umbrian cities were recovered for the Church, while Rienzi was playing out the last scene of his deplorable melodrama on the stage of the Capitol. While Charles IV was receiving the imperial crown from the hands of the Cardinal of Ostia, the indefatigable Spaniard was carrying his victorious arms into the Marches, against the Malatesta of Rimini, Astorre Manfredi of Faenza, Francesco degli Ordelaffi of Forlì and Cesena. The petty despots were either expelled from their States or forced to act as papal vicars

[1] M. Villani, v. 31–33, 37 ; *Cronica di Pisa*, coll. 1029–1033 ; *Cronica Sanese*, coll. 150, 152.

on the Cardinal's terms, who made his headquarters at Montefiascone as Rector of the Patrimony. Faenza, Cesena, and Forlì were taken. Defeated in the open field by the papal forces, Galeotto Malatesta was compelled to enter into an alliance with the Church.

An even more signal triumph was the recovery of Bologna. Hard pressed by the armies of Bernabo Visconti, Giovanni da Oleggio surrendered the city to Albornoz in March, 1360, and Bologna thus became subject to the direct dominion of the Holy See. The Cardinal's warlike nephew, Gomez Albornoz, was made governor. War between Bernabo and the Church followed; Bologna was invested by the forces of the Visconti and again hard pressed, until in June, 1361, Gomez Albornoz, with the aid of Galeotto and Malatesta Malatesta, completely defeated Bernabo's army on the banks of the Savena at San Rossillo. Thus was the work of recovering the temporalities of the Church practically accomplished, when, on September 11, 1362, Innocent VI died at Avignon.

A few years before his death, Innocent, at the advice of Albornoz (who had practically left the city alone, and had, perhaps, never entered its walls), had nominated a single foreigner (that is, not Roman) Senator of Rome, a kind of Podestà to hold office for six months—the first appointed being a Sienese noble, Raimondo de' Tolomei. This pleased the people, but about the same time (1360), taking advantage of the preoccupation of Albornoz with the affair of Bologna, they set up a popular government under seven *Riformatori* (in imitation of the Florentine Priors), *popolani* to hold office for three months. Nobles were excluded from the army as well as from the government—the popular forces of the Republic being reorganized, under the two *Bandaresi* (in imitation of the Gonfalonieri of the Companies in Florence) and four *Antepositi*, into a military guild, which was known as the *Felix Societas Balestrariorum et Pavesatorum Urbis*, the "happy society of the crossbowmen and shieldbearers of the City." The Bandaresi and Antepositi sat in the special council of the city, with the Riformatori and the heads of the

Rioni (the districts into which Rome is still divided). Later on, they formed, together with the Riformatori, the Signoria, which was called the Signoria of the Bandaresi. A force of three thousand well-armed plebeians waited on their biddings. It was their office to execute justice against powerful evildoers and refractory nobles, and all who should shelter criminals in their fortresses; and they began their work with the most rigorous severity. "There is no prince or baron in the jurisdiction of the Roman People," writes the Florentine chronicler, "who is not terrified thereat and does not hold them in great dread, and who for fear does not obey the governors of Rome and their rulers." [1] Such was the Roman Signoria with which Catherine of Siena, at a critical epoch in her life, was to have to deal. And better had it fared with the Church, if it had been only the temporal lords of Rome who trembled before it!

Amidst this turmoil of political faction and moral corruption, men and women arose who looked for righteousness; flowers of the spiritual life bloomed even in the bloodstained streets of Siena and on the arid desert of the seven hills of Rome. Catherine's work was, to some extent, anticipated by the Swedish princess, Birgitta (whom we now call St. Bridget), that flower of the north transplanted to the Eternal City, and by Giovanni Colombini, himself a Sienese.

Giovanni di Pietro Colombini was a rich merchant, belonging to the order of the Noveschi, one who had himself sat in the Signoria of the Nine. He was absorbed in mercantile pursuits and in the acquisition of wealth, until one day, to soothe his irritation when dinner was not ready and he wished to return to the warehouse, his wife bade him read a volume of the lives of the Saints. He chanced upon the legend of St. Mary of Egypt, and was completely converted by its perusal. Another of the Noveschi, who had also been one of the Nine, Francesco di Mino Vincenti, joined him, and the two consulted the pious Carthusian, Pietro Petroni, who bade them follow Christ in the most absolute

[1] M. Villani, ix. 87; Villari, *op. cit.*, pp. 234, 235; Gregorovius, English ed., VI. part II. pp. 403, 404.

poverty.[1] This appears to have been in 1355, the year of the downfall of the Nine. A few years later, they carried out Pietro's counsels, placed their daughters in the Benedictine monastery of Santa Bonda (of which the Abbess, Madonna Paola di Ser Ghino Foresi, was a sort of spiritual mother to this new movement), and gave away all their possessions to religion and the poor—Giovanni first making adequate provision for Monna Biagia, his wife. Even as they had punished their former avarice with poverty, they sought for shame where they had once received honour ; and for two months, the time during which they had sat in the supreme magistracy of the Nine, they performed all the menial work of the Palace, begging their food in the meanwhile through the streets.

Disciples came to them, who were received and clothed with rags at the Madonna of the Campo, and initiated into the spirit of these new *poverelli* by public humiliation through the streets of Siena—which one young noble who joined them confessed that he found as bitter as death.[2] Among the earliest of these *Gesuati* (as they were afterwards called) was Tommaso di Guelfaccio, one of the leading Noveschi, previously a man of soft and luxurious life, whom we shall meet again in Catherine's circle. Giovanni and Francesco then wandered over the Sienese contado, preaching Christ and Poverty, working everywhere a wonderful revival, stirring up a new life among the Franciscans and Dominicans themselves, who welcomed them with enthusiasm, especially at Asciano and Montalcino. Said a friar minor to Giovanni : "If religious will once more begin to speak only of God, the spirit of holy fervour will return among us, and we shall set the world on fire."[3] Banished from the Sienese dominions by the Twelve, they wandered to Arezzo, Città di Castello,

[1] Pietro Petroni died in 1361. A vision which he had upon his death-bed brought about the conversion of Boccaccio. Cf. Petrarca, *Rerum Senilium*, Lib. I. ep. 5 ; Bartholomaeus Senensis, *Vita B. Petri Petroni*, III. 1, 2, 11.

[2] Cf. *Lettere del B. Giovanni Colombini*, 87, the reception of Giovanni di Niccolò di Verdusa.

[3] *Ibid.*, 17.

and other Tuscan cities, converting sinners, enforcing reparation of fame and goods, healing feuds and factions. Pisa, too, gave them a glad welcome, and at length the Twelve, for very shame, revoked their sentence of banishment. Something of the mystical aroma of these days lingers yet in the letters of Giovanni and Francesco still preserved, and not the least pleasant feature in them is the beautiful and pathetic spiritual intercourse that still bound the former to his devoted wife, who, as she said, had prayed for rain, but had not quite expected such a flood.

A very different figure is Birgitta, whose revelation on the death of Clement VI we have already heard. Born about the year 1303, the daughter of Birger, lord of Finstad, and Ingeborge, his wife (both of whom were connected with the reigning house of Sweden), Birgitta, when little more than a child, was married to Ulf Gudmarsson, a Swedish noble of royal blood, to whom she bore eight children, of whom Charles, the eldest of her five sons, and Catherine, the second of three daughters, will play a part in this history. Her married life was (save for the enforced marriage of her eldest daughter to an unworthy man) one of almost ideal happiness. Alike in her husband's castle of Ulfasa and in the court of Magnus II, King of Sweden and Norway, she wrought for Christ and the salvation of souls. At her request, her confessor, Matthias of Linköping, translated the Pentateuch into Swedish. On their return from a pilgrimage to Compostela, Ulf Gudmarsson became a monk, in 1343, and died in the following year, Birgitta being with him at the last.

Then the spirit of prophecy fell upon her, and the same mystical Voice spoke in the heart of the Swedish princess that the dyer's daughter of Siena was to hear a few years later.[1] The wonderful book of *Revelations*, that Birgitta now began to dictate, is at once a spiritual autobiography, a collection of epistles, a record of graces and visions, a denunciation of the corruption of the times. It anticipates in many respects Catherine's political letters and her *Dialogue* alike. For a while, she returned to the court, as Mistress of the Palace, to preach repentance there ; a

[1] *Revelationes S. Birgittae*, II. 10.

little later she founded at Vadstena her order of the Holy Saviour, composed of women and men alike, each monastery containing two convents, the Abbess to be as the Virgin Mother in the midst of the Apostles. Then she looked southwards to Avignon and Rome, and the Voice spoke again in her heart, inspiring her with an eloquent letter to Pope Clement, rebuking him as "a lover of the flesh" for the cupidity and ambition that he suffered to flourish in the Church, urging him to be converted before it was too late.[1] At the end of 1349, she left her native land, and went, by Milan, Pavia, and Genoa, to Rome for the Jubilee.

With Italy the rest of Birgitta's life was to be associated. At Farfa, whither she had fled with her company during the interdict, she was joined by her daughter—the tall, silent, golden-haired Catherine, unhappy and mysterious, a prey to depression and to fits of terror which were only too well-founded. While at Farfa, Catherine heard of the death of her husband. Returning to Rome, the Swedish ladies took up their residence first in the palace of the Pope's brother, Cardinal Hugues Roger de Beaufort, at San Lorenzo in Damaso, and afterwards in the house still shown (now a Carmelite convent) near the Campo de' Fiori. In the anarchy that followed the Jubilee, Catherine ran fearful risks at the hands of the lawless Roman barons who attempted to get possession of her. At last one of the Orsini, hearing that the Swedish ladies were to go to S. Lorenzo fuori le Mura on the Saint's feast, laid an ambush for them between the basilica and the gate. Converted by a miraculous blindness, the young baron became their most ardent protector, and through him they acquired the friendship and support of his house, and especially of Niccolò Orsini, the Count of Nola.

The desolation of the Eternal City struck deeply into Birgitta's soul, and inspired pages of pure eloquence not unworthy of Petrarca himself. A Voice ever cried in her heart: "O Rome, Rome, thy walls are broken down; thy gates are left unguarded; thy vessels are sold and thy altars are desolate; the living sacrifice and morning incense are consumed in the outer

[1] *Revelationes*, VI. 63.

courts, and therefore the sweetest odour of sanctity rises no more from the Holy of Holies." But still she saw room for hope. "Rome is verily as thou hast seen," said the Voice; "the altars are desolate, the offertory is spent in the taverns, and they that offer serve the world rather than God. Know, nevertheless, that, from the time of Peter the humble even until Boniface ascended the seat of pride, innumerable souls have ascended to Heaven. Rome is still not without friends of God; let them call upon the Lord, and He will have mercy upon them."[1] And again she heard the high command: "Thou shalt remain in Rome until thou seest the Pope and the Emperor, and thou shalt speak to them in My name the words that I shall tell thee." So, with the exception of a pilgrimage to Assisi and the holy places of Naples, Birgitta remained in Rome, tending the sick in the hospitals, begging alms for the poor, labouring for the salvation of souls, while she waited for the promised advent of Pontiff and Emperor; and, in the meanwhile, "she had many revelations concerning the state of the City, in which our Lord Jesus Christ rebuked the excesses and the sins of its inhabitants, with grave threatening of chastisement. Which revelations, brought to the knowledge of the inhabitants of Rome, stirred up furious hatred against the blessed Birgitta. Wherefore some of them threatened to burn her alive, and others blasphemed her as a sorceress; but the blessed Birgitta patiently suffered their threats and insults."[2]

To this coming of Pope and Emperor the thoughts of all who looked for the salvation of Israel were soon to be directed; yet was it to prove but the song that "bore false witness of dawn."

[1] *Revelationes*, III. 27. [2] *Revelationes extravagantes*, 8.

CHAPTER III

THE VALLEY OF LILIES

"Virgo sacra, jam summo doctore docente imo etiam compellente, addiscebat quotidie amplius, et in lectulo florido frui Sponsi caelestis amplexibus et ad convallem liliorum descendere, ut foecundior redderetur; nec alterum pro altero dimittere aut diminuere."—Raimondo da Capua, *Legenda*, § 130.

It was probably in 1366 that Catherine, the mystery of her spiritual espousals being fulfilled, began to go forth from her cell, to join in the life of the family, to labour for the conversion of souls. The voice of the celestial Bridegroom sounded in her ears: *Open to me, my sister, my beloved, my dove;* which Fra Raimondo interprets: "Open for me the gates of souls that I may enter them. Open the path by which My sheep may pass in and out, and find pasture. Open for My honour thy treasury of divine grace and knowledge, and pour it forth upon the faithful." The gifts that she had received in the cell were now to be made manifest to the world.

Once more, and this time in the face of vigorous opposition from her family, Catherine devoted herself to all the humblest menial labours of the house. With her father's leave, she had full liberty to give as much as she thought fit of his substance to the poor. She tended the sick, in their houses and in the hospitals, day and night, and with the greatest zeal nursed those afflicted by the most loathsome diseases. From a poor woman named Cecca, dying of leprosy and deserted by all, who reviled and taunted her while she gave herself up to relieving the horror and loneliness of her last days, she took the dreadful malady, which spread over her hands; but, when the woman at length died and Catherine had prepared the body for burial, she was miraculously healed. One of her own sisters in religion, Suora Palmerina, had been among her chief detractors, and persecuted her still with her hatred when on her death-bed; converted at last by her prayers, Palmerina died in peace, and Catherine beheld her soul, which, "albeit it was not yet blessed, was so beautiful that no words could express." And, all this while, her conversation with the Divine Master and Spouse continued uninterrupted and increasingly ardent, although at times He came to her only in the guise of the beggar to whom she gave her cloak or the silver cross of her chaplet. "Taught, nay, rather compelled by her supreme Teacher, she learned every day more and more both to enjoy the embraces of the celestial Bridegroom in the bed of flowers, and to descend into the valley of lilies to make herself more fruitful, nor ever to leave or lessen the one for the sake of the other." [1]

Though suffering intolerable pains in her whole frame, she impressed all who approached her by her constant mirthfulness, her never-failing high spirits, her radiant happiness. "She was always jocund and of a happy spirit," says one of her intimates, "and especially when held down by any sickness; while that lasted, she was ever all laughing in the Lord and exultant and rejoicing." [2] To those who criticized her almost entire abstinence from human food, she would answer humbly: "God for my sins has smitten me with a singular infirmity, by which I am totally prevented from taking food; I would eat right willingly, but cannot. Pray for me that He may forgive me my sins, because of which I suffer every ill." [3]

From the beginning to the end of her life, Catherine desired to be subject to all, even to the servant in her father's house and the poor she encountered in the streets or in the hospital. She, in all sincerity, regarded herself as the vilest of creatures, and desired to be treated as such; again and again, we shall find her asserting that her sins are the cause of all the evil around her, and almost that she alone is responsible for all the corruption of the world. She would fain have her faults judged by comparison with the graces she received. "If I were perfectly inflamed by the fire of Divine Love," she said once to Fra Raimondo, "and

[1] *Legenda*, II. ii. 4 (§ 130).
[2] *Contestatio Fr. Thomae Caffarini*, *Processus*, col. 1258.
[3] *Legenda*, II. v. 9 (§ 174).

besought my Creator with ardent heart, would not He who is all merciful surely use mercy towards all these, and grant them all to be enkindled by the fire which would then be in me? And what is it that impedes such great good? Surely nought else but my sins. The fault cannot be on the side of the Creator, in whom there is no defect; it must, therefore, be in me and from me. When I consider how many and what great graces the Lord has so mercifully granted me, in order that I might become such as I have said, and still through my iniquities I am not such, which is clearly shown me in the evils that I see, I am wroth against myself and bewail my sins, albeit for this I do not despair, but always hope the more that He may pardon me and them."[1]

There were times, indeed, when she suffered much, needlessly, through this humility. Although bound by no vows (for the Dominican tertiaries did not then take the vows of Chastity, Poverty, and Obedience, even if there were many who, like herself, practised them in the highest degree), Catherine had resolved to render the most absolute obedience to the friar who, according to the time, was the director of the Mantellate and to their prioress, as also to her own confessor. And Raimondo tells us that she persevered so rigidly in this resolution that, as she lay dying, with all her tendency to self-accusation, she could not remember that she had ever even once not kept it. Indeed, he writes, "if this holy virgin had never had any other affliction while she lived, than what her very indiscreet directors inflicted upon her, she would, in some sort, have been a martyr by reason of her great patience. For they, in no wise understanding, and often not even believing the excellence of the gifts granted her from above, wished entirely to guide her along the road of the others who live in ordinary fashion, nor did they render honour to the presence of the Divine Majesty which was leading her by a wondrous way, albeit of that they continually saw the manifest signs; like unto the Pharisees, who in such wise, seeing signs and prodigies, murmured at the healings which the Lord worked on

[1] *Legenda*, Prologue I. (§ 13).

the Sabbath, saying: This man is not of God, because he keepeth not the sabbath day."[1]

Almost from the beginning, persecution had come upon her, of a more material kind than the assaults of the evil spirits in her visions, and it lasted all through the earlier years of her public ministry. The persons to whom she had thus made herself spiritually subject, and especially the women, misliked her mode of life and distrusted her conduct. "She could hardly exercise an act of devotion in public, without suffering calumnies, impediments, and persecutions, particularly from those who ought most to have protected her and even to have continually encouraged her in those very acts." Not only Suora Palmerina, but others of the Mantellate, her sisters in religion, reviled and slandered her, and called upon their superiors to correct her. They even gained over some of the Dominican friars to their side, who refused to have any dealings with her, often deprived her of the Blessed Sacrament in Communion, and even for a while took away her faithful confessor from her. At times, when they condescended to let her communicate in their church, they would insist upon her straightway leaving off her prayers of thanksgiving and going home; which was a sheer impossibility for Catherine, as she used to communicate with such fervour that, immediately afterwards, she would pass into the state of ecstasy, in which for hours she would be totally unconscious. On one occasion, finding her in this condition, they forcibly threw her out of the church at mid-day, and left her in the heat of the sun, watched over by some of her companions, until she came to her senses. One friar even brutally kicked her as she lay helpless. Of course we are told that he came to an evil end, as also did another friar of the same type, "religious in habit, but not in deeds," who, when the other friars were in the choir of San Domenico after dinner, catching sight of her in the church when she was in ecstasy, came down and pricked her in many places with a needle. Catherine was not aroused in the least from her trance, but afterwards, when

[1] *Legenda*, I. ix. 1 (§ 80).

she came back to her senses, she felt the pain in her body and perceived that she had been thus wounded.[1]

But all these things Catherine bore with her usual unalterable patience and humility. They did it all with holy intention and for the good of her soul, she said, and she ever prayed for her assailants as for kind and beloved benefactors. No complaint ever crossed her lips, even when a friar robbed her of the money she had for the poor. "On her tongue and in her heart she had nought save Jesus ; along the streets she walked with Jesus ; her eyes gazed fixedly upon Jesus, nor did they ever open through curiosity to behold other objects, unless they were such that could guide her to Jesus ; wherefore she was often seen rapt in ecstasy, and lifted up in wondrous abstraction and excess of mind." Later, when she was told that men called her a hypocrite and deceiver, she answered : "They speak sooth, for, if the world knew me, it would stone me. I am the greatest of all sinners ; and what remains but that you all pray for me, that God may illumine me, and bring me to humility and patience and to do penance for my sins ? Would that I could embrace and kiss the feet of those who know me so well ! "[2]

Hardest of all was it to bear when they deprived her of the Blessed Sacrament. Whenever she could, she communicated every day; not only was this the centre of her whole inner life, but her very bodily existence seemed to depend upon it. So great was her inflamed desire of being united to her celestial Bridegroom in this way, that it was physical, no less than mental agony, to be thus deprived of His embraces. "I am a miserable wretch," we find her writing to one of her friars, "for my sins are so manifold that, since you went away, I have never been worthy to receive the most sweet and venerable Sacrament. I tell you this in order that you may help me to weep, and pray that I may be aided, so that I may receive the fullness of grace. Pardon my ignorance, father, and remember me at your most holy Mass, and I will

[1] *Legenda*, III. vi. 12, 13 (§§ 406, 407) ; *Contestatio Fr. Simonis de Cortona* (Casanatense MS.), pp. 514, 515.

[2] Tantucci, p. 38 ; *Contestatio Fr. Barontis*, MS. *cit.*, pp. 509, 510.

receive the sweet body of the Son of God spiritually from you."[1] And not only her enemies, but even her confessor seemed against her. Sometimes Fra Tommaso himself bade her, under the duty of obedience, to mistrust her visions, to regulate her life more like those of others in order to avoid scandal, to force herself to eat. Humbly and patiently, she always obeyed him to the letter, and found the agony caused her by the attempt to eat and drink a new way of doing penance. "Let us go and execute this wretched sinner," she would say with a smile when the time came, and, though she simply masticated what little she took without swallowing any, the pain was so intolerable that, in after years, Fra Raimondo urged her not to continue the attempt, in spite of what was said. Nevertheless, she persevered in this until her last illness, though the torment it caused her grew almost daily more terrible and acute.

Friends and disciples, of both sexes, now began to gather round her. Her little cell in her father's house became a centre of religious life, an ever-burning spiritual lamp to all in Siena who looked for righteousness.

A little group of Mantellate became her constant companions. Chief among them were the two we still see supporting her in Bazzi's glorious fresco: Alessa Saracini and Cecca (Francesca) Gori; both widows of noble birth, who had given all their possessions to the poor, and taken the black and white habit of penance. The latter, an older woman, had three sons in the Dominican order, probably very young novices. Of the former, Fra Raimondo writes that, although she became her disciple later in time than some of the others, she was nevertheless, in his opinion, the first in perfection and Catherine's most faithful imitator. Both appear to have been educated women, and to have frequently written Catherine's letters for her. Closely associated with these was the Saint's beloved sister-in-law, Lisa, "my sister-in-law, according to the flesh, but my sister in Christ," the wife of her brother Bartolommeo—all the members of Jacomo di Benincasa's family then living under his roof. Her own sister

[1] Letter 70 (114).

Lisa, too, seems to have taken the habit. Another of the first of her companions was a certain Caterina di Ghetto (or Scetto), possibly the daughter of one of the Saint's brothers-in-law, one of the young unmarried women who, in imitation of Catherine, joined the Dominican tertiaries.

The earliest of Catherine's men followers were two young Dominicans: Fra Tommaso di Antonio Nacci Caffarini, a novice, then about seventeen years old, and Fra Bartolommeo di Domenico, who was slightly older and already a priest, and had been a companion in the novitiate with Fra Tommaso della Fonte. Next to Fra Raimondo, we owe most of our information about Catherine to the devotion of these two friars. It is possible that their first introduction to her, by Fra Tommaso della Fonte, was during the time of her strict seclusion and retreat in her cell, which still remained the centre of the spiritual life of all her fellowship.

Fra Bartolommeo gives us a detailed description of that cell, before she came out of it, while she conversed with no men save at the command or by the permission of her confessor. We see its door and window always closed, the hard couch of bare boards, the little lamps always burning day and night before the images of Christ, of the Blessed Virgin, and of the Saints which were painted there.[1] In words that curiously recall those of the *Vita Nuova*, but much less poetically and more crudely expressed, he tells us how—although he, too, was young, and evidently morbidly sensitive on this point—all carnal passion died away when he approached her, and that others, whose normal mode of thinking and feeling was quite alien from his own, had the same experience: "For her aspect and address seemed to pour forth a certain fragrance of purity, more angelical than human, and withal she was always joyful and merry of countenance." Even so had it been with Dante, when he went to behold the *nobili e laudabili portamenti* of Beatrice: "And albeit her image, which kept continually with me, was a power of Love to rule over me,

[1] *Contestatio Fr. Bartholomaei, Processus*, col. 1312.

it was, nevertheless, of so noble a virtue that it never suffered Love to sway me without the faithful counsel of reason." [1]

Nevertheless, there were certain things that Bartolommeo at first found hard to accept. He noticed that, when she returned to consciousness after her prolonged ecstasies, Catherine always seemed to know what her women companions had done in the meanwhile, and sometimes rebuked them for idle talk or waste of time. The friar, "in my stupidity, being as yet ignorant of the virtues of the holy virgin," could not at once believe that she did this by what he calls the prophetic spirit :—

"But, at that time, when once I came to her cell with her aforesaid confessor, after a long conversation she asked us what we were doing at the second and third hour of the night. But we, wishing to try her, said, questioning her : 'What dost thou think ?' And she answered : 'Who knows this better than you yourselves ?' Then her confessor rejoined, at my suggestion : 'I charge thee, on thy obedience, tell us if thou knowest what we were doing at that time.' But she humbly refused to do this, until her confessor charged her again on her obedience. Then, humbly bowing down her head, she said : 'You know well that there were four of you, and you were in the cell of the subprior, talking for a long while at that late hour.' We asked her who they were, and she named each ; and when we asked her what we said, she replied that, for the most part, we talked about things pertaining to the salvation of our souls, albeit at times we touched on other matters. I was amazed, but still doubted whether one of us four had not told her this. Wishing, therefore, to test whether she knew this by man or by the spirit of prophecy, I came to her on the following day, and in our conversation said : 'O mother' (for so we were wont to call her), 'how knowest thou what we do ?' And she : 'O son, since it has pleased our sweet Saviour to give me the sons and daughters which, by His gift, I have, nothing concerning you is hidden from me ; but He showeth me clearly everything that is done about them.' Then I rejoined : 'Thou knowest, then, what I was doing yesterday

[1] Cf. *Contestatio cit.*, col. 1314, with *Vita Nuova*, §§ 2 and 19.

evening at such an hour of the night?' And she answered me: 'Surely, for you were writing, and you were writing about such a matter.' All of which was so. And she added: 'Son, I always watch and pray for you, my children, and for others, until in your convent the bell rings for matins, and shows me what you are doing; nay, if you had good eyes, you would see me with you—as clearly as I see all and each of you, who you are, where you are, and what you are doing. Very often our sweet Saviour bears me company, while I say the Psalms and walk up and down this little cell, and He talks with me, instructing me about many things. But when He sees me wearied, He sits over there, and at His bidding I sit at His feet, and we talk together up to that hour. But when that hour comes, He gives me leave to sleep, saying: Go, daughter, and rest, whilst thy brethren, who are now rising to matins, praise Me in thy stead. And so I sleep. Then, after a brief while of slumber, I straightway rise.'"[1]

At first, Bartolommeo was not edified by her calling herself *misera*, *miserabile*, more wretched than all men, the cause of all the evils that were done. He thought she did not really mean what she said; until, to his question how this could be, as she manifestly abhorred the sins that many delighted daily to commit, she answered as she did later on to Fra Raimondo: "O father, I see you do not know my wretched state. For I, miserable woman, have received so many and such wondrous gifts from my Creator, that, as I think, there is no reprobate so vile that, if he had received such, would not be all aflame and burn with the love of his Creator. And, both by the example of his life and by the words of his teaching, he would so enkindle the hearts of men to the love of our celestial country and to the contempt of the present life, that they would cease from their sins. Since therefore I, wretched woman, endowed with so many gifts, do not do this, what can I in very truth say about myself, but that I am most ungrateful to my God, and that I am the cause of the ruin of all, who through me could be called back from evil and incited to good? If I did my duty, I should call them back by the food

[1] *Contestatio cit.*, coll. 1320, 1321.

of God's word, and animate them to act rightly by the example of a good life; and, because I have not done this as I might, surely I am guilty." [1]

These were Bartolommeo's last doubts. He became her most ardent follower and champion, and frequently acted as her confessor and that of all her spiritual company. A certain Franciscan friar, Fra Lazzarino of Pisa, was one of the first who followed him to her feet. An eloquent and popular preacher, a man of considerable learning, though by no means an exemplary Franciscan as far as his vow of poverty was concerned, Lazzarino was at that time lecturing on philosophy at Siena. He hated the very name of Catherine, abused her both in public and in private, and persecuted her friends. Knowing the devotion to her of Fra Bartolommeo, who was then lecturing occasionally on the *Sentences* of Peter the Lombard, he tried to make him unpopular with the students. Finding all his efforts against Catherine's reputation were useless, he began to preach publicly against her, and, when that failed, decided to visit her, under pretence of devotion, in order to catch her in her speech. With this intention, he came on the evening of the feast of St. Catherine, Virgin and Martyr, to Bartolommeo's cell, and asked him to bring him to her; and the Dominican, thinking his heart was touched, with leave of Fra Tommaso della Fonte, accompanied him to the house. Let Bartolommeo himself relate what followed:—

"When we entered her holy cell, Fra Lazzarino sat down upon a stool; she seated herself at his feet upon the floor, while I took a seat apart on the opposite side. Both kept silence for a while. At length he began: 'I have heard such good report of thy holiness and that thou art endowed by the Lord with the understanding of the Scriptures, that I have come to thee, hoping to hear somewhat to edify and comfort my soul.' But she answered: 'I am glad at your coming, for I believe the Lord has sent you in order that you, who have the knowledge of the holy Scriptures with which you daily feed the souls of the people, may be moved by charity to comfort my poor little soul; and so, for the love

[1] *Contestatio cit.*, coll. 1346, 1347.

of Jesus Christ, I pray you deign to do.' When, therefore, the time had passed in such conversation and night was at hand, he (not, indeed, mocking her, as he had thought to do, but nevertheless, in his heart, making little account of her) said: 'I see the hour is late, and therefore deem I had better go; I will return on another occasion at a more suitable hour.' And so he rose up to go. But, as he went away, the holy virgin followed him, and, kneeling with crossed arms, besought him to bless her; which he did. And, when she had his blessing, she besought him to remember her in his prayers. Then he, moved rather by shamefacedness than by devotion, asked her to pray for him, which she gladly promised she would do. He, therefore, went away, as I said, making small account of her, deeming her to be a good woman, but not worthy of her great reputation."

During the following night, Lazzarino rose to meditate upon the lecture which he was to deliver the next morning, and found himself overwhelmed by a flood of tears, which he was unable to check. In the morning, he forced himself to go to the schools and read his lecture perfunctorily, at once leaving the room when he had finished, because he could not contain his tears. So passed the day, until, in the night, he began to think that he had unwittingly offended God. Then a voice spoke in his heart: "Hast thou so soon forgotten that, the day before, thou didst scorn My faithful handmaid Catherine with so orgulous a mind, and that, albeit feignedly, thou didst nevertheless commend thyself to her prayers?" Before sunrise, he left San Francesco and hastened to Catherine's house. Catherine herself, "not ignorant of the things that were being worked in this man by her Spouse," opened the door. He fell at her feet; she knelt and implored him to rise. Entering the cell, he humbly sat down like her on the floor, and, after "a long and holy colloquy," besought her to adopt him as a son, and to direct him in the way of God. "But when she said that he knew the way of God better, by means of the holy Scriptures, he answered that he knew the rind, but she tasted the very pith. At length, constrained by his earnest prayers, she answered: 'The way of salvation for your soul is that, despising the pomp of the world and all its favour, casting away all money and superfluities, you follow Christ crucified and your father, Blessed Francis, in nakedness and humility.'"

Fra Lazzarino seemed changed into another man. He gave away all he had, even his books, excepting a commentary on the Gospels which he needed for his sermons, "and became really a true poor man of Christ." He became a zealous champion of Catherine's cause, and endured much persecution in consequence, especially from his own brethren, but triumphed over all and devoted himself to the conversion of souls. One of his fellow Franciscans tells us that he fled the society of the other friars to live in lonely hermitages, from which he would emerge at times to preach to the people, and that on these occasions his words were like flaming arrows to pierce the hearts of all who heard.[1]

Although Bartolommeo says that he became *valde domesticus* with himself, Lazzarino—perhaps because of his membership of the rival order—does not seem ever to have been closely associated with Catherine's spiritual family. We have, however, a dictated letter from Catherine to him, undated, but probably of a somewhat later epoch, a letter in which the Dominican tertiary, too, claims the seraphic Father of Assisi as hers :—

"Jesus hangs upon the Cross," she writes, "as our rule and our way, and as a written book in which all the unlearned and blind can read. The first verse of the book is hate and love; that is, love of the honour of the Father, and hatred of sin. Then, most beloved and dearest brother, and father by our reverence for the Sacrament, let us follow this sweet book, that so sweetly shows us the way. And if it befall that our three foes should assail us in the way, to wit, the world, the flesh, and the devil, let us take the weapons of hate, as did our father, St. Francis. In order that the world should not puff him up, he chose holy, true, and utter poverty. And so would I have us do. And if the demon of the flesh should rebel against the spirit, let us be angry with ourselves, and afflict and chastise our

[1] *Contestatio cit.*, coll. 1347–1351 ; *Contestatio Fr. Angeli de Salvettis* (O.F.M.), *loc. cit.*, col. 1367.

body; even as that father of ours did, who ever ran along this holy way with zeal and not with negligence. And if the devil should come with many illusions and varied fantasies and with servile fear, and wish to occupy our mind and soul, let us not be afraid; for these things are become powerless by the virtue of the Cross. O sweetest Love! They can do no more than God allows them; and God wills nought else than our good; He will not, therefore, give us more than we can bear. Take comfort, take comfort; and do not shun pain; but ever keep the will holy, so that it may repose in nought save in what Christ loved and in what God hated.[1] And our will, so armed with hate and love, will receive such fortitude that, as St. Paul says, neither the world nor the devil nor the flesh will be able to draw us back from this way. Let us bear, let us bear, dearest brother; for the more pain we bear down here with Christ crucified, the more glory shall we receive; and no pain will be so much rewarded, as mental pain and labour of the heart; for these are the greatest pains of all, and, therefore, are worthy of greater fruit."[2]

It is somewhat remarkable that Catherine seems never to have had any dealings with Giovanni Colombini. Although she frequently visited the monastery of Santa Bonda in the company of Lisa, and corresponded with two of the nuns there, she never makes any allusion to Giovanni in her letters. A cousin of his, however, Matteo Colombini, was among her correspondents, and Tommaso di Guelfaccio, whom we have met among the Gesuati, seems to have been one of the first to frequent her cell, and was afterwards, to some extent, associated with her labours.

[1] That is, keep the will steadfast in love of virtue and hatred of vice.

[2] Letter 225 (121). This letter was probably in answer to one of Lazzarino's to her, of which a mutilated fragment is preserved in the Biblioteca Comunale of Siena (MS. T. iii. 3), in which, as far as any connected sense can be made out of what is left, he appears to be complaining of the persecution he is receiving from his fellow Franciscans. It is dated "in Firenze lo dì dela pentecoste," and addressed to "Chaterina da Siena sposa di Jeso Cristo crocifixo et serva de suo servi et madre de suo fedeli devoti, in Pisa." Both letters are probably of the year 1375.

While the spiritual household of his daughter was thus being formed, Jacomo di Benincasa died. He had always been a tender and loving father, especially in these latter years, and Catherine "found his soul ready for the passage, nor kept back by any desire of the present life, for which thing she rendered immense thanks to her Saviour." In after years, she told Fra Raimondo that she had wrestled with the Lord in prayer that her father might not have to sustain the pains of Purgatory, and had at last obtained this grace for him, on the condition that she should bear them instead. At the instant he passed away, a grievous pain in the side assailed her, and never again left her until the end of her life: "But, as he expired, the holy virgin laughed for joy, saying: 'Blessed be the Lord, would that I were as you;' nor, whilst the others wept during the rites for the dead, could she show aught else save joy and gladness. She comforted her mother and the others, as though she was in no wise concerned at this death, for she had seen that soul pass out of the darkness of the body and enter immediately into the eternal light."[1]

Jacomo di Benincasa was buried at San Domenico on August 22, 1368. A man of the old regime, he died but a few weeks before the overthrow of his party in the State, which was also to reduce his own family to comparative poverty. A year before his death, a great event had filled all who looked for righteousness with hopes of a new era and renovation of the Church; hopes that Jacomo was not to see dashed to the ground; a Sovereign Pontiff had landed in Italy, and the successor of St. Peter had returned to Rome.

[1] *Legenda*, II. vii. 4 (§ § 220–222).

CHAPTER IV

THE COMING OF URBAN THE FIFTH

"Tu es qui venturus es, an alium expectamus"?—Matth. xi. 3.
"Colui che fece per viltà lo gran rifiuto."—Dante, *Inf.* III. 59, 60.

GUILLAUME DE GRIMOARD, Abbot of St. Victor of Marseilles, was at Florence, on his way to Naples on a mission from the Pope to Queen Giovanna, when the news reached Italy that Innocent VI was dead. "I dare to say," quoth the worthy monk, when he heard the tidings, "that if, by the grace of God, I were to see a Pope who would come to Italy, to the true papal seat, and would beat down the tyrants, I should be happy, if I had to die the next day."[1] On his return from Naples, he arrived at Marseilles at the end of October, 1362, to be met by a message from the Sacred College informing him that (owing to a deadlock in the conclave) he had been elected Pope. He was crowned at Avignon, under the title of Urban the Fifth.

The newly elected Pontiff was fifty-three years old. Never having been a cardinal, he was untainted by the corruption of the Curia. A man of simple and blameless life, learned and devout, he hated pomp and luxury, abominated simony and nepotism and all the vices he saw around him. His choice of a name, *Urban*, was held by the Italians to point towards Rome.[2] In the preceding year, he had been sent as ambassador to Bernabo Visconti, to urge the rights of the Church upon Bologna ; the tyrant, in one of his outbursts of bestial fury, had forced him to eat the fragments of the papal brief and driven him with contumely from Milan, according to one account with even grosser personal outrage. He knew then, by personal experience, what these tyrants of Italy were like. When Bernabo's ambassadors arrived to congratulate him on his election and to express their master's

[1] M. Villani, xi. 26.

[2] Cf. Petrarca, *Rerum Senilium*, Lib. VII. ep. I.

desire to come to terms, the Pope gravely answered that, when their lord had restored her cities to the Holy See and repented of his crimes, he would receive him back into the bosom of the Church.[1] His intention was to crush this chief despot first, and then send all Christendom forth to recover the Holy Places. But the realization of the scheme was impossible. Wars raged everywhere. France was at war with England, the Emperor on the point of hostilities with the King of Hungary, who in his turn was assailing the Venetians. Italy clung to her state of anarchy. Siena fought Perugia for the possession of Cortona and Montepulciano; Florence, with mercenaries under Galeotto Malatesta, made war on Pisa with mercenaries under Sir John Hawkwood. A general league against Bernabo effected little, and, in 1364, a peace was signed at Milan by which Bologna was left in the hands of the Church, but the Pope weakly consented to remove Albornoz to the southern legation.

Each peace, whether in France or in Italy, set loose fresh hordes of mercenaries, who moved over the lands almost unchecked, so admirably organized as to deserve the description that Gregorovius gives them, of "errant military states." In vain did Urban publish bull after bull, hurling anathemas at the companies and their leaders. The condottieri mocked at Rome's thunders. In the latter part of 1365, Duguesclin, on his way to Spain, besieged the Pope himself in Avignon, compelling him to pay an enormous ransom, and to absolve him and his followers from all censures.

It was, perhaps, this humiliation that induced Urban to carry out his old resolution of returning to Rome, to which the Romans had invited him at the beginning of his pontificate. The exhortations of the royal Spanish Franciscan, Peter of Aragon, who came to Avignon full of an impassioned dream of the reformation of the Church, no less than the eloquent appeal of Petrarca, made a deep impression on the Pope. The Emperor was favourable, and Albornoz urged him to make no delay. In

[1] M. Villani, xi. 31, 32. Cf. *Diario d'Anonimo Fiorentino* (edited by Gherardi), p. 296.

spite of the opposition of the King of France, Urban left Avignon on April 30, 1367, and, on June 4, he landed at Corneto, where a great throng of nobles and envoys from almost every State of Italy was waiting to receive him, headed by Albornoz himself and Birgitta's friend, the Count of Nola. In the midst of all this glittering show were Giovanni Colombini and Francesco Vincenti, with some sixty of their *poverelli*, clad in the most amazing rags. They had accompanied Albornoz from Viterbo, had invaded the Franciscan convent in which Urban was to stay, insisting upon making his bed, and those of the cardinals, and now, crowned with olive and carrying branches in their hands, they rushed madly to and fro, cheering frantically for Christ and the Pope. "It was the most lovely and devout thing that was ever seen," wrote Giovanni to the Abbess of Santa Bonda. They were accused of heresy, like that of the Fraticelli, the *frati della povera vita*, of whom there were many in Tuscany; but the Pope's brother, the "Cardinal of Avignon," Anglico de Grimoard, "who is like a lamb," and the papal secretary, Petrarca's friend Francesco Bruni, took them under their protection, and promised to befriend them with the Sovereign Pontiff.

At Corneto the Pope stayed for Whitsuntide, and received an embassy from the Romans, who conferred the full dominion of the City upon him, and gave him the keys of Sant' Angelo. Then he moved on to Toscanella, the *poverelli* running round him all the way. Urban bore it all with exemplary patience, but, when he got to his lodging, he sent for Francesco and told him he did not like their rags, but would clothe them in grey habits and white hoods at his own expense—whereat the "poor little men" sang psalms of praise.

The Pope entered Viterbo in state on June 9, 1367, "with such grace and exultation that it seemed the very stones would cry: Blessed is he that cometh in the name of the Lord." Here he took up his abode in the great fortress that Albornoz had built, and received the lords of the Italian cities that acknowledged his sway and the ambassadors of the Republics. To the unsophisticated eyes of Giovanni and Francesco, everything seemed ideal. "This Holy Father," they wrote to the Abbess and nuns of Santa Bonda, "is considered a good man, and we believe that God through him is working good and holy things. He has a brother who seems to us most holy and a good servant of God and right humble, and who keeps up his state unwillingly; he loves us right well; may Christ reward him and give him His grace. Think, Madonna and our mothers, that here is all the nobility of the world, with pomps and delights and goodly robes and lordship, and all lovely things and great are here. But, all the same, never was Poverty so dear to us as now, and never did she please us so." They were profoundly edified even by the papal courtiers. "You could not imagine how much virtue we find in these cardinals and in these great lords and many others, so much so that we are confounded at what they do. They have more humility in their great estate and in their vast wealth than we, poor and proud, in our vile and abject condition; we make the show, and they do the deeds." Cardinal Anglico gave them a rule of life, "which pleases us much, and, with the grace of God, will please all, for it is the true way of salvation."[1] But they would accept no bulls or privileges of any kind from the Pope. Their friend, the Bishop of Città di Castello, said to them: "Let virtues defend you, and not papal bulls."

With their order now confirmed, the seventy or more *poverelli* having doffed their rags and put on the new white and grey papal habit, Giovanni and Francesco left Viterbo towards the end of July. At Acquapendente, Giovanni fell ill. They tried to bring him back to Santa Bonda, but he died on the way at the abbey of San Salvatore on Monte Amiata, on the last day of July, 1367. He was buried in the church of the monastery of Santa Bonda. Fifteen days later, Francesco Vincenti followed him into the other world. Their order of the Gesuati, white-hooded and grey-gowned, lives now only on the canvasses of the painters of their native city.

One anxiety had clouded the last days of Giovanni's stay at

[1] *Lettere del B. Giovanni Colombini*, 90–93, 95, 108.

Lombardi

Giovanni Colombini.

Sano di Pietro

Accademia Siena

Viterbo. The Pope was arranging a league against the Visconti, and the Sienese ambassadors did not come. The only political letter of Giovanni and Francesco that has come down to us, dated Viterbo, July 18, is to the "magnificent lords, the Twelve, governors of the city of Siena," on this subject. Francesco Bruni has told them that his Holiness is amazed at their delay, and they implore them for their own good, lest they lose the Pope's favour, instantly to send the ambassadors.[1] On July 31, the very day of Giovanni's death, the league was signed in the Apostolic Palace, and, through the personal influence of the Marquis of Ferrara, the Republic of Siena joined it.[2] But, on August 20, the great Cardinal Albornoz died, followed to his grave by the admiration and reverence of friend and foe. At once his presence was missed in the papal counsels. An anti-French tumult broke out at Viterbo on September 5, and for three days Urban and his cardinals were besieged in the fortress by the insurgents. Florence and Siena, and even Rome itself, sent troops to his aid, but the Pope was glad at length to leave the turbulent capital of the Patrimony. Escorted by the Marquis of Ferrara with his men-at-arms, Urban left Viterbo on October 14. On October 16, he entered Rome in triumph, riding on a white mule, and was received with universal joy and acclamation. The Marquis of Ferrara, Count Amedeo of Savoy, the lords of the Malatesta family, and all the petty nobles of the Marches and Campagna accompanied him; the fierce soldier, Rodolfo Varano of Camerino, bore up the standard of the Church. Armed mercenaries, infantry and cavalry, surrounded the prelates and cardinals of the Curia. Such was the martial entry of the Vicar of the Prince of Peace; but the simple monk, who thus seemed the sovereign of the world, wept to see the desolation of the Sacred City, and threw himself in fervent prayer upon the ground at the tomb of the Apostle whose place he came to hold.

[1] *Lettere del B. Giovanni Colombini*, 110.

[2] See G. Sanesi, *Siena nella Lega contro il Visconti.* In the *Bullettino Senese di Storia Patria*, Anno I., 1894.

In the spring of the following year, 1368, the Emperor came again to Italy, as he had promised. He came with an army to carry out the designs of the league against the Visconti, joined forces with the papal troops and those of Queen Giovanna (to whom Urban had just given the Golden Rose), but effected nothing. Having made a truce with Bernabo and accepted a large sum of money from him, he moved southwards into Tuscany.

The rule of the Twelve in Siena was tottering. The party had split into two sections, one of which allied with the Tolomei and other nobles, while the other had the powerful support of the Salimbeni. Giovanni di Agnolino Salimbeni managed to prevent the two factions coming to open war, but, on his return from an embassy to the Emperor, he was killed by a fall from his horse on the way from Siena to his castle of Rocca d'Orcia. The nobles and Noveschi secretly brought troops into the city, and, on September 2, with the support of the populace, they forced the Twelve to surrender the Palace and the entire control of the State. Thirteen consuls were appointed, ten nobles and three Noveschi, who sent Messer Vanni Malavolti and two other ambassadors to the Emperor at Lucca. The Salimbeni and the Dodicini allied, and sent a rival embassy; Charles accepted their offers, and despatched Malatesta Malatesta to Siena with eight hundred horsemen. On September 24, the Salimbeni, shouting for the People and the Emperor, began a general rising against the new aristocratic régime, and admitted Malatesta and his cavalry. There was furious fighting from street to street, and a last mighty struggle in the Campo round the Palace, which was finally stormed by the imperial troops and sacked by the infuriated populace. The nobles fled the city with their families, while Malatesta fortified himself in the Poggio Malavolti, from which he ruled the city as imperial vicar. A popular council of a hundred and twenty-four plebeians was assembled, called the *Consiglio de' Riformatori*, which created a new Signoria of twelve "Defenders," representatives of all classes of the people. The Salimbeni were given Massa and five other castles in the Sienese contado, and declared *popolani.* The Emperor, passing through Siena on his way to join the Pope at Viterbo, knighted two of the family for their services, and accepted an enormous present of money from the Commune.

On October 21, the Pope and the Emperor entered Rome together, Charles leading Urban's mule on foot. This was the great event for which Birgitta had so long waited in patience, but, now that it had come, it brought her a personal trial and disappointment. She had communicated her visions concerning the reformation of the Church to the Pope. She had written to the Emperor, urging him to unite in this great work, and she now wrote again in the name of Christ, bidding him hearken to her revelations, and strive to make the Divine justice and mercy feared and desired upon earth.[1] But Charles simply ignored her, and Urban had no time at present to attend to a woman's admonitions.

The state of Siena was bordering upon anarchy. The banished nobles held the fortresses in the contado, burned and foraged up to the gates of the city, and absolutely declined to come to terms with the government of the Defenders, at whose sentences and decrees they mocked. Malatesta sent the army of the Commune against them, but it effected nothing. On December 11, there was a popular rising against the less democratic element in the new administration. The mob fired the gate of the Palace, broke in, and drove out the representatives of the Nine and Twelve from the Signoria. Ultimately, by a kind of compromise, under the authority of the imperial vicar, a new council of plebeian reformers instituted a fresh Signoria of fifteen "Defenders," eight of the *popolo minuto*, four of the Twelve, and three of the Nine. The Captain of the People and the "Gonfalonieri Maestri" (the Gonfalonieri of the three terzi of the city) were always to be of the *popolo minuto*, while the Captain was to have three counsellors, one from each order of the people, all together forming a supreme authority in criminal cases. Thus was established the

[1] *Revelationes*, IV. 45, VIII. 50, 51.

artisan government of the *Riformatori*, or *popolo del maggior numero*, in Siena.[1]

In the meanwhile, the Dodicini and the Salimbeni, who had instigated the rising for their own advantage and were naturally disappointed at the results, sent agents to the Emperor to implore his aid. Charles was now on his way back from Rome. On December 22, with the Empress, he entered Siena, "all armed save the head," with an imposing array of imperial troops, and alighted, as before, at the Palazzo Salimbeni. A few days later, the Cardinal Guy of Boulogne, a warlike French prelate whom the Emperor had made imperial vicar-general in all Tuscany, arrived at Siena with reinforcements. The adherents of the Twelve hailed him as a possible ecclesiastical despot to overthrow their enemies. Charles demanded the surrender into his hands of the towns and fortresses of Massa, Montalcino, Grosseto, Talamone, and Casole, with the intention of handing them over to the Cardinal. The Defenders summoned a council of more than eight hundred citizens, and returned a practically unanimous refusal. Neither would they make any fresh modification of their constitution at the Bohemian Caesar's bidding. The Noveschi and the populace alike were prepared to end the crisis by recalling the exiled nobles.

On the morning of January 18, 1369, there arose a sudden clamour through the streets of Siena: "Long live the People," "Death to the traitors who want the nobles back!" Led by Niccolò Salimbeni and his allies of the Dodicini, armed bands rushed through each terzo of the city, sacking and slaying as they went, while two other Salimbeni, Pietro and Cione, entered the Palace with their followers. The whole thing had been prearranged with the imperial authorities. Malatesta brought his soldiery into the Campo and called upon the Defenders, in the name of the Emperor, to expel their colleagues of the Nine. Summoned by the Salimbeni, Charles himself mounted, and moved towards the Palace with three thousand horsemen.

[1] Cf. O. Malavolti, *Historia de' Sanesi*, pp. 132, 132*v*.

All the bells of the city clashed out the alarm. The train-bands were in arms and poured into the Campo. Seizing the banner of the People, the Captain, Matteino di Ventura, left the Palace, put himself at their head, and drove the imperial forces back upon the Croce del Travaglio. In the narrow streets, assailed in all directions, deafened by the clanging bells, rained upon by stones and darts, the heavily-armed chivalry of the north was helpless. After an "incredible battle" of several hours, the Emperor was driven back to the Palazzo Salimbeni, with the loss of more than four hundred slain, including one of his own nephews. The three representatives of the Nine, who had left the Palace, were brought back in triumph in procession, to the sound of trumpets, crowned with garlands and bearing branches of olive. Pietro and Cione Salimbeni, in their turn, were made prisoners, and forced to yield up Massa to the Commune. A proclamation was issued forbidding any food to be sold or given to the Emperor or his people. Starved and terrified, protesting that he had been betrayed, the successor of Augustus pardoned the Commune everything, made the Defenders his vicars in perpetuity, meekly received back as many of his horses and as much of his property as the Captain of the People could recover, accepted a large sum of money, and went his way on January 25.[1] So cowed was the Emperor that a mere suggestion of trouble made him shrink from entering Pisa, where the upstart Doge had been overthrown and the old democratic government of the Anziani restored in the previous September. He passed on to Lucca, where he stayed till July, formally liberating that city for ever from the Pisan yoke.

In February, the Gambacorti—led by Piero and Gherardo and their sons—returned to Pisa in triumph, enthusiastically welcomed by the people in memory of the good government of their forebears. At the high altar of San Michele, Messer Piero swore love and fidelity to the Commune and People of Pisa, and he kept his oath. In the inevitable tumult against the Raspanti that

[1] *Cronica Sanese*, coll. 204–207

followed, he did his utmost to restrain the excesses of his adherents: "I have forgiven, as you know, the beheading of my kinsmen," he said, "and will not you forgive?"[1] In September, 1370, the citizens offered to make him absolute lord of Pisa, but he refused, and chose to be merely the chief salaried officer of the Republic, "Captain-General and Defender of the Commune and People." The administration of the twelve Anziani remained, but Piero Gambacorti was virtually the ruler of the State. He was a merciful and pacific man, an ardent Catholic and deeply religious, and his government was, in the main, of a paternal description. Lucca lay directly subject to the Roman Empire in the person of the Cardinal Guy of Boulogne, until in March, 1370, through the intervention of the Pope, the Cardinal surrendered his authority, and Lucca became a free Republic once more, with a Signoria of ten (nine Anziani and a Gonfaloniere of Justice) and the usual two councils. Like the government of the Gambacorti at Pisa, the new-born Republic of Lucca was decidedly papal in its tendencies and sympathies—a political fact of importance in the coming convulsions of Italy.

But, in Siena, things seemed little better under the new régime. There were risings and tumults within the city, in the main the work of the Salimbeni and the adherents of the Twelve, directed against the Noveschi; there was plundering and ravaging in the contado, the Marquis of Monferrato having failed in his attempt to reconcile the nobles with the popular government. Armed guards were set all over the city and at the gates: "And on the tower of the Campo many guards kept watch, day and night, and gave signals with fire and smoke when it was needful, and rang the bells to give the alarm." The Defenders appointed a new officer, the Executor of Justice, with full powers to enforce order, but with little result. "And thus all law and all justice was dead in the city of Siena, by the work of the Salimbeni and of the Twelve. To such a pitch it came that, in Siena and in the contado, men slew and plundered on every side."[2] The nobles

[1] *Cronica di Pisa*, col. 1052.

[2] *Cronica Sanese*, coll. 207, 208.

had sent Messer Vanni Malavolti, the government a certain Jacomo di Guido Guernieri (a swordsmith by trade), as ambassadors to Florence, and at length, in the spring of 1369, by Florentine intervention, a temporary peace was made between the nobles and the people, which was greeted with trumpets and salvos and great rejoicing.

Like most others that belonged to the order of the Dodicini, the family of Jacomo di Benincasa suffered heavily from the change of government. Catherine's elder brothers, Benincasa and Bartolommeo, were active members of their faction, and, either on the occasion of the September rising or in one of the later tumults, they were sought out by a band of the populace who meant to take their lives. A friend rushed into the house, telling them that the enemy were at hand, urging them to take refuge in the neighbouring church of Sant' Antonio, whither others of their faction had already fled. But Catherine sprang to her feet: "They must not go to Sant' Antonio," she said, "and I am sorry indeed for those who are there." She put on her mantle, and, bidding her brothers come with her and fear not, led them safely through their enemies, who lowered their weapons and reverently saluted her as she passed, to the hospital of Our Lady, where she left them in charge of the rector, telling them to stay in hiding for three days, and then return home in safety. And so it happened. All those who had taken shelter in Sant' Antonio were slain or made prisoners, but, after three days, the tumult subsided. Catherine's brothers were condemned to a fine of one hundred gold florins, which they paid, and were left in peace.[1]

As we have seen, the Twelve had still a small part in the new régime, and Benincasa and Bartolommeo were at first among the representatives of their faction that held office, the latter, it is said, having even sat in the Signoria as one of the Defenders for two months in 1370. But their condition had altered for the worse since their father's death. The revolution had ruined their business prospects, and, in the early autumn of this year, the two,

[1] The anonymous author of the *Miracoli*, quoted by Grottanelli in the notes to the *Leggenda minore*, pp. 209, 210.

together with Stefano, emigrated to Florence, and were admitted to the Florentine citizenship. Their family had business connections with Florence, and, apparently, had kept a workshop there for some considerable time previously.[1] In their adopted city they continued to exercise the art of dyers and tanners, but with little success, and were soon reduced to poverty. Catherine's beloved friend and companion, Lisa, naturally accompanied her husband.

Catherine followed them not only with prayers, but with letters. Writing to the three together, "I would see you always united," she says, "with the sweet bond of holy charity, so that neither demon nor word of man can separate you from it. I remember the word that Jesus Christ said: *he that humbleth himself shall be exalted*. Do thou, Benincasa, who art the eldest, wish to be the least of all, and thou, Bartolommeo, wish to be less than the least, and I pray thee, Stefano, to be subject to God and them; and so, sweetly, will you preserve yourselves in most perfect charity."[2] Patience and submission to the will of God is the note of her three letters to Benincasa. The blood of Christ will make him strong to bear with true patience every labour and tribulation, from whatever side they come: "It will make you persevering, so that, even until death, you will endure with true humility; because in that blood the eye of your understanding will be illumined by the truth, which is that God wills nought else save our sanctification, because He loves us ineffably; otherwise, He would not have paid so great a price for us. Be then content, be content in every time and place, for all are given you by the Eternal Love for love. Rejoice in your tribulations, and consider yourself unworthy that God should send you by the way that

[1] Grottanelli, *op. cit.*, pp. 211–213, gives the text of the petition of the three brothers (October 16, 1370) for admission to the Florentine citizenship, which was approved by 78 votes to 28. It is difficult to explain their claim to have been virtually Florentine citizens for so many years, unless it is a mere form of words and a recognized polite fiction. In Florence, the *Ars tinture guadi* was one of the minor guilds subjected to the great *Arte della Lana*, the guild of the wool-merchants.

[2] Letter 14 (252).

His Son trod, and in all things render glory and praise to His name." "Dearest brother, be a lover of virtue with holy patience, and go often to confession, which will help you to bear your burdens. I tell you that God will use His benignity and mercy, and will reward you for every burden that you have borne for love of Him."[1] But, presently, a coldness arose between Benincasa and those he had left behind in Siena ; in his tribulation, he thought that his mother ought to have helped him, while she, apparently, felt more in need of aid from him. Catherine naturally took Lapa's part, and held her brother ungrateful :—

"You must remember to correct yourself of your ingratitude and churlishness, in the matter of the duty you owe your mother, to whom you are bound by the commandment of God. As to your not having fulfilled the obligation of helping her, I hold you excused, because you have not been able ; but, even if you had been able, I do not know that you would have done it, seeing that you have been niggardly to her even in your words. In your ingratitude you have not considered how she bore you and gave you suck, nor all the care she has had of you and of all the others. If you tell me that she has not been tender to us, I say that it is not true, for she has been so tender to you, and to the other, that it costs her dear. But, even if it were true, you would be in her debt, and not she in yours. She took no flesh from you, but gave you hers. I pray you to correct this and your other defects, and pardon me my rudeness, for, if I did not love your soul, I would not say what I say to you."[2]

A little later, she sent a beautiful and tender letter of counsel to Benincasa's daughter Nanna, *sua nipote verginella*, on her taking the veil, interpreting for her the parable of the ten Virgins.[3] Afterwards, when her influence extended as far as Florence, she was able to help her brothers materially, by interesting the powerful Guelf politician, Niccolò Soderini, on their behalf.

Rome itself had seen but little of the Sovereign Pontiff during these few years. His health had been steadily failing, and he

[1] Letters 10 and 20 (249 and 251). [2] Letter 18 (250).
[3] Letter 23 (356).

had passed most of his time at Viterbo, and especially in the high-lying and salubrious Montefiascone.

The work of Albornoz had been left incomplete in one essential point. Perugia, the third city of the Papal States, was still unsubdued. Its subjugation was a very different matter from hunting out the tyrants of such places as Forlì or Imola: Perugia was a free and powerful Republic, only nominally subject to the Church. A conspiracy of the Baglioni in October, 1368, to surrender the city to the Pope, led to open war between it and the Holy See, in which the Benedictine Pierre d'Estaing, Archbishop of Bourges, had directed the papal forces; while the Perugians had been aided in their resistance by Bernabo Visconti, Giovanni di Vico, and Hawkwood's English mercenaries. They had at first been successful, and had even, in the following year, threatened the Pope himself in Montefiascone. Urban naturally answered with excommunications and interdict. In the October of this year, 1369, he received in Rome the Emperor of the East, Johannes V Palaeologus, who came to implore aid against the Turks. Thus the Pope, in the space of a year, had seen the successors of Charlemagne and Justinian alike at his feet; but found his power defied by a small Umbrian republic from its hill.

In April, 1370, Urban for the last time left Rome for Viterbo and Montefiascone. Giovanni di Vico submitted; the Perugians opened negotiations for peace. Then, at Montefiascone, the Pope suddenly announced his intention of returning to Avignon.

From the outset, Petrarca had hailed the papal return to Rome as the beginning of a new age for the Church—but only a beginning—and he had doubted the Pope's strength of will. He had greeted him on his arrival with the words of the Psalmist, *In exitu Israel de Aegypto:* "When Israel went out of Egypt, the house of Jacob from a barbarous people, there was joy among the Angels in heaven and among the faithful on earth. And lo! thou, most blessed Father, as far as in thee lies, hast rendered the Christian people happy. No longer will they now go wandering in search of their Lord or of His vicar; but the one they will find in heaven and within their own souls (for each is the seat of God), the other on earth and in his proper place, that place which the Lord chose, in which the first of His vicars dwelt when he lived, and still remains though dead. Thou hast restored brightness to our world, and, rising like the sun, hast put to flight the coldness of long night and the powers of darkness. The neglect of five pontiffs, equal to thee in rank but not in soul, and of more than sixty years, hast thou alone in a few days repaired." Urban has brought the Church back to her ancient seat; let him complete his work by restoring her to her old state of purity and dignity, and begin by reforming the luxury and pomp of the cardinals. Let him look to the legates and papal officials, who are usurping the lordship of the Italian cities, and ruling them with such unheard-of tyranny that Peter is amazed, and Christ, in indignant wonder, is threatening vengeance: "And, unless He from heaven and thou on earth come to the rescue (for the Italians seem drugged and lie in slumber), it will be all over with us; we shall soon see Italy reduced to servitude, and the Church literally militant, in arms and fighting for temporal sovereignty instead of for the faith; we shall see her triumphant, too, so that the fame thereof reaches heaven and the stars, and individual ecclesiastics ruling in triumph over this or that city—until, when those who now slumber are awakened, all things are overthrown and reformed by a terrible revolution." "Then turn not aside from the way by which thou hast started, for there is none straighter to salvation; the time is short, the journey long, and the hope of the reward will make the labour light. Beware of looking back; for thou knowest that *he who has set hand to the plough and looketh back, cannot enter into the kingdom of God*." "If I heard that thou wast departing, I should not believe unless I saw; and if I saw it with my own eyes, I should find it difficult to believe them. So great is the hope that I have set upon thee and upon thy virtues."[1]

This virile language found an echo in the Pope's heart. He urged the poet, both directly and through the Patriarch of

[1] *Rerum Senilium*, Lib. IX. ep. 1 (undated).

Jerusalem, to join him in Rome. Petrarca promised that he would come, and actually started in the spring of 1370, but was taken ill at Ferrara, and, when he recovered, the doctors forbade him to proceed.[1] He was probably at Padua, or in his retreat at Arquà among the Euganean Hills, when he heard that all was over, and that Urban was returning to Provence. In his last letter to the Pope, one of the noblest of his compositions, Italy herself addresses the fugitive successor of Peter :—

"When I was lacerated with deadly sores, thou didst descend to me to cure my wounds, and didst say with Peter : *I am an Apostle of Christ; have no fear of me, my daughter.* Thou didst begin to pour into them wine and oil, and now, without having bound them up or applied the remedies, thou art departing from me. Thou didst find, it may be, that my malady was such as seemeth to thee incurable, and for this thou art, perchance, deserting me, like a despairing physician who is ashamed to await the death of his patient. But who knoweth that He would not lay His hand upon me with thee, who healed the sick from all diseases? Who knoweth if he would not be with thee, at whose word the limbs of the infirm were made whole? Thou art the vicar of the one, the successor of the other ; thou holdest the keys of the Kingdom of Heaven. . . . If thou wilt not be moved by my entreaty, He will meet thee on thy way, who to Peter's words when he fled : *Lord, whither goest Thou?* answered : *I go to Rome to be crucified again.*"[2]

This letter was apparently written in the late spring or early summer of 1370. On May 22, an embassy from the Romans came to Montefiascone, to implore the Pope to reconsider his decision. "The Holy Spirit led me to Rome," he answered ; "it

[1] *Rerum Senilium*, Lib. XI. ep. 1, 16, 17, letters dated Padua, July 25 (1368), December 24 (1369), May 8 (1370), respectively.

[2] The original text of this letter (which is not found in the early editions of Petrarca's works) is given by A. M. Bandini, *Bibliotheca Leopoldina Laurentiana*, Tom. ii. (Florence, 1792), coll. 101–103. In Fracassetti's Italian version, it appears as the third of the *Lettere varie*. The words, *Ego sum Apostolus Christi*, etc., are those uttered by St. Peter to St. Agatha in prison, according to the legend of the latter saint, in the *Breviarium Romanum* for February 5.

now leads me away for the honour of the Church." Ill-health and the evil influence of the French cardinals were probably the real explanations; the only plausible excuse that Urban could have offered was that, Italy being now pacified, his presence was needed in Avignon to make peace between France and England, who had renewed hostilities. On June 7, he made two cardinals, both of whom were soon to touch Catherine's life very nearly: Pierre d'Estaing, with the title of Santa Maria in Trastevere, and the Bishop of Florence, Piero Corsini, the nephew of Piero degli Albizzi, whose faction had always favoured the league of Florence with the Church. He likewise appointed Pierre d'Estaing, who was a great-hearted and far-seeing man, of virtuous life and enlightened views, albeit of an aristocratic and somewhat overbearing disposition, to the southern legation in Italy; the northern legation, that called of Bologna, he had previously, in January, 1368, assigned to his own brother, Anglico de Grimoard. He now bade the Romans farewell, promising still to care for them as a father, urging them to remain at peace and not prevent his return, or the coming of his successor. "Nevertheless," he said, "we bear witness that we and our brothers, the cardinals of the Holy Roman Church, and our familiars and officers, have remained for three years with you and in the places round about, in great quiet and consolation; and you, collectively and individually, have treated us and our Curia with reverence and kindness."[1]

Birgitta had gone with her sons, Charles and Birger, to Amalfi. She returned, to find Urban on the point of departure, and resolved to make a last effort to see him. It was in July when she reached Viterbo and went out to Montefiascone, where the Pope was. With her came a man of high repute for sanctity, whom we shall meet again in connection with Catherine: the "hermit bishop," Alfonso da Vadaterra. Born of a Sienese father and a Spanish mother, Alfonso had begun a brilliant ecclesiastical career as Bishop of Jaen, but had renounced his bishopric, distributed his goods among the poor, and was now living at Rome

[1] Brief of June 26, 1370, in Raynaldus, vii. p. 190.

as an Augustinian hermit. He it was who wrote Birgitta's life, and apparently put the books of her *Revelations* into the form in which we now have them.

The Swedish princess on her mule climbed the high hill upon which Montefiascone stands, to the papal palace at the summit, overlooking the peaceful lake of Bolsena. There below her lay the island that had witnessed the martyrdom of Santa Cristina, and that other where Amalasuentha had been brutally done to death by her Gothic assassins ; further away lay the quiet little town with the church that had witnessed the mystical wonder that is celebrated still in the *Lauda Sion* of Aquinas and the marble glory ot Orvieto's Duomo. She was ushered into the presence of the Sovereign Pontiff—her friend Niccolò Orsini, the Count of Nola, apparently acting as interpreter. Urban received her kindly, granted her the authorization of her rule, but would not discuss the affairs of the Holy See. Presently, however, he sent a messenger after her, to ask her what was the Divine will in the matter. Then the visionary spirit seized again upon Birgitta, and the Blessed Virgin spoke in her heart to this effect :—

" Because of my prayer, he obtained the infusion of the Holy Spirit, that he should go through Italy to Rome, for nought else save to do justice and mercy, to strengthen the Catholic faith, to confirm peace, and thus to renovate Holy Church. Even as a mother leads her child to what place pleases her while she shows him her breasts ; so did I lead Pope Urban, by my prayer and the work of the Holy Spirit, from Avignon to Rome, without any danger to his person. What hath he done to me ? Now he turneth to me his back and not his face, and he intends to depart from me ; to this a malign spirit leads him with its fraud. For he is weary of his divine labour and lusteth for his bodily ease. Yea, the devil draws him with worldly delectation, for too desirable to him is the land of his birth in mundane fashion. He is drawn, too, by the counsels of his carnal friends, who consider his pleasure and will more than the honour and will of God, or the profit and salvation of his soul. If it should happen that he return to the regions where he was elected Pope, he will in a brief while receive such a stroke that his teeth will gnash; his sight will be darkened and grow dim, and all the limbs of his body will tremble. The ardour of the Holy Spirit will for a while grow tepid within him and depart, and the prayers of all the friends of God, who resolved to pray for him with tears and groans, will be numbed, and the love of him will grow cold in their hearts. And he will render account before God of the things which he has done in the papal chair, and of the things which he has omitted, but could have done to the honour of God in his great position." [1]

This revelation she delivered in person to the Pope, in the presence of the young French cardinal, Pierre Roger de Beaufort, the nephew of Clement VI.[2] But Urban went sadly on his way. On September 5, 1370, he sailed from Corneto, reaching France on the 16th. Three months later, on December 19, he died at Avignon, in the house of his brother Anglico, at his own wish stretched on the couch of poverty and dressed in the Benedictine habit. An ineffectual Pope, but a faithful monk to the end.[3] On December 30, Cardinal Pierre Roger de Beaufort was elected to succeed him; he was ordained priest on January 4, 1371, and, the next day, was crowned Pope under the title of Gregory XI.

A month before Urban's death, in November, 1370, a peace had been concluded at Bologna between the Church and Perugia, by the intervention of the ambassadors of Florence—the principal conditions of which were that the city of Perugia should recognize the Pope and the Church in perpetuity as its sovereign, and that

[1] *Revelationes*, IV. 138.

[2] The Cardinal had previously refused to present the revelation to Urban. Cf. Alfonso's testimony in Raynaldus, vii. p. 374.

[3] According to Birgitta, in spite of his great fall, Urban's soul finds mercy at the last because of his fidelity to his vows. Cf. *Revelationes*, IV. 144: "Visio quam habuit Sponsa Christi de judicio animae cujusdam Summi Pontificis defuncti." The Comtesse de Flavigny (*Sainte Brigitte de Suède*, p. 285) is clearly in error in supposing that Clement VI is the pontiff in question. Cf. Petrarca, *Rer. Sen.*, Lib. XIII. ep. 13. The Bolognese anticipated the judgment of the Church by at once venerating the dead Pope as a saint.

the Pope for his life-time should make the priors of the Republic his vicars, after they had formally surrendered the keys of the city to the commissaries of the Cardinal Legate, in sign and recognition of which they were to pay, during the life of the Pope, an annual tribute of 3,000 gold florins. The Perugians were still doubting about the meaning of the clause that spoke of the creation of vicars as only for the life-time of the Pope, while the recognition of the Church's sovereignty was perpetual, when Urban died, and the legate, Anglico de Grimoard, had no further powers to act. But the exiles who had been restored raised fresh tumults, the city lacked provisions, and Cardinal d'Estaing, confirmed in his legation by the new Pope, entered Perugia in triumph, on May 19, 1371, welcomed by the priors and citizens with palms and olive-branches.[1]

Thus, in appearance, was the work of Albornoz completed in the first year of the pontificate of Gregory XI ; but it was to prove a house built on sand, with no sure foundation in the love of the subjects that ostensibly accepted the papal rule. The year of Urban's desertion of Italy is the year of Catherine's entry into public life. The new pontiff, gentle, scholarly, sickly and suffering in his body, well-meaning, but weak and irresolute, fickle, and at times unexpectedly hard and obstinate, was to encounter the spiritual force of her whom He, whose vicar on earth he claimed to be, had wedded to Himself in the mystic bond of perfect Faith.

[1] Cf. Pellini, *Historia di Perugia*, I. pp. 1080–1085 ; Supplement to Graziani's Chronicle, pp. 208–217 ; Montemarte, *Cronaca di Orvieto*, I. p. 39.

CHAPTER V

THE SPIRITUAL FELLOWSHIP

"Amore non è altro che unimento spirituale dell' anima e della cosa amata."—Dante, *Convivio*, III. 2.

"Id quod amatur amore amicitiae, simpliciter et per se amatur."—St. Thomas Aquinas, *Summa Theologica*, I–II. Q. 26. A. 4.

CATHERINE was now nearly twenty-four years old: a wonderfully endowed woman. Gifts had been given her to fulfil the impassioned hunger and thirst after righteousness; a divination of spirits, and an intuition so swift and infallible that men deemed it miraculous, the magic of a personality so winning and irresistible that neither man nor woman could hold out against it, a simple untaught wisdom that confounded the arts and subtleties of the world; and, with these, a speech so golden, so full of a mystical eloquence, that her words, whether written or spoken, made all hearts burn within them when her message came. In ecstatic contemplation she passes into regions beyond sense and above reason, voyaging alone in unexplored and untrodden realms of the spirit; but, when the sounds of the earth again break in upon her trance, a homely common-sense and simple humour are hers, no less than the knowledge acquired in these communings with an unseen world.

It is stated by Orlando Malavolti, the sixteenth century historian of Siena, that Catherine had already written to Pope Urban V. But this is manifestly an error. Her time had not yet come to pass out of her hidden life into what a Pope of the Renaissance was to call the "game of the world." It is curious that, while she makes one reference to Urban in a letter to his successor,[1] she never mentions the hopes and fears that had been raised by his coming. Her entry into public affairs appears to have begun in those months that intervened between his flight from Italy and his death at Avignon.

All through this summer of 1370, the soul of Catherine was

[1] Letter 231 (7).

overwhelmed with visions and manifestations of divine mysteries. "To explain in our defective language what I saw," she said in after years, "would seem to me like blaspheming the Lord, or dishonouring Him by my speech; so great is the distance between what the intellect, when rapt and illumined and strengthened by God, apprehends, and what can be expressed with words, that they seem almost contradictory." As she prayed to the Lord for purity of heart that she might worthily receive the Blessed Sacrament of the Altar, it seemed to her that a torrent of mingled blood and fire was poured down upon her, to the mystical cleansing of body and soul. And, a day or two later, she believed that Christ had drawn her heart from her side, and given her His own in exchange, with which she was henceforth to live. "Do you not see, father," she said to Fra Tommaso della Fonte, "that I am no longer she who I was, but that I am changed into another person? Such gladness and such delight possess my mind, that I marvel greatly how my soul can stay in my body. Such ardour is in my soul that this material, exterior fire seems to me cold by comparison." Praying for this confessor and her other companions, that eternal life might be their portion, and seeking a sign from Christ that her prayers were heard, she felt the palm of her outstretched hand pierced through by an invisible nail of iron, and thus received the foretaste of the *stigmata*, the imprint of the five wounds of Our Lord in His passion, which afterwards—albeit invisible—were to be hers. "The abundance of graces and revelations and most manifest visions," writes Fra Raimondo, "at this time so completely filled the soul of this holy virgin, that she began utterly to waste away through the greatness of her love; and she became so weak that she could no more rise up from her bed, albeit she suffered nought else save only the love of her eternal Bridegroom, upon whose name she called continually, as though bereft of sense."

She prayed earnestly that she might soon be delivered from the body that kept her from the embraces of her Spouse, and that, if this might not yet be, in the meanwhile she might at least be united to Him by partaking in the sufferings that He endured on earth. At length it seemed that her heart was broken by the force of her love. "So great," she said, "was the fire of divine love and of the desire of uniting myself with Him I loved, that, if my heart had been of stone or of iron, it would have been broken in like manner." It was on a Sunday in the autumn of this year, 1370, when this mystical death fell upon her—a trance of some four hours' duration—in which her friends all thought her actually dead, and filled her cell with cries and lamentations. In this suspension of her bodily life, Catherine believed that she had really died, that her soul entered into eternity, tasted the blessedness of the vision of the Divine Essence, and, like Dante, beheld the spiritual lives of Heaven, Purgatory, and Hell. Like Dante, she was bidden repeat to the living what she had seen, *in pro del mondo che mal vive* :—

"Whilst my soul beheld all these things, the eternal Bridegroom, whom I thought fully to possess, said to her : 'Seest thou of what great glory they are deprived, and with what grievous torments they are punished, who offend Me ? Return, then, and make known to them their error, their danger, and loss.' And, for that my soul shrank with horror from this return, the Lord added : 'The salvation of many souls demands thy return, nor shalt thou any more keep that way of life that thou hast hitherto kept, nor shalt thou henceforth have thy cell for habitation ; nay, thou shalt have to go forth from thine own city for the welfare of souls. I shall be always with thee, and shall guide thee and bring thee back ; thou shalt bear the honour of My name and witness to spiritual things before small and great, the laity no less than the clergy and religious ; for I shall give thee speech and wisdom which none will be able to withstand. I shall lead thee, too, before the pontiffs and rulers of the Churches and of the Christian people, in order that, as is My wont, by means of the weak I may confound the pride of the strong.' "[1]

Fra Bartolommeo di Domenico tells us that he was preaching in San Domenico when the report was spread that Catherine had

[1] *Legenda*, II. vi. 1–9, 17, 20–23 (§§ 178–193, 206, 212–216).

died. After the sermon, he, too, heard the rumour, and rushed to her cell. It was so full of friars and women that he could hardly enter, and they told him she had been dead some hours before. She gradually came to life again in his presence, but for days could do nothing but weep, and bewail the sad fate of her soul that, having beheld with the Angels the face of her Creator, was sent down again to her carnal imprisonment. To the end, Catherine believed she had been really and truly dead, nor could she ever speak of this vision without tears. "Will you not have pity, father," she said to Fra Raimondo, "upon a soul that had been freed from the dark prison, and, after having seen a most blessed light, was again shut up in her former darkness? I am that wretched creature to whom this befell, for so did the divine Providence dispose because of my sins."[1] Nevertheless, this vision was the prelude to her public life—the mystical signification of her great and wonderful vocation.

Henceforth, Catherine's work was done openly in the eyes of the world, though for a while she did not, save in spirit, leave the territories of the Sienese Republic. A number of conversions marked the beginning of her public ministry. Andrea di Naddino Bellanti, a notorious sinner and blasphemer, struck down by illness in the flower of his manhood, was moved by her prayers to repentance and an edifying end. Francesco Saracini, the father-in-law of Alessa, a fierce and irreligious old noble of eighty years, at her bidding made peace with the enemy whom he hated to death, and became a model of simple-hearted devotion for the few months of life that remained to him. Jacomo Tolomei, the furious son of Francesco and Rabe Tolomei, "uomo assai maraviglioso e molto terribile," already twice a homicide and the terror of all the city, not only meekly submitted to his sisters, Ghinoccia and Francesca, taking the veil, but confessed his own sins to Fra Bartolommeo, and "was changed from wolf to lamb, from lion to watch-dog." A younger brother of his, Matteo Tolomei, became one of Catherine's spiritual household and entered the Dominican order.

[1] *Contestatio Fr. Bartholomaei*, coll. 1332–1333; *Legenda*, II. vi. 21 (§ 213).

But, among the men and women who gave up everything to become Catherine's followers and disciples, there were some very different from the Dominican tertiaries and the friars. Neri di Landoccio Pagliaresi, a vernacular poet, and by rank a noble of one of the lesser Sienese houses, who joined her about this time, is the first of a little group of youths of birth and learning who left their families to cleave to her and serve her as secretaries, binding themselves to her in worship and love of friendship ; a spiritual tie of whole-hearted devotion, which she describes in her *Dialogue* as the means chosen by God to raise a soul as yet imperfect in love to the perfection of love. By thus conceiving a spiritual and absorbing love for some one creature, such a soul frees herself from all unworthy passions, and advances in virtue, by this ordered love casting out all disordered affections. By the unselfishness and perfection of her love for such a friend, the soul can test the perfection or imperfection of her love for God.[1] It is like the love of Dante for Beatrice, but kindled at the foot of the Cross and consecrated at the steps of the Altar.

"You asked me to receive you for son," she writes to Neri, in the first of her letters to him ; "and, therefore, I—unworthy, miserable, and wretched as I am—have already received you, and receive you with affectionate love ; and I pledge, and will pledge myself for ever in the sight of God, to bear the weight for you of all the sins you have committed or might commit. But I pray you to fulfil my desire ; that is, that you conform yourself with Christ crucified, by entirely severing yourself from the conversation of the world ; for in no other way could we have this conformity with Christ. Clothe yourself, clothe yourself with Christ crucified ; for He is that wedding garment that will give you grace here, and afterwards will place you at the banquet of life eternal." [2]

A very different type from this highly-strung and sensitive poet (who to the end was tormented by terrible fits of despondency and depression, with a haunting fear lest he should not have

[1] *Dialogo*, cap. 144.

[2] Letter 99 (272). In all subsequent letters, Catherine addresses him as *tu*.

grace to persevere) was his friend and companion, Francesco di Messer Vanni Malavolti, the son of one of the most influential of the great Sienese nobles.

"I was then about twenty-five years old," writes Francesco, "not a little fiery and daring by reason of my kindred and my birth, well furnished with temporal goods, and, impelled by my still youthful age, I was living lasciviously and unrestrainedly in the wretched delights of the world and the flesh, as though I were never to die, recklessly pursuing my inordinate lusts with all my power. But it chanced that, as I had conversation and fellowship with many like me in age and birth, among my other dear and beloved companions, there was a noble youth of Siena called Neri di Landoccio di Messer Neri de' Pagliaresi, with whom I spent much of my time, both because he was very virtuous and pleasant, and because he was an excellent composer of beautiful poems, in which at that time I took the greatest delight. This Neri, after we had been friends for a long while, had heard often (without my knowledge) of the fame of that glorious virgin Catherine, and had even spoken to her, whereby he had become wondrously changed and made another man. Pitying me because of the lascivious life I led, and desiring the salvation of my soul rather than of my body, he many times besought me to go with him to speak with the said virgin Catherine. But I, caring little for these words and prayers, nay, rather deriding them, for a long time would not in the least consent to his will; but at length, constrained by his prayers, and unwilling to distress him because of the bond of singular love by which he was bound to me, I told him that I was ready to satisfy his desire; albeit, in my inmost heart, I was not going thither from any devotion, but rather with contempt, and intending, if she preached to me about the spirit and especially about confession, to answer her in such wise that she would never speak to me any more. And so, with this intention, I prepared to go to her. But, when we both came to the glorious virgin, no sooner had I seen her face than a terrible fear entered me, with so great a trembling that I almost fainted; and, albeit (as I said) I had no thought or intention of confessing, God so wondrously changed my heart at her first word that I went straightway to confess myself sacramentally; and that first visit was so efficacious that I became all the contrary to what I had been before." After a few more visits to her, he completely abandoned his former mode of life; and so great was the change that, whereas hitherto his own wife, "a noble damsel, fair and beautiful according to the flesh, but far more according to virtue and spirit," had not sufficed him, "but I was striving also, according to my power, to have several other women," he now, with her consent, lived for a long time with her in chastity, and, shunning the worldly pleasures in which his soul had delighted, he found his joy in the churches and in conversing with the servants of God, and began to frequent Catherine's house and listen to her teaching.

Nevertheless, shortly after, he fell into a grave sin—known, he says, only to God. "Immediately after the commission of this sin, touched by God, I went to the virgin's home, and, as soon as I had entered her house, before I had come to her presence, beyond her wont she had me called to her; and, having sent out all the others who were with her, she made me sit down near her, and said to me: 'Tell me, how long is it since thou didst go to confession?' To which I answered: 'Last Saturday.' And this was perfectly true, for such was the custom of all of us who conversed with her. Then she: 'Go and confess at once;' to which I: 'My sweet mother, I will confess to-morrow, which is Saturday.' But she repeated the same thing, saying: 'Go, and do what I tell thee.' And when I sought some delay, and refused to do it just then, she, with face glowing and enkindled, said to me: 'How, my son, dost thou think that I have not my eyes ever open over my children? You could not do or say anything without my knowing it. And how dost thou think to hide from me that thou hast just now done so and so? Go therefore, immediately, and cleanse thyself from such great misery.' Then, when I heard her tell me exactly all that I had done and said, confused and full of shame, without any other answer, I straightway heedfully fulfilled her command and went to confession; and not only then, but on many other occasions, did she manifest to me, with modest and humble words, not only my hidden deeds, but also the thoughts that were passing in my heart, the good as well as the evil." [1]

On a later occasion, Catherine was to write to Francesco: "I can well call thee dear; so much art thou costing me in tears and labour and in much bitter sorrow." But, for the present, the young man was in the first fervour of his conversion. "From being a bestial man and well-nigh demoniacal," he says, "I had come to true knowledge and to life according to the spirit." His relations and associates strove by all possible means to draw him from his new mode of living. Two especially misliked his change to good—"and this, as I deem, because we had previously been the most concordant in the lascivious vanities of the world." One of these was a connection by marriage, Neri di Guccio degli Ugurghieri (a member of the oldest feudal family of Siena), and the other a companion, Niccolò di Bindo Ghelli. Whenever they met Francesco, they would abuse Catherine, and declared themselves ready to say the same to her face. "Come then," said Francesco at last, "and I will introduce you to her. If you convince her, I promise to return with you to my old life; but take good heed, for, if you go to her, before you depart she will convert you, and make you both go to confess your sins." That, the two protested, Christ Himself could not induce them to do; but, nevertheless, a few days afterwards, they accompanied him to the Saint's house. And, whereas they had come with the intention of saying everything bad against her, when they were in her presence, they found they could not utter a word:—

"Then she sweetly began to reprove them for many words which they had used many times against me, even as though she herself had been bodily always present when they said these things, albeit she had never heard anything about them from me, of which may God be my witness. Having heard these words of the virgin, they were touched and confused, and began to weep bitterly, nor did they answer anything but this: 'Tell us, lady,

[1] *Contestatio Francisci de Malavoltis*, cap. i., Casanatense MS., pp. 430–433.

what you would have us do, for we are disposed and ready to do whatever you think fit to command.' To which the virgin answered, saying: 'I wish you instantly to go to confession; and do thou, Francesco, lead them to my father, Fra Tommaso.' And, departing thence, we went together straight to the convent of the Friars Preachers of Siena, where the said father was, and there, with the greatest devotion and with tears, both the two confessed their sins. And so completely did they correct their lives, that, throughout the whole of that Lent, they were always present at holy preachings, put aside all evil conversations, and lived honestly and with the fear of the Lord. And thus it appears manifestly how wondrously these two, who fled her so, nevertheless could not escape out of the hands of that holy little virgin Catherine." [1]

Other lay disciples who joined Catherine's spiritual family at this time were Gabriele di Davino Piccolomini, a married man, and Nigi di Doccio Arzocchi, apparently a youth, both members of noble houses. Less closely associated with her, but a fervent believer in her sanctity and mission, was Tommaso di Guelfaccio, the follower of Giovanni Colombini, a man in whom the government of the Republic placed much confidence. A man of a very different stamp, who became her disciple through Neri di Landoccio and Nigi di Doccio, and who has left us his memoirs, was Ser Cristofano di Gano Guidini, a notary. Cristofano belonged to the faction of the Riformatori, held various small offices under the government, and in after years sat twice in the chief magistracy as one of the fifteen Defenders. After he had associated for some time with Catherine and her circle, he desired to abandon the world and enter the religious state, but yielded to the prayers of his mother and determined to marry. He has preserved to us the letter of advice that Catherine wrote to him on the choice of a wife, gently blaming him for his decision in abandoning the call to a higher life, but bidding him, in all he does, seek the honour of God and the salvation of his soul. [2] A simple and straight-

[1] *Contestatio Francisci de Malavoltis*, cap. iii., MS. *cit.*, pp. 439, 440.

[2] Letter 43 (240). Cf. *Memorie di Ser Cristofano di Gano Guidini*, pp. 31–33,

forward man, not without learning, he was, perhaps, the most practical member of the fellowship.

It was probably through Ser Cristofano that a more important personage was brought into Catherine's sphere of influence : the painter and democratic politician, Andrea di Vanni. Andrea di Vanni had taken part in the revolutionary movement that had brought about the supremacy of the Riformatori, and was a man of weight in the counsels of the new magistrates of the Republic, much employed in important embassies. He was intimate with the worthy notary, and stood godfather to his eldest son. There is no reason for supposing that he actually became one of Catherine's spiritual family, and her letters to him, written when he was filling the office of Captain of the People, are of a later date. He was a loyal and conscientious politician according to the lights of his day, and a virile painter, with a noble and striking ideal of the Blessed Virgin in his art.[1] The most important of his surviving works is the large altar-piece in the church of Santo Stefano, on the Lizza ; but, restored and repainted though it be, he would be graceless indeed who could look unmoved upon that strange, unearthly, almost uncouth, but immeasurably touching and appealing portrait of Catherine from his hand that still watches over the Cappella delle Volte in San Domenico.

That a young woman should thus be surrounded with men, some of them no older than herself, gave food to cynical thoughts and slanderous tongues. The bitterest of all accusations for Catherine to bear was made against her. A woman named

and Grottanelli, *Orazioni di Santa Brigida* (Siena, 1867), p. 4. Cristofano wrote a life of Giovanni Colombini, translated Catherine's *Dialogo* into Latin, and had an Italian version of the *Revelations* of St. Bridget copied for the Confraternity of Our Lady.

[1] Cf. F. M. Perkins, *Andrea Vanni*, in the *Burlington Magazine*, vol. ii. (London, 1903). He seems to have called himself "Andrea di Vanni," Vanni becoming a family name in later times. Various documents concerning his public life, with certain of his letters to the Signoria when ambassador to the Pope (1373, 1384, 1385), are given by G. Milanesi, *Documenti per la Storia dell' Arte Senese*, vol. i. docs. 90–95, 137, and Borghesi and Banchi, *Nuovi documenti*, pp. 27, 54, 55.

Andrea, whom she was tending while dying slowly of cancer, accused her to the prioress and sisters of the Mantellate as guilty of unchastity. In spite of Lapa's vehement indignation, Catherine nursed her traducer lovingly to the end, and at last gained her soul, too, for her Divine Bridegroom. In the first pang of the lying accusation, she had prayed to Him with tears to prove her innocence; but when, in answer, He bade her choose between the crown of pearls and the crown of thorns, she eagerly and ardently pressed the latter upon her brows. It was on this occasion that, to punish herself for a momentary fit of aversion caused by the horrible physical state of the patient's body, Catherine subjected herself to an ordeal too dreadful to be set down in this place.

"Sweetest daughter," said the Divine Voice in her heart, on another occasion, "the time to come of thy earthly pilgrimage will be full of such wondrous new gifts from Me that it will cause stupor and incredulity in the hearts of the ignorant and carnal; and many, too, that love thee will doubt, and will think that what will befall thee through My exceeding love is delusion. For I will pour such abundance of grace into thy soul that it will overflow wondrously even in thy body, which will thereby acquire an all unwonted mode of life. Thy heart will be so mightily inflamed towards the salvation of thy neighbours that, forgetting thine own sex, thou wilt utterly change thy former way of conversation, nor wilt thou any more shun the company of men and women; nay, for the salvation of their souls, thou wilt expose thyself to every labour according to thy power. At these things many will be scandalized, and by them shalt thou be spoken against that the thoughts of many hearts may be revealed. But be not thou disturbed, nor fear at all; for I shall be ever with thee, and shall deliver thy soul from deceitful tongues and from the mouth of those that lie. So execute manfully whatever the Holy Spirit instructs thee, because through thee I will deliver many souls from the jaws of Hell, and, by means of My grace, bring them to the Kingdom of Heaven."[1]

[1] *Legenda*, II. v. 1 (§ 165).

It was probably about this time that a last attempt from the religious portion of the city was made to hinder Catherine's work, and it came from two men in Siena who were, in Francesco Malavolti's words, "religious of very great worth according to the world." One, Fra Gabriele da Volterra, a Franciscan and then minister of the province, a "Master in Sacred Theology," with a great reputation for learning and preaching, was a sort of petty Brother Elias, who lived sumptuously in the convent of San Francesco like a great prelate. The other was a friar of the order of Augustinian hermits, Fra Giovanni Tantucci (usually known as Giovanni Terzo, to distinguish him from two other "Brother Johns" who had preceded him in his convent), also a "Master in Sacred Theology," who had been to England, where he had taken his doctor's degree at the University of Cambridge. These two murmured against Catherine, in orthodox pharisaical fashion, saying that she was an ignorant woman, seducing simple persons with false expositions of holy Scripture, and leading them to hell with herself. They resolved to make her recognize her errors, and came one day to visit her, with two companions, intending to silence her by difficult theological questions. A number of men and women were with her when they arrived; Fra Tommaso della Fonte, Fra Matteo Tolomei, a certain Niccolò di Mino, Tommaso di Guelfaccio, Neri di Landoccio, Gabriele Piccolomini, Alessa, Lisa, Cecca, and others, including Francesco Malavolti, who tells the tale of what happened.

"While we were thus listening to the saintly and wonderful words and doctrine of that holy virgin, she suddenly broke off in her speech, and, becoming all enkindled and with countenance all glowing, she raised her eyes to heaven, and said: 'Blessed be Thou, sweet and eternal Bridegroom, who dost find so many new ways and paths by which to draw or lead souls to Thyself.' And she said many other words, which I do not remember exactly, and would not be able to repeat in the form in which they were uttered by her. But we were all attention, considering what she did, for her motions and all her words were full of mystery nor without particular cause; so we were expecting the end that the matter must needs have. Then the father Fra Tommaso, her confessor, said to her: 'Tell me, daughter, what is the meaning of what thou hast just done? What dost thou mean? Let us understand something about it.' But she, like an obedient daughter, answered: 'My father, you will soon see two great fishes caught in the nets'; and said no more. We still by these words did not know what she meant to say; but, while we were thus in suspense and expecting the end of the affair, one of the virgin's women companions, who lived in the house with her, said: 'Mother, there is here below Master Gabriele da Volterra of the Friars Minor, with a companion, and Master Giovanni Terzo of the friars of St. Augustine, also with a companion, who wish to come to you.'"

As Catherine was going to meet them, the two came into the room. They sat down, and the others grouped themselves round, as they said that they wished to say nothing to her in secret. Then, "like two furious lions," the Franciscan and the Augustinian in turn began to ply her with the most difficult theological questions, hoping to put her to confusion before her friends and disciples. "But the Holy Spirit, who deserteth none that trust in Him, did not desert this humble handmaiden of His, but granted her so great wisdom and fortitude, that if there had been not only two such men, but even a thousand or ten thousand, she would have overthrown all, and won a magnificent triumph over them, even as that same Holy Spirit said through the mouth of David: *A thousand shall fall at thy side, and ten thousand at thy right hand.*" All aflame with divine zeal, yet with the utmost reverence for her two opponents, Catherine rebuked their inflated and unprofitable science, their setting their hearts upon the praises of creatures, and spoke so winningly of the love of Christ that the two were instantly converted. Master Gabriele was living in such pomp that in his convent he had made himself one cell out of three, and furnished it so sumptuously that it would have been excessive for a cardinal, including "a most noble bed with a silk covering and curtains round it, and so many other things that, together with his books, they would be worth hundreds of ducats.

Taking the keys from his girdle, he said before us all : 'Is there no one here who will go to distribute and give away for the love of God what I have in my cell?' Then uprose Niccolò di Mino and Tommaso di Guelfaccio, and, taking the keys, they said to him : 'What would you have us do?' And Master Gabriele answered them : 'Go into my cell, and whatever you find therein distribute and give away for the love of God, so that nothing be left me in it save my breviary.'" They took him at his word, distributed his books among the other friars of the convent who were students, and gave the rest to the poor, leaving only what was sufficient for a humble Franciscan friar of the strict observance. Gabriele himself shortly after went to Santa Croce at Florence, and there set himself to serving the friars in the refectory and other acts of humility, although he was still the minister of the province. Master Giovanni, also, gave away all he had, keeping only the breviary, and became one of Catherine's immediate followers, afterwards accompanying her in her travels until her death. He was one of the three confessors who were deputed by the Pope to hear the confessions of those who were converted by her means.[1]

It was doubtless through Maestro Giovanni Tantucci that Catherine was brought into touch with the hermits of Lecceto. The convent of San Salvatore di Lecceto was the head house in Tuscany of the Augustinian hermits, "a blessed place," writes its seventeenth century historian, Ambrogio Landucci, "in which the Most High chose to work so many wonders." It lies beyond Belcaro, a few miles westward of Siena, in what still remains of a once glorious forest of ilex trees. The place was originally known as the Convento di Selva, the Convent of the Wood, which was also called the *Selva di Lago*, because of the lake or swamp (afterwards drained) that lay at the foot of the hill upon which, solitary and austere, the convent still rises. From remote middle ages, wonderful legends had lingered round the convent and forest. Miraculous waters had gushed out of the arid soil; the stones had taken mystical colours in commemoration of Him

[1] *Contestatio Francisci de Malavoltis*, cap. iii., MS. *cit.*, pp. 441–445.

who was crucified ; the flowers of the forest had wonderful healing properties, "all evident signs that here flourished a continual spring of Paradise." Angels had descended in human form to eat with the hermits in their refectory, or to succour them in their need ; Christ Himself had appeared in the wood to confirm the young friar, Giovanni di Guccio, in his vocation ; but fiends lurked in it, ready to ensnare the souls of the unwary, even as the young Sienese knight, Ambrogio Sansedoni, walking heedlessly under the ilexes, had been confronted with what seemed a beautiful girl bound by two ruffians to a tree, who was only revealed in her true nature at the sign of the Cross.

The great days of the convent, however, were a thing of the past, although the house was still ruled by Fra Niccolò Tini, the prior whose sweetness of disposition, boundless humility and charity, are so lovingly extolled by his novice, Filippo Agazzari. Both Fra Niccolò Tini and Fra Filippo must have been living at the convent during the whole time of Catherine's life ; but she appears to have had no dealings with the former (to whom she refers indirectly only in one letter), nor does the latter, in his fascinating *Assempri*, ever make any mention of her or any of her followers. It is, indeed, somewhat startling to find a contemporary Sienese, evidently of holy life and devout conversation, who must have frequently seen Catherine, or, at least, have heard all about her, in after years picturing the religious and social life of his day as though no such person had ever existed.[1] There was evidently a party opposed to Catherine in the convent. It is, at least, certain that none of the friars in Lecceto who now became Catherine's disciples—William Flete, Felice de' Tancredi (known as Fra Felice da Massa), Antonio da Nizza, or Giovanni Tantucci himself—make any appearance in Fra Filippo's pages,

[1] Fra Niccolò Tini (said to have been a Marescotti) was prior of Lecceto from 1332 till 1388. His life is related in Fra Filippo's *Assempro* 41. Filippo entered under him as a novice in 1353, began to write his *Assempri* in 1397, and was elected prior in 1398. Giovanni Tantucci (who died in 1391) apparently succeeded Fra Niccolò as prior. Cf. Carpellini, *Gli Assempri di Fra Filippo da Siena*, pp. xxvi., xxvii., and Landucci, *Sacra Leccetana Selva*, pp. 103–109.

and the first of these, at least, was a man of some fame in those days.

William Flete was an Englishman from Cambridge, who had settled down among the Augustinian hermits at Lecceto, led, perhaps, to that spot by his acquaintance with Giovanni Tantucci, who had probably been his fellow-student by the banks of Cam. In Catherine's circle these two scholars were usually spoken of by their academic degrees, Giovanni being the "Master," and William the "Bachelor." In the wood of ilexes, he led a life more austere than his rule enjoined upon him ; devoting himself to works of penance and to study ; avoiding all intercourse with outsiders, and associating but little with the other friars, returning only to the convent in the evening or for the offices of the Church.[1]

It is clear from one of Catherine's letters to him that it seemed to her that the good hermit of England attached too much importance to mortification for its own sake. There are those, she tells him, "who have set their desire more in mortifying the body than in slaying their own will. These are fed at the table of penance, and are good and perfect ; but, if they have not a great humility and do not take consolation in judging according to the will of God and not according to that of men, they often mar their perfection by making themselves judges of those who do not go by the same road as they. And this befalls them because they have set more zeal and desire in mortifying the body than in slaying their own will. Such as these ever wish to choose times and places and mental consolations in their own way, as also the tribulations from the world and the assaults of the demon ; saying, to deceive themselves, being deceived by their own will (which is called spiritual will) : 'I would have this consolation, and not these assaults and turmoils of the demon ; not, indeed, for my own sake, but to please and possess God more, because it seems to me that I possess Him better in this way than in that.'

[1] Cf. *Memorie di Ser Cristofano*, etc., p. 34. William Flete had previously known Giovanni Colombini, who sends a message to him and to the prior, *Lettere del B. Giovanni Colombini*, 80.

And thus such a one often falls into pain and weariness, and becomes thereby unbearable to himself; and so mars his perfect state. The taint of pride lies within this, and he perceives it not. For, if he were truly humble and not presumptuous, he would surely see that the first sweet Truth gives state, time, place, consolation, and tribulation, according as it is necessary for our salvation, and to complete in the soul the perfection to which she is chosen. And he would see that it gives everything for love, and therefore with love." The souls that have this perfect light, enamoured and panting with love, run to the table of holy desire. "They lose themselves, stripping off the old man, that is, their own sensuality, and they clothe themselves with the new man, Christ sweet Jesus, following Him manfully. These are they who are fed at the table of holy desire, and who have set their solicitude more in slaying their own will than in slaying or in mortifying the body. They have, indeed, mortified the body, but not as their chief aim, but merely as an instrument to aid them in slaying their own will; for their chief aim should be, and is, to slay the will, so that it neither seek nor will aught save to follow Christ crucified, seeking the honour and glory of His name and the salvation of souls. These are ever in peace and in quiet. No one can scandalize them, because they have got rid of the thing by which scandal cometh, to wit, their own will. All the persecution that the world and the devil can give flows under their feet; they stand in the water, holding fast to the branches of inflamed desire, and are not submerged. Such a soul rejoices at everything; and she does not judge the servants of God, nor any rational creature; nay, she rejoices at every state and every way that she sees, saying: 'Thanks be to Thee, eternal Father, who hast many mansions in Thy house.' And she rejoices more at the diverse ways she sees than if she saw all going along one path; because she sees the greatness of God's goodness more clearly revealed. She rejoices at everything, and draws the perfume of the rose from all. And she does not pass judgment even upon what she expressly sees to be sin, but is touched with true and holy compassion, saying: 'To-day it is thou, and to-morrow it would be myself, were it not for the divine grace that preserves me.' "[1]

And, a little later, we find her urging him and Frate Antonio (the hermit of Nice who, Cristofano di Gano tells us, was the Englishman's chosen companion) not to let their love of solitude draw them from their duties of obedience and charity :—

"I tell you, in the name of Christ crucified, that not only should you say Mass in the convent sometimes in the week when the prior wishes it, but I want you to say it every day, if you see that it is his wish. Because you lose your consolations, you do not lose the state of grace ; nay, rather, you acquire it, when you lose your own will. I want us (in order that we may show ourselves eaters of souls and tasters of our neighbours) not to attend only to our own consolations ; we must also care and have compassion for the labours of our neighbours, and especially for those who are united in one same bond of charity. If you did not so, it would be a very great fault. And, therefore, I wish you to be sure to listen to the troubles and needs of Frate Antonio, and I wish and pray Frate Antonio to listen to yours. And so I beseech you, in Christ's name and mine, to do. In this way you will preserve true charity in yourselves, and, otherwise, you would give room to the devil to sow discord."[2]

Another early member of the spiritual family was Messer Matteo di Fazio de' Cenni, "a notable servant of God," who, after a dissolute youth, had been converted by the influence of William Flete, and was now devoting himself to an active life of charity as rector of the Casa della Misericordia, one of the chief Sienese hospitals. Sano di Maco, a plebeian who had business connections with the Benincasa family and was a person of some influence with the artisan government, also became one of Catherine's sons in religion. An old hermit, Fra Santi da Teramo, "holy alike in name and in deeds," an anchorite from the Abruzzi who had been intimately associated with Pietro Petroni and Giovanni Colombini, likewise joined the circle. "In his old age," writes Raimondo, "finding this precious pearl, the virgin

[1] Letter 64 (124). [2] Letter 77 (128).

Catherine, he left the quiet of his cell and his former mode of life, in order that he might help others as well as himself, and followed her, especially because of the signs and wonders that he daily saw both in himself and in others ; declaring that he found greater quiet and consolation of mind, as also greater advance in virtue, by following her and listening to her teaching, than he had ever found in the solitude of his cell."[1]

Two others, whose names were destined to be linked more intimately with that of Catherine, were still needed to complete the fellowship : Raimondo da Capua himself, and that young countryman and beloved disciple of the saintly maiden, to whom at the last he could appeal in testimony of the truth of the whole of his Life of their spiritual mistress : "He is the witness of almost all this narration, in such wise that I can say with John the Evangelist : *he knoweth that he saith true.* He, that is, Stefano the Carthusian, knoweth that Raimondo of the order of Preachers saith true, who, albeit unfit and unworthy, has composed this Legend."

[1] *Legenda,* III. i. 10 (§ 340). Cf. Bartholomaeus Senensis, *Vita B. Petri Petroni,* III. 6.

CHAPTER VI

FROM THE CELL TO THE WORLD

> "Buscando mis amores,
> Iré por esos montes y riberas,
> Ni cogeré las flores,
> Ni temeré las fieras,
> Y pasaré los fuertes y fronteras."
> San Juan de la Cruz, *Canciones entre el Alma y el Esposo.*

THESE were stormy days for Siena. Plots against the supremacy of the Riformatori were incessant, and the government retaliated by torture and executions. At the beginning of 1371, a conspiracy was discovered, and two culprits were sentenced to be *attanagliati*, that is, torn by hot pincers on a cart all through the city to the place of execution. Catherine was in the house of Alessa, when the dreadful pageant passed through the street below; at her prayers, the horrible shrieks and despairing blasphemies of the condemned men were hushed at a vision of Christ that came to meet them at the gate of the city, "and they went to death as joyously as though they were invited to a banquet."

In the July of this year, a formidable rising of the *Compagnia del Bruco*, a secret association of the wool-carders, who were subjected to the Guild of Wool, and forbidden the right of combination, shook for a moment the whole fabric of the State. It was a curious anticipation of the tumult of the *Ciompi* in Florence, seven years later. For several days the insurgents held the city at their mercy, and compelled the government to put seven of their own number into the Signoria. This was followed by a counter conspiracy of the Dodicini and their allies, with the connivance of the Captain of the People, Francesco di Naddo, supported by the Salimbeni. There was a sanguinary massacre in the Costa d'Ovile on July 30; but, in spite of the defection of their chiefs, the armed companies of the city kept loyal to the government, and, with the aid of the Noveschi and nobles, the rising was crushed. The Captain of the People, robed in scarlet, was beheaded on a scarlet-covered scaffold in the middle of the Campo. The Dodicini were excluded from the administration, the central magistracy now consisting of twelve of the "People of the Greater Number" and three Noveschi. Among the citizens condemned to pecuniary penalties was Nanni di Ser Vanni Savini, "famous among those who were devoted to the world and full of the prudence of the flesh," as Fra Raimondo says of him, who was sentenced to pay a fine of five hundred florins; a little later, we shall find him among Catherine's disciples.[1]

Almost immediately after leaving the seclusion of her father's house, we find Catherine in touch with the politics of her native city, and with the great questions that were agitating the whole Church. Not only are the spears and swords of contending factions lowered before her as she passes along the streets of Siena, but the princes and potentates of Italy seem to realize instantly that a new spiritual power has arisen in the land, and from Avignon the Pope himself would fain know the secrets that Christ had hidden from His vicar to reveal to the simple maiden whom He had made His bride.

This was in part due to the effect produced upon Gregory's mind by the revelations of Birgitta. From the beginning of his pontificate, the Swedish princess had exhorted the new Pope to repair the scandal caused by the defection of his predecessor. In a vision she heard the voice of the Blessed Virgin, promising that, if Gregory will restore the papal chair to Rome and reform the Church, her prayers will flood his soul with spiritual joy from her divine Son; if not, he will assuredly feel the rod of Christ's indignation; his life will be cut short, and he will be summoned to the judgment of God. She wrote to bid the Pope come to Italy by the beginning of the following April (apparently of 1372) at the latest, if he would still have the Blessed Virgin as a mother and escape the judgments of God. There will be no peace in France until the people appease God by some great works of humility and piety; as for the expedition which the Pope is organizing to redeem the sepulchre of Christ with mercenary

[1] *Cronica Sanese*, col. 228. Cf. *Legenda*, II. vii. 17 (§ 235).

soldiers, that will no more please Him than did the worship of the Golden Calf.[1]

At Birgitta's bidding, the hermit-bishop Alfonso brought this letter to Perugia, and entrusted it to the Count of Nola for transmission to the Pope. A copy was shown to the Count and to a sinister personage, of whom more presently, the papal nuncio, the Abbot of Marmoutier, and then destroyed, after its contents had been communicated to Cardinal d'Estaing, as also to Gomez Albornoz, who had been converted by Birgitta and was then holding Spoleto for the Church. But there was one significant passage in the revelation which was reserved for Gregory alone. "Unless the Pope," said Birgitta to Alfonso (speaking in the person of the Blessed Virgin), "comes to Italy at the time and in the year appointed, the lands of the Church, which are now united under his sway and obedience, will be divided in the hands of his enemies. To augment the tribulation of the Pope, he will not only hear, but will also see with his own eyes that what I say is true, nor will he be able with all the might of his power to reduce the said lands of the Church to their former state of obedience and peace. These words that I now say to thee are not yet to be told or written to the Abbot, for the seed is hidden in the earth until it fructifies in ears of corn."[2] This prophecy was soon to be fulfilled to the letter, and in part at the Abbot's cost.

Gregory, who had bidden the Abbot demand an explanation of the first revelation, returned no answer to the second; and Birgitta, seeing no hope of his present coming, started for the Holy Land, in the autumn of 1371, accompanied by Alfonso, her two sons, Birger and Charles, and others. At Naples, Charles fell in love with the still beautiful Queen, and Giovanna, allured by the splendid manhood of the young northern warrior, returned his passion. Both of them were married, but the Queen is said to have contemplated obtaining a divorce and to have suggested the same to him. An adulterous connection of this kind seemed

[1] *Revelationes*, IV. 139, 140.

[2] *Ibid.*, IV. 140. Cf. Comtesse de Flavigny, *Sainte Brigitte de Suède*, pp. 397–402.

Alinari.

St. Bridget giving her rule.

G.A. Sogliani — Uffizi. Florence.

to Birgitta worse than death, and when, before any steps had been taken, Charles died at the beginning of March, she welcomed it as his deliverance.[1] She left Naples immediately after the funeral, and, going by way of Cyprus, reached Jerusalem early in May. In October, she was back in Naples, where she found the pestilence raging in that gayest and most licentious of cities. Here she began, apparently at the request of the Queen and Archbishop, to preach repentance, urging the latter to attempt a complete reformation of the Neapolitan church by correcting the immoral lives of its prelates and priests. She exhorted Giovanna herself to confession and a complete amendment of life, warning her to set the affairs of the kingdom in order, for that God had declared that she would have no heir of her body :—

"Let her acquire greater humility and contrition for her sins, for in My sight she is a robber of many souls, a lavish squanderer of My goods, a rod and a tribulation to My friends. Let her have continual fear in her heart, for all her time she has led the life of a harlot rather than of a queen. Let her devote the rest of her time, which is brief, to My honour. Let her fear, and so live that she incur not My judgment. Otherwise, if she will not hear Me, I will judge her, not as a queen, but as an ungrateful apostate."[2]

Praying for the Pope on the feast of St. Polycarp, January 26, 1373, Birgitta had a vision of Christ, who told her that Gregory was fettered by his excessive love for his own kindred and his coldness of mind towards Him, but that, through Our Lady's prayers, he would overcome all obstacles and come to Rome. "But whether thou shalt see him come or not, is not lawful for thee to know." In February, she despatched the hermit-bishop to Avignon with a long letter to the Sovereign Pontiff, describing another vision, in which she beheld Gregory himself standing before the throne of the heavenly Judge, and heard the terrible rebuke addressed to him : "Why hatest thou

[1] Cf. Comtesse de Flavigny, *op. cit.*, pp. 411–415. Giovanna's third husband, James of Majorca, died in 1375. *Cronicon Siculum* (ed. J. de Blasiis), p. 28.

[2] *Revelationes*, VII. 11.

Me so? Why is thy daring and thy presumption so great against Me? For thy mundane court is plundering My celestial Court. Thou in thy pride dost take My sheep from Me; thou dost unlawfully seize upon the goods of the Church, which are Mine own, and the goods of the subjects of the Church, to give them to thy temporal friends. Thou dost rob My poor for the sake of thy rich. Too great is thy audacity and presumption. What have I done to thee, Gregory? I patiently permitted thee to ascend to the Supreme Pontificate, and foretold to thee My will, and promised thee a great reward. How hast thou repaid Me for all My benefits? Why dost thou make reign in thy court such great pride, insatiable cupidity, and the lust that I hate, and likewise the most horrible simony? Moreover, thou dost rob Me of innumerable souls; for almost all who come to thy court dost thou cast into the hell of fire, in that thou dost not attend to the things that pertain to My Court, albeit thou art the prelate and pastor of My sheep. The fault is thine, because thou dost not wisely consider what is to be done for their spiritual salvation, and what to be corrected. And albeit I could with justice condemn thee for these things, yet do I still admonish thee, for the salvation of thy soul, that thou come to Rome, to thy seat, as quickly as thou canst. Come, then, and do not delay. Come not with thy wonted pride and mundane pomp, but with humility and ardent charity; and, after thou art thus come, extirpate and root out all the vices from thy court. Put far from thee the counsels of thy carnal and worldly friends, and humbly follow the counsels of My spiritual friends. Rise up manfully, put on thy strength, and begin to renovate My Church, which I acquired with My own blood; let it be brought back in spirit to its primitive holy state, for now it is a house of shame that is venerated rather than Holy Mother Church. But, if thou dost not obey My will, I will cast thee down from the Court of Heaven, and all the devils of hell shall divide thy soul, and for benediction thou shalt be filled with eternal malediction. If thou dost obey Me in this way, I will receive thee like a tender Father; I will be merciful to thee, and will bless thee, and will robe and deck thee with the pontifical vestments of a true Pope; I will clothe thee with Myself, so that thou wilt be in Me and I in thee, and thou shalt possess eternal glory."[1]

The Queen, whose heart had been for a little moved by Birgitta's words, supplied her with means to return to Rome, which she reached at the beginning of Lent. Here the Count of Nola and the Abbot of Marmoutier came to her from the Pope, to ask for light, and, like the Pharisees of old, to demand a sign, now that the renewal of hostilities between the Church and Bernabo Visconti seemed to raise a fresh obstacle to his return. In answer, early in July, Birgitta wrote her last letter to Alfonso, which he was to show to the Pope. Let Gregory do what lies in him for the honour of God, the salvation of souls, and the renovation of the Church, and he will have a sign of eternal consolation. But, if he does not come, he will have a sign of another kind, in the loss of things both temporal and spiritual, and in the remorse of his own conscience. As to the discord between the Pope and Bernabo, with such danger to innumerable souls, let the former come to terms. "For, even if the Pope were expelled from the popedom, it were better that he should humble himself and make peace on whatever occasion it could be done, rather than so many souls perish in eternal damnation." Let him trust in God alone, and, though all dissuade him from coming to Rome, and do all in their power to hinder him, none of them shall prevail over him. "Thus saith the Lord: Since the Pope doubts whether he should come to Rome for the establishment of peace and the reformation of My Church, I would have him come by all means in the coming autumn. And let him know that he can do nothing more pleasing to Me than coming to Italy."[2]

A few days later, on July 23, 1373, Birgitta died. Her daughter Catherine took the body to Sweden, and then returned to Rome, to await the coming of the Pope that her mother had promised. Petrarca died in the following year. And, in the meanwhile, the other Catherine had taken up the work that the

[1] *Revelationes*, IV. 141, 142. [2] *Ibid.*, IV. 143.

Italian poet and the Swedish princess alike had left uncompleted, beginning with those two formidable prelates of the Church Militant whom we have seen meeting over Birgitta's revelations —Cardinal d'Estaing and the Abbot of Marmoutier.

Cardinal d'Estaing, although upright and strenuous, had proved a stern and unpopular ruler of Perugia. At the end of 1371, the Pope appointed him to the legation of Bologna, in succession to Cardinal Anglico de Grimoard, while his place at Perugia was taken by Cardinal Philippe de Cabassole, Petrarca's friend, the Patriarch of Jerusalem, a mild-tempered and amiable prelate who won golden opinions from the Perugians during the few months of his government. In January, 1372, d'Estaing made a pompous triumphal entry into Bologna, received with acclamation by the inhabitants, who saw in him the champion of their liberty against Bernabo Visconti: "He was reputed a very great and upright man," says the chronicler, "and they said that he had great legatorial powers, and more authority from the Pope than had ever been given to any other representative of the Church."[1] In the following August, Cardinal de Cabassole died, and was succeeded by the Abbot of Marmoutier (who had come to Italy in the preceding year as treasurer general of the Church), who now governed Perugia and the Patrimony and Spoleto, with the title of vicar apostolic, the troops being still under the command of Gomez Albornoz.

Now begins the series of Catherine's letters. And among the first of them that we can date with any approach to certainty are the two to Cardinal d'Estaing, in his capacity of legate of Bologna and chief representative of the Pope in Italy. They are, as it were, the frontispiece to the whole mystical volume of her epistles. They give us at once the essence of her spiritualized political doctrine. Italy is the prologue, peace the epilogue. Love of Charity is the rule; self-love and servile fear the enemies to be overthrown. The philosophy that she has learned from the Prince of Peace in her cell of self-knowledge is applied to the political state of the Church and of the world. Already is

[1] *Cronica di Bologna*, coll. 491, 492.

her soul overwhelmed by that impassioned dream of a reformation of the Church down to its very foundations—*infino alle fondamenta*, to use her own words—which is soon to lead her across the Alps, the ambassador of Christ as well as of Florence, the maiden image of the Italian people, to reconcile the Pope with Italy, to bring him back to Rome.

It was early in 1372 that Catherine first addressed a letter to Cardinal d'Estaing, opening with a play upon the words *legato* and *Legato*, which it is impossible to render in English. "Dearest and reverend father in Christ sweet Jesus," she begins; "I, Catherine, servant and slave of the servants of Jesus Christ, write to you in His precious blood, with the desire of seeing you bound in the bond of charity even as you have been made Legate in Italy,[1] as I have heard, and at which I have been greatly and singularly delighted, considering that by this you will be able to do much for the honour of God and the weal of Holy Church. But you know that we can effect no work of grace in ourselves, nor for our neighbour, without charity; charity is that sweet and holy bond which binds the soul with her Creator; it bound God in man and man in God. This inestimable charity kept God and Man fastened and nailed upon the wood of the most holy Cross." It is charity alone that unites the separated, enriches the poor in virtue, makes wars to cease, gives patience and perseverance, and can never be shaken, because it is founded on the living Rock, on Him who is the way, the truth, and the life. Bound in this love, let the representative of the Sovereign Pontiff follow in the footsteps of Christ:—

"I would have you then, like a true son and servant bought back by the blood of Christ crucified, follow His footsteps, with manly heart and ready zeal, never turning aside by reason either of pain or pleasure, but persevering even to the end in this, and in every other work which you undertake to do for Christ crucified. Strive to extirpate the iniquities and the miseries of the world, which come from the many sins that men commit, by which the name of God is shamed; do your utmost, as one

[1] *Legato nel legame della carità sì come sete fatto Legato.*

hungry for His honour and for the salvation of your neighbour, to find a remedy for all this. I am certain that, if you are bound in the sweet bond of charity, you will use your legation, which you have received from the Vicar of Christ, in this way. But, without the first bond of charity, you cannot use it so, nor do what you ought; and, therefore, I pray you to try to have this love in you. Bind yourself with Christ crucified, following His footsteps with true and royal virtues, and bind yourself with your neighbour by deeds of love. But I would have us think, dearest father, that, unless our soul is stripped of all self-love and worldly affection, we can never come to this true and perfect love, the bond of charity; because one love is so contrary to the other, that the one separates us from God and our neighbour, while the other unites us; one gives life, and the other death; one gives darkness, and the other light; one war, and the other peace. Self-love so narrows the heart that it leaves no room for you or your neighbour; but divine charity enlarges it, receiving into itself friends and enemies and every rational creature, because it is clothed with the love of Christ and therefore follows Him. Miserable self-love abandons justice and commits injustice, and has a servile fear which does not let it do justly what it should, either because of flatteries or for fear of losing its state. This is that perverse servitude and fear that led Pilate to slay Christ. I would have you, then, utterly lay aside this kind of love, and be founded in true and perfect charity, loving God for His own sake, inasmuch as He is worthy of being loved, because He is the supreme and eternal Goodness, and loving yourself for Him and your neighbour for Him, and not for your own advantage. Thus, then, my father, legate of our lord the Pope, would I have you bound in the bond of true and most ardent charity, and this does my soul desire to see in you."[1]

[1] Letter 7 (23). The Palatine MS. 56 states that this letter was sent to the Cardinal "in Corneto, essendo nuovamente fatto ine legato." Students of the *Inferno* may remember that it was this legate, "vir magnae virtutis et scientiae," who, at the instigation of Benvenuto da Imola, made the stern, but ineffectual attempt to stamp out unnatural vice in the University of Bologna. Cf. Benvenuto, *Comentum*, I. pp. 523, 524, where for 1375 we should probably read 1373.

And she follows this up with a second letter, "with desire of eeing you a virile and not cowardly man, so that you may nanfully serve the Spouse of Christ, using both spiritual and emporal means for the honour of God, as this Spouse hath need n these times." Let him open the eyes of his understanding to ee her necessities, and let him beware of servile fear (a favourite loctrine of Catherine's, which we find her repeating again and gain in almost the same words). Let him look upon the immaculate Lamb, who sought nought save the honour of the Father, and feared nothing, not even the shameful death of the Cross. "We are the scholars, who have been sent to this sweet nd gentle school." And the time has come to put these lessons nto practice :—

"Strive manfully, to the utmost of your power, to bring about he peace and union of the whole country. And if, for this holy work, it were necessary to give the life of the body, it should be given a thousand times, if it were possible. It is a terrible thing o think and hear and see that we are at war with God, by reason of the multitude of the sins of the subjects and their pastors, and lso in corporeal war by reason of the rebellion that has arisen gainst Holy Church.[1] Where all faithful Christians should be reparing to make war upon the infidels, false Christians are waging it against each other ; and the servants of God cannot ontain themselves for grief and bitterness at seeing the damnation of souls who are perishing for this, and the demons are rejoicing, ecause they see what they want to see. Verily, then, it is time o give our lives in imitation of the Master of Truth, and to care ought for honour or shame that the world would give us in ainful torments and death of the body. I am certain that you will do this manfully, if you are clothed with the new man, Christ esus, and stripped of the old, to wit, of your own sensuality ; for hen you will have cast off servile fear ; in no other way would ou ever do it, but would rather fall into the very sins I have

[1] *i. e.* the war between Bernabo Visconti and the Holy See. Catherine, in er letter to Bernabo himself, describes it in the same way as "rebellion against Ioly Church."

named. Considering, then, that it was necessary for you to be a virile man, and without any fear, and freed from self-love (for you are put by God in an office that demands no fear save that which is holy); therefore, I said to you that I desired to see you manful and not timorous. I hope in the Divine Goodness that He will grant grace to you and to me, that is, to fulfil His will and your desire and mine. Peace, peace, peace! Dearest father, make the Holy Father consider the loss of souls more than that of cities; for God demands souls more than cities." [1]

A man of a very different stamp from that of this great-hearted and zealous Cardinal was the other director of the papal policy in Italy. Gérard du Puy, Abbot of Marmoutier and nephew to Pope Gregory, was one of the worst of those rapacious wolves in sheep's clothing to whom the pastors of Avignon had entrusted their Ausonian flocks. While d'Estaing in his Bolognese legation was vigorously pursuing the campaign against the Visconti, without oppressing the subjects of the Church committed to his rule, the Abbot, supported by Hawkwood's mercenaries, was governing Perugia with the most detestable tyranny. To secure his hold upon the turbulent city, he was building two great fortresses, connected by a large covered way supported by arches, over which troops could pass to and fro. He ground down the people with taxes, excluded all the citizens, high and low, from his counsels, and ruled the province with corrupt notaries and foreign captains. He connived at the most outrageous licence of his officials, in which a nephew of his own was the worst offender, and to the protests of the injured parties returned an answer disgusting in its brutal cynicism.[2] Nevertheless, this detestable monk had been the intermediary between the Pope and Birgitta, and now, probably immediately after the latter's death in July, 1373, he was bidden approach Catherine in the same way; his papal uncle, unabashed by the rebuke of the Swedish prophetess,

[1] Letter 11 (24). Cf. Petrarca's canzone, *Italia mia*: "I' vo gridando: Pace, pace, pace."

[2] Cf. Pellini, I. pp. 1111, 1112; Supplement to Graziani, pp. 217–219; Montemarte, I. p. 41; *Chronicon Regiense* (*Rer. It. Script.*, xviii.), col. 85.

ras still seeking a sign like the Pharisees of old, and the fame of ıe maiden of Fonte Branda (probably through the report of the ɛgate of Bologna) had penetrated even into the papal palace of ɩvignon.

We do not know by what means his appeal was conveyed to ;atherine, nor whether she was aware of the character of the cclesiastic with whom she was now dealing; but her answer is xtant, and it is one of the most striking of her political letters. Γo this wicked man, too, she writes in the precious blood of ɜod: "with desire of seeing you a true priest, and a member ɔound in the body of Holy Church." The first part of the letter s an impassioned hymn to charity, by whose milk the soul lives, he love that binds the soul to Christ even as it bound the Son of ɜod to the Cross, the fire that burns away vice and sin and love ɔf self. All must follow this rule of love, purifying memory, ɹnderstanding, and will in this divine fire. Above all, God lemands from men in the position of the Abbot a zeal and solicitude for the salvation of souls. "This is the way of Christ crucified, who will always give us the light of peace. But, if we hold another way, we shall go from darkness to darkness, and ultimately to eternal death." Her answer to the Pope is that two things in particular are disfiguring the Church, and must be taken away: nepotism, "excessive tenderness and solicitude for kinsmen," and leniency in dealing with the wickedness of the clergy. "Christ specially hates three perverse vices: impurity, avarice, and the puffed-up pride which reigns in the Spouse of Christ, that is, in the prelates, who attend to nought save pleasures and states and excessive riches. They see the infernal demons carrying off the souls of their subjects, and they reck not of it, because they have become wolves and sellers of the divine grace." "I say not that the Spouse of Christ will not be persecuted; but I believe that she will remain in flower. It is necessary, for her complete reformation, that she should be pulled down even to her foundations." As to the Abbot's own professed repentance: "I, your unworthy daughter, have taken and will take the debt of your sins upon myself, and we shall burn yours and mine together in the fire of sweet charity, where they are consumed. Hope and be assured that the divine grace has pardoned you them." "You must chiefly labour together with the Holy Father, to the utmost of your power, in removing the wolves and incarnate demons of pastors who attend to nought save eating, and goodly palaces, and stout horses. Alas, that what Christ acquired upon the wood of the Cross is spent upon harlots! I pray you that, even if you have to die for it, you tell the Holy Father to find a remedy for such great iniquities, and, when the time comes to make pastors and cardinals, not to make them for the sake of flattery nor for money nor for simony; but, with all your power, pray him to heed and consider whether he finds virtue and good and holy repute in the man, and not to consider whether he is noble or plebeian; for virtue is the thing that makes man noble and pleasing to God."[1]

This year, 1373, was marked by innumerable dissensions and homicides, especially among the religious and clergy. The Sienese chronicler declares that the Augustinian friars murdered their provincial at Sant' Antonio (a convent of the order in the Sienese contado near the Bagni of Petriuolo); that, at Assisi, the Friars Minor fought with knives, and fourteen were killed; and at Siena a young friar in San Domenico killed another, and every convent was divided against itself. The same thing went on outside the convents; every order in the State was rent with plots and petty treasons; "and so the world is one darkness."[2] The new Senator of Siena, Count Lodovico da Mogliano from the Marches, who entered upon office in February—"a man of discreet years, pacific and wise, who gave good hope to all the citizens"—attempted to restore order by impartial executions of noble and plebeian criminals alike; but the only result was a series of riots, in which his own life was threatened, and all his household ran great risks of being massacred by the Sienese populace.[3]

Three of Catherine's letters bear the impress of these events. Writing to Pietro, priest of Semignano in the Sienese contado,

[1] Letter 109 (41).
[2] *Cronica Sanese*, col. 238.
[3] *Ibid.*, coll. 235, 236; O. Malavolti, p. 141.

'ho was at mortal feud with another priest and apparently leading scandalous life in other respects, she sets before his eyes the ignity of the priesthood which he is outraging with his impurity nd his hatred, and threatens him with the judgments of God, if e does not amend and make peace. "What a scandal it is to ee two priests keep in deadly hatred! It is a great miracle that God does not command the earth to swallow you both up. Come, hen, while you are still in time to receive mercy; hasten to Christ crucified, who will receive you benignly, if only you wish t; and think that, if you do not so, that sentence will fall upon ou which was given to the unjust servant to whom his master ıad forgiven his great debt, and who then would not remit a small ne to his fellow-servant." And, in like manner, she bids the Provost and Jacomo di Manzi, two ecclesiastics of Casole, to ollow the footsteps of the Lamb who made peace between God nd man by shedding His blood upon the Cross, to turn their hate ıpon their own sins, and make peace with God and their neighbour. "I beseech you, in the name of Christ crucified, not to leny me this grace." To Madonna Mitarella da Mogliano, the vife of the Senator, who had written to her in terror, after the nob had assailed her husband, that she had "no faith nor hope ave in the prayers of the servants of God," she sent words of gentle comfort, and a reminder that not a leaf can fall from the ree without the permission and will of God.[1]

But letters were the smallest part of Catherine's activity at this ime. Wherever men and women in Siena were in suffering or n need, she was always there. The sick were healed, the dying omforted when she stood by them; hardened sinners were noved to repentance at her bidding, and heard the sweet assurance from her lips: "Fear not; I have taken your sins upon nyself." "I never saw any person," writes Francesco Malavolti, "however badly disposed, of whatever condition or state, come to his virgin, whom the Holy Spirit had chosen, who ever departed rom her without being first converted to good and without at once going to confess himself sacramentally, laying aside all evil works

[1] Letters 59 (47), 3 (43), 31 (333).

and becoming entirely a new being."[1] Pietro di Giovanni Ventura tells us how, at the instance of his sister, he went to visit Catherine. He had not been to confession for seven years. "That virgin, raising her hands to heaven, then said: 'Pietro, I will take all thy sins upon myself, and do penance for them, and make satisfaction for them instead of thee. But I wish for this grace, Pietro, from thee—that thou confess thy sins.' To which I answered, saying: 'It is only a few days since I confessed them.' And she: 'It is not so, for I know that it is seven years since thou wert confessed in the least.' And she added: 'Why wilt thou not go to confession?' And, albeit I had told no one of that matter, nevertheless she manifested it all to me, and even the cause for which until then I had been unwilling to confess."[2] After that meeting Pietro became one of Catherine's most devoted followers and disciples, and, though once, for a brief moment, he wavered and asked for a sign, he was one of the little band that shared her fortunes down to the end. It was, perhaps, a foreknowledge of that moment's weakness that made Catherine address him a beautiful letter upon love and perseverance in the service of the beloved.[3]

In northern Italy, Cardinal d'Estaing was strenuously carrying on hostilities against the Visconti: "he was a right valiant man," says the chronicler of Bologna, "and made more war upon the lords of Milan than any other legate who was here had done, save only him of Spain."[4] But the Tuscan Republics wavered between Bernabo and the Pope. At the beginning of November, 1373, two ambassadors from Bernabo and Galeazzo came to Siena. The latter seems to have soon returned to his master; but Bernabo's envoy stayed on "in the hostelry of the Ocha," until the following January, when, the Sienese regarding his presence as compromising, he was requested to leave the city, the Gonfaloniere of the Terzo di Camollia escorting him

[1] *Contestatio Francisci de Malavoltis*, cap. iii., MS. *cit.*, p. 440.

[2] *Contestatio Petri quondam Johannis Venture de Senis*, MS. *cit.*, p. 482.

[3] Letter 47 (235).

[4] *Cronica di Bologna*, col. 496.

remoniously out of the gate.[1] While in Siena, he sought an terview with Catherine, in the name of Bernabo and his nbitious wife, Beatrice della Scala—possibly with the idea of ›nvincing her of the good intentions of his master, with a view › influencing the public opinion of the Sienese through her, now ıat fresh processes were being instituted against the Visconti : the papal court on account of their cruel oppression of the Iilanese clergy. If this was his object, the ambassador was ıanifestly unsuccessful.

Catherine promptly dictated to her secretaries the two long :tters to Bernabo and Beatrice which we still possess. Unfor-ınately, the passages at the end of the letters, in which she irectly answers their requests or questions, were regarded by er contemporaries as of merely ephemeral interest, and have, ıerefore, not been preserved, either in the printed editions or ı any of the manuscripts ; but, reading between the lines of er letter to Bernabo, we gather that the tyrant of Milan had :ied to represent himself to the simple Sienese maiden as a :ind of scourge of God, divinely ordained to punish the iniquities f the pastors of the Church.

To this most sanguinary and grasping of all the despots of taly, Catherine expounds the law of Love, as shown in the ıystery of the Redemption. She speaks of the vanity of all arthly lordship, which may pass away in a moment, in com-ıarison with the lordship of the city of the soul, in which God ests, and which, defended by free-will, is impregnable against ll the assaults of the world, the flesh, and the devil. But to ›reserve or regain this spiritual liberty, man must be washed in he blood of Christ ; this blood is kept in the body of Holy Church, to be administered by the hands of Christ's vicar ; and ve cannot partake of it save through him. " I tell you, dearest ather, and brother in Christ sweet Jesus, that God does not vish you, nor any one else, to make yourself the executioner ›f His ministers ; for He has reserved this to Himself and

[1] *Cronica Sanese*, coll. 238, 239.

committed it to His vicar. And if the vicar does not do what he should (and it is bad if he does not), we must humbly await the punishment and chastisement of the Supreme Judge, God eternal, even if our possessions are taken from us by these men. I pray you, in the name of Christ crucified, concern yourself no more with this. Possess your own cities in peace; punish your own subjects when they do wrong; but never touch those who are the ministers of this glorious and precious blood, which you can have by no other hands than theirs. Without it you will not receive the fruit of that blood, but you will become a putrid limb, cut off from the body of Holy Church. Now no more, father; humbly would I have us put our head upon the lap of Christ in heaven in affection and love, and of Christ on earth, who holds His place, to show reverence for the blood of Christ, of which blood he bears the keys; to whom he opens, it is opened, and to whom he shuts, it is shut; he has the power and the authority, and there is no one who can take it out of his hands; because it has been given him by the first sweet Truth."

Let Bernabo, then, become a faithful son of the Church. "But what amends shall we make for the time that you have been outside? For this, father, it seems to me that a time is preparing in which we shall be able to make sweet and gracious amends; for, as you have disposed your body and temporal substance to every peril and death in war with your father, so now I invite you, in the name of Christ crucified, to true and perfect peace with that father, benign Christ on earth, and to war upon the infidels, preparing to give your body and substance for Christ crucified. Make yourself ready, for it befits you to make this sweet amends; even as you have gone against him, so now go to his aid, when the Holy Father raises on high the banner of the most holy Cross. I wish you to be the first to invite and urge the Holy Father to make haste, for it is a great shame and disgrace to Christians to suffer wicked infidels to possess what by right is ours. But we act like fools and base of heart, who make war only upon each other; we are divided ɩgainst each other by hate and rancour, whereas we should be ɔound by the bond of divine and most ardent charity."[1]

And to Beatrice, whose pride and avarice were notorious :hroughout Italy, she writes "with desire of seeing you clothed n the robe of most ardent charity, so and in such wise that you nay be the means and instrument of reconciling your husband vith Christ sweet Jesus and with His vicar, Christ on earth. I ɩm certain that, if the virtue of charity is in you, it is impossible ɔut that your husband will feel the warmth of it."[2] From a etter addressed to Catherine by Elizabeth of Bavaria, the wife ɔf Bernabo's son Marco (Petrarca's godson), we find that she ɩad thoughts of coming in person to Milan. Elizabeth expresses ɩer deep disappointment at hearing that the Saint has changed ɩer plans, and humbly commends her husband and little four-ʳear-old daughter Anna to her prayers.[3]

With these first political letters, Catherine entered into the ɩational life of her country. The lords of Italy and the prelates ɔf the Church had learned by now that her words had a power ɩot their own, nor was either party unprepared or unwilling to nake use of it for their own ends and advantage.

In the letters to the Cardinal of Bologna and his Milanese .dversary alike, Catherine refers to the Crusade. From the ɔeginning of his pontificate, Gregory had urged the powers of Christendom to make peace among themselves, and turn their .rms against the Turks and Saracens. In particular, he had ɔesought King Louis of Hungary, as the persecutor of infidels .nd defender of the Catholic Faith, to use the great power that he Lord had given him, "for the defence of His people whom He has redeemed by the shedding of His most precious blood,

[1] Letter 28 (191). In the bull of the Pope against Bernabo and Galeazzo, ʳhich is dated January 7, 1373 (Raynaldus, vii. pp. 235–237), the former accused of having tortured certain priests to death with appalling atrocity. 'he matter is evidently that to which Catherine refers, and the date of the apal bull, together with the authenticated presence of Bernabo's envoy in iena, seems to fix this as the occasion of her letter.

[2] Letter 29 (319).

[3] *Lettere dei discepoli di S. Caterina*, 2.

and so from a perishable earthly kingdom pass to an eternal one."[1] But, before anything could be effected, war broke out between Venice and Genoa, between the latter power and Cyprus; Bernabo Visconti continued to keep all the forces of the Church engaged in Italy; all the Pope's efforts to make peace between France and England proved in vain.

Nevertheless, at the beginning of 1373, Gregory proclaimed the Crusade. Birgitta, as we saw, had from the outset raised the voice of prophecy against the scheme, as one that merely afforded at once an excuse to the Pope for neglecting his more immediate duty, and an opportunity to the mercenary soldiers for plundering and ravaging on a more extensive scale than was possible in Christendom. But Catherine, on the contrary, was fired with enthusiasm at the papal announcement. She saw in the proposed expedition at once the liberation of the sepulchre of Christ and the deliverance of Italy from these armed pests that, like the eagle upon Prometheus, were feeding upon her vitals; visions passed before her eyes of crowds of martyrs offering up their blood for the redemption of the Holy Land, of men who had hitherto fought for Mammon putting on the sign of the Cross, expending their fierce strength and ardour in battling for the Faith. So when, a little later, the papal summons and invitation were repeated, and fresh briefs from Avignon arrived in Italy, her voice rang out, *sicura, balda e lieta*, from the "City of the Virgin," as had Dante's of old from the ruddy sign of Mars.

But already the cloud was gathering on the horizon that was to render the Pope's design abortive and even Catherine's eloquent pleading of no avail. Early in the following year, 1374, the Pope recalled Cardinal d'Estaing, and appointed Guillaume de Noellet, known as the Cardinal of Sant' Angelo, to take his place as legate in Italy and papal governor of Bologna. The new legate entered Bologna on March 15: "He came through Tuscany, and, when he arrived at Florence, the Florentines showed him great honour; but here we did not welcome him as we had done the others, because this novelty of changing cardinal

[1] Raynaldus, vii. pp. 201, 202, 223.

was too frequent. May God have sent us one who will be good for this city."[1] It was a most unfortunate choice. Cardinal de Noellet was a tyrannical and incompetent French prelate of the usual type furnished by Avignon ; he and his colleague, the Abbot at Perugia, were speedily to drive their Italian subjects to desperation.

This was a dark and dismal year for all Italy, and especially for Catherine's native city : "In Siena," writes one of her chroniclers, at the opening of his records for this year, "there was pestilence, war, and very great scarcity, so that the bushel of grain was worth two golden florins."[2]

In the spring, a fierce war on a small scale broke out in the contado. One of the Salimbeni, Andrea di Niccolò, had seized Perolla, a castle of the Sienese Maremma near Massa, and hurled the daughter of its late lord, Geri (apparently himself a kinsman of the Salimbeni), to whom it rightfully belonged, down from the battlements. Secure in this stronghold, he gathered bandits and exiles round him, murdered and plundered all through the Maremma, levying blackmail up to the very gates of Siena. With aid from the Florentines (to whom in like manner they had rendered assistance in subduing the Ubaldini in the preceding year), the Sienese got together a large army, under their Senator (the Count Lodovico da Mogliano already mentioned), and, on April 23, forced the place to surrender. The Senator returned to Siena with twenty-nine prisoners, including Messer Andrea Salimbeni himself. Sixteen were executed, but the Senator, either by reasons of friendship or for fear of the Salimbeni, shrank from doing justice on the chief offender. Upon this the populace armed and assailed the Palace of the Signoria, demanding justice with threats of raising the whole city. The Defenders, intimidated, gave authority to the leader of the mob, one Noccio di Vanni, a saddler by trade, to do what seemed to him to the advantage of the Republic. Noccio at once led his followers to

[1] *Cronica di Bologna*, col. 495.

[2] *Annali di Siena dal* 1300 *al* 1400. Biblioteca Comunale di Siena, MS. A. iv. 1., f. 18.

the palace of the Senator, who fled at their approach, and, breaking in, took his seat on the bench as judge, and condemned Andrea to instant execution. He was promptly beheaded ; but when, a month or so later, Noccio tried to repeat this process with one of Andrea's associates, the government interfered, and deprived him of the authority they had so strangely given.

With some difficulty the tumults were thus appeased in the city. But, indignant at the affront offered to their house, the Salimbeni rose in arms in the contado. Niccolò di Niccolò Salimbeni seized Montemassi, Cione di Sandro Salimbeni harried the district of Montepulciano, Agnolino di Giovanni Salimbeni, the virtual head of the house, ravaged the hills and valleys about Montalcino ; while others of the family with their adherents made war elsewhere in the contado, and defied the forces of the Republic. From Perugia, the Abbot of Marmoutier sent agents to both parties, offering to mediate, but was suspected (with good reason) of having a secret understanding with the Salimbeni. A more genuine pacific offer from the Florentines was rejected by the latter, who would hear of no terms while their kinsman's blood was unavenged. Within Siena itself, the faction of the Dodicini was secretly favouring the rebels. The Signoria appointed a magistracy of ten to carry on the war, imprisoned twenty-five of the Dodicini, extorted a heavy sum of money from them in fines, and sent for aid, which was promptly granted in horse and foot, to Florence and to Lucca.

It was at this time that Catherine first left the territory of her native city. Moved by the conflicting reports that had reached his ears, the General of the order, Fra Elias of Toulouse, summoned her to attend the chapter-general which met at Florence in May. "There came to Florence," writes an anonymous Florentine contemporary, "in the month of May, 1374, when the chapter of the Friars Preachers was held, at the command of the Master of the order, one wearing the habit of the sisters of penance of St. Dominic, who was called Caterina di Jacomo di Benincasa of Siena, who was of the age of twenty-seven years, and whom we deemed to be a great servant of God. And with her she had three other women, dressed in her habit, who went in her company. Hearing her fame, I managed to see her and to gain her friendship, in such wise that she ofttimes came here into my house."[1] We have no clue to the identity of the writer, nor any record elsewhere of this first visit of Catherine to the great city with whose political turmoils she was soon to be associated. Probably on this occasion she made the acquaintance of various Florentine citizens, of all classes in the State, and more particularly of Messer Angelo Ricasoli, who had succeeded Cardinal Piero Corsini as bishop, and Niccolò Soderini, a wealthy and influential man, of a deeply religious mind, one of the "popolani grassi" and a leading spirit in the Parte Guelfa. She left Florence on June 29, and returned to her mother's house at Siena, to find the pestilence raging and a partial recurrence of the horrors of 1348 within the city.

This frightful scourge had appeared in May, and it ravaged Tuscany all through the summer until September, spreading thence through northern and central Italy even across the Alps. While attacking all ages and classes, the mortality was particularly terrible among the children. And the black shadow of famine dogged its footsteps. There was fearful scarcity of everything—bread, wine, meat, and oil were at unheard-of prices. In the great Tuscan cities, the government collected all the materials that could be made into bread, and doled it out by ticket; but, even so, there was not enough to go round. At Siena, the Spedale di S. Maria della Scala acted up to its great traditions and devoted all its resources to succouring the poor; and it was heroically supported by the Casa della Misericordia and the Disciplinati of Our Lady. The death-carts went from street to street, gathering up the dead; the priests, who tended the dying and buried the victims, in many cases shared their fate. The pestilence was already at Florence when Catherine was there, and

[1] *Miracoli e transito di Santa Caterina*, Biblioteca Riccardiana, MS. 1267, f. 190. This little work was printed by Grottanelli in 1862, under the title *Alcuni miracoli di Santa Caterina da Siena, secondo che sono narrati da un Anonimo, suo contemporaneo.* Cf. Augusta Drane, I. pp. 216–218.

lasted from March to October; but the devastation was on a less dreadful scale than among the Sienese; out of a population of 60,000, some 7,000 Florentines perished, and, although we have not the exact figures, the mortality in Siena was evidently much greater.[1]

Two of Catherine's brothers, Bartolommeo, who had accompanied her back from Florence, and Stefano, who had gone to Rome, her sister Lisa, and eight of her nephews and nieces, Lapa's grandchildren, died. With her own hands Catherine prepared the bodies for burial, saying over each: "This one, at least, I shall not lose." With her companions, she passed through the streets of the city, seeking out the most infected districts, entering the houses and the hospitals, tending the stricken, comforting and converting the dying, laying out the dead—many of whom she is said to have buried with her own hands. Not a few—including the hermit, Fra Santi, and the devoted rector of the Casa della Misericordia, Messer Matteo Cenni—gained such strength from her ministrations that they rose up healed at her word, and followed her to render service to the others.

Foremost among her fellow-labourers was the noble and holy Dominican friar who now became her spiritual director, and afterwards her biographer: Fra Raimondo delle Vigne of Capua; he whom, in her last letter, she was to call "father and son given me by that sweet Mother Mary." A man of aristocratic birth and great learning (among whose ancestors was that ill-fated Piero delle Vigne, the chancellor of the Emperor Frederick II, whose fame Dante had so nobly vindicated in a famous canto of the *Inferno*), Raimondo had in some mysterious way—to which he vaguely refers as miraculous—been called in his youth to the Dominican order, and had rapidly become a personage of importance among the friars. He had been prior of the Minerva at Rome in 1367, and shortly after (it being the practice of the

[1] Marchionne di Coppo Stefani, *Istoria Fiorentina*, Lib. IX. rubr. 745, who gives the Florentine mortality, says that Florence suffered less in proportion to its inhabitants than any other town in Tuscany, and that elsewhere a third of the population died.

order, with a view to avoiding all possibility of heresy or scandal, to appoint only friars of established fame and doctrine to such offices) had been made director of the convent of Dominican nuns of Santa Agnese at Montepulciano, where he had spent two years, and where, at the request of the nuns, he had written the life of their blessed patroness which still appears in the *Acta Sanctorum* for her feast. Thence he had been sent to San Domenico at Siena, as lector or professor of theology, and there (though he did not for some time see anything miraculous in her, nor put much credit in her revelations) he had at once espoused Catherine's cause, and insisted that she should on no account be hindered from communicating as often as she pleased.[1] To him she found she could open her heart as to no other man, and, with the cordial and humble assent of Fra Tommaso, he now took his place as her chief confessor and spiritual director.

"Considering," as he writes, "that Christ is far more powerful than Galen, and grace than nature," Raimondo led a devoted band of friars into the thickest fury of the pestilence, to lay down their lives for their people if such was God's will. Day and night, he was to be seen in the hospitals, or visiting the stricken in infected houses, bearing the Blessed Sacrament, hearing their last confessions, performing the rites for the dead. Both he and Fra Bartolommeo were among those who took the infection, and believed that Catherine's miraculous intervention had raised them up from the bed of death. But all the three Dominican sons of her companion, Cecca Gori, died.

Many others, priests and religious, had deserted the city, like those of the laity who could find a safer refuge. Fra Filippo tells a striking story of one of these latter, a man he knew, a great usurer and oppressor of the poor, who, at the first approach of

[1] *Legenda*, II. xii. 8 (§ 314). It was apparently on the feast of St. John the Baptist, when he acted as deacon at High Mass in San Domenico at Siena, that Catherine first saw Raimondo. Cf. Augusta Drane, I. p. 224, and Tantucci, p. 122. This must have been in the preceding year, if the author of the *Miracoli* is right in his statement that, in 1374, Catherine was at Florence till June 29.

the pestilence, converted all he had into ready money and fled to Massa, where he waited until he heard that it had abated. Then he returned to the city, and, drinking and laughing with his friends, began to boast that he had jockeyed God. "And, raising his eyes on high, he cried out at the top of his voice: *Thou thoughtest to catch me, Domenedio, but Thou hast not got me!* But no sooner had he said this word, than he said another in a lower tone: *Woe's me, Thou hast indeed got me, for I feel the swelling.*" And straightway he went to his house and died.[1]

A fresh recruit to Catherine's mystical army at this time was a young novice of San Domenico, Fra Simone da Cortona. From his own account of himself, he was a melancholy and sensitive youth, tormented by shyness, self-consciousness, and religious scruples. While the other younger friars of the convent, for fear of infection, shrank from associating with the fathers, Raimondo, Tommaso Caffarini, and Bartolommeo, who visited the sick, Simone eagerly sought their company and joined them in their work; and they, "as though to reward me for my labour," brought him to Catherine, "which to my taste was, indeed, a magnificent reward." "O how gladly did I see her, and how eagerly did I listen to her burning words! Verily, for her sake, all labour was turned for me into rest." But once, when they were visiting her, the other friars forgot all about him, and left him outside; Catherine called for him, and he, abashed and mortified, would not go in. Afterwards, when they had left, Catherine said to her companions: "My son has gone away troubled, because he could not speak with me, but I will go to him this very night." He went to bed, very angry and miserable; but she appeared to him in a dream, and gave him sweet comfort. Afterwards, when he accompanied Fra Bartolommeo, who was preaching a mission at Asciano, Catherine, fearing that the youth might again think himself neglected, always remembered him in the postscripts to the letters she addressed to the elder friar, and excused herself for not having had time to write directly to him. "Tell Frate Simone, my son

[1] *Assempro* 57, *Come un uomo diceva che Dio non l'aveva gionto.*

in Jesus Christ, that the son is never afraid to go to his mother; nay, he runs to her, especially when he thinks himself hardly used; and his mother takes him in her arms, and clasps him to her breast, and comforts him. And, although I am a bad mother, nevertheless I will always bear him at the breast of charity."[1]

Worn out by her labours, Catherine herself fell dangerously ill on the feast of the Assumption of this year, 1374, and with all joy prayed for death, until restored by a vision of the Blessed Virgin, who showed her all the souls whom, if her life were prolonged, she would yet guide to eternal life.[2] It having been, as she believed, revealed to her that she would ultimately be the special companion in paradise of Agnese of Montepulciano, she felt a keen desire to visit her shrine in that town. Thither she now went, on her recovery, followed by Fra Raimondo and another of her confessors; and Girolamo del Pacchia's masterpiece still preserves the legend of how, as Catherine bent down over Agnese's incorrupt body to kiss her feet, one of them raised itself to meet her lips. The painter has united this with a similar episode which is said to have occurred a little later, when Catherine came again to Montepulciano, accompanied by her sister-in-law Lisa (who had returned to Siena after her husband's death and taken the habit of the Mantellate), to place the latter's two daughters in the convent; while she laid her face to the silk covering that was over the dead face of Agnese, "Lisa and the others, lifting up their eyes, saw a very white and very minute manna, that, like rain, descended from on high in such great abundance that it covered the body of Agnese, and the virgin Catherine, as also all the others who were present, in such wise that Lisa filled her hands with those little grains."[3]

It was during their first stay at Montepulciano that Fra Raimondo's last doubts were dispelled concerning the divine origin

[1] *Contestatio Fr. Simonis*, MS. *cit.*, pp. 511–516; Letter 105 (113). Cf. Dante, *Par.* xxii. 1–9.

[2] So the author of the *Miracoli*, quoted by Augusta Drane, I. p. 237.

[3] *Legenda*, II. xii. 17–19 (§§ 327, 328). Cf. Raimondo, *Vita S. Agnetis de Monte Politiano* (*Acta Sanctorum*, Aprilis tom. ii.), pp. 793, 794.

of Catherine's works and revelations, which, till then, had been keeping his mind in suspense: "for I remembered that it was now the time of that third beast with the leopard's skin, by which is signified hypocrisy, and in my days I had met with hypocrites, especially among women, who are more easily and readily seduced by the Enemy, as is shown in the case of our first Mother." At her intercession, he obtained a mental vision of his own sins so clear, and a contrition so overwhelming, that he was convinced could proceed from nothing save from the grace of the Holy Spirit. A little later, when he doubted again of the truth of what she was revealing to him, he saw her face transformed into the face of Christ, and experienced a wonderful illumination of mind concerning the matter of which she spoke.[1] Nevertheless, the good father, who, like Dante, "*seco* avea di quel d'Adamo," was still unable always to follow her etherial flights, and he confesses it with some little humour. On one occasion, when she was discoursing at great length upon the divine mysteries, he fell asleep: "But she, who, while she thus spoke, was all absorbed in God, went on with her discourse for a long time before she perceived that I was asleep. At last she noticed it, and then woke me up by saying with a loud voice: 'Ah, why do you lose your soul's profit by sleeping? Am I talking about God to a wall or to you?'"

Montepulciano lay close to the fiefs of the rebellious Salimbeni, but it seems more probable that Catherine's relations with that family belong to a later epoch in her life. Nor do I think that her mediation in the local feuds and dissensions should be assigned to this date. She appears to have been ill with fever during most of this visit to the monastery of Santa Agnese, and, as soon as was possible, she probably returned to Siena.

In spite of the pestilence, the war between the Republic and the Salimbeni had continued. In October, the latter, in a sudden sally from their beleaguered fortress of Boccheggiano, completely defeated the Sienese forces, although outnumbered by nearly three

[1] *Legenda*, I. ix. 6, 7 (§§ 87–91). Cf. *Par.* xxvii. 105, where Dante says of Beatrice: "che Dio parea nel suo volto gioire."

to one, capturing their captain and all their munitions of war. The government retaliated by expelling all members of the family from Siena, proclaimed them rebels, and ordered their palaces and houses to be dismantled. But in the following March, 1375, the Florentines intervened, and sent Buonaccorso di Lapo Giovanni, Leonardo Strozzi, and Carlo Strozzi as ambassadors to bring about peace. The three came first to Siena and then went on to confer with the Salimbeni in Val d'Orcia. At the end of April, it was proclaimed to the sound of trumpets throughout Siena and in the lands of the Salimbeni that the whole matter had been referred to the decision of the Priors of the Commune of Florence.

The representatives of both parties were at Florence, engaged in the final negotiations, when news reached Tuscany of a more momentous peace having been made in northern Italy. On June 7, a courier rode into Pisa bearing an olive branch from Cardinal de Noellet, with the tidings that he had concluded at Bologna a truce for a year between the Holy See and Bernabo Visconti. Four days later, the symbolical olive and the official announcement of the truce was brought to Siena. In both cities the news was received with sorrow and apprehension ; men doubted the intentions and the good faith of the papal legate ; sinister rumours were spreading as to the movements of Hawkwood's mercenaries, whom the Church had dismissed from her service and who were approaching the Tuscan frontiers. "From this truce," writes the chronicler of Pisa, "there resulted such great evil that war followed through almost all the world."

CHAPTER VII

UNDER A DARKENING SKY

"Then in her sacred saving hands
She took the sorrows of the lands,
With maiden palms she lifted up
The sick time's blood-embittered cup,
And in her virgin garment furled
The faint limbs of a wounded world.
Clothed with calm love and clear desire,
She went forth in her soul's attire,
A missive fire."

A. C. Swinburne, *Songs before Sunrise.*

CATHERINE was by this time no longer at Siena. Other cities in Tuscany were now claiming her spiritual ministrations, and her great political work had fairly begun.

It was probably in the latter part of 1374 that Birgitta's confessor, the hermit-bishop, Alfonso da Vadaterra, returned to Italy from Avignon. He came to Siena, and sought an interview with Catherine in the name of the Pope, from whom he brought her the apostolic benediction, to enlist her ever-increasing spiritual influence for the papal intentions. "The Pope," writes Catherine to Fra Bartolommeo and Fra Tommaso Caffarini, who were then at Pisa, "has sent here one of his vicars—the spiritual father of that Countess who died at Rome. It is he who renounced the bishopric for love of virtue, and he came to me in the name of the Holy Father, bidding me offer up special prayers for him and for Holy Church; and for a sign he brought me the holy indulgence. Rejoice then and be glad, for the Holy Father has begun to attend to the honour of God and of Holy Church. I have written a letter to the Holy Father, beseeching him, for the love of that most sweet blood, to give us leave to expose our bodies to every torment. Pray to the supreme eternal Truth that, if it is best, He may vouchsafe this mercy to us and to you, so that we may all together give our lives for Him."[1] To Alfonso

[1] Letter 127 (117). Cf. Cristofano di Gano, *Memorie*, p. 34. This letter about the Crusade, which was apparently Catherine's first to Gregory XI, has not come down to us.

it must have seemed that the spirit of his dead friend lived again in the Sienese maiden, and he now associated himself with her spiritual fellowship.

The two friars had spread Catherine's fame through Pisa, and she received repeated invitations to come thither, especially from certain nuns who greatly desired to see and to hear her, and who assured her that she could win many souls to God in that city—invitations that had been supported by a letter from no less a person than Piero Gambacorti, the ruler of the Pisan Republic, himself. Her answer to the latter, admonishing the upright man who was holding earthly lordship by so doubtful and unstable a title, to detach himself from the delights of the world and keep his eyes fixed upon Divine Justice in governing, is extant; at the end she excuses herself from coming, on the grounds of her bad health and the risk of causing scandal—relations being then somewhat strained between Messer Piero and the Sienese, in consequence of the refusal of the Pisans to help their nominal allies against the rebellious Salimbeni, whereas Florence and Lucca had loyally corresponded to their bond.[1]

Nevertheless, early in the new year, 1375, Catherine believed herself to have received a divine command to delay no longer, and accordingly set out for Pisa. With her went Alessa, Lisa, Cecca, and others of her women, as also her mother, Monna Lapa herself, who would not again be parted from her daughter. Fra Raimondo, Fra Tommaso della Fonte, and Fra Bartolommeo accompanied her, to hear the confessions of those whom she was to convert to God.

At Pisa the little band of Sienese received a royal reception, being met by Piero Gambacorti himself, the Archbishop (Francesco Moricotti di Vico), and the chief religious and political notabilities of the State. Catherine was entertained and lodged in the house of Gherardo Buonconti, a leading citizen of Pisa, and one of a large family of brothers and sisters, several of whom became her disciples. The house stood on the Arno, near the little

[1] Letter 112 (193). Cf. *Legenda*, II. viii. 17 (§ 257), and *Cronica Sanese*, col. 240.

church or chapel of Santa Cristina. Here the same wonders were enacted as had been done at Siena: the sick were healed; men of evil life were brought to repentance. "I saw her speak to certain sinners," wrote Giovanni Dominici, the famous Cardinal of Ragusa, then a young Dominican novice, to his mother, "and her words were so profound, so fiery and potent, that they straightway transformed these vessels of contumely into pure vessels of crystal, as we sing in the hymn of St. Mary Magdalene that our Lord Jesus did to her."[1] A new breath of spiritual life seemed given to that decaying city, whose days of political independence were drawing to a close.

There were, as usual, some that murmured, and others that professed themselves scandalized at Catherine's mode of life and at the reverence with which she was treated, especially at the way in which many of the men and women who approached her knelt and kissed her hands. Two learned men of the city, Maestro Giovanni Gutalebraccia, a physician, and Ser Pietro di Messer Albizzo, a lawyer of repute who was a leading spirit among the adherents of the Gambacorti, came to her, much as Fra Lazzarino and Maestro Gabriele had done in Siena, and attempted to bewilder her with theological problems. To all their questions she answered simply, that only one thing was necessary: to know that Christ, the true Son of God, had assumed human nature for our salvation, had suffered and died for our liberation; and she spoke to them so sweetly of the love of Him that they were moved to tears. But the hostile comments on the reverence shown her increased, until Fra Raimondo (Fra Bartolommeo being also present) hinted that she should stop it, asking her if it did not move her mind to vainglory. "I hardly notice what they do," she replied, "and, through God's grace, it does not please me; I consider only the good affection that brings them to me, and thank the Divine Goodness that thus moves them, praying that He may perfect and fulfil those desires which He has inspired.

[1] This letter, written from Constance in 1416, is included in Biscioni, *Lettere di Santi e Beati Fiorentini*, and there is a Latin version of it appended to the *Processus*.

I marvel how a creature, knowing itself to be a creature, can have vainglory."[1]

But there was one, whom Bartolommeo styles "a certain man of no small reputation among spiritual persons," who, in all sincerity, trembled for the safety of Catherine's soul. This was the poet of the Gesuati, Bianco dall' Anciolina, known as "El Bianco da Siena," but sometimes called "El Bianco da Firenze," or "El Bianco da Città di Castello," from the place where he had lived as an anchorite after the death of his master, Giovanni Colombini. "Now beware, Catherine, my sister," he sang, "lest thou fall in great ruin; if thou hast the divine grace, take heed to preserve it. Beware lest, through thy great fame, thou becomest hungry for it. If thou art indeed the bride of Christ, thou canst verily deem thyself blessed; but if such praise pleases thee, I fear lest the demon rejoice; beware lest thou be caught in his snares. Many have been the saints to whom men have flocked, who, lest they should be wounded by pride, have fled to the cell. I hear that thou claimest that the Holy Spirit is guiding thee; if it is true, I thank God who has so exalted thee. Beware, beware, beware, lest thou become a liar or cowardly through vanity. Beware lest the temptation of prophetical speech enthrall thee. Lay aside the fantasies of vain prophecy; if thou goest by their ways, thou wilt find thyself ensnared. Thou art proclaimed to be of holy life; thou art already called a saint. If the Holy Spirit is leading thee, seek not earthly praise, which undoes the soul that desires it. Shouldst thou fall, many will lose their faith; beware, poor woman, lest thou be overthrown. May the loving divine light so guard thee along its way that thy soul may take her stand upon the truth alone."[2] This poem, or *lauda*, El Bianco seems to have actually sent to Catherine at Pisa, together with a long letter, blaming her severely for allowing such honours to be paid her, generally censuring her mode of life as dangerous

[1] *Contestatio Fr. Bartholomaei*, *Processus*, coll. 1352, 1353.

[2] Poem in 32 stanzas, headed "Questa seguente lauda mandò el Bianco alla Beata Caterina da Siena" (No. 72 in the printed collection of the *Laudi spirituali del Bianco da Siena*).

and objectionable, urging her to shun publicity and to seek solitude, since the latter was the way of the Saints, while hers was that of hypocrites and seekers of their own praises. Raimondo and Bartolommeo attempted to keep the letter from Catherine, intending to send a sharp answer on their own account; but she insisted upon hearing it, professed the warmest gratitude to the writer for his solicitude for the welfare of her soul, and rebuked the two friars for their uncharitable interpretation of his good intentions. Her own answer is extant, written, she tells him, "with the desire of seeing us united and transformed in that sweet, eternal, and pure Truth, which takes from us all falsehood and lying":—

"I thank you cordially, dearest father, for the holy zeal and anxiety that you have for my soul. You seem to be in great doubt at what you hear about my life. I am certain that nothing moves you save desire of the honour of God and of my salvation, for you fear that I may be assailed and deluded by the devil. I do not wonder, father, at your having this fear, especially in the matter of eating; for I promise you that it is not only you who are afraid about it, but I myself tremble for fear of deception by the devil. But I put my trust in the goodness of God, and mistrust myself, knowing that upon myself I cannot rely. Not only in this, but in all I do, I always fear because of my own frailty, and because of the astuteness of the devil, thinking that I may be deceived; for I know and see that the devil lost blessedness, but not wisdom, and with that wisdom, or rather astuteness, he could deceive me. But I turn, then, and cling to the tree of the most holy Cross of Christ crucified, and thereto I would be fastened; and I doubt not that, if I be fastened and nailed to it with Him, through love and with deep humility, the devils will have no power against me, not because of my virtue, but by the virtue of Christ crucified. You bid me specially pray to God that I may eat. I tell you, my father, and I tell you in the sight of God, that I have always tried in every possible way, once or twice a day, to take food; and I have prayed continually, and do pray to God, and will pray that He may give me grace in this matter to live like other creatures, if it is His will, for it is mine. I pray you to pray that supreme eternal Truth that, if it is more for His honour and the salvation of my soul, He may give me grace and enable me to take food, if it pleases Him. And I am certain that the goodness of God will not despise your prayers. I beseech you to write to me what remedy you see for it, and, if only it be to the honour of God, I will gladly adopt it. And I beseech you, too, not to be hasty in judging, unless you are quite sure that you see things as they are in God's sight." [1]

The desire that Catherine had expressed in this letter, that she might "be fastened and nailed to the tree of the most holy Cross of Christ crucified with Him, through love and with deep humility," was now to be mystically fulfilled. The church of Santa Cristina stands on the Lung' Arno, not far from the little Gothic gem of Santa Maria della Spina, which she, who had chosen a crown of thorns for a crown of pearls, must have seen in all its fresh beauty. Although Santa Cristina in its present form is in the main a building of the nineteenth century, prosaic alike in its surroundings and its interior, there stands still, by the first altar to the right of the entrance, a fragment of one of the pillars of the older church, with the inscription: *Signavit Dominus servam suam Catharinam hic signis redemptionis nostrae*: "Here the Lord signed His servant Catherine with the signs of our redemption." For here, on the fourth Sunday of Lent, 1375, the Sunday known as *Laetare Sunday* from the text of Isaiah sung as Introit ("Rejoice ye with Jerusalem, and be glad with her, all ye that love her"), while rapt in ecstasy after Communion, Catherine of Siena in a measure received the same

[1] Letter 92 (305), which is one of those included in the Harleian MS. Cf. *Contestatio Fr. Bartholomaei*, *loc. cit.*, coll. 1354, 1355 (f. 142 in the Sienese MS.). The poem, or *lauda*, previously quoted, which has hitherto curiously escaped the notice of all the biographers of St. Catherine, leaves no doubt as to the identity of the person who wrote to her. For the life of El Bianco at Città di Castello, see the *Vita d'alcuni servi di Giesù Cristo* appended to Belcari's *Vita del B. Giovanni Colombini*.

mystical revelation which had been stamped in all the fulness of its seal upon the members of Francis of Assisi one hundred and fifty years before. Fra Raimondo and the others saw her gradually rise up from her prostrate position to her knees, with face all glowing, stretch out her arms, and then, after remaining a while steadfast in this attitude, fall suddenly to the ground as though mortally wounded. "I saw," she said, "the crucified Lord coming down to me in a great light, and for this, by the impetus of the mind that would fain go forth to meet its Creator, the body was constrained to rise. Then from the marks of His most sacred wounds I saw five blood-red rays coming down upon me, which were directed towards the hands and feet and heart of my body. Wherefore, perceiving the mystery, I straightway exclaimed: *Ah, Lord my God, I beseech Thee, let not the marks appear outwardly on my body.* Then, whilst I was yet speaking, before the rays reached me, they changed their blood-red colour to splendour, and in the semblance of pure light they came to the five places of my body, that is, to the hands, the feet, and the heart. So great is the pain that I endure sensibly in all those five places, but especially within my heart, that, unless the Lord works a new miracle, it seems not possible to me that the life of my body can stay with such agony, and that it will not end in a few days."

They brought her back to her room, in what appeared a dying condition. But it seemed that, in answer to the united prayers of all the fellowship, this new miracle was wrought, and when, on the following Sunday, she received the Blessed Sacrament again from Raimondo's hands, her strength was, as it were, supernaturally renewed. "O Father of ineffable mercy," writes the good friar, "what wilt Thou do for Thy faithful servants and for Thy beloved children, when Thou dost show Thyself so benign to such afflicted sinners as us? I said to her: 'Mother, does the pain still last of the wounds which were made in thy body?' And she answered: 'The Lord has heard your prayers, albeit to the affliction of my soul, and those wounds not only do not afflict my body, but even fortify it; so that, instead of receiving torment from them, albeit I feel them still, they bring me strength.' "[1]

While staying at Pisa, Catherine for the first time saw the sea. On the island of Gorgona, some twenty miles from Livorno, there stood a Carthusian monastery, of which a certain Don Bartolommeo Serafini of Ravenna was then prior: a man of holy life and spiritual conversation, who believed profoundly in Catherine's mission, and was eager for the monks under his charge to hear her words. At his repeated instance, supported by Fra Raimondo, Catherine visited the island, with a number of her companions and friends from Pisa. They arrived at evening, and, while Raimondo and the others were entertained at the convent, the prior found rooms for Catherine and her women without. The next day, at the earnest prayer of the monks, Catherine spoke to them of the temptations of the monastic life and of its trials, in such a profound and illuminating fashion that all were amazed, and the prior, turning to Raimondo, declared that, if she had heard the confession of each (as he had done), she could not more appositely have healed the soul of every one. Bartolommeo himself bears witness to the great spiritual fruit that she wrought among them. He tells us how she left the island in the convent boat, and how, when they had reached the Pisan shore, the monks asked her blessing before rowing back, and believed that, through her intercession, they were miraculously delivered from a sudden storm that rose. He speaks, too, of her parting warning to him concerning a scandal which the devil would shortly try to cause in his flock, which was soon verified in the attempted suicide of a young monk, who was only liberated from temptation by the touch of the mantle that Catherine had left behind her, and by calling on her name.[2]

The simplicity with which Don Bartolommeo in his old age tells these stories is a revelation of the character of the man, and

[1] *Legenda*, II. vi. 10, 11 (§§ 194–198). Cf. Lombardelli, *Sommario della disputa a difesa delle Sacre Stimate di Santa Caterina*, p. 13.

[2] *Legenda*, II. x. 20 (§ 296); *Contestatio Dom. Bartholomaei de Ravenna*, *Processus*, coll. 1304–1307.

it is evident that Catherine was as delighted and edified by him as he had been impressed by her. "God is calling you by holy and good inspirations," she wrote to Ippolito degli Ubaldini, a Florentine noble who sought her advice about entering religion, "and He has prepared a holy and devout place for you, utterly cut off from the world, with a father, the Prior of Gorgona, who is veritably an angel, a mirror of virtue, with a good and holy family. Tell him your intention fully, and make a steady, firm, and true resolution. And if you decide to enter that holy and devout place (which will be the life of your soul), or whatever you determine, if you dispense your substance to the poor, give some of it to that place of Gorgona. For the convent needs to be put into shape, if it is to conform to the rule of the Carthusian order." [1] Two of the most beautiful of her spiritual letters are addressed to one of the monks of this convent, Francesco Tebaldi of Florence, who is apparently the same young man who had been so sorely tempted to take his own life. "We have all had a great desire to hear news of you," she says at the end of the first; "it seems to me that the demon has not slept, and is not sleeping with regard to you; at which I am very glad, because I see that, by the goodness of God, the battle has not been to death, but to life. Thanks, thanks, to the sweet God eternal, who has given us so much grace! Now you will begin to know that you are nothing, and to realize that your being, and all grace that is founded upon your being, comes from Him who is. To Him let all thanks and praise be rendered; for it is His will that we give the flower to Him and that the fruit be our own." [2]

A man of a more virile type than the gentle Prior of Gorgona, who is said to have first met Catherine at this time, and afterwards came under her influence, was the Florentine hermit of Vallombrosa, Don Giovanni dalle Celle, whose name runs through so much of the religious life of the Trecento. His spiritual

[1] Letter 130 (271). The convent of Gorgona was a Benedictine house that had recently been made over to the Carthusians, and would, therefore, need the building of separate cells for the monks.

[2] Letters 150 (62), 154 (63).

letters, still only in part collected, extend from the forties to the nineties of the century. Giovanni had become a monk of the Vallombrosan rule at an early age, and, while superior of S. Trinità in Florence, had committed a peculiarly scandalous and infamous crime, for which (after release from imprisonment) he did penance all the rest of his long life. In his earliest extant letter, he beseeches the saintly Augustinian hermit, Fra Simone da Cascia, as a most experienced physician of souls, to heal "the execrable wound of my mind": "I was what I am not; I used to do penance; but now, by looking back, I have become a statue of salt. I used to taste what now, in my wretchedness, I hardly remember. I have fallen, and cannot rise of myself; I strive to return to the man I was, but dare not, for my mind is overwhelmed by remorse and confounded by the shame of my sins. Receive me, then, crying to thee from the abyss, and begin to build up in me what I have destroyed."[1] After this he took the name of Giovanni dalle Celle, "John of the Cells," from the solitude above Vallombrosa to which he retired, but from which he issued at intervals to labour in Florence and elsewhere for the good of souls. Men and women alike appealed to him for direction; but his special work of this kind seems to have been the guidance of a confraternity of young men, known as his adopted sons, whom he trained in the religious life; at the same time, through his friend Guido dal Palagio (a man of devout life and great charity, known to students of Italian literature by a noble patriotic canzone, and dear to lovers of the beautiful for the Franciscan convent above Fiesole which he founded), he kept in touch with the government of the Republic.

It has frequently been stated that Catherine had come to Pisa by the express wish of the Pope, to carry out certain negotiations

[1] This letter, with Fra Simone's answer, is given by P. Nicola Mattioli, *Il Beato Simone Fidati da Cascia* (Rome, 1898), pp. 392–410, and must have been written before 1348, the year of Simone's death. Giovanni's crime, as described by Girolamo of Vallombrosa, in B. Sorio, *Lettere del B. Giovanni dalle Celle*, p. 7, curiously illustrates Catherine's words about the wicked practices of certain monks, in her *Dialogo*, cap. 129.

on his behalf, with the object of preventing the Republic from joining the league that was being formed against the Holy See. There is no warrant for this in Raimondo's narrative, and it seems chronologically an anticipation of what was to take place some months later. If Catherine had any more definite mission than that of her Divine Spouse for the conversion of souls, it could only have been in connection with the proposed Crusade; she was apparently to use Pisa as a headquarters from which to stir up enthusiasm among high and low in Italy, alike by letter and by spoken word, for "the holy passage."

The Pope was trying gradually to feel his way in this matter, which he probably had sincerely at heart. Among the numerous bulls despatched from Avignon was one addressed to the provincial of the Dominicans in Tuscany, the minister of the Friars Minor, and to Fra Raimondo, empowering them to investigate the will and disposition of the faithful, to enroll those who were ready to give their lives in the great undertaking, and to report to the Pope thereon, so that he might know upon what support he could rely from Italy when the banner of the Cross should actually be raised. There had been some immediate response from individuals, three of the Buonconti, for instance, having enrolled themselves; but it was imperative to secure the adhesion of the heads of the maritime States of the Mediterranean: Naples, Genoa, Pisa, and Sardinia; especially as the practical intervention of Venice in the enterprise seemed doubtful, and Louis of Hungary, in spite of his alleged pledges to the contrary, showed small disposition to move his powers in defence of the threatened Greeks and their Emperor, notwithstanding an urgent brief from Gregory inciting him to act with vigour.[1] A little later, these exhortations were renewed, and a friar of great eloquence, one of the few immediate links between Petrarca's circle of correspondents and that of Catherine, Fra Bonaventura Badoara of Padua, an Augustinian hermit, was sent to inflame the

[1] Brief of January 28, 1375. Raynaldus, vii. p. 263. The Pope was flattering himself that the Greeks were prepared to submit to the Roman obedience in return for armed Hungarian protection.

King's lagging zeal.[1] But the official invitations of the Pope and the eloquent exhortations of his Augustinian emissary seem frigid and perfunctory, when compared with the fiery-hearted enthusiasm, the white and glowing passion, with which Catherine threw herself into the undertaking.

From the house of the Buonconti, she despatched letters and messengers in all directions, to princes and rulers of republics, to captains of mercenaries and to private citizens alike, urging each in his own degree to support the papal design, and to be ready to lay down his life for the Cross when the summons should come. One of the first to whom she appealed was Queen Giovanna of Naples, whose ambiguous character and dangerous position stirred her imagination and excited her compassion. In words of touching tenderness, the maiden of the people implores the daughter of kings, who had won from men the title of *regina meretrix*, to repent and amend her life, thereby becoming "a true and perfect daughter of God," to contemplate the ineffable love that God bears her, and plant the tree of the Cross in the garden of her soul. "Rise up, then, manfully, sweetest sister! It is no longer time for sleep, for time sleeps not, but ever passes like the wind. For love's sake, lift up the standard of the most holy Cross in your heart. Soon must we uplift it, for, as I understand, the Holy Father will proclaim the war against the Turks. And, therefore, I pray you to make ready, so that we may all go together to die for Christ. I beseech and urge you, in the name of Christ crucified, to support His Spouse in her need, with your possessions, your person, and your counsel; in all that is possible, show yourself a faithful daughter of sweet and holy Church."[2] And to Bartolommeo di Smeduccio, the tyrant of San Severino in the Marches, a young condottiere whose growing reputation as a soldier was giving him a power and importance far beyond that derived from the forces actually at his disposal, she wrote: "Let your heart and soul be enkindled in Christ sweet Jesus, with love and desire of paying Him back for so much love by giving life

[1] Brief of October 27, 1375. *Ibid.*, p. 264.

[2] Letters 133 (312) and 138 (314).

for life. He has given His life for you, and do you give your life for Him, blood for blood. I invite you, in the name of Christ crucified, to give your blood for His, when the time comes which the servants of God are expecting, for going to win back what has been taken from us: namely, the holy place of the sepulchre of Christ, as well as the souls of the infidels, who are our brothers, bought back by the blood of Christ even as we; to redeem the place from their hands, and their souls from the hands of the demons and from their infidelity. I invite you not to be negligent nor tardy, when the Holy Father raises the standard of the most holy Cross, and orders the sweet and holy expedition. I beseech you, by the love of Christ crucified, to await with gladness and desire the invitation to these sweet and glorious nuptials, where impurity will be left behind, and the soul, free from sin and penalty, will be fed at the table of the Lamb. You would indeed be foolish to keep away from such great delight. It seems to me that any one who could not go upright should go there crawling, to show his love for God by giving Him life for love of life. Make amends for your failings and for your sins with the instrument of your body, even as with the instrument of your body you have offended."[1]

As far as words went, the response to Catherine's appeals was prompt. Mariano d' Oristano, who ruled the island of Sardinia under the title of Judge of Arborea, promised to join the Crusade in person, and to supply two galleys, a thousand horsemen, three thousand foot-soldiers, and six hundred crossbowmen, for ten years. The Genoese seemed enthusiastic.[2] Giovanna professed herself more than ready. "My venerable mother," wrote Catherine to the Queen, "I will pray, to the utmost of my feeble powers, the supreme and eternal goodness of God that He may give you perfect light for this and all your good works, and that He may increase desire upon desire in you; so that, enkindled with the fire of love, you may come from the sovereignty of this miserable and transient life to that perpetual city of

[1] Unpublished. Appendix, Letter I.

[2] Letter 66 (125).

chese egli fussi uenuto accio col-
lui costui non seguita la natura
sua / ma p la sua cechita neuscito
fuori . // Veramente cosi /e/ caro
padre in cristo dolce Jesu che lanima naturalmente insemedes-
sima de amare & seguitare il suo
padre creatore dio eterno che
uedendo che dio la creata solo p
amore sentesi trarre uerso di-
lui & non puo sostenere le ingiurie che gli sieno fatte . Vuolne fare la uendecta p amore che gli a
al padre & questa /e/ la ragione
p che lanima uuole sempre fare uendecta contra la parte sensitiua che /e/ suo nimico mortale . Pero che colui che ua drieto
a essa sensualita egli rimane morto di morte eternale crucifigge
cristo unaltra uolta che uoi sapete che solo p lo peccato egli mo-
ri / si che lanima inamorata di
dio sommo eterno padre uuole
seguitare la natura sua / lamo-
re gli fa pdere [illegible] lamore fa uē-
decta di se medesimo percoten-
do la falsa passione sensitiua .
El dimonio el mondo & la carne percotendo col coltello dellodio & della more / odio & dispiacimento del peccato amore delle uirtu dilectandosi di quello che dio amo odiando quello
che egli odio . Allora rende lanima il debito suo al padre seguita la sua natura gia mai non cesare . Guarda gia che non ci mec-
tessi il ueleno della more pprio
di se medesimo da marsi fuori
di dio / ponendo lo studio suo &
nelle delitie stati & dilecti del mō-
do fare della carne sua uno dio /
tenendola con disordinato dilecto & dilicatezze . Questo tale non tanto che faccia uendecta del nimico che gli a morto il-
padre / ma esso medesimo luc-
cide . Or non uoglio che sia in
uoi : ma uoglio che seguitiate
lanima gentile nostra che dio
ua data con amore & libero arbitrio . Vistrignete & ui legate
questo uestimento che non sa-
ra dimonio ne creatura che uel
possa torre . Cosi uestito & armato delle uirtu col coltello /
dellodio & della more pdere-
te il timore seruile / possederete la citta dellanima uostra none schiferete mai i colpi di ue-
runa tribulatione o pena che
potessi sostenere / ne uolgerete
il capo adrieto a ripigliare il-
uomito de peccati mortali . Nō
uoglio cosi / ma con una uera p

A PAGE OF THE HARLEIAN MS. 3480, SHOWING A PORTION OF SAINT CATHERINE'S LETTER TO BARTOLOMMEO DI SMEDUCCIO.

[*To face p.* 140.

Jerusalem, the vision of peace, where the Divine Clemency will make us all kings and lords, and will reward every labour to whoso endures it for His most sweet love."[1]

To the Queen Mother of Hungary, too, Elizabeth of Poland, Catherine wrote, telling her that Giovanna's support had been secured, imploring her to use her influence with her son, King Louis, to induce him to accede to the Pope's request, and serve the Church with his arms. "The Church has need of your human aid, and you have need of her divine aid. Be assured that, the more you give her of your aid, the more you will partake of the divine grace, the fire of the Holy Spirit, which is contained in her. I, wretched, miserable woman, have nothing wherewith to aid her; but if my blood could be of any avail, I would gladly shed it all. But I will do this much: I will give her that little particle that God gives me, that it may be helpful to her, albeit I see nought in me that is useful that I can give, save tears and sighs and continual prayer. But you, mother, and my lord the King, your son, can aid her with prayers through holy desire, and can also at your will and with love support her by human aid. Do not shun, then, for the love of God, this labour; but embrace it for Christ crucified, for your own utility and exaltation, and to work out your salvation. And pray your dear son earnestly to offer himself for love to serve Holy Church."[2]

But, in the meantime, the political horizon in central Italy had been growing darker and darker. The two papal legates, Cardinal de Noellet at Bologna, the Abbot of Marmoutier at Perugia, were steadily filling the cup of their iniquities to the brim, and the prophecies of Birgitta and Petrarca were soon to be fulfilled to the letter. In the summer of this year, 1375, the storm burst with dramatic suddenness.

From the outset of Gregory's pontificate, the Florentines had been alarmed by the subjugation of Perugia, and had attempted

[1] Letter 143 (313), dated August 4. Giovanna, as the descendant of Charles of Anjou, bore the title of Queen of Jerusalem.

[2] Letter 145 (311).

to form an alliance with Siena, Pisa, Lucca, and Arezzo, for the defence of Tuscany against the supposed sinister designs of the papal representatives. They had hitherto, however, found these other communes unwilling to enter into any league in which the Church was not included. Their growing suspicions that the two legates were plotting against the liberties of the Republic, already excited by the aid that they had given to the Salimbeni and Ubaldini, were brought to a head in June, when, on the conclusion of the truce at Bologna between the Church and the Visconti, Hawkwood's mercenaries were dismissed from the service of the former. There had been great scarcity of food during the spring throughout Florence and the contado (as well as elsewhere in Italy) ; but, in spite of the express command from the Pope to the contrary, Cardinal de Noellet refused to allow grain to be sent thither from the places under his dominion. He now wrote to the Signoria that Hawkwood was collecting troops, and that, unless Florence would lend him at least sixty thousand florins to hire them, he would be unable to prevent these mercenaries from assailing the territory of the Republic. The Signoria having expressed their inability to find the requisite sum, Hawkwood arrived with his company at the Florentine frontier.

There can be little doubt that the ruling faction in Florence had been for some time desiring a rupture with the Church, partly from really patriotic motives, partly with a view to weakening the power of the Parte Guelfa in the Republic. In spite of the explicit allegations of Florentine historians, it is most unlikely that either the Pope or his legates had any intention of undertaking so impossible a task as the subjugation of Tuscany, though it may well be that they contemplated the overthrow of the democratic governments, and the establishment of a régime less hostile to the aggrandizement of the temporal sovereignty of the Church. Cardinal de Noellet probably spoke the truth when he declared that he had no longer any control over Hawkwood's movements, and he was, perhaps, really unable to supply the Florentines with grain from the cities of Romagna. Gregory could protest, with much show of reason on his side, that the Florentines had not the smallest right to object to the truce with the Visconti, seeing that they themselves had not contributed their share to the payment of the mercenaries, as they were bound by the terms of their treaty with the Church.[1] Nevertheless, the evil government and iniquitous policy of the papal representatives in Italy was calculated to arouse the worst apprehensions, and the Florentines could not look on with indifference while the neighbouring cities, hitherto practically free or ruled by friendly potentates, bound to their Republic by the Guelf league, were reduced to mere units in a powerful and consolidated State. The Pope wrote to the Signoria, complaining of their unworthy suspicions of him, protesting his great affection for the Florentines, and urging them to come to some agreement with the Cardinal to prevent Hawkwood's soldiers from harming their cities or those of the Church.[2] But it was now too late. On June 21, the Florentines made terms on their own account with Hawkwood and his *Societas Anglorum*, purchasing a five years' peace with them for the sum of 130,000 gold florins. A few days later, the anti-papal feeling in the city was roused to a height of frenzy by the discovery of a plot (which, apparently, was revealed by Hawkwood himself) to betray Prato to Cardinal de Noellet; two of the conspirators, a notary and a monk in priest's orders, were tortured to death through the streets of Florence with appalling cruelty. It was further alleged that an agent of the Cardinal had been in Florence, to spy out a site for the erection of a papal fortress.[3] Hostilities were now inevitable. On July 24, the Florentines took the politically astute, but morally indefensible step, of entering into an alliance for five years with Bernabo Visconti. The next day, pleading the danger

[1] Brief of August 8, 1375. Raynaldus, vii. p. 268. Cf. Capponi, *Storia della Repubblica di Firenze*, I. pp. 319–322; Marchionne Stefani, Lib. IX. rubr. 751; Ammirato, I. 2. pp. 691, 692.

[2] Briefs of June 16 and 21. Gherardi, *La Guerra dei Fiorentini con Papa Gregorio XI*, docs. 4 and 5.

[3] *Diario del Monaldi*, p. 507; Ammirato, I. 2. p. 693.

caused by the coming of the English as their justification, they informed the Republics of Pisa, Siena, Lucca, and Arezzo of what they had done, and called upon them to join the league.

Having thus blackmailed the Florentines, Hawkwood, in July, came into the contado of Pisa and then into that of Siena, compelling each of these communes to make similar terms. Pisa paid 30,000 florins, and Siena 35,500 (of which Montepulciano contributed 3,000). "In order that the Commune should not suffer for what the pastors of the Church had wrongly made them pay," the Florentines and Sienese imposed a heavy tax on the ecclesiastics to raise the money, a levy which, in the case of the clergy of Siena, amounted to two-thirds of the whole sum.

Catherine was apparently still at Pisa while these things were being done. Hawkwood had previously made a sort of promise that he would join the Crusade; the time seemed ripe for her to call upon him to fulfil his word, and so leave Tuscany in peace. She accordingly sent Fra Raimondo to the English camp, with a letter to Hawkwood and his captains, exhorting them to abandon the service and pay of the devil, and become soldiers of Christ crucified. "I pray you sweetly in Christ Jesus that, since God and our Holy Father have ordered the expedition against the infidels, and you delight so much in making war and fighting, you war no more upon Christians, because it offends God; but go against those others. How cruel it is that we who are Christians, members bound in the body of Holy Church, should persecute one another! I am much amazed that, after having promised (as I have heard) to go to die for Christ in this holy enterprise, you should now be making war here. This is not the holy disposition that God demands from you." This letter is, however, merely the credentials for Fra Raimondo, who is to give them her full message by word of mouth. "My father and son, Fra Raimondo, is bringing you this letter. Trust what he tells you, for he is a true, faithful servant of God, and will not advise or tell you anything save what is for the honour of God, and the salvation and glory of your soul." So much were Hawkwood and his captains impressed by the friar's exhortations, that they

.ll took a solemn oath that, if the Crusade really started, they vould go, and Raimondo returned to Catherine with their signed ınd sealed promises to this effect.[1]

In August, the Florentines elected eight magistrates, two for ·ach quarter of the city, known as the *Otto della Balìa*, or *Otto lella Guerra*, to carry on the conflict with the Church. These ncluded representatives of each order in the State : one noble, Alessandro de' Bardi ; one artisan, Giovanni di Mone ; six ɔurghers, Giovanni Dini, Giovanni Megalotti, Andrea Salviati, Tommaso Strozzi, Guccio Gucci, Matteo Soldi. They were ıll men of mark, able and experienced, animated by sincere patriotism, haters of the prepotency of the Parte Guelfa ; such popularity did they acquire by their energetic management of the task committed to them, that they were called the *Otto Santi*. Eight other officials, known as the *Otto di livelli*, were appointed, to tax the clergy and the churches for the defence of the city.[2] Mercenaries were hired, German cavalry obtained from Bernabo, and a German condottiere, Conrad Wertinger, who was in the service of Galeazzo Visconti, was elected captain-general of the forces of the Republic. The Abbot of Marmoutier having arrested the Florentine ambassador at Perugia, the Florentines seized and imprisoned the papal nuncio, Luca Bertini, Bishop of Narni, who was returning from Avignon to the Patrimony.[3]

[1] Letter 140 (220).

[2] Cf. Gherardi, *op. cit.*, p. 23 ; Marchionne Stefani, Lib. IX. rubr. 752, 753 ; and, for a hostile contemporary view of "citizens who had such presumption as to consent to be called *santi*," Sercambi, *Croniche*, I. p. 213.

[3] Cf. Raynaldus, vii. p. 279 ; *Cronica Sanese*, col. 246. The statement made by Augusta Drane (I. p. 347), and copied from her by more recent writers, that "the mad Ghibelline mob, encouraged by their 'Eight Saints,' after slaughtering the inquisitors, seized the papal nuncio and flayed him alive in the streets of Florence," is entirely inaccurate. The papal bull (Raynaldus, *loc. cit.*) merely says that the nuncio was *aliquandiu crudelissimo carcere detentus*. For an account of this personage, who was afterwards Bishop of Siena, see G. A. Pecci, *Storia del Vescovado di Siena*, pp. 288–290. Augusta Drane has, perhaps, confused him with the monk Niccolò who had been so horribly put to death, probably unjustly, for the affair of Prato.

Nevertheless, war was not openly declared against the Church, and a show of diplomatic relations was maintained with the papal legates. The other Tuscan communes showed no eagerness to enter the league. Piero Gambacorti was divided between his religious feelings and his need of Florentine support; Siena had differences concerning boundaries with Pisa and Arezzo, which latter State was the first to adhere to Florence; Lucca still regarded the Church as her liberator from the foreign yoke, and was most unwilling to commit herself to any hostile action. "Do not allow yourselves to be deceived by any flatteries," wrote the Pope to the government of Lucca, "nor corrupted by any sedition, nor terrified by any threats from those who are, perchance, striving to disturb your peace and pervert your devotion, and who reduce the liberty of their neighbours to servitude when they can; but, like most devoted sons, be columns of the Church which desires and seeks your liberty." [1]

Catherine was still at Pisa at the beginning of September, where we find her, on the second day of the month, dictating to Fra Raimondo a letter to the new Senator of Siena, the Marchese Pietro del Monte Santa Maria, a religious and upright noble from Umbria, through whom she was able to keep in constant touch with the government of her native city during her absence at this time.[2] Shortly after, however, she returned with her spiritual family to Siena, Fra Raimondo apparently remaining at Pisa, where he was still busy with the affairs of the Crusade. But her stay at Siena was very brief. The City of the Virgin could look after herself, and was too powerful to be coerced, while the position of Pisa and Lucca was difficult in the extreme. Almost immediately, probably through the medium of Alfonso da Vadaterra, Catherine received a command from the Pope to repair to Lucca, to confirm that Republic in its tottering allegiance to the Holy See.

Tommaso Caffarini and Neri di Landoccio are the only two of Catherine's household that we know for certain accompanied

[1] Brief of August 10, 1375. Pastor, *Geschichte*, I. doc. 3.

[2] Letter 135 (209). Cf. *Cronica Sanese*, coll. 244, 250.

ier to Lucca, and it is to the pen of the former that we owe the .ccount of her visit to this most beautiful of Tuscan cities, with its ʼines and olives and distant hills of marble, where Ruskin, almost :xactly five hundred years later, saw "one glow of calm glory ınd perfect possibilities of human life." The rulers of the Republic and private citizens alike received her with every nanifestation of reverence and affection; for the signs and wonders, both spiritual and material, that she wrought here as previously at Siena and at Pisa, together with the burning words :hat she uttered, convinced them that she "taught as one that had authority, and not as the scribes."[1] A little group of letters still preserved, addressed by her after her departure to women of Lucca with those beautifully sounding names, Mellina, Colomba, Caterina, Chiara, Bartolommea, Lagina, shows us the intense personal love for herself that she aroused in their hearts, to such an extent that her presence had become all in all to them. "My beloved daughters," she says in one, "love God without any intermediary. And, if you wish to love Him through me, wretched and miserable woman as I am, I will teach you where to find me. That you may not depart from this true love, go to that most sweet and venerable Cross with the sweet enamoured Magdalene; there you will find the Lamb and me, where your desires can be fed and nourished and fulfilled. In this way would I have you seek me and all created things; let this be your standard and your consolation. And do not think, because my body is far from you, that my affection and my care for your salvation is taken from you; nay, it is greater when I am absent bodily than when present. Know you not that the holy disciples knew and felt their Master more after His departure than before? For they took such delight in His humanity that they sought no further; but, after His presence had gone, they began to know and understand His goodness. Therefore said the first Truth:

[1] Caffarini's account of Catherine's stay at Lucca is in his *Supplementum*, Tantucci, pp. 107, 108. Neri di Landoccio, in his *capitolo* in praise of St. Catherine (printed at the end of Toresano's edition of the Letters) refers to a promise she made him there.

pedient for you that I go away; for if I go not away, the rter will not come unto you. So say I: it was expedient that ould go away from you, in order that you should set yourves to seeking God in truth, and not with any intermediary. I tell you that you will fare better now than before, if you enter into yourselves to think upon the words and the teaching that has been given you, and in this way you will receive the fulness of the grace of God."[1] In these letters, there are constant references to the love of Mary Magdalene for her Divine Master, and it is fitting that the one memorial of Catherine in Lucca to-day should be the great picture by Fra Bartolommeo della Porta, which represents the Magdalene and Catherine together in ecstatic adoration of the sovereign mystery of the Christian faith.

We do not know how long Catherine stayed at Lucca. Her mission was to the magistrates of the Republic rather than to the women, and, as soon as she thought she had confirmed them in their resolution of not joining the league, she passed on to Pisa, where her influence over Piero Gambacorti secured the neutrality of that State and a promise that Lucca would be protected by its power, if necessary. She had, apparently, anticipated that her absence from Siena would be a brief one, but she now found it impossible to leave Pisa. "I am afraid," she wrote to Fra Tommaso della Fonte, "that I must obey the orders that have been given me; for the Archbishop has asked the General for me to remain still some days. Beseech that venerable Spaniard to obtain grace for us that we may not return empty. But, by the grace of God, I do not think I shall return empty."[2]

At the end of October, a Florentine citizen renowned for eloquence and patriotism, Donato Barbadori, arrived at Pisa as ambassador from the Commune of Florence, bearing a letter from

[1] Letter 164 (348).

[2] Letter 139 (106). Cf. Dante, *Par.* xi. 129. I am inclined to think that this *venerabile Spagnuolo* is not Alfonso da Vadaterra (as supposed by the editors of the Letters), but St. Dominic himself, as we find Catherine elsewhere asking Dominicans to invoke his intercession in similar language. Cf. below, p. 319.

the Signoria, expressing their amazement that the Pisans had rejected their overtures. His instructions were to exhort Messer Piero and the Anziani to enter the league, and, if they refused, to warn them in strong language of the indignation this would arouse in Florence. He was then to do the same at Lucca, where, if the citizens answered that they would enter the league only when the other communes of Tuscany had done so, he was to tell them openly that he had had a favourable reply from Pisa (if it were so), and to add that the Sienese were most ready to follow the same course. And indeed, on November 27, Siena formally joined the league, stipulating that it should not last less than four years, that she should not be bound to keep more than one hundred and fifty lances in its service, and that none of the confederates should aid the Aretines against her.[1] Nevertheless, Pisa and Lucca both stood firm, albeit the latter State gave way so far as to allow a free passage through its territory to a body of men-at-arms that Bernabo Visconti was sending to Florence.

The Florentines had at length realized that, even with the doubtful adherence of the other Tuscan communes, the assistance of Bernabo Visconti alone would not suffice to enable them to fight against the Pope—especially as Hawkwood, in spite of the enormous bribe that he was still receiving from the Republic, had gone back, in September, to the service of the Church. In addition, at the beginning of October, the Pope (as, indeed, he had done several times before) announced his intention of returning very shortly to Rome. This the Florentines resolved to prevent. With the consent of the Signoria, the Otto della Guerra undertook to stir up a general rebellion of all the cities and towns of the Papal States. Envoys and letters were despatched, offering all the forces of the Republic to aid them, and promising to preserve their liberty. Let them remember that they are Italians, whose portion it is to command and not to obey. Let them contrast the sweetness of liberty with the tyrannical rule of the barbarians whom the pastors of the Church have sent from Gaul to oppress them. Let them shake off the shameful

[1] Gherardi, *op. cit.*, p. 20, docs. 83 and 84.

yoke of the foreigner, and show themselves worthy of liberty and the Italian name.[1]

There was an immediate and almost unanimous response to this appeal. The exactions and misrule of the papal officials had passed the limit of endurance, and the indignation of the Perugians had been further aroused by the death of the wife of one of their citizens, who, to escape from the violent hands of a nephew of the Abbot of Marmoutier, had thrown herself from the window of her house, and been dashed to pieces on the pavement below. On December 3, with the aid of Florentine troops, the inhabitants of Città di Castello began the revolt. Viterbo followed. The Abbot promptly sent his English mercenaries against the rebels, upon which, on December 7, the whole people of Perugia, nobles and populace alike, rose in arms, "in the name of God, of His Mother Mary, and of the blessed Saints Ercolano, Lorenzo, and Costanzo," shouting "Death to the pastors of the Church!" There was a general rush of all the papal officials and adherents to the citadel, to which Gomez Albornoz, after a vain attempt to beat back the insurgents, also retreated. The connecting wings of the fortress were broken down, and the Abbot, with Gomez and the rest, were kept closely blockaded, continually harassed by the rudimentary artillery of the epoch, especially a formidable *trabocco*, or ballista, which hurled gigantic stones, and was christened *caccia-preti*, the "priest-hunter."[2]

Gubbio, Sassoferrato, Urbino, Todi, Forlì, and other cities rose in rapid succession. In ten days, more than eighty cities and towns in the Patrimony, Umbria, and the Marches had been lost to the Church. Of the larger cities, Rome, Ancona, and Orvieto alone did not move. The Malatesta at Rimini and the Trinci at Foligno still declared for the Church, and the soldiery of Gomez Albornoz still held Ascoli. Messenger after messenger rode into Florence, bearing the branch of olive from the revolted cities.

[1] Gherardi, *op. cit.*, doc. 103.

[2] There is a vivid account of this liberation of Perugia "from the hands of the accursed pastors of the Church" in the Supplement to Graziani's Chronicle, pp. 220–224.

The bells were rung and the city was illuminated. Horse and foot were promptly despatched to support the insurgents, and to each town the Florentines sent a red standard with *Libertas* emblazoned upon it in white letters, which, together with the flag of the Commune, floated in front of their troops. Each place as it rose was received into the league; but, although the Florentines rigidly abstained from gaining any advantage to themselves, they cared less for the liberation of the people than for the expulsion of their pastors. Without any protest from them, the former tyrants, whom Cardinal Albornoz had expelled, in many cases returned; Francesco di Vico seized Viterbo for himself, Sinibaldo degli Ordelaffi (the son of the formidable Francesco) entered Forlì, the Alidosi retook Imola, and the Polentani Ravenna, while Count Antonio da Montefeltro occupied Urbino.

Catherine was still at Pisa when the news of the revolution in the Papal States reached the city. She was at that time staying in a hospice in the piazza di Santa Caterina, near the convent and church of the Dominicans. Fra Raimondo and his companion, Fra Pietro da Velletri, told her the news. "This is milk and honey," she said, "in comparison with what is to follow. Thus, father, do the lay folk act now, but soon you will see how much worse will be the deeds of ecclesiastics. When the Roman Pontiff will strive to correct their wicked lives, they will cause a universal scandal in the whole Holy Church of God, which, in the fashion of a pestilent heresy, will divide her and torment her."[1] Thus, Raimondo assures us, did Catherine foretell the schism which they were both soon to witness.

After this overwhelming triumph for the Florentines, it became increasingly dangerous for Pisa and Lucca to resist their overtures. It was probably before leaving Pisa that Catherine made a fresh appeal to the Anziani of Lucca by letter, not to forsake the cause of the Church. "If you tell me that it seems that she is failing and cannot even help herself, much less her children, I answer that it is not so, although it may seem like it to the outward show. If you look within, you will find that strength of

[1] *Legenda*, II. x. 8–10 (§ § 284–286).

which her enemies are deprived. I pray you, then, by the love of Christ crucified, dearest brothers and sons of Holy Church, to keep ever firm and persevering in what you have begun." She urges them at length, by every argument she can muster, to face every danger rather than join the league, and concludes with a promise of help from Pisa. "I tell you that, if you were to remain alone, you should stand firm in this field, and not look back; but, by the grace of God, there is another there too. There are the Pisans, your neighbours, who, if you stand firm and persevere, will never fail you, but will ever aid you and defend you until death from whosoever would injure you. Ah, sweetest brothers, what demon will be able to coerce those two members who are bound together, in order not to offend God, in the bond of charity?" [1]

[1] Letter 168 (206).

CHAPTER VIII

BETWEEN FLORENCE AND AVIGNON

"E crescendo in me il fuoco, mirando vedevo nel costato di Cristo crocifisso intrare 'l popolo cristiano e lo infedele; e io passavo, per desiderio e affetto d'amore, per lo mezzo di loro; ed entravo con loro in Cristo dolce Gesù, accompagnata col padre mio santo Domenico, e Giovanni singolare con tutti quanti i figliuoli miei. E allora mi dava la croce in collo e l'olivo in mano, quasi come io volessi; e così diceva che io la porgesse all' uno popolo e all' altro."—St. Catherine, Letter 219 (87).

To one endowed with the prophetic spirit, a sinister sign of the times must have appeared in the creation of cardinals, the second since Gregory's elevation to the pontificate, which took place on December 21 in this year, 1375. Among these nine new princes of the Church were three of the Pope's own kinsmen, including Gérard du Puy, the infamous Abbot of Marmoutier, who was still besieged in the citadel of Perugia. All were French, with the exception of Simone Brossano, the archbishop-elect of Milan, and Pedro de Luna, a young Spanish prelate of noble birth, great learning, and apparently sincere piety, who held a professorship in the University of Montpellier. "Take heed," said Gregory to Pedro de Luna, "lest thy moon suffer eclipse." Yet, judged by what might have seemed the higher standard, the Cardinal of Aragon, as he was called, was the only one of the nine not unworthy of his elevation.

Gregory's choice of cardinals utterly destroyed all hopes in a possible reformation of the Sacred College. To Catherine, who had just returned to Siena when the news reached Italy, it seemed a cruel act of cowardice on the Pope's part, a putting ointment upon a mortifying wound where the steel and the cautery were needed for the life of the patient. So we gather from the first of her letters to Gregory which have been preserved to us, evidently written about the beginning of the following year, 1376, "with desire of seeing you a fruitful tree, planted in the soil of true knowledge of yourself." Love of self has corrupted prelates and subjects alike, and no one dares begin the work of reform. "The sick man is blind, for he knows not his own need, and the pastor, who is the physician, is blind, for he considers nothing save his own pleasure and advantage, and, in order not to lose that, does not employ the knife of justice nor the fire of most ardent charity. Such a one is truly a hireling shepherd, because not only does he not draw his little sheep out of the hand of the wolf, but he himself devours them; and the cause of all this is that he loves himself without God, and does not follow sweet Jesus, the true Shepherd, who has given His life for His sheep. O *babbo mio*, sweet Christ on earth, follow that sweet Gregory, for it will be as possible to you to quench self-love as it was to him, for he was of the same flesh as you; and the same God is now who was then; we only need virtue and hunger for the salvation of souls. This is our remedy, father; that we lift up this love above ourselves and every creature outside God; let us think no more of friends and kinsmen, nor of temporal necessities, but only of virtue and of the exaltation of spiritual things; for temporal things are failing you for no other reason save that you have abandoned the care of spiritual things." "I beseech you to send to Lucca and to Pisa, dealing with them like a father as God will teach you, helping them in whatever can be done, and inviting them to stand firm and persevere. I have been at Pisa and at Lucca until now, inviting them, to the utmost of my power, not to make a league with the putrid members who are rebels to you. But they are in great perplexity, because they have no encouragement from you, and are being continually urged with threats by the other side to join it. But, up to now, they have not entirely consented. I beseech you also to write forcibly to Messer Piero, and do it zealously and do not delay. I have heard that you have made some cardinals. I believe that it would be more to the honour of God, and better for yourself, if you would always take care to make virtuous men. If the contrary is done, it will be a great insult to God and the ruination of Holy Church. And let us not wonder afterwards, if God sends His chastisements and His scourges upon us, for it is just. I beseech you, do what you have to do manfully and with fear of God." [1]

Already the dyer's daughter of Siena could address the Sovereign Pontiff in terms almost dictatorial. And, indeed, Gregory had need of such virile counsellors. His newly created Cardinal du Puy had been compelled to surrender the citadel of Perugia to the insurgents, on January 1, 1376. A fortnight later, the Florentine force returned to Florence in triumph, crowned with garlands of olive, to the sound of music and the pealing of bells. Hardly had Catherine returned to Siena when, on the very day of the surrender of the citadel of Perugia, Donato Barbadori again appeared as ambassador at Pisa, sent by the Eight to that city and to Lucca, once more to demand the abandonment of their neutrality. And, on March 13, the Signoria of Florence wrote exultantly to Bernabo Visconti: "Yesterday, by the grace of God, we concluded the league with the Pisans and the Lucchese." [2] Nevertheless, in thus joining the league under compulsion, neither Piero Gambacorti nor the Anziani of Lucca intended to undertake any hostile measures against the Pope, and the latter Republic had expressly stipulated that none of the confederates should be compelled to help any other who should occupy possessions of the Church.

Immediately after the surrender of the citadel of Perugia, the Signoria of Florence addressed an impassioned appeal to the Romans, through Coluccio Salutati, the famous chancellor of the Republic, one of whose letters in after years was to seem more formidable to Gian Galeazzo Visconti than an army of twenty thousand men. God has had compassion upon Italy, he wrote, and has raised up the spirit of her peoples against the most foul tyranny of barbarians. This must be particularly pleasing to the

[1] Letter 185 (1), corrected by the Harleian MS. Catherine wrote simultaneously to the Archbishop of Otranto, urging him fearlessly to tell the Pope the truth about what seemed to him to be for the honour of God and the renovation of the Church; and to the papal secretary, Niccolò da Osimo, offering Fra Raimondo for the Church's service. Letters 183 (33) and 181 (40).

[2] Gherardi, *op cit.*, doc. 183.

Romans, whose love of liberty made them masters of the world. Let them rise, too, and aid in expelling this abomination from Italy, for this will be a truly Roman work. Let them not be seduced by the suggestions of the priests that, if they support the state of the Church, the Pope will bring back the Roman Curia to Italy. Surely the Romans will not suffer Italy to be trampled under foot for their own gain. The example of Urban V has shown how little such promises can be trusted, and, indeed, if the Pope comes, he will set his seat at Perugia instead of Rome. "Therefore, dearest brothers, consider their deeds, not their words; for not your advantage, but their lust of domination is bringing them back to Italy. Be not deceived by honeyed words, and do not suffer your Italy, which your forefathers with the cost of so much blood made the head of all the world, to be subject to barbarians and foreigners. Repeat once more the saying of the famous Cato: We do not so much desire to be free as to live with freemen."[1]

But the Romans were resolved to do nothing to prevent the restoration of the Apostolic See to the Eternal City. "We had firmly intended," wrote Gregory to all the States and peoples of Italy, a few days later, "to return with the Roman Curia to the Supreme City and our other towns in Italy, and to live and die among you, and to relieve you of the heavy burdens which, on account of the whirlwinds of warfare, you have borne, to our great displeasure and that of our predecessors, and to preserve you in peace, and rule you with beneficent government with the aid of the Most High."[2] He further appointed a Roman, Cardinal Francesco Tebaldeschi, a good man but enfeebled by age and illness, to succeed the Cardinal Abbot of Marmoutier as vicar-general of the Church in the Papal States. Simultaneously, he attempted to come to terms with the league, through the intervention of the Queen of Naples and the Doge of Genoa, who sent two ambassadors, Niccolò Spinelli and Bartolommeo Giacoppi, to Florence. But, before they arrived, Gregory, on February 11,

[1] Letter of January 4, 1376. Pastor, *Geschichte*, I. document 4.

[2] *Litterae hortativae pro parte domini nostri papae*, etc. Dated Avignon, January 6, 1376. Biblioteca Vaticana, *Cod. Vat. Lat.* 6330, f. 430.

formulated a terrible process against the Florentines, which they described as too atrocious to be addressed even to schismatics and infidels, enumerating their real or alleged offences against the Holy See, summoning by name all the citizens who had held office since June to appear in person at Avignon before the last day of March. A few days later, with Florentine aid, the city of Ascoli, upon which the liberty of the whole of the Marches depended, rose against the Church, and Gomez Albornoz, who had taken refuge here after the surrender at Perugia, found himself besieged in the citadel.

From Siena, Catherine watched the course of events with agonized dismay: *Io muoio di dolore e non posso morire*, she writes; "I am dying of grief and cannot die." It seemed to her that the jaws of hell were opened, and that the devils were carrying off the souls of men on every side. While admitting to the full that the iniquities and oppression of the papal officials were the real cause of the war, and that, humanly speaking, the rising of the cities of the States of the Church had ample justification, she regarded rebellion against the Pope as in itself a mortal sin, and, in consequence, the policy of the Florentines as almost diabolical. Her soul is rent in twain between Italy and the Church, between liberty and religion, and hence comes what at times seems the exquisite inconsistency of the letters with which she attempted to win the contending parties to counsels of charity and peace.

Niccolò Soderini had been elected one of the priors of the Florentine Republic who held office for the first two months of 1376, and found himself most reluctantly forced into an attitude of hostility towards the Church. To him Catherine wrote, "with desire of seeing you a member bound and united in the bond of true charity, in such wise that you may partake of this true love, and that, now that you have been made head and set in signory, you may be the means to help to bind all these members, your citizens, so that they may not stay in such peril of the damnation of soul and body." Whoso goes against the Church, cuts himself off from the sacraments, and despises the blood of Christ. If they will humble themselves, the Pope is ready to receive them ; he is inviting them to peace, notwithstanding the injury he has received from them. They are misled if they think themselves the offended parties, for the sins of God's ministers should have been left to Him to punish. "I beseech you, Niccolò, by that ineffable love with which God has created and so sweetly ransomed you, to strive with all your power (for God has not given it to you save for some great hidden end) to bring about peace and union between your fellow-citizens and Holy Church, in order that yourselves and all Tuscany may not be imperilled." [1]

And to the Pope she wrote, bidding him win back the revolted cities by love alone :—

"O my sweet, most holy babbo, I can see no other means for you to have back your little sheep, who like rebels have strayed from the fold of Holy Church. Wherefore I pray you in the name of Christ crucified, and I would have you do this mercy for me, conquer their malice with your benignity. We are yours, O father ; and I know that they all in general realize that they have done wrong ; but, albeit they have no excuse for working evil, nevertheless, because of the hardships and cruel injustice that they suffered by reason of bad pastors and governors, it seemed to them impossible to act otherwise. For when they perceived the stench of the life of many of their rulers, who you know are demons incarnate, they came into such exceeding fear that they have acted like Pilate, who slew Christ in order not to lose lordship ; and so have they done, for they have persecuted you in order not to lose their state. I crave mercy, then, father, from you for them. Do not look at the ignorance and pride of your sons ; but, with love and kindness, giving what gentle punishment and benign rebuke that will please your Holiness, render peace to us, wretched children who have offended. I tell you, sweet Christ on earth, in the name of Christ in heaven, that, if you act thus, without storm or strife, they will all come in sorrow for the offence committed and will lay their heads in your lap.

[1] Letter 171 (217). Cf. Marchionne Stefani, Lib. IX. rubr. 762. From 1344, the Florentine priors began their two months of office from the calends, instead of the 15th day as in Dante's time.

Then you will rejoice, and we shall rejoice; for with love you will have put back the sheep that was lost into the fold of Holy Church. And then, my sweet babbo, you will fulfil your holy desire and the will of God in carrying out the holy enterprise; to which I invite you in His name, to do it soon and without negligence. And they will join with great affection, for they are disposed to give their lives for Christ. Ah, God, sweet Love! Uplift soon the banner of the most holy Cross, babbo, and you will see the wolves become lambs. Peace, peace, peace; so that the war may not postpone this sweet time. But if you wish to execute vengeance and justice, wreak it upon me, miserable and wretched woman, and give me every pain and torment that you like, even unto death. I believe that, through the odour of my own iniquities, many defects and many disasters and discords have come. Then upon me, your miserable daughter, inflict whatever punishment you will. Alas, father, I am dying of sorrow and cannot die. Come, come, and no more withstand the will of God which calls you; the starving sheep are awaiting your coming to hold and possess the place of your ancestor and champion, the Apostle Peter; for, as vicar of Christ, you are bound to repose in your own place. Come, then, come, and delay no more; take heart and fear nought that could befall, for God will be with you."[1]

The Florentines had already appealed to the Cardinals Piero Corsini and Jacopo Orsini to take their part in the papal court, and promised to send ambassadors to prove their innocence. Catherine likewise wrote to these two prelates, imploring them to use their influence in hastening the Pope's coming to Italy and the beginning of the Crusade; she urged the Florentine Cardinal to labour for the reformation of the Church by his own word and example, and the Roman to press the Pope to make peace with the revolted cities.[2] But the Florentines made no show of laying down their arms, while town after town in the Papal States, including Assisi at the beginning of March, rose against the ecclesiastical officials and joined the league. The two papal

[1] Letter 196 (4). [2] Letters 177 (29) and 223 (28).

ambassadors at length arrived from Bologna, and made three alternative offers on behalf of the Pope : a truce for five years with Bernabo and the Florentines and their allies, the rebellious cities, in the meanwhile, to pay their usual tribute to the apostolic treasury ; a perpetual peace with Bernabo and the Florentines, and a truce of five years with the others, who would, as in the former case, still pay their tribute ; a general peace with the whole league, the question of the rebellious towns to be referred to the arbitration of the King of Hungary, the Queen of Naples, or the Lord of Padua, at the choice of the Florentines themselves.[1] These terms were rejected by the Florentines. Their agents were busy in Bologna, where Cardinal de Noellet was suspected of being about to pawn the fortresses of the Commune to Hawkwood, as he had already done with Bagnacavallo, to pay the English. On the night of March 20, the Bolognese nobles, led by Taddeo Azzoguidi, rose against the legate, while the petty signori of the contado, with Florentine aid, entered the city with their armed retainers. Taken by surprise, the Cardinal surrendered the keys of the gates and castles, and his mercenaries made no resistance. The news caused wild exultation in Florence, for, says the Bolognese chronicler, "all that they had done to overthrow the state of the Church would have been of no avail, if Bologna had not rebelled." [2] A strong force of troops with the banner of liberty, under Conrad Wertinger, was at once despatched to Bologna, and received with enthusiasm. The government of the city was put into the hands of sixteen Anziani, four for each quarter, and the Cardinal escorted to Ferrara, where the Marquis held for the Church.

Bagnacavallo and Faenza were still in the hands of the *papa-*

[1] Cf. Gherardi, *op. cit.*, p. 43 *n.*, where it is shown that there is no foundation for the usual statement that the Pope offered to leave Perugia and Città di Castello at liberty, provided the Florentines proceeded no further and did not molest Bologna. The financial side of the whole question was of vital importance to the Holy See. From Bologna, alone, the Pope drew the annual sum of 200,000 florins. Cf. *Cronica di Bologna*, col. 498.

[2] *Cronica di Bologna*, coll. 499–501.

lini, the former under Hawkwood, the latter ruled by a French prelate under the title of Count of Romagna. Fearing for his position, this latter sent for Hawkwood and the English, who burst into Faenza, shouting *Viva la Chiesa*, sacked the town, and expelled all the inhabitants, save a number of women whom they kept for their own lusts. Two of Hawkwood's captains or *caporali* were fighting together for the possession of a beautiful young girl, a novice from one of the convents, who cried upon her divine Bridegroom and His Mother to deliver her, when Hawkwood came upon the scene. Unable to separate them, he stabbed the girl to death with his own dagger. "And so," writes Fra Filippo, "the Virgin Mary heard her and delivered her; virgin and martyr and bride of her Son, she bore her away to the realm of life eternal, as it is written in the Psalm: *lest the righteous put forth their hands unto iniquity*."[1] Shortly after, Hawkwood sold both Bagnacavallo and Faenza to the Marquis of Ferrara, to obtain the arrears of pay that were owed him by the Church.

In spite of the expulsion of the legate from Bologna, the position of the Florentines was highly critical. If the Pope were to promulgate his sentence and could induce the nations to enforce it, the whole mercantile traffic of the Republic would be destroyed. Rumours had already reached them of papal galleys being equipped in haste at Marseilles to prey upon their commerce, of a great army of formidable Breton mercenaries being taken into the pay of the Church. It was, above all, imperative to gain time. "Because of the process," writes Fra Raimondo, "they were compelled to treat for peace with the Sovereign Pontiff, through the means of persons who they knew were acceptable to him. They were informed that the holy virgin, by reason of the fame of her sanctity, was most pleasing in the Pope's sight. Therefore they ordained that I should first go to the said

[1] *Assempro* 58: "Come una vergine fu guardata da la Vergine Maria per martirio." The sack of Faenza was on March 28, 1376. Cf. *Cronaca Riminese* (*Rer. It. Script.*, xv.), col. 914; *Cronica di Bologna*, coll. 501, 502. There was little actual bloodshed.

Sovereign Pontiff, in the name of Catherine, in order to mitigate his indignation." The friar was apparently to dispose the Pope in favour of the two Florentine ambassadors, who were already on their way. He started about the fourth week in March, accompanied by Giovanni Tantucci, Felice da Massa, and others of Catherine's household, with the letter of credentials from Catherine to the Pope which we still possess, beseeching the wavering Pontiff to make himself, with the aid of divine grace, the instrument for the pacification of the entire world. She bids him, in the name of Christ crucified, extirpate the evil pastors and rulers, "full of impurity and cupidity, puffed up with pride," the foul plants who are poisoning the garden of the Church; and plant in their stead "sweet smelling flowers, pastors and governors who will be true servants of Jesus Christ, who will attend to nought else save the honour of God and the salvation of souls, and who will be fathers of the poor." Hitherto, the luxurious lives of the prelates have been shamed by comparison with the virtues of many of the laity: "But it seems that the supreme and eternal Goodness is having done by force what has not been done for love; it seems that He is allowing states and pleasures to be taken from His Spouse, as though to show that He wished Holy Church to return into her primitive state of poverty, humility, meekness, as she was in that holy time, when they attended to nought else save the honour of God and the salvation of souls, caring for spiritual things and not temporal. For, since she has aimed more at temporal than at spiritual things, her affairs have gone from bad to worse." But let the Pope take heart and fear nothing; if only he will come to Italy and raise the standard of the Cross, all will be well. But he must come like a meek lamb, "using the arms of the power of love alone, aiming only to have the care of spiritual things":—

"Answer the summons of God, who is calling you to come to hold and possess the place of the glorious pastor St. Peter, whose vicar you are. Lift up the banner of the holy Cross. Come, and you will reform the Church with good pastors. You will give her back the colour of most burning charity which she has lost; for so much blood has been sucked from her by iniquitous devourers, that she has become all pallid. But take heart and come, father, and do not make the servants of God wait, who are afflicted with desire. And I, miserable, wretched woman, can wait no more; living, I seem to die in pain at seeing God so outraged. Do not postpone the peace because of what has happened at Bologna, but come; for I tell you that the fierce wolves will lay their heads in your lap like meek lambs, and crave you to pardon them, father. I say no more. I beseech you, father, to hear and listen to what Fra Raimondo will tell you, and the other sons who are with him, who are coming in the name of Christ crucified and in my name; for they are true servants of Christ and children of Holy Church." [1]

And, a little later, she wrote to Raimondo and his companions: "I am dying and cannot die, I am bursting and cannot burst, with the desire that I have for the renovation of Holy Church, for the honour of God, and the salvation of every creature, and of seeing you and the others robed with purity, burned and consumed in His most ardent charity. Tell Christ on earth not to make me wait any longer. And when I see him, I shall sing with that sweet old man Simeon: *Lord, now lettest Thou Thy servant depart in peace, according to Thy word.*" [2]

All immediate prospects of a reconciliation between Italy and the Holy See seemed dashed to the ground by the revolt of Bologna and the sack of Faenza. On the last day of March, Jacopo di Ceva, the fiscal advocate of the Curia who had formulated the process, demanded in full consistory that sentence should be pronounced against the Florentines. Their two ambassadors, Donato Barbadori and Alessandro dell' Antella, duly

[1] Letter 206 (5), amended by the Harleian MS. Raimondo's own words, *Legenda*, III. vi. 26 (§ 420), might be taken as meaning that he was sent to the Pope *after* the promulgation of the sentence against the Florentines; that is, in April; but the internal evidence of this and Letter 219 (87) seems to fix the date of his starting between March 21, the day after the revolt of Bologna, and April 1, when Catherine had the vision of the cross and olive-branch.

[2] Letter 211 (88).

appeared to represent the Commune and the citizens implicated, who (they said) could not appear in person, as they were all in prison at Florence. They protested the innocence of the Republic, painted a lurid picture of the evil deeds of the papal legates, and implored an extension of the time that they might fully answer all accusations. In reply, Gregory solemnly put Florence under the interdict, revoked all privileges granted by his predecessors, declared the goods of each Florentine confiscated, their possessions and persons to be the free prey of any who could make themselves masters of them ; he forbade, under the same penalties, any private person, community or prince to have any dealings with them or favour them in any way, all previous obligations being cancelled, and threatened to invoke the arms of all the powers of Christendom upon the entire nation. The Eight, together with fifty-one other citizens named (among whom was Niccolò Soderini), were excommunicated, and, together with their sons and grandsons, formally deprived of all civic rights and legal protection, unless they appeared at Avignon by May 30. Against this sentence, Donato Barbadori uttered an impassioned and solemn protest, in the name of the Republic; turning to the great Crucifix that hung opposite the papal throne, he appealed from the Sovereign Pontiff to Christ Himself: "Look upon me, O God of my salvation, and be Thou my helper ; do not Thou forsake me, for my father and my mother have forsaken me." [1]

But, while these things were being done at Avignon, Catherine at Siena had a vision, in which it seemed to her that the Divine Bridegroom bade her, with the Cross on her shoulders and the olive-branch in her hand, intervene between the Church and her opponents :—

"On the night of the first of April," she writes to Raimondo and his companions, "God more specially revealed His secrets,

[1] Cf. Gherardi, *op. cit.*, pp. 44–46, documents 198, 199 ; St. Antoninus, *Chronicorum*, III. pp. 379–382. On April 5, Charles IV put Florence under the ban of the Empire ; but his previous exploits at Siena had taught the Florentines what his imperial threats were worth.

manifesting His wondrous mysteries in such wise that my soul seemed not still to be in the body, and received such fulness of delight that no tongue can tell it; for He explained and in part set forth the mystery of the persecution which Holy Church is now enduring, and of the renovation and exaltation which she is to have in the time to come, and said that the present time is permitted in order to restore her state to her.[1] And the first sweet Truth quoted two words that are in the Holy Gospel: *It must needs be that offences come into the world; but woe to that man by whom the offence cometh;* as though to say: 'I suffer this time of persecution in order to extirpate the thorns of My Spouse, for she is all full of brambles; but I do not suffer the evil cogitations of men. Knowest thou what I am doing? I am doing as I did when I was in the world, when I made the scourge of small cords, and cast out them that sold and bought in the Temple, not suffering that My Father's house should be made a den of thieves. So I tell thee I am doing now; for I have made a scourge of creatures, and by that scourge I am casting out the merchants —impure, greedy, avaricious, and puffed-up with pride—who sell and buy the gifts of the Holy Spirit.' Thus I understood that He was casting them out by the scourge of human persecution; that is, by means of tribulation and persecution, He would free them from their disordered and impure living. And, while the fire of holy desire increased within me, as I gazed, I saw the Christian people and the unbelievers enter into the side of Christ crucified; and I, by desire and the affection of love, passed through the midst of them, entering with them into Christ sweet Jesus, accompanied by my father St. Dominic, and my special John with all my children.[2] Then He laid the Cross upon my neck and put the olive into my hand, even as though I wished it, and bade me offer them to one people and to the other; and He said to me: 'Say unto them:

[1] *i.e.* her primitive state of purity, not her temporal possessions.

[2] *Giovanni singolare con tutti quanti i figliuoli miei.* My translation is intended to suggest that "Giovanni singolare" is Fra Raimondo himself, who tells us that Catherine called him "John." Cf. *Legenda*, Prologue I. (§ 6).

I bring you tidings of great joy.' Then my soul was filled; she was drowned with the truly blessed in the Divine Essence by union and affection of love, and so great was the delight that my soul possessed that she no longer beheld the past sorrow of seeing the offence against God, but said: 'O happy and fortunate fault.'"[1]

In the light of this vision, a few days before Easter, which this year fell upon April 13, Catherine offered her services to the Republic of Florence as mediator between it and the Pope: "remembering the word that our Saviour said to His disciples: *With desire I have desired to eat this passover with you before I suffer*." The passover which she would fain eat with the Florentines is that of peace and union with the Church, within whose body alone can they receive the paschal mysteries, the fruit of the blood of Christ and the heritage of eternal life.

"You know well," she wrote, "that Christ left us His vicar for the cure of our souls; for in nought else can we have salvation, save in the mystical body of Holy Church, whose head is Christ, and we are the limbs. And whoso is disobedient to Christ on earth, who holds the place of Christ in heaven, does not partake the fruit of the blood of the Son of God; for God has decreed that this blood and all the sacraments of Holy Church, which receive life from this blood, should be communicated and given to us through his hands. We cannot go by another way, nor enter by another gate; for the first Truth said: *I am the way, the truth, and the life*." He who rebels against the Church is a rotten member, and what is done to His vicar on earth, be it reverence or insult, is done to Christ in heaven. "Then, if God is at war with you, because of the injury you have done to our father and His vicar, I tell you that you are weakened; for you have lost His aid. Let us grant that there are many who do not believe that they offend God in this, but think that they are offering Him a

[1] Letter 219 (87), amended by the Harleian MS., from which we learn that Felice da Massa was one of those who accompanied Raimondo and Giovanni Tantucci to Avignon.

sacrifice in persecuting the Church and her pastors, and who say in self-defence: 'They are wicked, and do everything evil.' But I tell you that God wills, and has commanded so, that, even if the pastors and Christ on earth were incarnate demons (whereas the latter is a good and benign father), we must be subject and obedient to him, not for their sake for what they are, but to be obedient to God because he is Christ's vicar." If only they will be reconciled with him, all Tuscany will have spiritual peace and repose, and the war will be turned against the infidels; otherwise, "you and all Tuscany will have the worst time that ever our ancestors had. Think not that God is sleeping over the injuries that have been done to His Spouse." Let them, then, eat this passover of peace and union in the body of the Church, where the food of the soul is found and the wedding-garment for the nuptials of eternal life. "Pardon my presumption, and impute it to the love that I have for your salvation, both of soul and of body, and the grief that I have at the damage you are receiving, spiritually and temporally. And think that I had sooner say it you by word of mouth than by letter. If through me anything can be done for the honour of God, to unite you with Holy Church, I am ready to give my life, if it should be needed." [1]

Catherine had just received news from Raimondo at Avignon which filled her with peace and exultation. He had, like many others, probably been impressed by the mildness of the Pontiff's reception, and had over-estimated his pacific disposition. "Rejoice, rejoice, and exult," she writes in her paschal letter to the friar and his companions, "for the time is at hand when the spring will bring us sweet-smelling flowers. And do not wonder if you see the contrary coming, but be then more certain than ever. I would fain never rest until I see a knife pass through my throat for the honour of God, so that my blood may remain sprinkled in the mystical body of Holy Church." And, in a postscript, she suggests, subject to Raimondo's approval, that Neri di Landoccio

[1] Letter 207 (198). Capecelatro and Augusta Drane refer this letter to Catherine's second embassy to Florence, but Tommaseo seems to me undoubtedly right in assigning it to this earlier occasion.

should be sent to the papal court, "to work for the peace of those decayed members who have rebelled against Holy Church."[1]

Neri could now be spared more readily from Catherine's side, as her spiritual family had just received a new member of the same kind, who soon became her chosen friend and best-loved disciple: Stefano di Corrado Maconi. Born in 1347, Stefano was of the same age as Catherine herself; his parents, Messer Corrado and Madonna Giovanna Bandinelli Maconi, belonged to conspicuous houses among the lesser nobility of Siena, a former member of the family having even found a place in the *Inferno* of the great Florentine. Young and gallant, educated to a degree presumably rare among the nobles of that day, Stefano was likewise distinguished for his sweetness and purity of character, although sharing to the full in the social life of his order and city. Through a dispute on a point of honour at some social gathering, the Maconi had become involved in a feud with the potent families of the Tolomei and Rinaldini, and Stefano had felt himself compelled in honour to lead the retainers of his own family. The Maconi would willingly have made peace, but, in spite of the intervention of many influential citizens, the Tolomei and Rinaldini would hear of no reconciliation. At length Stefano's pious mother, Giovanna Maconi, persuaded him to have recourse to Catherine, and a certain noble friend of theirs, Pietro Bellanti, who had himself been reconciled to a deadly foe by her means, offered to bring him to her. "I visited her, therefore, and she received me, not like a bashful maiden as I expected, but with most loving charity, as though welcoming a brother on his return from distant regions. At this I was amazed, and listened to her efficacious and holy words by which she compelled, rather than induced me, to go to confession and to live virtuously. I said: 'The finger of God is here.' And when she had heard the cause of my visit, she answered confidently: 'Go, dearest son, and trust in the Lord, for I will gladly labour until you have an excellent peace; and do you suffer me to take the

[1] Letter 226 (89).

whole weight of this business upon my head.'" Stefano merely tells us that, by her means, they obtained peace in a miraculous fashion, even against the will of their adversaries ; but we owe to the pen of his Carthusian biographer the dramatic story of how, when Catherine had fixed the day for all the parties to meet at the church of San Cristoforo in the Piazza Tolomei, and Corrado and Stefano with their kinsmen came as arranged, the Tolomei and the Rinaldini, with a view of adding a fresh insult and rendering reconciliation impossible, did not appear. "They will not hear me," said Catherine, "but, when God speaks, they will have to listen." As she prayed and was rapt in ecstasy before the altar, a mysterious force drew the Tolomei and the Rinaldini, each independently of the other, to the church ; a divine light irradiated the emaciated kneeling figure in the black and white habit ; and the factious nobles, seeing a sign from God, committed all the controversy into her hands, listened meekly to her words, and exchanged forgiveness and the kiss of friendship with those who, an hour before, had been their deadliest foes.[1]

While Catherine was engaged upon this reconciliation, Stefano frequently visited her, and sometimes, to his ineffable delight, she asked him to write letters for her at her dictation. Soon he became heart and soul hers, enkindled by the divine love that ever burned in her ; he exulted when he was made a mark for the jests of the city in consequence, and idlers shouted *Caterinato* after him as he passed through the streets. In return, Catherine loved him with so special an affection that, as he tells us, many of her other followers took it ill, and bore him a certain envy—among whom, however, Neri was not included, for, from the outset, he and Stefano had contracted an ardent friendship which was only to end with the former's death. Stefano now became, for a time, the chief of Catherine's secretaries. "After a short while," he

[1] *Epistola Domni Stephani*, §§ 2, 3 ; Bartholomaeus Senensis, *De Vita et Moribus beati Stephani Maconi*, Lib. I. cap. 4–6. Bartholomaeus Senensis assigns the beginning of the feud to the year of pestilence, 1374, and Augusta Drane, evidently rightly, supposes the reconciliation to have occurred early in 1376.

writes, "that most holy virgin said to me in secret: 'Know, most beloved son, that the greatest desire thou hast will soon be fulfilled.' At this I was astonished; for I could think of nothing that I longed for in the world, while I was prepared to reject all that it could offer. Therefore I said: 'O dearest mother, what is the greatest desire that I have?' 'Look,' she said, 'into thy heart.' And I answered her: 'Certainly, most beloved mother, I can find no greater desire in myself than to keep always near you.' And she straightway replied: 'And this will be.' But I could not comprehend the way in which this could suitably happen, considering our different conditions and position; but He, to whom nothing is impossible, ordained in a wondrous way that she should go to Avignon to Gregory XI; and so, albeit unworthy, I was accepted as one of this holy company, thinking it a little thing to leave parents, brothers, sisters, and kindred, and deeming myself blessed in the enjoyment of the presence and familiar friendship of the virgin Catherine."[1]

It was probably from Florence that Neri di Landoccio started for Avignon. "To thee, most beloved and dearest son in Christ sweet Jesus," Catherine wrote to him, while he was waiting at Pisa for the ship that was to take him to Marseilles, "I write in His precious blood, with the desire of seeing thee united and transformed in the fire of most burning charity, so that thou mayest be a vessel of love to carry the name and the word of God, with His great mysteries, into the presence of our sweet Christ on earth, and mayest bear fruit by inflaming his desire." He was the bearer of a letter imploring the Pope to imitate Christ, the Good Shepherd, in his dealings with the rebels, to make peace with them, and devote his powers to the reformation of the Church. "I beseech you, reverend father, to give and

[1] *Epist. cit.*, §§ 4, 5, 9. Bartholomaeus Senensis, *op. cit.*, Lib. V. cap. 1, tells a curious story of how Stefano, after joining Catherine's family, was led into attending a secret meeting against the government in the vaults under the Spedale, in which several of the aristocratic members of the confraternity of Our Lady's *disciplinati* were involved, and of the penance which he inflicted upon himself at her bidding for the seditious words that he had uttered.

grant what Neri, the bearer of this letter, will ask you, if it is possible to you and according to your will. I beseech you to give him audience, and believe what he will tell you. And because sometimes it is impossible to write what one would wish, I add, if you want to send to tell me something secret, tell him by word of mouth with confidence (for you can) whatever can be accomplished by me. If it were necessary to give my life, I would gladly give it for the honour of God and for the salvation of souls."[1]

Catherine's appeal had reached the Florentines in an auspicious moment. Although Niccolò Soderini was no longer in the government, the Signoria that held office for March and April contained at least one moderate man: Buonaccorso di Lapo Giovanni. The need was pressing; papal envoys from Avignon had been sent in all directions, ordering every sovereign and commonwealth to break off relations with the Florentines and expel them from their dominions, and many States had obeyed; papal galleys were intercepting Florentine ships, and making booty of their merchandise; the Breton mercenaries were quickly gathering together. Catherine's offer of mediation was accepted, and, at the beginning of May, accompanied by Stefano Maconi, Fra Bartolommeo di Domenico, and her usual company of men and women, she came to Florence. The new Signoria was less pacifically inclined than its predecessor, and included Giovanni Dini, one of the Eight. Nevertheless, the Priors came out of the gate of the city to meet her, and besought her to go on their behalf to Avignon, to secure at least a favourable hearing for the ambassadors they were about to send.

During the few weeks that Catherine now stayed in Florence, while the diplomatic arrangements were being made, she put herself in touch with every class in the State, and made spiritual disciples in every direction. She was already acquainted with Messer Angelo Ricasoli, the luke-warm, time-serving bishop, and with Niccolò Soderini, the upright and devout republican; possibly also with Carlo Strozzi, a wealthy burgher of the Parte

[1] Letters 228 (278) and 218 (3).

Guelfa, whose wife Laudamia was one of her correspondents. Buonaccorso di Lapo Giovanni seems to have been her chief link with the popular side. The family of the Canigiani (kinsmen of Petrarca's mother, Eletta Canigiani) became especially devoted to her. The head of the family, Piero di Donato Canigiani, and his son, Messer Ristoro (a learned lawyer), were men of great character and personality, wealthy and influential burghers, leading spirits in the counsels of the Parte Guelfa. A younger brother of Ristoro, Barduccio di Piero Canigiani, although little more than a boy, had devoted himself to a religious life and was one of the "adopted sons" of Don Giovanni dalle Celle. Among the lower orders, a tailor, Francesco di Pippino, and his wife, Monna Agnese, were Catherine's ardent disciples. Francesco does not seem to have been by birth a Florentine, but a native of San Miniato al Tedesco, who had settled in the capital and probably become a Florentine citizen. In spite of his humble position, he was a man of some importance among all in Florence who looked for righteousness; and in later years, in his own unobtrusive way, he made his little house near the Piazza del Grano, in the quarter of Santa Croce, a centre of religious life in the city. With them were closely bound in ties of friendship a high-born couple, Bartolo Usimbardi and his wife, Monna Orsa, who likewise took Catherine as their supreme guide in the spiritual life.

Although vigorously continuing the campaign against the papal officials in Italy, the Florentines were prepared to yield to the Pope's authority in spiritual matters, and obeyed the interdict. "To-day," writes a contemporary, "on the eleventh day of May, 1376, they left off singing the Mass in the city and contado of Florence, and no longer celebrated the Body of Christ to us, citizens and contadini. But we see Him with our hearts, and God knoweth that we are not Saracens nor pagans, but are and shall remain true Christians, the elect of God."[1] Another tells us how a passion of devotion swept over the citizens, who found themselves thus for secular reasons deprived

[1] *Diario d' Anonimo Fiorentino*, p. 308.

of the supreme consolation of their religion : *Lo pan che il pio padre a nessun serra.* Men and women thronged the churches to sing psalms and hymns ; incessant processions were made through the streets, bearing relics of the saints ; as many as five thousand flagellants passed along, scourging their bare shoulders, while twenty thousand persons followed ; the commandments of the Church were kept as they had never been before, and for every one that practised his religion when the Mass was said, there were now a hundred. A number of noble and wealthy young men formed a confraternity which met at Fiesole, devoting themselves to austerity and works of charity, especially labouring to convert fallen women, whom they clothed and provided with means to live an honest life ; others gave up everything, and went about begging alms for the poor : "And this matter was so spread abroad that it seemed verily that they wished to conquer the Pope by humility, and to be obedient to the Church."[1] The government looked with great suspicion upon this movement, but took no active steps to check it. There was simultaneously a recrudescence of activity among the Fraticelli, those *frati della povera vita*, who held that the condemnation of poverty by John XXII had been "the condemnation of the life of Christ," and that neither he nor his successors were lawful popes. Poverty being the law of Christ, the Court of Avignon was the devil's synagogue. The sacraments were invalid if administered by an unworthy priest.[2] Numbers of Florentines, men and women, began to affect their doctrines, especially now that they seemed justified by the attitude of the papal court towards the Italians.

The fact was that, at this stage in the conflict, all Florence was united against the Pope ; adherents of the Parte Guelfa were agreed with those of the Otto della Guerra that the Republic must defend her rights and liberties. Men like Don Giovanni dalle Celle had no doubt as to where the duties of every citizen lay. "I have heard news of thee

[1] Marchionne Stefani, Lib. IX. rubr. 757. Cf. Dante, *Par.* xviii. 127–129.

[2] Cf. Tocco, *I Fraticelli*, pp. 341-353.

for this holy Easter," he wrote to Guido dal Palagio, shortly before Catherine's arrival in Florence, "and I have heard that thou art compelled to take certain offices of the Commune, for which matter I believe that questions often arise in thy heart, because of the war which you have with the Holy Father. But thou hast no need to doubt, as long as thou directest thy intentions first to the honour of God, and then to the good state of thy city; it is lawful for thee to aid her and defend her and counsel her, so that she may never fall into the hands of her enemies. If thou payest the loan, let not thy intention be to act against the Pope, but to defend thy country, and with this holy intention thou canst pass through all the offices of the Commune without mortal sin. Excommunications are made for those who sin mortally, and therefore hold for certain that no innocent man can be excommunicated; and if, nevertheless, thou wert excommunicated, it would not be valid in the sight of God, who only confirms the sentence of pastors who bind and loose justly, with lawful cause. Only, thou must beware of giving advice or voting that the Pope, or any other cleric or religious, should be taken or slain. I should have said much to thee on this matter, did I not fear lest my letter should come into the hands of those who care little for the good state of that city."[1] But he was equally emphatic by word and letter against the Fraticelli, and prepared to defend the whole hierarchy of the Church against them. "What matters it to thee," he wrote to a Florentine artisan who had joined them, "whether Christ was poor or rich, as long as thou believest that He is thy Saviour, thy Redeemer, thy Food, the price of thy Redemption, and thy Reward? I certainly believe that Christ was poor, and I would go through the fire for this, saving always all that our holy mother, the Catholic and Apostolic Church, holds."[2] Like Birgitta before him, the monk had profoundly mistrusted the papal designs for a Crusade. "If thou hast Christ in the Sacrament of the Altar," he wrote to a young nun named

[1] Letter in Tocco, *I Fraticelli*, p. 348.

[2] Wesselofsky, *Il Paradiso degli Alberti*, I. doc. 14.

Domitilla, who had taken Catherine's exhortations as meaning that she, too, was to go to the Holy Sepulchre, "even as He came forth from the womb of the Virgin Mary and as He hung upon the Cross, why wouldst thou abandon Him to go to see a stone?" This led to a correspondence with William Flete, who supposed that he had attacked Catherine herself, with the result that Don Giovanni, a little later, formally joined her spiritual fellowship. "It will be glorious for me," he wrote, "to be called a heretic with her, that, even as Christ who was reputed a heretic by the Pharisees because He made Himself the Son of God, I may bear the cross of His passion. O most sweet heresy of celestial Catherine, who makest just men out of sinners, and, the friend of publicans and sinners, dost make the Angels smile and heaven rejoice!"[1]

In the meanwhile, the Florentines continued to foment the rebellion in the Papal States, and even put a price upon the head of Gomez Albornoz, who was making a valiant defence of the citadel of Ascoli. Nor was the papal court resting on its arms. On May 27, the company of Bretons, six thousand foot and four thousand horse, under the Cardinal Robert of Geneva, left Avignon, with orders to march straight upon Florence. They boasted that, if the sun entered Florence, they would, and that they would make the Pope's brother, the Vicomte de Turenne, lord of the city.

It must always remain a question whether the sending of Catherine to Avignon was the result of a temporary victory of Niccolò Soderini and the peace party in the counsels of the Republic, or a mere device on the part of the others to gain time. The Florentine archives apparently hold no record of the matter, and we can only gather what happened from Catherine's own

[1] *Lettere del B. Giovanni dalle Celle*, 19, with which compare Catherine's letter to Monna Pavola, 144 (371). Don Giovanni's letters to William Flete (together with a third, defending Catherine against the Augustinian, Giovanni da Salerno) are given by Gigli at the end of the *Opere*, vol. ii. pp. 985–997. They are included, with three others and a letter from William to Raimondo, in the Palatine MS. 60.

letter to Buonaccorso di Lapo Giovanni. According to this, the Signoria and the Eight had assured her that they were repentant for having gone against the Church, and ready to throw themselves on the Pope's mercy. "See, my lords," she said, "if you really intend to use all humility in deed as well as word, and that I should offer you up before your father like sons that were dead, I will labour in this to the utmost of your wish. In no other wise would I go." They declared emphatically that this was their intention, and that they would instruct the ambassadors, whom they were going to send after her, to confer with her about everything. "We do not believe," said one of those present, apparently Buonaccorso himself, "that this peace can ever be brought about, save by the hands of the servants of God."[1] Upon this understanding, in the latter part of May, Catherine accepted the mission. "It seems to me," she wrote to the Pope, "that the Divine Goodness is making the great wolves become lambs. I am now coming to you at once, to lay them humbled in your lap. I am certain that you will receive them like a father, notwithstanding the way they have injured and persecuted you; learning from the sweet first Truth who says that the Good Shepherd, when He has found the sheep that was lost, takes it upon His shoulders and brings it back to the fold. So will you do, father; now that your lost sheep is found again, you will take it on the shoulder of love, and put it into the sheepfold of Holy Church. Then, at once, our sweet Saviour wills and commands you to raise the banner of the most holy Cross against the infidels, and that the whole war should be turned against them. Keep back the soldiers whom you have hired to come hither, and do not suffer them to come; for they would ruin everything, rather than put it straight. My sweet father, you ask me about your coming; and I answer and tell you, in the name of Christ crucified, that you must come as soon as you can. If you can do so, come before September; and, if you cannot come before, do not delay longer than until September

[1] Letter 234 (215). Cf. below, p. 191.

And do not consider any opposition that you may meet; but come, like a virile man and without any fear. But take heed, as you value your life, not to come with armed men, but with the Cross in your hand, like a meek lamb. If you do so, you will fulfil the will of God; but, if you came in another wise, you would not fulfil, but transgress it. Rejoice, father, and exult; come, come."[1]

[1] Letter 229 (6).

CHAPTER IX

FROM THE BABYLON OF THE WEST

"Novi expertus ut nulla ibi pietas, nulla caritas, nulla fides, nulla Dei reverentia, nullus timor, nihil sancti, nihil iusti, nihil aequi, nihil pensi, nihil denique vel humani. Amor, pudor, decor, candor inde exulant."—Petrarca, *Epist. sine titulo*, XVI.

CATHERINE started from Florence towards the end of May. She was accompanied by Fra Bartolommeo di Domenico, Stefano Maconi, Gherardo Buonconti with his brothers, Tommaso and Francesco, and a number of other disciples; Alessa, Cecca, and Lisa were also of the party. No details have been preserved of the journey, and it is even uncertain what course they took. A local tradition speaks of Catherine passing through Bologna, while a passage in a letter from Giovanni dalle Celle to Fra Giovanni da Salerno seems to show her on her way along the Riviera. In any case, we know from one of her own letters that she reached Avignon on June 18, 1376.

Into this Babylon of the West, the mystical bride of Christ and her companions came as messengers from another world. Avignon had altered but little since Petrarca had invoked the fire from heaven to fall upon it. "I know by experience," he wrote, "that there is no piety there, no charity, no faith, no reverence for God nor any fear of Him, nothing holy, nothing just, nothing worthy of man. Love, purity, decency, candour are banished from it. All things are full of lies and hypocrisy. The voices of angels conceal the designs of demons." [1] The only change for the better since Petrarca wrote these words was that, instead of a strong pontiff, enslaved to vice and luxury, there now sat on the papal throne a weak Pope, who, in his sincere but ineffectual way, looked for righteousness.

Two days after her arrival, the Pope admitted Catherine to what appears to have been a private audience, only Fra Raimondo

[1] *Epist. sine titulo*, XVI.

being present. Gregory knew no Italian and Catherine no Latin, the friar acting as their interpreter. In spite of the correspondence that had passed between them, the Pope had been prejudiced against her; but he was unable, now that he saw her face to face, to withstand the magic of her personality. "In order that thou mayest see clearly," he said, "that I desire peace, I put the matter entirely into thy hands; only be careful for the honour of the Church." He assigned to her what Stefano Maconi calls "a fine house with a beautifully decorated chapel," where, for the three months that she stayed in Avignon, he lodged and supported her whole household at his own expense.[1]

But the Florentine ambassadors did not appear, and rumours reached the court—rumours greedily accepted and spread abroad by the prelates of the Curia—that new and oppressive taxes were being imposed upon the clergy at Florence. The three ambassadors—Pazzino Strozzi, Alessandro dell' Antella, and Michele Castellani—had been nominated in May, and their coming formally notified to the Pope. Their original commission had reference only to getting the ecclesiastical censures removed, but this had been extended, at the advice of Bernabo Visconti, to include the whole question of peace.[2] Nevertheless, the counsels of the Signoria were divided, and at least some of the Eight were unwilling to come to terms with the Church until the whole of her temporal power was completely destroyed. The matter lingered on in this way through all June. Catherine, who had understood that the ambassadors were to follow her immediately, with full powers to confer with her and arrange terms with the Pope through her, and that, in the meanwhile, all hostilities on the part of the Florentines would be suspended, was amazed and indignant. "Believe me, Catherine," said the Pope, "they have deceived and will deceive thee; they will not send the ambassadors, or, if they do, it will be such a mission that it will amount to nothing." Already a fresh process was preparing

[1] *Legenda*, III. vi. 26 (§ 420); *Processus*, col. 1337; *Epistola Domni Stephani*, § 11.

[2] Gherardi, *op. cit.*, docs. 221, 228.

against them, threatening them with the most fearful spiritual and temporal penalties, including the papal anathema and the proclamation of a crusade against them throughout the entire world. On their part, the Florentines were preparing vigorously to push on the campaign, alike against Albornoz in the Marches and against the Cardinal of Geneva, who was daily expected in the Bolognese.

To the Eight, on June 28, Catherine wrote an emphatic letter, beseeching them not to turn back, but to approach the Pope with true humility of heart, "imploring life like the son that was dead." She complains strongly of the new tax upon the clergy, if it is true that they have imposed it, as calculated to alienate those of the cardinals who desire peace and still further to inflame the anger of the Pope against them. "I tell you, dearest fathers, and pray you not to impede the grace of the Holy Spirit, which, albeit you do not merit it, our sweet Christ on earth is disposed in his clemency to give you. And you would be putting me to shame and reproach. For what save shame and confusion could result, if I tell him one thing and you do quite another? I beseech you not to let it happen again. Nay, strive in word and deed to show that you desire peace and not war. I have spoken to the Holy Father. He listened to me graciously, through God's goodness and his own, and showed himself lovingly affected towards peace, acting like a good father in not so much considering the offence that his son has committed against him as whether he has become humble, so that he may be able to pardon him completely. My tongue could not tell how singularly glad he was. After I had talked with him for a good space of time, he said at the end of our conversation that, if what I had laid before him concerning you were so, he was ready to receive you as his children, and to do in this matter what I should think right. It did not seem to the Holy Father that he should give any more definite answer, until your ambassadors arrive. I am amazed that they have not yet come. As soon as they arrive, I shall be with them, and shall then go to the Holy Father; and I will write to you according to how I find the matter proceeding.

But you, with your levies and changes, are spoiling what I am sowing. Do no more so, for the love of Christ crucified and for your own advantage." [1]

The three ambassadors had probably already started when this letter reached Florence. A new Signoria entered office on the first day of July, and had decided to despatch the three citizens named as syndics, "to make truce or peace with the Pope, or with his commissary, upon what conditions they shall think fit." Their decision was confirmed in the Council of the Captain and People on July 4, and in the Council of the Podestà and Commune on July 5; and, on July 7, the Signoria wrote to Cardinals Orsini and Corsini, calling God to witness that they had only acted to defend their own liberty, asking them to use their influence with the Pope on behalf of their ambassadors, to whom they would shortly send the mandate for peace.[2] As soon as they arrived at Avignon, Catherine sent to bid the three come to her, and, in the presence of Fra Raimondo, reminded them of what the preceding Signoria had promised her; she told them that the Pope had put the peace into her hands, and that they could have good terms if they desired it. The ambassadors brusquely answered that they had no commission to confer with her, nor to make the acts of submission she suggested.[3] No shadow of resentment or personal mortification seems to have entered Catherine's mind at finding herself thus discarded; although bitterly disappointed at what she probably regarded as the perfidy of the Republic, she continued to beseech the Pope to deal with them mildly, acting not as a judge but as a father.

Nevertheless, the Florentines were probably in earnest. The Mantuan representative at the papal court, Cristoforo da Piacenza, writing to his master, Lodovico Gonzaga, on July 17, tells him of the arrival of the ambassadors, and that they are very desirous of peace. They have not been able to see the Pope, but have visited the cardinals, and are expecting a formal

[1] Letter 230 (197); in the Harleian MS.

[2] Gherardi, *op. cit.*, docs. 273, 274; *Diario d'Anonimo Fiorentino*, p. 309.

[3] *Legenda*, III. vi. 27 (§ 421).

audience. Three ambassadors from Pisa (including Benedetto Gambacorti, one of Piero's sons), and two from Lucca, had previously come to beseech the Pope to make peace with the Florentines. The Pisans had effected nothing; but to the ambassadors of Lucca, who had protested that the Lucchese had never forgotten how the Church had delivered them from the hands of Pharaoh, the Pope returned a most gracious answer. He said he loved their city, and was convinced that they had only entered the league under compulsion; but he could see no possibility of peace between the Church and the Florentines, as they had not power to restore the cities and towns that they had induced to rebel against her, nor to indemnify her for all she had lost and suffered; the vicar of Christ was bound to have peace with the contrite of heart alone, and not to encourage sinners in their sins.[1] Nevertheless, yielding probably to the united appeals of Catherine and the ambassadors of Lucca, Gregory ultimately delegated two cardinals, Pierre d'Estaing and Gilles Aycelin de Montaigu, to treat with the Florentine ambassadors.

But Catherine felt that her mission was a higher one than that she had received from Florence. Disavowed by the Eight, she was still in Avignon as the ambassador of Christ, to bid the Pope return to Rome and reform the Church. She continued at the same time to urge on what she regarded as the holy and pacific work of the Crusade. When his first prejudices were overcome, Gregory heard her gladly—the faithful Raimondo always acting as interpreter. In one of their first interviews, Catherine spoke her mind concerning the shameful vices of the Roman Curia, and the Pope, after a feeble attempt to rebuke her, listened in silence, and made no comment at the end, though Raimondo was amazed at the boldness and authority with which she had spoken. On another occasion, Gregory questioned her about his return to Rome. "It is not meet," she answered, "that a wretched little woman should give advice to the

[1] Despatch dated Avignon, July 17. Osio, I. doc. 124. It is curious that the writer should make no mention of Catherine.

Sovereign Pontiff." And the Pope: "I do not ask you for advice, but to tell me the will of God in this matter." And, while she still made excuses, he charged her on her obedience, to say if she knew anything of the will of God in this affair. "Then she, humbly bowing down her head, said: 'Who knoweth this better than your Holiness, who vowed to God that you would do this thing?' When he heard this, he was overwhelmed with amazement, for, as he said, no living man save himself knew that he had made this vow." [1]

There were the usual petty persecutions and trials, for all the corrupt members of the papal court and their dependants were naturally against her. Soon after her arrival, three prelates of the Curia came to Catherine, and made a prolonged attempt to ensnare her in her speech, hoping apparently to discredit her growing influence with the Pope by convicting her of having come under false pretences as ambassador for Florence, or of heresy in the doctrines she professed. Foiled in their object, they candidly reported to the Pope that they had never found a soul so humble and so illumined; but the attempt, especially with a view to an accusation of heresy, had been a serious one. "I can tell you," said the Pope's physician, Francesco Casini, to Stefano Maconi, "that, if they had not found this virgin Catherine had a solid foundation, she would never have made a more unfortunate voyage." [2] This Francesco di Bartolommeo Casini, a Sienese by birth, who had been one of Petrarca's friends and correspondents, now attached himself to Catherine's circle; a man of great reputation in his own art and of considerable influence in the papal court, his friendship stood the whole fellowship in good stead. Another influential person who conceived a great affection and devotion for Catherine was the Pope's sister, the Countess of Valentinois, who expressed a desire to be present when she received Communion. Coming one Sunday morning, at Raimondo's

[1] *Legenda*, II. iv. 7 (§ 152); *Processus*, col. 1325. Gregory during the conclave had made a vow that, if elected Pope, he would return to Rome.

[2] *Epistola Domni Stephani*, §§ 22–24.

invitation, to her house for this purpose, she brought with her amongst others the young wife of the Pope's nephew, Dame Elys de Turenne. After Mass, while Catherine was rapt in ecstasy, this young woman thought she was feigning, and, under pretence of kissing her feet, leant over and stabbed them through and through with a needle, or some other sharp instrument. Catherine remained insensible and motionless; but, when she came to herself, she suffered such great pain from the wounds that she was scarcely able to walk, and her companions then, for the first time, perceived what had been done.[1] On another occasion, the mistress of one of the cardinals, either to gratify her curiosity or to test the Saint's intuition, insisted upon speaking with her, and made a great show of being a person of spiritual life; but Catherine resolutely kept her face averted from her, and the unfortunate woman had to depart without even seeing her features.

We have, rather curiously, no record or tradition of Catherine coming into contact with any of the French cardinals, though, doubtless, she made the acquaintance personally of d'Estaing, whom she had previously known by letter. Perhaps, from the outset, she foresaw that the time would soon come for her to class all the rest together as *dimoni incarnati.* The political situation would have led her into direct intercourse with two of the Italians, Jacopo Orsini and Piero Corsini, the former of whom was the official protector (salaried by the Republic) of Siena at the papal court. Almost certainly, too, she met, and was doubtfully impressed by, the Cardinal of Aragon, Pedro de Luna, in whom the "servants of God" (to adopt the quaintly expressive phraseology of the age) put great hopes. We are told also of another prelate, not a cardinal, who at first opposed her, but was ultimately won over to her side—one who was to play a pre-eminent part in the drama of her latest days,

[1] *Epistola Domni Stephani,* § 11. Fra Bartolommeo, *Processus,* col. 1327, says that the injuries inflicted were more serious than Stefano describes, and that Catherine suffered much in consequence for many days.

ırtolommeo Prignano, then Archbishop of Acerenza, and sistant to the Vice-Chancellor of the Holy See.

In the meanwhile, Gregory was ostensibly pushing on the 'eparations for his journey to Italy; but the most careful ›servers doubted whether he would have the strength of mind overcome the obstacles that confronted him. In his despatch July 17, Cristoforo da Piacenza informed Lodovico Gonzaga .at a number of the papal officials had already started, and that rancesco Orsini was on the way to Rome to acquaint the omans with the Pope's intentions, and to bid the feudatories of e Church be ready to meet his Holiness with fitting reverence some port near Rome on September 20. "Nevertheless, he finding great obstacles to his setting out, for all the cardinals this nation are against it, as also his own father and brothers, ıd I hear that the Duke of Anjou is coming to prevent his oving, if he can. I know not what to say. I see many signs ıat point to his going; for the Lord Otho has already come ith seven galleys and seven smaller ships, which are now at Iarseilles. I hear that the galley belonging to the Commune Ancona, upon which the Pope is to travel, is at present at Iarseilles." [1]

Louis, Duke of Anjou, brother of the French king, an nbitious and unstable prince, arrived at the papal court, and ›und Catherine in possession of the Pope's mind. Gregory ›ld him that, at all costs, in spite of his love for his native nd, he was compelled, in the interests of the Church of God, return to Rome. Either because his heart was really touched because he hoped to use her influence for his own ends, ouis persuaded Catherine to come with him from Avignon to s castle of Villeneuve, to console his wife with her ministrations. atherine stayed three days at Villeneuve, and so inflamed the 'uke with ardour for the Crusade that he promised that, if the ope called upon him to do so, he would himself raise an army ıd lead it across the seas at his own expense. He besought

[1] Osio, I. doc. 124. Otho of Brunswick was the fourth husband of the ueen of Naples.

her to go with him to the King of France. When she humbly refused, he induced her to write to the King the eloquent letter we still possess, urging him to reform his kingdom, no longer to let his wars with England hinder the redemption of the Holy Land, but to make peace and enable the Duke to carry out his holy purpose.[1] She wrote at the same time exultantly to the Pope that at last God had sent the means to begin "the holy passage," as they had found a prince who would be a good head. But God bids him undertake another crusade as well; to raise the standard of the Cross against the corrupt and wicked ecclesiastics, and provide the Church with good pastors and rulers instead.[2] A little later, after her return to Avignon, hearing that Louis had narrowly escaped death through the fall of a wall at a banquet, Catherine wrote exhorting him to bear what had happened ever in his memory as a sign from God of the vanity of earthly pleasure, to keep his heart and desire fixed and nailed to the Cross, and formally to take the Cross in the presence of the Pope before the latter set out.[3] But already the Duke's resolution and aspirations were fading away, and his subsequent career, had Catherine lived to see it, would have seemed to her the betrayal of all the hopes she had set on him.

Catherine had returned to Avignon to enter into a desperate struggle with the French cardinals for the soul of the Pope. In spite of his preparations, Gregory was wavering. "Tell him," Christ had seemed to say in her heart when he asked for a sign, "that I give him this excellent sign that it is My will that he should go: the more his going is opposed and contradicted, the more will he feel such a strength increasing in him as no man will be able to take from him; which is contrary to his usual way."[4] In the Sacred College, Cardinal d'Estaing, alone among his countrymen, was supporting the Pope in his preparations; Orsini, Corsini, and Pedro de Luna were neutral; but the rest were emphatically opposed to the move, and the whole influence of the King of France was at their back.

[1] *Processus*, col. 1337; Letter 235 (186).
[2] Letter 238 (9).
[3] Letter 237 (190).
[4] Letter 238 (9).

It would seem that the Pope was too much afraid of these latter any longer openly to admit Catherine to his presence; communications between them were now, for a while, confined to messengers and letters. Once the Pope sent her a short note, saying that the cardinals alleged that Pope Clement IV undertook nothing without the counsels of the Sacred College, and always followed their advice, even if his own opinion was different. "Alas, most holy Father," she answered, "these men quote Pope Clement IV to you, but they tell you nothing about Pope Urban V, who asked their advice about things, when he was in doubt whether it was better to do them or not; but when a thing was absolutely clear to him, as your going is to you (about which you are certain), he took no heed of their counsel, but followed his own, and did not care although they were all against him. Follow the counsel of those who think of the honour of God, the salvation of souls, and the reformation of Holy Church, not that of men who only love their own lives, honours, states, and pleasures. I beseech your Holiness, in the name of Christ crucified, to make haste. Adopt a holy deception; let it seem that you are going to delay for a time, and then do it swiftly and suddenly, for, the more quickly it is done, the sooner will you be freed from these torments and troubles. Once before they made you fall into their snares, when you delayed your coming, snares which the demon had spread in order that the loss and evil should result which has resulted. You, like a wise man, inspired by the Holy Spirit, will not fall into them again."[1] Then Gregory bade Raimondo tell her to pray to God for light to see whether he would meet with any obstacle. She answered that she had already prayed, before and after Communion, and she saw no danger of any kind in the way. "I have prayed, and will pray our sweet and good Jesus that He may take away all servile fear from you, and that only holy fear may remain. May there be in

[1] Letter 231 (7). A Latin translation of this letter, probably what Raimondo actually presented to the Pope, is in the Palatine MS. 59; but there is not the slightest foundation for Augusta Drane's statement (I. p. 378*n.*) that all the letters which Catherine wrote to Gregory at Avignon "are in Latin, not Italian.

you such an ardour of charity as will not let you hear the voices of those incarnate demons, nor follow the counsel of those perverse counsellors founded in self-love, who, as I understand, are trying to frighten you and so prevent your coming, by saying that you will be slain. And I tell you in the name of Christ crucified, sweetest and most holy Father, that you have absolutely no cause for fear. Come with confidence; trust in Christ sweet Jesus; for, if you do what you ought, God will be with you and there will be no one against you. Up, manfully, Father! For I tell you, you have no need to fear. If you did not do what you are bound to do, you would have need to fear. You are bound to come: come then! Come, sweetly, without any fear. And if any of your household strive to impede you, say to them boldly what Christ said to Peter, when, through tenderness, he sought to draw Him back from going to His passion: *Get thee behind me, Satan: thou art an offence unto Me: for thou savourest not the things that be of God, but those that be of men.*"[1]

The beautiful prayer that Catherine offered on this occasion was taken down by Tommaso Petra, an Italian protonotary attached to the papal court, who became one of her disciples, and was afterwards secretary to Gregory's successor, and has thus been preserved to us. "O supreme and ineffable Deity," she prayed at the end, "I have sinned and am not worthy to pray to Thee, but Thou hast power to make me worthy; punish my sins, O Lord, and consider not my miseries. I have one body, which I offer up to Thee; here is my flesh, here is my blood; let my veins be emptied, my body destroyed, my bones scattered, for those for whom I pray to Thee; if it is Thy will, let all my frame be ground up for Thy vicar upon earth, the bridegroom of Thy Spouse, for whom I pray Thee to deign to hear me, that he, Thy vicar, may consider Thy will, may love and fulfil it, so that we may not perish. Give him a new heart, that he may

[1] Letter 233 (8). She had previously written to him: "God has given you authority and you have taken it: you are bound to use your strength and power; and, if you do not wish to use it, it would be more to God's honour and your soul's salvation to resign what you have taken." Letter 255 (13); Harleian MS.

continually grow in grace, strong to uplift the banner of the most holy Cross." [1]

From the outset, the Florentines had pushed on the war—as, indeed, they were compelled to do in the face of the coming of the Bretons. Rodolfo Varano, Lord of Camerino, a feudatory of the Church, had been appointed captain-general of the League, and despatched to Bologna. Bartolommeo di Smeduccio had likewise been taken into the service of the Republic, and had had the campaign in the Marches committed to him. Bartolommeo was a personal enemy of Rodolfo's, and the two would not work in harmony ; but he bore a more deadly hatred towards Gomez Albornoz, who had attempted to deprive him of San Severino by treachery, and he could be trusted to use all his power for the reduction of the citadel of Ascoli. The Bretons had arrived at Borgo di Panicale in the Bolognese contado on July 12, had taken and sacked Crespolano, and were ravaging all the country round with fire and sword—the Cardinal of Geneva urging them on and applauding their worst excesses. Rodolfo, though at the head of a powerful force, contented himself with holding Bologna, and made no serious efforts to take the field against them. Elsewhere, the Florentines were feeling the heavy weight of the papal censures. The expulsion of their merchants and the imprisonment of their other citizens at Avignon had cut them off from their profitable commerce with Provence and the papal court. Although France, Spain, and England did not carry out the papal decrees to the letter, enough was done in the first two countries to inflict immense damage upon the commerce of the Republic, and expelled Florentine merchants returned to the city from all parts of the world.[2] The Pisans refused to take any active steps in the matter ; but, after some delay, the Queen of

[1] *Orationi* I. and II.

[2] The Bishop of London, William Courtenay, published the bull against the Florentines, but was compelled by the King and Chancellor to retract the publication. Cf. *Dict. of National Biography*, XII. p. 343. In the following June, 1377, we find the Signoria thanking the King and the Duke of Lancaster for favours granted to Florentines in England. Gherardi, *op. cit.*, doc. 357.

Naples decided to expel all the Florentines from her dominions, and to take up arms on behalf of the Church. When the news reached Florence, on August 16, Ristoro Canigiani and Benedetto Strozzi were instantly sent as ambassadors of the Commune to induce Giovanna to reconsider her decision; and the inclusion of Messer Ristoro in the embassy is a striking sign of the unity of all parties among the Florentines for the defence of the Republic.[1] They were unsuccessful in their mission; but, in September, the forces of the Queen, advancing to the relief of Ascoli, were completely routed and driven back by Bartolommeo di Smeduccio. At the beginning of the same month, a conspiracy was discovered to betray Bologna to the Cardinal of Geneva and the Marquis of Ferrara; several Bolognese citizens were executed, others put under bounds.

The actual rupture of the negotiations came from the Pope. According to the Florentines, the terms offered them amounted to the desertion of their allies, the revolted cities of the Papal States, and the payment of an indemnity of three million florins. Even to the papal delegates, Cardinals d'Estaing and Aycelin, this seemed excessive, and they proposed certain modifications, to which Gregory answered that he would rather suffer the martyrdom of St. Bartholomew than consent. He sent the chamberlain, Pierre de Cros, with an abrupt order to the ambassadors instantly to depart from the court. The three arrived at Florence on September 22, and their report, formally delivered before the Signoria and a council of a number of chief citizens, *richiesti*, raised the utmost indignation and alarm throughout the city. On the day after their arrival, the Eight wrote to Bernabo Visconti that the coming of the Pope to Italy was now certain, and that it

[1] *Diario d' Anonimo Fiorentino*, pp. 313, 314. But, with regard to another disciple of Catherine, we may notice that the Eight wrote to the Bolognese on August 19, exhorting them to prorogue to another time the election of Pietro, Marchese del Monte Santa Maria, as their captain, not because for his virtues he is not a man worthy of the greatest honours, but only because of his excessive devotion to the Church, and because he is closely related to the Ubaldini, their deadly enemies. Gherardi, *op. cit.*, document 294.

ıs more than ever necessary to strengthen their forces, for, less his powers were utterly broken, they would never be able extort a fitting peace from him. A few days later, the Signoria ·ote to the Emperor, the King of Hungary, the Doge of enice, and the Doge of Genoa, enclosing copies of the terms e Pope had offered, declaring that the conditions would be trageous if the city had been subjected to a long siege, and the ctor were already lording it within her walls. It was decided to nfiscate and sell the goods of the churches for money to carry ı the war.[1]

"Alas, alas! dearest brother," wrote Catherine to Buonaccorso Lapo Giovanni, "I am grieved at the methods that have been opted in asking peace from the most holy Father; for there s been a show of words rather than of deeds. I say this cause, when I came thither to you and to your lords, they owed in their words that they were repentant for the fault mmitted, and it seemed that they would humble themselves ıd crave mercy from the Holy Father; for when I said to em: 'See, my lords, if you really intend to use all humility deed as well as word, and that I should offer you up to your ther like sons that were dead, I will labour in this to the utmost your wish. In no other wise would I go'; they answered me at they were content. Alas, alas! dearest brothers, this was the ıy and the gate by which it befitted you to enter; and there is › other; and if you had followed this way in deed as in your ›rds, you would have had the most glorious peace that ever y one had. I say not this without cause, for I know what the sposition of the Holy Father was like; but since we began to ıve that way, following the astute methods of the world, rrying into effect something quite different from what was first ofessed by word, the Holy Father has been given grounds, not r peace, but for more anger. For when your ambassadors came re, they did not adopt the fitting method which the servants of

[1] Gherardi, *op. cit.*, documents 304–307 (Sept. 23 to Sept. 28, 1376); *ario d'Anonimo Fiorentino*, p. 323, where the Pope is represented as saying: "O disfarò al tutto Firenze, o Firenze disfarebbe la santa Chiesa."

God had suggested to them. You have gone on in your own fashion; and I was never able to confer with them, although, when I asked for the letter of credentials, you told me that you would tell them that we should confer together about everything. Your humble words proceeded more from fear and need than from the spirit of love and virtue. But do you not see how much evil and how many untoward things have come from your obstinacy? Alas, alas! loose yourselves from the league of pride, and league yourselves with the humble Lamb; do not despise or act against His vicar. No more so, for the love of Christ crucified! Do not scorn His blood; but do in the present time what has not been done in the past. Do not conceive bitterness or indignation, if it should seem to you that the Holy Father demands what appears to you very hard and impossible to do. He will not want more than lies in your power. But he is acting like a true father who punishes his son when he does wrong; he rebukes him severely to make him grow humble and acknowledge his fault; and the good son is not angry with his father, because he sees that what he does is done for love of him. So I say to you, in the name of Christ crucified, that, as often as you are spurned by our father, Christ on earth, so often must you fly back to him. Trust in him, for he is right.

"And now he is coming to his spouse, to the place of St. Peter and St. Paul. See that you run to him at once, with true humility of heart and amendment for your faults, following the holy beginning with which you began. If you do so, you will have spiritual and bodily peace; but, if you act in other fashion, our ancestors never had such great woes as we shall have; for we shall be calling the anger of God upon us, and shall not partake of the blood of the Lamb. I say no more. Be as zealous as you can, now that the Holy Father will be at Rome. I have done, and will do, all that I can, even to death, for the honour of God and for your peace, and in order that this obstacle may be taken away, for it impedes the sweet and holy passage. If no other evil resulted from it, we should be worthy of a thousand hells. Take comfort in Christ, our sweet Jesus, for I hope in

The Ecstasy of St. Catherine.
Detail from Bazzi's Fresco San Domenico Siena.

His goodness that, if you will adopt the course that you ought, you will have a good peace."[1]

Catherine would gladly have left Avignon before, but the Pope, still feeling his spiritual powers too weak, wished to have her there until the very day of his departure. And not without reason. The French cardinals made a last effort to draw him back, and produced a letter, apparently anonymous, but which they ascribed to some person with a reputation for sanctity and prophecy (possibly the Franciscan, Peter of Aragon, for whom he had a great esteem), commending the Pope's intention of returning to Rome, but warning him that an attempt would be made to poison him if he came to Italy, advising him to postpone starting until the matter could be investigated, and, in any case, to begin the Crusade first. The letter was apparently shown to Catherine, probably by Fra Raimondo, at the Pope's request. She instantly wrote to Gregory, denouncing it in no measured terms as the work of an incarnate demon, "the sower of the most deadly poison that has for a long time been sowed in Holy Church," and a manifest forgery on the part of the devil's counsellors, who wish to impede the reformation of the Church for their personal ends. "I conclude that I do not believe that the letter sent to you issues from that servant of God who has been named to your Holiness, nor that it was written very far away; but I believe that it comes from near at hand, from the servants of the devil who have little fear of God. If I believed that it came from him, I should not consider him a servant of God, unless I saw other proofs of it. Pardon me, father, if I have spoken too presumptuously; I humbly pray you to forgive me, and to give me your benediction. Remain in the holy and sweet charity of God. I beseech His infinite goodness to grant me the grace of soon seeing you, for His honour, set your foot outside the portals, with peace, repose, and quiet of soul and of body. I beseech you, sweet father, to give me audience, when it pleases your Holiness; for I would fain come into your presence

[1] Letter 234 (215).

before I depart. The time is short; so that, if it pleased you so, I would fain it were soon."[1]

We have no record of what passed at this interview between Catherine and Gregory—her farewell to him until they should meet again (but once only, as it was to prove) upon Italian soil. At last the Pope's resolution was fixed. The galleys, that for weeks had lain waiting at Marseilles, were secretly made ready, and Gregory suddenly, to the incredulous dismay of the Sacred College, announced his intention of departing instantly.

On September 13, 1376, Gregory came out of the papal palace of Avignon, to return to the seat of the Apostles. A mournful crowd in silence watched the departure. At the door of the palace his aged father, Count Guillaume de Beaufort, threw himself at his feet, crying: "My son, whither art thou going? Shall I never see thee more?" "It is written," answered the Pope, "*thou shalt trample upon the asp and the basilisk.*" And he passed over the prostrate body of his father—so well had he learned the lesson Catherine had striven from the outset to impress upon him, that *tenerezza dei parenti* was one of the first things that Christ wished His vicar to root out from his heart.[2] From the beginning, evil omens seemed to attend the Pope's departure. His mule started and backed, and could not be made to stir, but another was brought, and Gregory steadfastly went on his way. Six cardinals—including the Cardinal of Pamplona (Pierre de Montirac, Vice-Chancellor of the Church), Gilles Aycelin, and Anglico de Grimoard (who, as archbishop of the city, was staying at his post)—remained at Avignon. The rest, with the other papal officials, accompanied the Sovereign Pontiff in the state procession that moved by slow stages to Marseilles, which they reached on September 20. Here the papal fleet—twenty-two galleys and a number of smaller ships, under the supreme command of the Grand Master of the knights of St. John—lay in

[1] Letter 239 (10), corrected by the Harleian MS.

[2] Cf. Capecelatro, pp. 262, 263. The story is told in the *Quarta Vita Gregorii XI*, Baluze, I. col. 481, in which the Count's action is wrongly assigned to the Pope's mother, who was already dead.

readiness ; but it was not until October 2 that the Pope actually embarked. It seemed that he had wished to postpone his departure from his beloved native land as long as possible. "O God," writes Pietro Amelio da Alete, the Augustinian Bishop of Sinigaglia, "who could ever imagine how copious and bitter were the cries and wailing and lamentations that arose! Never was such sorrow known. The Pope himself wept. Every cheek was wet with tears ; the hearts of all seemed breaking."[1] The fleet moved slowly from port to port along the Riviera, encountering terrible weather at sea, and at length, on October 18, reached Genoa.

And here Catherine and her company were awaiting the Pope's coming. She had left Avignon on the day of his departure, September 13, and thence travelled by land, for which the Pope and the Duke of Anjou had provided her with the requisite means. We have glimpses of her on the way at Toulon, where, writes Fra Raimondo, "albeit we were silent, the very stones seemed to cry that the holy virgin had arrived in the city," and where she miraculously healed a child ; and again at Voragine (the modern Varazze), which she found depopulated by the pestilence. She promised the survivors a brighter future for their town, commending it to the special protection of the Blessed Trinity and the Madonna.[2] Early in October, she reached Genoa; where, with all her company, she stayed for a month in the house of a noble lady of the city, Madonna Orietta Scotti, whose husband, Messer Barnaba Scotti, is said to have been descended from a Scotch soldier of fortune who came to Italy in the days of Charlemagne.

The tossing on the seas had shaken the Pope's nerves, and the news he received on landing increased his dismay. On October 12, the Eight had written from Florence to the Romans, professing astonishment at their belief in the coming of the Pope, who was lingering at Marseilles and looking for an excuse to

[1] *Itinerarium Domini Gregorii Papae XI*, a long and detailed composition in leonine verses, in *Rer. It. Script.*, iii. 2.

[2] Cf. Augusta Drane, II. pp. 6–8.

return to Avignon : "And, if he comes, it will not be in peaceful guise, but accompanied by martial fury ; we are absolutely convinced that his presence will bring you nothing save war and devastation."[1] There were popular tumults in Rome ; the Florentines continued to carry on the war round Bologna and Ascoli. Although the reception of the Curia by the Genoese had been cordial and enthusiastic, the Doge, even in the Pope's presence, declared himself unable to publish the papal processes against the Florentines in the city. The French cardinals exaggerated every report, represented the stormy weather as a divine warning, and urged the Pope to reconsider the situation. A consistory was held, at which it was proposed that they should return to Avignon, and Gregory was about to give way.

But the Pope still thought of Catherine, whom, apparently, he had not seen since his arrival. He feared to summon her to his presence, because of the comments and opposition this would excite among the cardinals, and thought it derogatory to his dignity to visit her openly in the day, when throngs of people were pressing to see her and hear her words. In the evening, on the day of the consistory, he went in disguise to the house of Orietta Scotti. Catherine fell at his feet ; he bade her rise, for that he himself was a suppliant, and besought her to obtain him the grace to know what course he should adopt. After a long colloquy with her, Gregory departed, full of edification and with his courage restored.[2] He at once informed the cardinals of his resolution to proceed, and ordered the fleet to put to sea. On October 29, he set sail from Genoa, and Catherine was destined never again to see his face in this life.

Catherine herself was delayed at Genoa for some weeks after the Pope had left, partly by her unceasing labours for the salvation of souls, partly by an outbreak of sickness among her fellowship. Stefano Maconi tells us that they were almost all

[1] Gherardi, *op. cit.*, doc. 309.

[2] This incident is recorded only by Fra Tommaso in the *Supplementum ;* Tantucci, pp. 48, 49. Cf. *Oratione* III., the prayer that the Saint offered on this occasion.

taken ill, and that Madonna Orietta watched most anxiously over them, calling in two physicians every day to their aid. Neri di Landoccio and Stefano himself, who had nursed the others, suffered most of all, the former being brought very near to death's door, and both seemed miraculously restored to health by Catherine's prayers and her spiritual power upon them.[1] "Take comfort sweetly and be patient," she wrote to Giovanna Maconi, Stefano's mother, "and do not be troubled because I have kept Stefano too long; for I have taken good care of him. Through love and affection I have become one thing with him, and therefore I have taken what is yours as though it were mine own. I am sure that you are not really displeased. For you and for him together I would fain do my very utmost, even unto death. You, mother, have given birth to him once; and I wish to give birth to him and you and all your family, in tears and in labour, through continual prayer and desire for your salvation."[2]

And to her own mother, Lapa, who bewailed her daughter's long absence and complained that she had been deserted, she wrote a tender letter of comfort, "with desire of seeing you the true mother, not only of my body, but of my soul." "Dearest mother, you know that I must follow the will of God; and I know that you wish me to follow it. It was His will that I should set out on this journey, which has not been without mystery nor without fruits of great usefulness. It has been by His will that I have stayed, and not by the will of man; and, if any one said the contrary, it is false and not the truth. And so I shall have to go, following His footsteps in what way and at what time shall please His inestimable goodness. You, like a good and sweet mother, should be content and not distressed at bearing all burdens for the honour of God, and your salvation and mine. Remember that you did this for the sake of temporal goods, when your sons left you in order to acquire temporal riches; but now, to acquire life eternal, it seems to you such a burden that you say you will vanish, if I do not answer you at once. All this

[1] *Epistola Domni Stephani*, § 13; *Legenda*, II. viii. 21–24 (§ § 261–264).

[2] Letter 247 (355).

befalls you because you love that part which I have received from you, that is, your flesh with which you clothed me, more than that which I have received from God. Raise, O raise your heart and affection to that sweet and most holy Cross, where every burden becomes light; be willing to bear a little finite pain, to escape the infinite pain which we deserve for our sins. Now take comfort, for the love of Christ crucified; and do not think yourself abandoned, either by God or by me. Nay, you will be consoled and will receive full consolation; your sorrow has not been so great, but that the joy will be greater. We shall soon come, by the grace of God." [1]

Early in November, Catherine and her company left Genoa by sea. After narrowly escaping shipwreck on the way, they landed at Livorno and went on thence to Pisa, where Lapa, Fra Tommaso della Fonte, and others met them. From Pisa, Catherine sent Stefano to Siena, with letters and messages, to prepare the way for their return; [2] and, probably about the middle of December, she found herself once more in her native city.

In the meanwhile, Gregory had proceeded on his way, tossed by storms at sea and assailed by sinister rumours wherever he touched shore. At Livorno, which he reached on November 10, he was received by Piero Gambacorti and his sons, who, together with the ambassadors of Lucca, again besought him to make peace with the Florentines. But the Pope would not listen to a word on the subject, but ordered fresh processes to be published against them. A fearful tempest arose and scattered the fleet; the galleys of the Cardinals of Amiens and Glandèves sank, but their lives were saved; the greater part of the ships got to Port' Ercole. Gregory himself with six galleys was driven to the island of Elba, from which he despatched a letter to the cardinals, "bidding them take heart, for these tempests which he had suffered

[1] Letter 240 (169).

[2] Two letters from Stefano at Siena to Neri at Pisa ("al luogo de' frati di San Domenico, o vero di Santa Caterina"), dated November 29 and December 8, 1376, are published by Grottanelli in the *Lettere dei discepoli*, 5 and 6, full of little playful touches.

on the sea were the sign of a great victory, and no prince had ever come to Italy without enduring storms and tribulations at sea, if he were afterwards to prove a conqueror, as was shown by the example of Aeneas and King Charles."[1] At length, on December 5, the Pope reached the shores of the Papal States, and landed at the port of Corneto.

At Corneto the Pope stayed for nearly six weeks, to keep Christmas, and to come to terms with the Romans, whom the Florentines were inciting to insurrection. Here he received a characteristic letter from Catherine, written shortly after her return to Siena, exhorting him to constancy, fortitude, and patience, assuring him of the good disposition of the Sienese, urging him to proceed with confidence.[2] Nevertheless, ill tidings poured in. On December 14, the citadel of Ascoli, from which Gomez Albornoz had escaped in a vain effort to procure reinforcements, was compelled to surrender to the forces of the league. A week later, an attempt to gain back Città di Castello for the Church failed; Uguccione and Francesco, sons of the Marchese Angelo del Monte Santa Maria, were beheaded; and Benedetto Strozzi and Ristoro Canigiani (a further proof of the solidarity of all parties in Florence for the defence of the Republic) were sent to confirm the city in its friendship with the Commune of Florence, "and with a word from the Eight of the War."[3] Bolsena revolted from the Church; and, at the beginning of January, a papal force composed of troops supplied by the Queen of Naples, which had been sent against Viterbo, was completely defeated by Francesco di Vico and the Florentines.[4]

But this was more than counterbalanced by the submission of Rome itself. On December 21, an agreement was made between

[1] Despatch from Cristoforo da Piacenza to Lodovico Gonzaga, dated Rome, December 13, 1376. Pastor, *Acta Inedita*, doc. 1.

[2] Letter 252 (11).

[3] *Diario d'Anonimo Fiorentino*, p. 327.

[4] Luigi delle Vigne, a brother of Fra Raimondo, was one of the Queen's knights who were taken prisoners on this occasion. In Letter 254 (284), to Pietro di Jacomo Tolomei, Catherine begs him to use his influence with the Prefect to get Luigi set free without ransom.

Cardinals d'Estaing, Corsini, and Tebaldeschi, in the name of the Church, and the government and people of Rome, by which the full dominion of the city was offered to the said cardinals, as representing the Pope, in the same manner and form as had been offered to Urban V. The whole of Trastevere and the Leonine city was put into the hands of Cardinal Tebaldeschi as papal legate ; the Pope on his part undertaking to preserve and maintain the Signoria of the Bandaresi, "the society of the executors of justice and four counsellors, the crossbowmen and shieldbearers," while stipulating that the right of reforming the said society should be recognized as pertaining to him.[1] The last obstacle to the return of the Sovereign Pontiff to the seat of the Apostles was thus removed. On January 13, the fleet sailed from Corneto. A fair and prosperous voyage to Ostia raised the hopes and expectations of the Pope and his court ; and, on January 16, they sailed up the Tiber to San Paolo fuori le Mura, where they were received with every demonstration of enthusiasm and exultation by the Bandaresi and the people of Rome. The next day, January 17, 1377, Gregory made his triumphal entry into the Eternal City : "Verily," writes the Bishop of Sinigaglia, "I never thought in this world to see such glory with my own eyes."

[1] Convention in Raynaldus, vii. p. 283.

CHAPTER X

THE ANGEL OF PEACE

"Per altro non venni se non per mangiare e gustare anime, e trarle delle mani delle dimonia. La vita voglio lasciare per questo, se io n'avessi mille. E per questa cagione anderò e starò secondo che lo Spirito Santo farà fare."—St. Catherine, Letter 121 (201).

It is evident from Catherine's letters that she had no thought or desire of seeing Gregory return to Rome as a temporal sovereign. She dreamed of the Pope as a purely spiritual power, coming unarmed in poverty and humility, conquering all opposition by the might of love alone. The spectacle of the Church fighting against the Italians with mercenary arms, for the recovery of the revolted cities of the Papal States, was to her an utter horror and abomination, a veritable war against God.

To the Sovereign Pontiff, shortly after his return to Rome, she addressed a letter which gives impassioned utterance to the aspirations of all those Catholics who, at any epoch in the history of the Church, have prayed that their pastors might realize that Christ's kingdom was not of this world, and, for the salvation of souls, consent at length to lay down the Christless burden of temporal power (even if existing merely in unrealizable and vaguely formulated demands)—only to be confronted by the papal *non possumus*, the declaration that he who sits on the throne of the Fisherman cannot renounce what the Church has once possessed, or claimed to possess, as her own. God demands peace from the Pope, she writes, and that he should not be so intent upon temporal lordship and possessions as not to see how great is the destruction of souls and the outrage to God that results from war. "You could indeed say, Holy Father: 'I am bound in conscience to preserve and recover what belongs to Holy Church.' Alas, I confess that it is true; but it seems to me that one must still more guard what is more dear. The treasure of the Church is the blood of Christ, given in ransom for the soul; for the treasure of the blood is not paid for temporal substance, but for the salvation of the human race. So that, supposing that you are bound to conquer and preserve the treasure and the lordship of the cities that the Church has lost; much more are you bound to win back so many little sheep, who are a treasure in the Church. It is better to let the mire of temporal things go than the gold of spiritual things. Peace, peace, for the love of Christ crucified." What is the loss of the temporal power compared to the evil of seeing grace perish in men's souls, and the obedience die away that they owe the Pope? How can he reform the Church while he remains at war, and squanders upon soldiers what belongs to the poor? "You have need of the aid of Christ crucified; set, then, your affection and your desire upon Him; not on man and on human aid, but on Christ sweet Jesus, whose place you hold; for it seems that He wishes the Church to return to her sweet primal state. O how blessed will your soul be and mine, when I see you begin this great good work, and when what God is now permitting by force shall be accomplished in your hands by love!"[1]

As soon as Catherine got back to Siena, certain Florentines waited upon her—apparently on behalf of the Parte Guelfa—wishing to hear from her lips what she had done for them at Avignon, and what were the dispositions of the Pope. She answered that Gregory was ready to receive them into his grace, if they would give proof of their submission to the Holy See,

[1] *i.e.* the return of the Church to her primitive state of poverty and purity by the loss of her temporal possessions. Letter 209 (2), corrected by the Harleian MS., which states that this letter was sent to the Pope "poi che fu giunto a Roma," as is confirmed by internal evidence; Gigli and Tommaseo are clearly in error in assigning it to an earlier date. The postscript in the MS. reads: "I believe that Fra Jacopo da Padova, the bearer of this letter, is a true and sweet servant of God; I commend him to you, and beseech your Holiness to be pleased to see him and the others always near you." Fra Jacopo of Padua was an Olivetan monk, one of Catherine's correspondents, who was afterwards prior of San Bartolommeo outside Florence.

and urged them to send ambassadors to him as soon as he should have arrived at Rome. They besought her to come again to Florence, to give a formal account of her legation and appease the minds of the Parte Guelfa ; this, however, Catherine refused to do, as compromising the dignity of the Church after what had passed at Avignon, though she ultimately consented to send Stefano Maconi in her stead. When he arrived at Florence, Niccolò Soderini, Piero Canigiani, and Stoldo di Bindo Altoviti (a prominent member of the Parte Guelfa, who played a considerable part in the internal politics of the Republic) accompanied Stefano to the Eight, to whom he delivered Catherine's message, detailing all that had been done in Avignon and urging them to make peace. But a rumour spread through the city that "a certain Catherinated Sienese" was inducing the Eight to subject the government to the Pope ; a tumult was raised, "so that not otherwise than of old the Jews gnashed on the blessed levite Stephen with their teeth, so did many of the people with murderous fury upon our Stephen, and they would without doubt have assailed him, had not the authority of most influential men intervened."[1] Nevertheless, Stefano's biographer assures us, his words had not been lost. But events were to render all immediate prospects of peace out of the question.

Almost all the States of Italy, even those at war with the Holy See, sent ambassadors to congratulate the Pope on his arrival. The Sienese were also charged with the task of making excuses for their having joined the league, and of obtaining from the Pope the restitution of Talamone, which had been seized by the prior of the Pisan knights of St. John with aid from the Church. With them went Tommaso di Guelfaccio, the Gesuato, bearing a letter from Catherine to the Pontiff, once more exhorting him to make peace with the Tuscan communes and the revolted cities, for the pacification of all Italy. By love alone can he hope to win the souls of the Italians.

[1] Barth. Senensis, *op. cit.*, Lib. I. cap. 8. This is our only authority for this embassy, which, from the wording of Catherine's answer, was evidently while the Pope was at Corneto.

"The Sienese ambassadors are coming to your Holiness, and, if there are any folk in the world who can be caught with love, these are they. And, therefore, I pray you to strive to take them with this hook. Accept their excuses for the fault which they have committed, for they are sorry for it, and it seems to them that they are in such a position that they know not what to do. I beseech you, sweet babbo mine, if you see any way by which they could satisfy your Holiness without their being involved in war with those with whom they are allied, you would be pleased to adopt it. Bear with them, for the love of Christ crucified. I believe that, if you do this, it will be a great boon for Holy Church and obviate much evil."[1] The Pope received them kindly for Catherine's sake, but would only answer in generalities—with the result that the ambassadors doubted his pacific intentions, and concluded that he meant to hold Talamone as a pledge for the loyalty of the Sienese in his coming campaign for the reconquest of the Papal States.

The three Florentine ambassadors arrived in Rome on January 26. They were Pazzino Strozzi, Alessandro dell' Antella, and Michele Castellani—the same three who had been to Avignon—and they bore a mandate to congratulate the Pope and to treat for peace. Gregory received them kindly, but would only offer practically the same terms as before: they must pay an indemnity of more than a million florins to the apostolic treasury within four years, and virtually abandon their colleagues in the league.[2] The indemnity was more than excessive, and an appalling event, that happened a few days later, enabled the

[1] Letter 285 (14), amended by the Harleian MS. The ambassadors were Andrea di Conte, Giovanni Vincenti, and three others. Cf. O. Malavolti, pp. 143*v.*, 144, and the *Cronica Sanese*, col. 252. On November 25 (1376), the Signoria of Florence had requested the Sienese to suspend the sending of the ambassadors, as the time was at hand in which all the confederates were to meet to consider the general utility of the league. Gherardi, *op. cit.*, doc. 321.

[2] Gherardi, *op. cit.*, pp. 71, 72. St. Antoninus states (III. p. 384) that the Pope had written from Corneto to the Florentines, bidding them send him the same ambassadors that had been to Avignon ; but there is documentary evidence that they had been already appointed in November.

Florentines to give a sinister interpretation to the second papal demand.

Foiled at Bologna, the Cardinal of Geneva had taken the Bretons into winter quarters at Cesena, the only large town in Romagna that now remained faithful to the Church. The overbearing brutality of these ruffians, backed by the Cardinal, who gave them leave to take what they needed from the citizens without payment, brought about an armed rising in Cesena on February 1, in which some three or four hundred of the Bretons were killed, and the rest driven from the city, or forced to take refuge with the Cardinal in the citadel. There was no thought of rebellion against the Pope: "Viva la Chiesa," had been the shout of the populace, no less than "Muoiano i Brettoni"; and, on the following day, trusting in the pacific declaration of the Cardinal, the insurgents laid down their arms. But already, at the former's summons, Hawkwood and his English were hastening from Faenza; joining forces with the infuriated Bretons, they entered Cesena at night by the citadel, and were ordered to put the inhabitants to the sword. To do him justice, Hawkwood hesitated, and made some sort of remonstrance; but the Cardinal insisted. On the next day, February 3, an appalling massacre followed. Men, women, and children were slaughtered indiscriminately; the English were chiefly bent on plunder, but the Bretons, thirsting for vengeance, did not even spare the infants at the breast or in the cradle, and committed unspeakable horrors of every description. The churches were desecrated, those of the friars who attempted to give sanctuary to the fugitives were murdered with the rest. At least four thousand of the inhabitants of Cesena were thus butchered; fifteen thousand survivors, starving and perishing with the cold, fled in utter destitution, to die on the way, or find shelter, as best they could, in the neighbouring towns. A thrill of horror ran through all Italy—it is impossible to set down on paper even a small part of the unutterable atrocities that the common report of the time ascribed to the mercenary soldiers of the Church. "Nero himself never committed such cruelty," writes the

Franciscan chronicler of Bologna; "it was enough to make folk believe no more in pope or cardinals." In all the cities of the league, Masses were offered up, and men and women thronged the churches to make offerings, and to pray for the repose of the murdered citizens of Cesena.

If such was the fate of the faithful adherents of the Church, what might not the rebels expect at her hands, if deserted by their Florentine allies? Coluccio Salutati wrote, in the name of the Republic, to the States of Italy and to the princes of Christendom, declaring that what had happened had thoroughly justified the policy of Florence. "This is the unhappy fate of peoples that obey the Church! This is the deplorable state of Italy, which these rulers for the Church are destroying and defacing! But we do not accuse the humanity of the Sovereign Pontiff of these things, for we believe that he is cordially displeased by this and many others, about which we are silent; but we lament exceedingly that he still finds no remedy for so many and such horrible deeds."[1] Nevertheless, Gregory seems to have taken no steps publicly to dissociate himself from the unutterable horrors done in his name. In his eloquent canzone to the Pope, Franco Sacchetti bewails "the innocent blood of Cesena, shed with such fury by these wolves of thine": "Woe to whoso is under thee and does not rise! For there is just cause to free oneself from him who is fain to feed on human blood."

Nowhere in Catherine's letters does she make any explicit reference to the massacre of Cesena. But, doubtless, the fresh remembrance of the blood of these unhappy victims to the lust of the pastors of the Church for temporal sovereignty must have given terrible actuality to her letter to the Pope, written ten weeks after the event, pleading for peace at any price:—

[1] The fullest account of the massacre is given in the *Cronica di Bologna*, col. 510; the *Cronica Sanese*, coll. 252–254; and by St. Antoninus, III. p. 383, who to some extent exonerates the English of the worst horrors. For the whole subject, cf. *L'eccidio di Cesena del* 1377 *di anonimo scrittore coetaneo*, ed. G. Gori (Archivio Storico Italiano, N. S. vol. viii. part 2), and Canestrini, *op. cit.*, p. xlvi. *n.* Contemporary authorities differ considerably as to the details and the numbers killed on either side; that 4000 of the inhabitants perished in the massacre is the lowest estimate.

"Have mercy upon so many souls and bodies that are perishing. O pastor and keeper of the cellar of the blood of the Lamb, let not trouble nor shame nor the abuse that you might think to receive, nor servile fear draw you back, nor the perverse counsellors of the devil who counsel you to nought else save wars and misery. Consider what great evils are resulting from this wicked war, and how great is the good that will be the result of peace. Alas! babbo mio, my soul is full of woe, for my iniquities are the cause of every ill. It seems that the devil has taken the lordship of the world, not by himself, for he can do nothing; but in as much as we have given him. On whatever side I turn, I see that each one has given him the keys of free will by his perverse desires; laymen, religious, and clergy are proudly pursuing delights and states and worldly riches, with much impurity and misery. But, above all other things that I see, the most abominable in the sight of God are the flowers that are planted in the mystical body of Holy Church—which should be flowers of sweet odour, and their life a mirror of virtue, hungry lovers of the honour of God and of the salvation of souls. They are befouled with every misery, lovers of themselves, uniting their own sins with those of the others, and especially in the persecution that is being dealt to the sweet Spouse of Christ and to your Holiness.[1] Alas! we have fallen under the sentence of death, and we have made war upon God. O babbo mio, you are given us as the mediator to make this peace; and I do not see how it can be done, unless you carry the cross of holy desire. We are at war with God, and your rebellious children are at war with God and with your Holiness. God wills and demands of you that, according to your power, you should take the lordship from the hands of the demons. Set yourself to freeing Holy Church from the foul smell of her ministers; weed out these stinking flowers, and plant sweet-smelling flowers therein, virtuous men who fear God. Then I pray your Holiness to be pleased to grant peace and to accept it, in whatever way it can be had, always without injury to the Church

[1] That is, the wickedness of the priests and ecclesiastics is giving strength to the opponents of the Holy See.

and your conscience. God would have you attend to souls and to spiritual things more than to temporal."[1]

Catherine dates this letter from "the new monastery which you have granted me, entitled Santa Maria degli Angeli." This was on the site of the present villa of Belcaro, that most romantically placed castle, embedded in its noble grove of ilexes, from the battlements of which the Sienese contado lies outstretched before our eyes away to the Maremma and distant Monte Amiata. It had been given her by Nanni di Ser Vanni Savini, who, after an unfortunate and turbulent career as a politician of the faction of the Twelve, had been finally converted to a religious life. While at Avignon, the Pope had granted her the necessary faculties; and on her return to Siena, the Signoria, in answer to her petition of January 25, 1377, had authorized her to turn the dismantled fortress into a monastery, for the reception of "religious sisters, who will continually pray for the city and citizens and inhabitants of Siena and its contado."[2] The Abbot of Sant' Antimo, Fra Giovanni di Gano of Orvieto (a monk in whom Catherine had great confidence, and who occasionally acted as one of her confessors), formally blessed the beginning of the monastery as papal commissary, in the presence of all Catherine's spiritual family, and William Flete came over from the neighbouring Lecceto to say the first Mass. Catherine returned to Siena on April 25, the feast of St. Mark.

We have lost sight of Francesco di Vanni Malavolti during these months. During Catherine's absence at Avignon, he had drifted back to his former dissolute way of life, and, on her return, at first shrank from visiting her. She implored him to come to

[1] Letter 270 (12). The date, April 16, 1377, is given by the Harleian and Palatine MSS.

[2] It was forbidden to alienate fortified places without leave of the Commune, but the Saint represents in her petition that the castle is in ruins, and that she will do nothing save with the permission of the Defenders. The petition was approved by the General Council of the Bell by 333 votes to 65. Cf. the document given by Grottanelli, notes to *Leggenda minore*, pp. 219–222, and *Legenda*, II. vii. 17–20 (§§ 235–238). There was a Carthusian convent in the vicinity, of which several of the monks were among Catherine's disciples and correspondents.

her. "Dearest and beloved son in Christ sweet Jesus," she wrote, "I, Catherine, servant and slave of the servants of Jesus Christ, write to thee in His precious blood, with desire of finding thee again, my little lost sheep, and I have a very great desire of putting thee back into the fold with thy companions. It seems to me that the devil has so robbed me of thee that thou dost not let thyself be found; and I, thy miserable mother, go seeking and sending for thee, because I would fain take thee upon my shoulders, by reason of the bitter sorrow and compassion that I have for thy soul. Open the eye of thy understanding, dearest son, raise it from the darkness, and recognize thy fault, not with confusion of mind, but with knowledge of thyself and with hope in the goodness of God. See how miserably thou hast spent the substance of grace that thy heavenly Father gave thee. But, even as that son did, who, when he had wasted his substance and began to be in want, realized his fault and had recourse to his father for forgiveness, so do thou; for thou art impoverished and in want; thy soul is dying of hunger. Go to thy Father for forgiveness; He will succour thee, and will not despise thy desire, if it is founded in sorrow for the sin committed—nay, He will fulfil it sweetly. Alas, alas! where are thy sweet desires? O my unhappy soul! I have found that the devil has stolen thy soul and thy holy desire. The world and its servants have spread the snares with its disordinate pleasures and delights. Up, now, take the remedy, and sleep no more. Comfort my soul, and be not so cruel, for thy salvation, as to grudge me one visit. Do not let thyself be deceived by the devil through fear or shame. Break this entanglement. Come, come, dearest son: I can well call thee *dear*, so much art thou costing me in tears and labour, and in much bitter sorrow. Ah, come, my sweet son, and return to thy fold. I plead my excuse before God, for I can do no more. In coming and staying, I am asking nothing from thee, save that thou wouldst do the will of God. I say no more. May Christ Jesus console thee with thyself and me with thee."[1]

[1] I follow the Palatine MS. 59, which gives a better text of this letter than

Francesco tells us that he at once went to her, "albeit not without great shame and fear. But she, like a most benign and sweetest mother, received me with a joyful countenance, giving the greatest comfort to my weakness. And a few days afterwards, when I went to her again, and one of the virgin's women companions said to her, as it were in blame of me, that I had little stability, she said with a smile: 'Never mind, my sisters, for he cannot escape out of my hands, let him go by what way he will; for when he thinks that I am far from him, I shall put such a yoke upon his neck that he will never be able to slip out of it.' At this time, I had both wife and children. The sisters, and I with them, laughed at these words, and we made merry, nor did any of us then think any more about them."[1]

At Siena, Catherine had again taken up her apostolic mission, labouring for the conversion of souls, making peace between enemies, tending and comforting the afflicted. Above all, at this time, the prisoners and those doomed to death by the law claimed her ministrations. The government lived in daily apprehension of conspiracies; the prisons were full; executions were incessant. At the beginning of this year, 1377, a young noble of Gubbio, Gaddo Accorimboni, had been made podestà, and, in the hope of obtaining the senatorship, he set about his work with the most ruthless severity, caring less for justice than for winning a reputation as an inflexible and vigorous magistrate. We have still the beautiful letter that, on the Thursday in Holy Week, Catherine addressed to the prisoners under his heavy hand, exhorting them to gain true patience in the contemplation of the blood of Christ crucified.[2] It was probably now that the episode in her life occurred that is known to so many that know nought else of Catherine, by Bazzi's fresco and Mr. Swinburne's poem. A young Perugian noble, apparently little more than a youth, Niccolò di Toldo, attached to the household of the Senator or

Gigli (266) or Tommaseo (45). It is also one of those included in the Bolognese edition of 1492.

[1] *Contestatio Francisci de Malavoltis*, cap. i., MS. *cit.*, p. 433.

[2] Letter 260 (309). Cf. *Cronica Sanese*, col. 251.

Podestà, was sentenced to death for some rash words he had uttered against the State. Fra Tommaso Caffarini found him in the prison of the Commune, raging with despair, refusing to make his confession or to hear a word about the salvation of his soul. He had never received the sacraments since his first Communion. Then Catherine came to his cell, bringing him such mystical consolation that he became "like a meek lamb led to the sacrifice," and died with Christ's name and hers on his lips, she receiving his severed head into her hands. "He met his death," writes Fra Tommaso, "with such wonderful devotion that it seemed not that of one condemned for any crime of man, but rather the passing away of some holy martyr. All who witnessed it, among whom I was one, were moved to such intense compunction of heart, that never, until then, do I remember having been present at any funeral where there was so much devotion as at his."[1] I will return presently to the wonderful letter in which Catherine informs Fra Raimondo of every detail in the tragedy turned triumph ; for it is one of those that most vividly illustrate the words of Stefano Maconi, that in her letters we may perceive "the living image of that divine virgin, expressed in the most true features of her holiness."

In the summer of this year, Catherine left the city, to carry on her spiritual ministry in the Sienese contado. The immediate occasion of her going was a feud that had arisen between two of the principal members of the great house of the Salimbeni, Agnolino di Giovanni di Agnolino and Cione di Sandro, which was threatening to set the whole district once more aflame with civil war. A dispute concerning the possession of a castle, in which they both claimed a share, was the ostensible cause of the quarrel, but there was also a political difference between the two nobles. Cione, a restless and turbulent spirit, inclined to support the policy of the papal legates in Tuscany, from whom he was always looking for aid against the liberties of

[1] *Contestatio Fr. Thomae, Processus,* col. 1266. The story is one of Fra Tommaso's additions in the *Leggenda minore*, pp. 93, 94, as Fra Raimondo, being then absent from Siena, does not mention it. See below, chapter xvi.

his fellow-citizens; while Agnolino, the head of the family, although he had joined in the rebellion of 1374, had inherited the traditions of his famous father, Giovanni di Agnolino Salimbeni, who for so many years had been a power for peace in the State, and was ready to serve the Republic against all her enemies. Agnolino's widowed mother, the venerable Madonna Biancina Salimbeni, a sister of the lords of Foligno, had been for long the devoted worshipper of Catherine, who was also in correspondence with Madonna Stricca, the wife of Messer Cione. It was probably at the invitation of these two ladies that Catherine intervened in the dispute, though she was doubtless glad of such an opportunity to pursue the same apostolic work for her divine Master and Bridegroom among the people of the contado that she had already accomplished, for so many years, within the walls of Siena itself.

Several of Catherine's letters to the Salimbeni have been preserved. Besides Biancina and Stricca, she was in correspondence with Agnolino's two sisters, the Countess Benedetta and Madonna Isa, both of whom were at this time widows, and whom she was persuading to enter the religious life.[1] To Benedetta, whose second betrothed had died before the wedding, and upon whom her family were urging a third marriage for political reasons, she wrote urging her not to give herself to the perverse service of the world, but to take the two rebuffs it had given her as a sign that she was called to be the bride of Christ, and advising her to enter the new monastery of S. Maria degli Angeli at Belcaro. And in a longer letter, on divine love contrasted with the love of men, she invites her to the enclosed garden of self-knowledge, planted in the soil of true humility. "I know," she writes to Agnolino, "that much evil has been said and will be said to you about the Countess, because she wishes to be the servant and bride of Jesus Christ. She and you would be very foolish, if she did not answer, now that the Holy Spirit

[1] In the *Cronica Sanese*, under 1373, we read: "Agnolino di Giovanni Salimbeni ne mandò a marito due sue sorelle di Dicembre. El Comune di Siena mandò gente a far lo' scorta" (col. 236).

is calling her. And she has seen that the world rejects her and drives her to Christ crucified." And to Madonna Isa, who ultimately became one of the Mantellate, she suggests that Benedetta should come to the Rocca—Rocca d' Orcia or Rocca di Tentennano, the chief fortress of the Salimbeni, where Agnolino usually resided with their mother—before she herself came thither.[1]

It was already August when Catherine left Siena, accompanied by her usual band of disciples and women, which included Fra Raimondo, Fra Tommaso della Fonte, Fra Bartolommeo, Fra Matteo Tolomei, Fra Santi, Stefano, Neri, the newly regained Francesco Malavolti (from whose pen comes the most vivid description of these months), Gabriele Piccolomini, with Alessa, Cecca, Lisa, and others of the Mantellate. Monna Lapa—familiarly known as *nonna*, or "granny," by the members of her daughter's spiritual family—seems to have come as far as Montepulciano. She and Cecca were left among the nuns of the monastery of Santa Agnese, where Cecca had a daughter, Giustina, a novice; while Catherine went on her mission, first to Cione Salimbeni at his stronghold of Castiglioncello del Trinoro, and thence to Agnolino at the Rocca. "And in a short space of time," writes Francesco Malavolti, "she brought both of them to perfect concord, which many other barons and potent men had hitherto been unable to effect." From the Rocca, Catherine visited the Abbey of Sant' Antimo, at the request of her friend the Abbot, who found himself involved in a quarrel with the archpriest of Montalcino, who claimed jurisdiction over him. In like fashion, at Montepulciano, it was her task to pacify Spinello Tolomei and others of his family, who were in a chronic state of hostility towards both the Salimbeni and the Republic, and divided among themselves. In this latter attempt, however, she had only a partial and temporary success; for, in the following spring, in spite of the intervention of the new Bishop of Siena (Luca Bertini, the papal nuncio whose imprisonment at Florence has

[1] Letters 112 (329), 113 (330), 114 (267), 115 (332).

been already mentioned), Spinello rose in arms, harried the lands of the Salimbeni, and renewed the fierce factions of the two houses.

For more than four months Catherine remained in these parts, making Rocca d' Orcia her headquarters. No traces of this once famous castle remain to-day. It stood on an eminence above the Orcia, some twenty-three miles from Siena on the way to Rome, between Montepulciano and Montalcino, and (like so many similar *castelli* that we still see in southern Tuscany and in the Roman Campagna) was practically a small town centred round the great fortress of the feudal lord. It was also known as the "Isola della Rocca," apparently from its isolated position. Here, the pacific work for which they had come being accomplished, Madonna Biancina showed herself the most loving and devoted of hostesses to Catherine and her followers, while men and women poured in from the hills and country round, to hear the Saint's words and be healed of their maladies. Wonderful stories are told us by Fra Raimondo and by Francesco Malavolti of her power in casting out demons from the bodies of the possessed,[1] but even more remarkable were the conversions that she effected in men's souls. "I sometimes saw," writes Fra Raimondo, "a thousand or more persons, men and women, come together from the mountains and other regions of the Sienese contado, to see and hear Catherine, as it were summoned by an invisible trumpet; and there, not only by her words, but at the mere sight of her, they were straightway moved to compunction for their misdeeds; weeping and bewailing their sins, they hastened to the confessors, of whom I was one, and made their confessions with such great contrition that no one could doubt that a great abundance of grace had descended from heaven into their hearts."[2]

Eating souls, or devouring demons, was Catherine's playful term for converting sinners. "We must work for the honour

[1] *Legenda*, II. ix. 7–9 (§§ 274–276); *Contestatio Francisci de Malavoltis*, cap. iv., MS. *cit.*, pp. 446–453. Cf. Augusta Drane, II. pp. 61–66.

[2] *Ibid.*, II. vii. 21–22 (§§ 239, 240). Cf. *Processus*, col. 1271.

of God, even as the holy apostles did," she writes to Caterina dello Spedaluccio and Giovanna di Capo, two of her women who had been left behind in the city, and who repined at her long absence; "after they had received the Holy Spirit, they separated from each other and from that sweet Mother Mary. Albeit it would have been their greatest delight to have stayed together, nevertheless they gave up their own pleasure, to seek the honour of God and the salvation of souls. This is the rule that we must adopt for ourselves. You are in Siena, and Cecca and the *nonna* are at Montepulciano. Fra Bartolommeo and Fra Matteo have been there, and will be again. Alessa and Monna Bruna are at Monte Giovi, eighteen miles from Montepulciano; they are with the Countess and Madonna Isa. Fra Raimondo and Fra Tommaso and Monna Tomma and Lisa and I are at the Rocca among evil-doers, and they are eating so many incarnate demons that Fra Tommaso says that he has bad pains. And, with all this, they cannot have enough; their appetite increases, and they are finding work that is highly paid. Pray the Divine Goodness to give them big and sweet and bitter mouthfuls."[1] And to Lapa herself, the "nonna" at Montepulciano, she wrote: "You know, dearest mother, that I, your miserable daughter, have been placed on earth for nought else save the honour of God and the salvation of souls. To this my Creator has called me. I know that you are content that I should obey Him. I beseech you, if you think that I am staying longer than you would wish, to be content; for I cannot do anything else. I believe that, if you knew the case, you yourself would send me hither. I am here to heal a great scandal, if I can. It is not the fault of the Countess; and, therefore, you must all pray to God and the glorious Virgin that they send us a good result. Do you, Cecca and Giustina, drown yourselves in the blood of Christ crucified; for now is the time to prove virtue in the soul."[2]

[1] Letter 118 (175).

[2] Letter 117 (167). Catherine's mother was by this time herself one of the Mantellate. A brief from Gregory XI grants special spiritual favours to Lapa,

In fact, Catherine's prolonged sojourn in the contado was arousing political suspicions as well as perplexing and distressing her friends, and troubles of every kind seemed gathering round her. While she was at Sant' Antimo, the archpriest of Montalcino, impelled thereto by his hatred of the Abbot Giovanni di Gano, laid complaints against both her and him before the government. Catherine at once despatched Pietro di Giovanni Ventura in her name to Siena with a letter to the Defenders and the Captain of the People, warning them not to set "the servants of God" against them by listening to slanderous tongues. She declared that the Abbot was "as great and perfect a servant of God as there has been in these parts for a very long time," and that they ought to reverence and assist him in his work. "You complain every day that the priests and other ecclesiastics are not corrected, and now, when you find those who would fain correct them, you prevent it and raise complaints." As to the accusations against her and her company, they ought to turn a deaf ear to them. "We have sought and are continually seeking the salvation of your souls and bodies, not heeding any labour, but offering sweet and loving desires to God, with abundance of tears and sighs, to prevent the divine judgments falling upon you which we deserve for our iniquities. I have not enough virtue to do aught but what is imperfect; but the others, who are perfect and attend only to the honour of God and the salvation of souls, are those who do it. But neither the ingratitude nor the churlishness of my fellow-citizens shall prevent me labouring even to death for your salvation. We shall learn from that sweet Paul, who says: *Being reviled, we bless; being persecuted, we suffer it*; we shall follow his rule. The truth shall be what will set us free. I love you more than you love yourselves; and I love your pacific state and your freedom, even as you do. So do not believe that anything against it is being done, either by me or by any other of my company. We are put to sow the word

Cecca, Lisa, and Alessa, "Sienese widows, sisters of penance of the Blessed Dominic." Cf. Tommaso Caffarini, *Tractatus super informatione*, etc., p. 13.

of God and to gather the fruit of souls. Every one is bound to be keen for his own art; this is the art that God has given us; we must, therefore, exercise it and not bury our talent, for then we should be worthy of a great rebuke, but employ it at every time and in every place and on every creature. For God is no respecter of places or of creatures, but accepts holy and true desires. I came for nought else save to eat and taste souls, and draw them from the hands of the devils. For this I would lay down my life, if I had a thousand, and for this reason I shall go and stay according as the Holy Spirit shall direct."[1]

The murmuring continued while she was at Montepulciano and the Rocca. Madonna Rabe Tolomei, misliking that her son, Fra Matteo, should be lingering with Catherine among the hereditary enemies of her house, wrote that her daughter Francesca was very ill, and that Matteo must come instantly to her, on pain of her curse.[2] Others declared that Catherine and Raimondo were plotting with the Salimbeni against the State, and so wrought upon the Defenders that they despatched Tommaso di Guelfaccio with a letter ordering them to return to Siena, where there was some more important peace to be effected by her means. In her answer, a long and eloquent letter, Catherine rebukes their self-love and cowardly fear that leads them to mistrust those who are labouring indefatigably for their welfare and the peace of the State, at the same time craving pardon for her presumption in thus addressing them, and promising to obey their summons as soon as she can.[3] To Salvi di Pietro, a goldsmith in Siena who had weight with the government, she wrote that, in spite of the murmurs and suspicions that had arisen against her and Fra Raimondo, God had bidden her stay until her work was accomplished, and that she rejoiced in being thus persecuted. "Whether the demon likes it or not, I shall continue to exercise my life in the honour of God and the salvation of souls, for the entire world and particularly for my native city. The citizens of Siena do a most shameful thing in

[1] Letter 121 (201). [2] Letter 120 (344).
[3] Letter 123 (202).

believing or imagining that we are engaged in weaving plots in the lands of the Salimbeni, or in any other place in the world. We are only plotting to defeat the devil, and to deprive him of the lordship that he has assumed over man by mortal sin, and to take hate from man's heart and pacify him with Christ crucified and with his neighbour. These are the plots that we are weaving, and that I wish to be woven by whoever is with me. I am sorry for our negligence, whereby we do this only in lukewarm fashion. And therefore I pray thee, sweet son, and do thou pray all the others, to pray to God that I may be more zealous in doing this and every holy work for His honour and the salvation of souls. Poor calumniated Fra Raimondo begs you to pray to God for him, that he may be good and patient."[1]

Catherine was now, to her great sorrow, compelled to sever herself from her *poverello calunniato.* She sent Raimondo from the Rocca to the Pope: "with certain proposals," he says, "which would have been good for the holy Church of God, if they had been understood;" and, at Rome, the General of the order compelled him to resume the office of prior of the Minerva, which he had already held under Urban V, whereby he was unable to return to Catherine. And, indeed, save for a few weeks, she was never again to be united, save in spirit, with her "most beloved and most dear father and son in Christ Jesus, given me by that sweet Mother Mary." For three years, his spiritual ministrations had been of the utmost consolation to her; she could confide in him as in no other of her confessors; and the parting was most bitter to her, although no word of complaint passed her lips.

The anonymous author of the *Miracoli* tells us of a certain man, a friar apparently, whom he does not name, who had sought Catherine's friendship and wondered at her holy life, but whose devotion towards her changed into carnal love; until at last, "when she never showed him any other semblance than what was pure and holy," his passion so maddened him that he attempted to take her life in church. "A few days afterwards,

[1] Letter 122 (304).

this religious left his order, threw aside the habit, and returned to his house in a village some way from Siena, and there he lived half desperate. And she, when she knew that he had gone away, prayed God for him that He would have mercy upon his soul. But at last this man, persevering in his despair, hanged himself by the neck."[1] One of Catherine's letters is directed to a religious who had left his order, a sweet and most loving letter throughout, ending: "If I were near at hand, I would know what demon has stolen away my little sheep, and what is the bond that keeps him bound, so that he does not return to the flock with the others. But I will strive to see it by means of continual prayer, and with this knife to cut the bond that holds him; and then will my soul be happy."[2] But this is probably another man.

Among the correspondence of Catherine's disciples, we find two piteous letters addressed at this time to Neri di Landoccio at the Rocca. In one, the writer, in answer to an affectionate message conveyed to him by Gabriele Piccolomini, wonders that Neri remembers him, now that he has become "a vessel of contumely," and is ashamed to write to any servant or friend of God. "I was once thy very dear brother," he says in the other, "but now, for a long time, I have found myself dismissed and cancelled from the book in which I felt myself so sweetly fed. Do not wonder if I have not written to thee, or if I write to thee no more, until I return to gather the fruit of true obedience, of patience, and true humility. But I have so long wandered from the true way, that I almost judge it impossible for me ever to find or taste that food, or to reach a place of repose. And this has happened to me because I have kept the eye of my understanding closed with darkness, and driven the light away from

[1] See Grottanelli, notes to the *Leggenda minore*, pp. 354, 355, and cf. the different story in the *Legenda*, III. vi. 14 (§ 408).

[2] Letter 173 (134). An almost contemporary Latin version of a portion of this is in the Vatican, *Cod. Vat. Lat.* 939. Cf. Letter 192 (275), where Catherine assures Neri di Landoccio, who was always in dread about his own final perseverance, "that God will not permit in thee what He permitted in that other."

my soul. I have no more hunger or appetite for what is good." The first is signed "F. S."; but, at the end of the second letter, he says: "I do not put my name here, because I know not if I still have a name."

It has frequently been supposed that the author of these two letters was the unhappy man mentioned above; but an examination of the original manuscript, and a comparison with the authentic text of one of Catherine's own letters, make it quite certain that they were written by Fra Simone da Cortona, in one of that young friar's chronic fits of depression and spiritual misery.[1] Indeed, Catherine's letter to Simone is manifestly in answer to what he had written to Neri. Addressing him as "Dearest son *without a name* in Christ sweet Jesus," she exhorts him to fight, "like a virile knight," against all obstacles and temptations, the battle in which we cannot win the victory "unless the light of most holy faith is in us; and we cannot have this light, unless the earth of all terrene affection is drawn out from the eye of our understanding, and the cloud of self-love is cast away; for it is that perverse cloud which utterly takes from us every light, spiritually and temporally." She urges him, in all his troubles, to trust in the love of God, who permits these things for love of us—though sometimes we cannot see it. Through lack of light, because self-love has covered up the pupil of the eye of faith, "we believe ourselves to be cast off by God, and, because of this, we come to a confusion of mind, whereby we leave off doing our work, as though we think we are not accepted by God, and we come to weariness, and are insupportable to ourselves." But in the blood of Christ we shall learn that God does not let us be tried beyond our endurance. Let him embrace the Cross, and not abandon his prayers and spiritual exercises, but, without negligence or confusion, serve God and obey the rules of his order, and find the holy desire of the honour of God and the salvation of souls in

[1] They are contained in the MS. of the Biblioteca Comunale of Siena, T. iii. 3, and printed by Grottanelli in the *Lettere dei discepoli*, 7 and 8.

the blood of Christ crucified : "And I tell you that then you will have your name, and I shall find my son again."[1]

In the meanwhile, after an ineffectual attempt on the part of Piero Gambacorti, at the beginning of March, to mediate between the Florentines and the Pope, the war had continued. In April, Hawkwood, with his whole company of English, passed over to the side of the league ; but this was counterbalanced by the defection of Rodolfo Varano, a few months later, who, when the Florentines refused to let him keep Fabriano for himself, threw up his command and entered the service of the Church. After some wavering, the Bolognese finally submitted to the Pope in May.[2] Francesco di Vico similarly left the league, and made peace on his own account with the Church. Foiled in an attempt to recover Talamone by force of arms, the Sienese avenged themselves by wasting the territory of the Count of Nola, upon which the Cardinal of Geneva sent a portion of his Bretons to attack Grosseto and ravage the Sienese Maremma. These dreaded mercenaries had shown themselves of little use in the open field, and, at the end of September, they were routed by Hawkwood, whom the Florentines had despatched to the aid of their allies.

Trincio de' Trinci, Lord of Foligno and Gonfaloniere of the Church, the son-in-law of the Marquis of Ferrara (whose daughter, Jacoma d' Este, he had married), was vigorously carrying on hostilities in Umbria against the adherents of the league, and kept harrying the Perugians with the ecclesiastical forces. Trincio and his brother Corrado were ferocious despots of the usual mediaeval type, but Catherine felt a special solicitude for them as the brothers of her beloved Madonna

[1] Letter 58 (86), but none of the printed editions (save the Bolognese of 1492) has the true opening of the letter, which connects it with what Simone had written : *Carissimo figliuolo senza nome in Cristo dolce Gesù :* as in the MS. 102 of the Biblioteca Nazionale V. E. of Rome.

[2] Cf. Catherine's rather vague letter, 268 (200), to the Anziani and Consuls and Gonfalonieri of Bologna, which seems to have been written in this year. The Bolognese, while acknowledging the papal sovereignty, retained their republican liberties.

Biancina Salimbeni. On September 14, the feast of the Exaltation of the Cross, she addressed a long letter to the two, on the love of God, shown above all in the mystery of the Redemption by the Crucifixion, concealed only from the eyes of the lovers of self, who are absorbed in the things of the world, or plunged into the mire of sensuality. While congratulating them on their fidelity to the Church, she urges them to a complete amendment of life.[1] Trincio had already received a similar admonition from the Franciscan tertiary and prophet, Tommaso Unzio, whom he had threatened to burn alive, and who had warned him that he would live as long as the great bell of the Commune remained intact. He was apparently sincerely moved, but had little time for amendment. At the approach of Count Lucio di Lando, one of the condottieri of the league, who was leading a Florentine force against Camerino, the enemies of the Trinci rose; and, on September 28, as the great bell cracked when it sounded the signal to the conspirators, they broke into Trincio's palace, stabbed him to death, and hurled the still quivering body down from the balcony into the piazza below, where it remained for some days unburied. Corrado was at Anagni when this happened. He hurried to Spoleto to await his chance, and thence, on December 6, at the invitation of the people, entered Foligno. There was a general massacre of the enemies of the Trinci, and Corrado was declared lord of the city.

"Keep close to Christ crucified," Catherine had written to the widowed Jacoma d' Este, when the news of Trincio's death reached her, "and begin to serve Him with all your heart and with all your soul; and bear with true patience the holy trial that He has laid upon you, not for hate, but for the love He bore to the salvation of his soul, upon which He had such mercy that He permitted him to die in the service of Holy Church. God, who loved him with a special love, wishing to ensure his

[1] Letter 253 (194). For the ingratitude of the Pope and the alleged treachery of the Cardinal of Geneva (to which Catherine distantly refers in the letter), cf. the *Anonimo Fiorentino*, pp. 337, 338, and Manni's *Cronichetta d' Incerto*, p. 213.

salvation, allowed him to be brought to this fate which was sweet for his soul. And you should be the lover of his soul rather than of his body; for the body is mortal and a finite thing, but the soul is immortal and infinite. The supreme Providence has provided for his salvation, while it gives you these sorrows to bear in order to have something for which to reward you in eternal life. I promise you, dearest sister, that, if you do so, God will even put you back into your temporal house, and you will ultimately return to your native land, Jerusalem, the vision of peace."[1]

There were further negotiations for peace during the summer, which failed because of the excessive demands made by the Pope. After four months at Anagni, whither Gregory had gone at the end of May, the Florentine ambassadors returned and described the situation as hopeless. On the morning of October 6 (1377), the Signoria summoned a parliament, a general council of all the citizens to meet in the Palazzo Vecchio, to hear the report of the ambassadors. They found the whole assembly unanimous in declaring that the Pope's terms must be rejected and the war continued at all costs. Ristoro Canigiani, Catherine's zealous disciple, who spoke in the name of the College of the Ten of Liberty, was as emphatic as Donato Barbadori himself, who was the speaker of the College of the Gonfalonieri. It was decided that the war should be carried on until a better peace could be obtained, that the interdict should be disregarded, and Mass said again throughout Florence and the contado. The clergy who had left the dominions of the Republic were ordered to return under the heaviest penalties, and all citizens bidden attend Mass, under pain of denunciation, no excuses being accepted. The Eight were confirmed in office for another year, and a new magistracy of ten appointed to levy fresh taxes upon the priests and religious,

[1] Letter 264 (324). Cf. St. Antoninus, III. pp. 385, 386; Durante Dorio, *Istoria della famiglia Trinci* (Foligno, 1638), pp. 165–174; Pellini, I. pp. 1188–1190. Corrado ruled Foligno until 1386, when he died childless, and Ugolino, the son of Trincio and Jacoma, succeeded him, added Montefalco to his dominions, and in 1392 received investiture as papal vicar from Boniface IX.

and to compel citizens to buy the goods of the churches. The defiance of the interdict was solemnly carried out on October 18. The Madonna of the Impruneta was brought into Florence and carried in procession, with the head of St. Zanobius, to the Piazza della Signoria, where Mass was sung at an altar set up on a platform, and one of the Augustinian friars of Santo Spirito preached an impassioned sermon to the crowd from the ringhiera of the palace.[1]

Gregory had, in fact, put himself into an impossible position. He had still further alienated the Sienese by imprisoning the ambassadors they had sent to him at Anagni. He had squandered the moneys of the Church upon the mercenaries, who were daily deserting his banners. We find him piteously writing to Queen Giovanna, on October 12, that, considering the great aid he has had from her, it is very grievous to him to burden her more, but Christ is his witness that he knows not to whom to have recourse save her.[2] On October 29, Bartolommeo di Smeduccio, with Count Lucio di Lando and Francesco da Matelica, utterly routed Rodolfo Varano, who had been reinforced by Bretons from the Pope, and pressed the pursuit up to the walls of Camerino. Several hundreds were killed, a thousand taken prisoners, and the captured banners brought in triumph to Florence and dragged through the streets.

Like other weak men in a similar position, Gregory seems to have vented his anger upon those who would not offer any resistance. Whatever those proposals were, "useful for the Church, if they had been understood," which Fra Raimondo brought with him from Catherine to the Pope, the latter would not accept them. He was exceedingly angry with Catherine, who, he apparently thought, ought to have gone to Florence or come to Rome, instead of labouring for souls in the Sienese contado, or, at least, to have done something that she had not done; and Raimondo, especially during the Pope's absence at Anagni, found himself looked upon with much suspicion and disfavour. "Take

[1] *Anonimo Fiorentino*, pp. 339–341; *Cronichetta d' Incerto*, pp. 212, 213.

[2] Brief of October 12, 1377. Pastor, *Acta Inedita*, doc. 2.

comfort," wrote Catherine to him ; "God has provided for you, and will provide, and His providence will not fail you. In all things have recourse to Mary, embracing the holy Cross ; do not let yourself ever fall into confusion of mind, but sail over the tempestuous sea in the bark of the Divine Mercy." For her part, she humbly confesses that the Pope is right if he complains of her negligence, and promises to obey his commands more fully for the future. May God give His vicar grace to throw himself like a lamb into the midst of the wolves, setting aside and putting away from himself the care of temporal things, to attend only to spiritual. "If he does this (which the Divine Goodness demands of him), the lamb will lord it over the wolves, and the wolves will become lambs ; and thus shall we see the glory and praise of God, the welfare and peace of Holy Church. In no other way can it be done ; not with war, but with peace and benignity, and with that holy spiritual punishment that a father should give to his son when he does wrong."

Then, suddenly, Catherine turns to address the Pope directly. "Alas, alas, alas! most holy Father, would that you had done this the first day that you came to your own place ! I hope in the goodness of God and in your Holiness that you will do what is not done, and in this way both temporal and spiritual things will be gained back. This is what God bade you do (as you know that you were told), to bring about the reformation of the Church by punishing what was wrong and planting virtuous pastors, and that you should seize a holy peace with your undutiful children, in the best way and the one most pleasing to God that could be found ; so that you could then begin to restore, by lifting up the banner of the most holy Cross against the infidels. I believe that our negligence and not doing what can be done, not with cruelty nor with war, but with peace and kindness (always punishing those who have sinned, not according to their deserts, but according to what they can bear), are, perhaps, the cause of such great ruin and loss and irreverence towards Holy Church and her ministers having come upon us, as now is. And I fear lest, unless the remedy is applied of doing what has not been done, our sins may merit so much that we shall see worse disasters come; such, I mean, that would distress us more than the loss of temporal things. Of all these evils and of your sorrows, I, wretched woman, am the cause, through my little virtue and through my great disobedience. Most holy Father, mitigate your anger against me with the light of reason and with truth—not for my punishment, but for your anger.[1] To whom shall I have recourse, if you abandon me? Who would succour me? To whom can I fly, if you drive me away? The persecutors are persecuting me, and I fly to you and to the other sons and servants of God. And if you abandon me, conceiving displeasure and indignation against me, I will hide myself in the wounds of Christ crucified, whose vicar you are; and I know that He will receive me, because He wills not the death of the sinner. And if I am received by Him, you will not drive me away; nay, we shall stay in our place to fight manfully with the arms of virtue for the sweet Spouse of Christ. In her am I fain to end my life, with tears, with sweat, and with sighs, and to give my blood and the marrow of my bones. And if all the world should drive me away, I will not care, for I shall find rest, with weeping and with bearing much, on the breast of that sweet Spouse. Pardon me, most holy Father, for all my ignorance and for the offence I have committed against God and against your Holiness. Let the truth excuse me and set me free: Truth eternal. I humbly ask your blessing."[2]

Raimondo had had no opportunity of seeing the Pope in person until the latter's return to Rome, on November 7. He then appears to have satisfied him concerning Catherine's conduct, as we find her declaring herself consoled by letters she had received from the "dolce babbo" and himself.[3] She seems to have passed this Advent at the Rocca, much afflicted in body

[1] That is, "punish me as much as you will, but do not be unreasonably angry." I adopt the reading *miticate col lume*, as in Aldo and Toresano, instead of the *mirate* of Gigli and Tommaseo.

[2] Letter 267 (91).

[3] Letter 272 (90).

and mind, but exulting in the new gift of writing which she believed she had miraculously acquired. "Thou hast written to me," she writes to Alessa, "that it seemed that God was compelling thee to offer up prayers to Him for me. Thanks be to the Divine Goodness which shows such ineffable love to my miserable soul. Thou tellest me to write thee if I am suffering, and if I have my usual infirmities at this time; to which I answer that God has provided wondrously, within and without. In the body He has done much for me this Advent, making me relieve my sufferings by writing; and it is true that, through His goodness, they have been worse than they used to be. I wish suffering to be my food, tears my drink, sweat my ointment. I wish suffering to make me fat, suffering to heal me, suffering to give me light, suffering to give me wisdom, suffering to clothe my nakedness, suffering to strip me of all love of self, spiritual and temporal. What I have suffered in being deprived of the consolations of all creatures has made me know my lack of virtue and my own imperfection, and the most perfect light of the sweet Truth, who provides and accepts holy desires and not creatures; He has not withdrawn His goodness from me because of my ingratitude, my little light and knowledge; but He has only looked upon Himself, who is supremely good. I beseech thee, by the love of Jesus Christ crucified, most beloved daughter mine, not to slacken prayer; nay, redouble it, for I have greater need of it than thou seest; and to thank the goodness of God for me. And pray to Him that He may give me grace to give my life for Him."[1]

About the beginning of the new year, 1378, Catherine seems to have returned to Siena. But her stay there was again of brief duration. Hardly had she arrived when she received a papal command, through Fra Raimondo, to go at once to Florence.

[1] Letter 119 (178). For her learning to write at this time, see below, chapter xvi.

CHAPTER XI

CATHERINE'S LAST EMBASSY TO FLORENCE

"Non fu adempito il desiderio mio di dare la vita per la verità, e per la dolce Sposa di Cristo. Ma lo Sposo eterno mi fece una grande beffa. Onde io ho da piangere, perocchè tanta è stata la moltitudine delle mie iniquitadi, che io non meritai che il sangue mio desse vita, nè alluminasse le menti accecate, nè pacificasse il figliuolo col padre, nè murasse una pietra col sangue mio nel corpo mistico della santa Chiesa."—St. Catherine, Letter 295 (96).

In spite of the rupture of the negotiations in October and the violation of the interdict at Florence, neither party had entirely abandoned the hope of a compromise. The financial position of the Florentines was little better than that of the Church, and their unity was more apparent than real. Before Fra Raimondo left Tuscany, Niccolò Soderini had come to Siena and assured him that the majority of the Florentines sincerely desired peace, but were being prevented by the action of the minority who held the government. The remedy he suggested was that the religious citizens should make common cause with the captains of the Parte Guelfa, and deprive these few of their offices, as enemies to the public good, the "admonishing" of four or six of such persons being in his opinion sufficient.[1] The friar repeated this conversation to the Pope, but without any immediate result.

Simultaneously with the Pope's return to Rome from Anagni, Friar John of Basle, an Augustinian hermit, came to Florence. In spite of the resolution previously taken not to discuss peace until Gregory had revoked all his processes, he was allowed to confer with the Eight, to whom he proposed that the Florentines should choose Piombino or Viterbo or Pisa, as a place for a general congress to be assembled.[2] The Pope's desperation at this time is vividly pictured in a brief to his

[1] *Legenda*, III. vi. 28 (§ 422).

[2] Gherardi, preface to the *Anonimo Fiorentino*, p. 237.

nuncio at Naples. No tongue nor pen, he declares, can adequately express his urgent needs; the provinces are in anarchy, the mercenaries are clamouring for pay, he is tormented inwardly more than it is fitting to write, and Queen Giovanna herself seems beginning to favour the enemies of the Church.[1] His counsels had been further weakened by the loss of the loyal and strenuous Cardinal Pierre d'Estaing, who died in November. At the beginning of the new year, 1378, Gregory took the extreme step of appealing to Bernabo Visconti, and sent the Bishop of Urbino to propose their own ally to the Florentines as arbitrator. He resolved simultaneously to win over the Parte Guelfa to his side, by means of Catherine. "It has been written to me," he said to Fra Raimondo, "that, if Catherine of Siena goes to Florence, I shall have peace." The friar answered that they were all ready, in obedience to his Holiness, to encounter martyrdom. "I do not wish you to go," replied the Pope, "because they would maltreat you; but I do not believe that they will harm Catherine, for she is a woman and they hold her in reverence."[2] At the Pope's bidding, Raimondo at once drew up the necessary bulls and credentials, and despatched them to Catherine, who, "like a daughter of true obedience," instantly started for Florence.

The exact date is uncertain, but it was at least not later than the beginning of March, 1378, that Catherine thus, for the third time, found herself within the walls of Florence. It is clear that her mission on behalf of the Pope was less to the Commune or People as a whole, than to the Parte Guelfa. Following the hint that Niccolò Soderini had given Fra Raimondo, she was to use her moral influence in support of the measures adopted by the captains of the Party to prevent the extreme spirits on the opposite side from interrupting the peace negotiations, that had already begun, and to ensure that this time the Republic should seek peace with deeds no less than

[1] Brief to Pietro Raffini, dated Rome, December 26, 1377. Pastor, *Geschichte*, I. doc. 8.

[2] *Legenda*, III. vi. 29 (§ 423).

words. To avoid attracting notice and exciting anti-clerical feelings, none of her friars or priests, excepting Fra Santi, came with her. Besides Lisa and Giovanna di Capo, her only other companions appear to have been Neri and Stefano. When the last-named, in April or May, was obliged to return to Siena in obedience to his parents, his place was taken by Cristofano Guidini.[1]

This is one of the few episodes in Catherine's life concerning which we have external contemporary (and, for once, hostile) evidence. "In this year," writes Marchionne Stefani, under 1377 (the Florentines, it will be remembered, began their new year on March 25), "it happened that there was in Florence a woman named Catherine, the daughter of Jacopo Benincasa, who, being held of most holy, pure, and good and chaste life, began to blame the opponents of the Church. Those who managed the Party welcomed her right gladly; and among the others the chiefs in this affair were Niccolò Soderini, who had made a room for her in his house, in which she had sometimes stayed, Stoldo di Messer Bindo Altoviti, and Piero Canigiani; these were those who praised her to the skies. And it is true that she knew ecclesiastical matters, both by her natural talents and by what she had acquired, and she spoke and wrote very well. Piero Canigiani, too, was having a habitation built for her up at the foot of San Giorgio, and was collecting money from all his faction, men and women, buying stone and wood, and bringing it up there. Either maliciously by her own will, or introduced by the instigation of these men, she was brought many times to the meetings of the Party, to declare that it was right to admonish, in order that they might take measures to stop the war. By those of the Party she was reputed a prophetess, and by the others a hypocrite and a bad woman; and many things were said of her, by some for treachery, and

[1] Cf. Letter 298 (254), and the letter from Stefano, dated Siena, May 22 1378, to Neri di Landoccio, "Florentie apud sanctum Georgium," in *Lettere dei discepoli*, 9.

by others because they thought to speak well by speaking evil of her."[1]

As soon as Catherine arrived, she began to urge upon the principal citizens the need of making peace with the Pope. Niccolò Soderini brought her to speak with the officials of the Parte Guelfa, to whom she declared that it was absolutely right to deprive of their office those who were attempting to prolong the war, as such men were not rulers, but destroyers of the city. Among the captains of the Party who held office from March 20 to May 20 of this year were Stoldo Altoviti, Ristoro Canigiani, Tommaso Soderini, Alessandro Buondelmonti, and Benedetto Peruzzi. They readily agreed to put all possible pressure upon the Signoria to work for peace, "not only with words, but with deeds." Unfortunately, they needed no instigation from her to "admonish" citizens whom they professed to consider obnoxious. The complaint had already been raised that it was less dangerous in Florence to blaspheme God than to blaspheme the captains of the Party. The more violent of their adherents seized the first opportunity for each to admonish his private enemy as a Ghibelline, "even if he were more Guelf than Charlemagne."[2]

Among the Florentines who at this time became Catherine's disciples, two need special notice: Barduccio di Piero Canigiani and Giannozzo di Benci Sacchetti. Barduccio, whom we have already mentioned as one of the "adopted sons" of Giovanni dalle Celle, was a consumptive youth, who now clung to Catherine heart and soul, entered her spiritual family as one of her secretaries, and never again left her. "He was young in years," writes Fra Raimondo, "but old in life; by birth of the city of flowers, but adorned with all the flowers of virtue. The sacred virgin loved him, it seemed to me, more tenderly than the

[1] Lib. IX. rubr. 773. Marchionne's statement, about Canigiani afterwards adopting the subscriptions for his own use, is obviously a partisan falsehood. After Catherine's death, even this adherent of the Eight practically acknowledges her sanctity. *Ibid.*, Lib. XI. rubr. 866.

[2] *Ibid.*, Lib. IX. rubr. 767, 788.

others, and this, I think, was because of his great purity of disposition."[1] Giannozzo, the brother of Franco Sacchetti, was a converted spendthrift and wastrel; a poet of no mean order in the vernacular, whose *laudi* were being sung by the people in their processions, when deprived of the sacrifice of the Mass by the papal interdict. One of these compositions, *O divina carità*, reads like a rendering into verse of a letter of Catherine's own; another, beginning *Maria dolce che fai*, frequently attributed to others, is a classic of its kind.[2] He had been one of those young men who had joined the confraternities that met at Fiesole at the beginning of the interdict; and, although Marchionne Stefani denounces him (in the light of later events) as "a man of evil sort and a hypocrite," there can be no doubt of the sincerity of his conversion. Unfortunately, he continued to fish in the troubled waters of political intrigue, and at the same time to assail his political opponents with poetical lampoons, and his subsequent fate was one of the many tragedies that saddened Catherine's life.

In the meanwhile, Sarzana had been chosen as the place of the peace conference, under the presidency of Bernabo Visconti. The Pope was represented by Jean de la Grange, the Benedictine Cardinal of Amiens, and two other French prelates of the Curia. Venice, France, Naples, and the adherents of the league sent ambassadors; Otho of Brunswick attended in person. The Florentine procurators—Pazzino Strozzi, Alessandro dell' Antella, and Benedetto Alberti, with two of the Eight, Andrea Salviati and Simone Peruzzi—had started on March 3. All seemed going well. On March 20, Strozzi, Alessandro dell' Antella, and Andrea Salviati, came back to Florence to confer with the Signoria, returning to the Cardinal and Bernabo on the 22nd.[3] The delegates had already agreed on the amount

[1] *Legenda*, III. i. 11 (§ 341).

[2] Cf. F. Palermo, *Rime di Dante Alighieri e di Giannozzo Sacchetti*, pp. ciii.–cxxx.; Marchionne Stefani, Lib. X. rubr. 821; O. Gigli, *Sermoni Evangelici e Lettere di Franco Sacchetti*, doc. 1.

[3] *Anonimo Fiorentino*, p. 351.

of the indemnity (less than half what the Pope had originally demanded), and were on the point of coming to terms on the other conditions.

On the evening of March 27, two hours after sunset, there came a knocking at the Porta San Frediano, and a cry: *Open quickly to the messenger of peace.* The guards drew back the bolts, but saw no one. But the cry spread through the city: *The olive has come, the peace is made.* Men rushed from their houses repeating it, carrying torches, and began to illuminate the city. The priors, having no tidings, issued a proclamation bidding every one go quietly home, and not leave his house again till the morning. A few days later, the news reached Florence that Pope Gregory had died at that very hour.[1] Men said that it was the Angel of God that had come; but was it not rather the Pontiff's own unquiet ghost, seeking a reconciliation with the city that he had cast out of the bosom of the Church?

For the first time for seventy-four years, a new Pope was elected in the Vatican, on April 8. Couriers rode into Florence with the news that the Roman cardinal, Francesco Tebaldeschi, had been raised to the papacy.[2] Quickly followed the official notification that not Tebaldeschi, but "the Lord Bartolommeo of Bari" had been made Sovereign Pontiff, and had taken the title of Urban VI. What this meant, and what had happened, will be seen presently.

On the news of Gregory's death, the papal representatives left Sarzana, the peace negotiations having thus come to an end without result. In May, the Florentines sent eight ambassadors, two from each quarter of the city, to honour the new Pope Urban. Four of these envoys, Donato Barbadori, Alessandro dell' Antella, Pazzino Strozzi, and Stoldo Altoviti, together with Filippo Corsini (the brother of the Cardinal of Florence), were further named as procurators of the Republic to conclude peace with the Holy See.

[1] *Anonimo Fiorentino*, p. 352; Manni's *Cronichetta d' Incerto*, p. 215; *Historia Sozomeni Pistoriensis* (*Rer. It. Script.*, xvi.), col. 1104.

[2] *Cronaca di Ser Nofri*, Corazzini, *I Ciompi*, p. 7.

Rumours of strange movements in Rome and in the Sacred College had doubtless already reached Catherine from Raimondo, who represented Pedro de Luna as the chief factor in the election of Urban VI. Since the death of Pierre d'Estaing, the Cardinal of Aragon had become Catherine's chief hope among the great prelates of the Curia. To him the Saint now wrote, "with desire of seeing you a sweet lover of the truth which sets us free," giving him a pitiful picture of the spiritual state of Florence under the violated interdict; where "the religious and secular clergy, and especially the mendicant friars, who have been put by the sweet Spouse of Christ to announce and proclaim the truth, forget that truth and deny it from the pulpit. Not only have they broken the interdict, but they advise the others to celebrate with a good conscience, and the laity to attend, and they say that whoso does not do this commits a sin. They have plunged the people into such great heresy that it is pitiful even to think of it, not only to behold it. And they are led to do and speak thus by the servile fear of men and human pleasure, and by the desire of offerings." "I would have you enamoured of the truth, sweet father mine; and, in order that the holy beginning that you made (when, knowing that the Spouse of Christ had need of a good and holy pastor, you exposed yourself fearlessly to everything for this) may come to effect with perseverance, I beseech you to keep close to Christ on earth, and sound this truth continually into his ears; so that he may reform his Spouse in the truth. With a manful heart, bid him reform her with holy and good pastors, in reality and in truth, not only in the sound of words. Let him then, for the love of Christ crucified, with severity and with sweetness, root out vices and plant virtues, according to his power. And may it please him to pacify Italy, so that afterwards, in a goodly company, we may uplift the banner of the Cross, and make a sacrifice of ourselves to God for love of the truth."[1]

[1] I follow the text of the Palatine MS. 56, as the printed editions of this letter (Gigli, 25; Tommaseo, 284) are corrupt. Catherine's denunciation of the mendicant friars is interesting, as showing that the Franciscans, or, at least, some of them, took the popular side, even against the Pope.

The violation of the interdict had, from the outset, been repugnant to the religious instincts of the majority of the Florentines, and, now that Gregory was dead, Catherine persuaded the Signoria to propitiate his successor by revoking their decree for the compulsory celebration of the offices of the Church. "It seems to me that the first streaks of dawn are beginning to come," she wrote to William Flete, "for our Saviour has illumined this people so that they are delivered from the perverse darkness of the offence they committed by having Mass celebrated by force. Now, by the divine grace, they are observing the interdict and beginning to be obedient to their father." [1] And she wrote at the same time, in a similar strain, to Alessa, who had not accompanied her to Florence: "Have special prayers offered in the monasteries, and tell our prioress to bid all her daughters make special prayer for peace, so that God may have mercy upon us, and that I may not return without it; and for me, her wretched daughter, that God may give me grace to be always a lover and proclaimer of the truth, and to die for that truth." [2]

But, in Florence itself, the dissensions were growing daily more intense, and a complete rupture between the Parte Guelfa and the Signoria seemed imminent. As the prospects of peace drew near, the power of the adherents of the Eight decreased, and the captains of the Party waxed more arrogant and vigorous in their admonitions. And in the background, scarcely heard or heeded by either faction, were sounding the ominous rumblings of a coming storm; the artisans and unemployed of the lowest orders, the *Ciompi*, were exchanging fierce and secret oaths, preparing the general uprising that was to overwhelm the whole city a few weeks later.

The Parte Guelfa was guided by a small group of fanatical and overbearing partisans, among whom Lapo da Castiglionchio, Bettino Ricasoli, and Piero degli Albizzi were the most prominent; they swayed the voting at the meetings where it was decided to admonish such or such individuals; and the sentences which the captains, at their instigation, pronounced were published by night:

[1] Letter 227 (126). [2] Letter 277 (181).

"either to avoid tumult, or to increase the alarm by assuming the appearance of a secret tribunal."[1] Even men of such high character as Ristoro Canigiani and Stoldo Altoviti pursued the same policy. From the outset, Catherine had fallen into the hands of this faction, which by tradition claimed to be that of the Church, and it is clear that its more unscrupulous members were simply making her a tool for their private ends, dragging her name into their campaign of excluding their own personal enemies from office. Niccolò Soderini's well-meant suggestion to Fra Raimondo, and Catherine's own unfortunate speech to the officials of the Party, were, indeed, bearing bitter fruit. It was in vain that she sent Stefano Maconi to individual members to plead for moderation, in vain that she herself implored them not to pervert the means of securing peace to a cause of civil war, in thus giving vent to their own hates. The number of those who, during these months that Catherine was in Florence and Ristoro Canigiani held office as one of the captains of the Party, found themselves excluded from office, without explanation or appeal, was daily increasing. All through March and April the work went on. At length, on April 22, the captains took the extreme step of admonishing Giovanni Dini, the powerful member of the Eight, and, on April 30, among seven other prominent citizens, they admonished Piero Donati, who had been drawn as one of the priors, and Maso di Neri, who was one of the Twelve.[2] This brought things to a crisis.

In the new Signoria that came into office on May 1, 1378, Salvestro de' Medici—a strong Guelf, but intensely obnoxious to the Party—was Gonfaloniere of Justice. While openly declaring his intention of overthrowing the prepotency of the faction, he was ardently in favour of peace with the Church, and it was, perhaps, on his initiative that the ambassadors to Rome were empowered

[1] Capponi, *Storia della Repubblica di Firenze*, II. p. 2. Cf. Rodolico, *La Democrazia Fiorentina*, pp. 171–176.

[2] *Anonimo Fiorentino*, pp. 351–353; Ammirato, I. 2, pp. 713, 714; *Legenda*, III. vi. 30, 31 (§§ 424, 425), where Fra Raimondo seems to imply that Catherine approved the admonishing of Giovanni Dini.

to make terms. Not daring to admonish him, and relying upon the fact that five of his colleagues were their adherents, the captains of the Party offered to meet him half-way, by promising that in future no one should be admonished upon mere suspicion, unless he were really a Ghibelline, nor any name put to the ballot for admonishing more than three times. These pledges were flagrantly violated a few weeks later (Ristoro Canigiani, be it noted, being no longer in office), when Bettino Ricasoli, who was then *proposto* of the captains, wishing to admonish two of Salvestro's adherents, had the doors of the palace locked and the voting repeated twenty-two times until he had his will. The more violent spirits in the faction, led by Lapo da Castiglionchio, proposed to surprise the Palazzo Vecchio and reform the State in favour of their party. Piero degli Albizzi, however, induced them to postpone the execution of this treacherous plan until the feast of St. John, when the Signoria would go to see the palio run, the palace would be deserted, and the city would swarm with men from the contado. Then would be the time to bring out the old lily standard of the Guelfs, occupy the palace with arms, and raise the whole city to the cry of *Viva il Popolo e la Parte Guelfa.*

But they were anticipated. On June 18, Salvestro, being *proposto* of the Signoria for that day, assembled the Colleges and the Council of the People, the former in the Palazzo Vecchio, the latter in the adjoining palace of the Captain, and presented a petition to the Signoria, praying that all the provisions against the magnates of the city and contado, especially the Ordinances of Justice, should be renewed and enforced. It was vigorously opposed in the Colleges, and Buonaccorso di Lapo, speaking for the Twelve, denounced the proposal as altogether inopportune.[1] Salvestro then rushed down to the palace of the Captain, and appealed to the Council of the People against his colleagues. A furious tumult arose in the council chamber. A shoemaker, Benedetto di Carlone, laid violent hands on Carlo Strozzi: "Carlo, Carlo, the matter will go otherwise than thou thinkest,

[1] *Anonimo Fiorentino*, pp. 243, 504.

and your predominance must be utterly destroyed." Benedetto Alberti called from the window to the crowd in the piazza: "Shout, all of you, *Viva il Popolo!*"

The alarm spread through the city; all the shops were shut; the people began to arm. The captains of the Parte Guelfa and their adherents, nobles and *popolani* alike, had secretly armed, and were assembled in the palace of the Party to take measures against the Gonfaloniere. Among those present were Lapo da Castiglionchio, Piero degli Albizzi, Niccolò Soderini, the hated Bartolo Siminetti, and both Piero and Ristoro Canigiani. But, hearing the tumult, they quietly dispersed and returned to their own homes. Overborne by the clamour, the Colleges passed the measure; and, on the following day, but by a very narrow margin, it was approved by the requisite two-thirds in the Council of the People and the Council of the Commune.

For three days things hung thus in suspense, the city guarded at night, the shops closed, while the Signoria, the representatives of the Guilds, and the captains of the Party engaged in fruitless negotiations. On Tuesday, June 22, the "antevigil" of St. John, the Guilds rose in arms, and came with their banners into the piazza, shouting: *Viva il Popolo!* The Signoria empowered the magistrates and Colleges to reform the city and abolish the unpopular laws of the Parte Guelfa; but, in the meanwhile, led by the men of the Guild of the Furriers with their banner, the populace had begun to take vengeance on their own account. Instigated, if not actually by the government, at least by those who had been admonished, they assailed the houses of the leaders of the Parte Guelfa. The houses of Lapo da Castiglionchio and his family overlooking the Ponte Rubaconte were first attacked, Messer Lapo himself escaping into the Casentino disguised as a friar. The houses of Carlo Strozzi near the Porta Rossa, of Bartolo Siminetti in Mercato Nuovo, of the Albizzi near San Piero Maggiore, of Filippo Corsini, and others, were successively looted and given to the flames. Then the mob passed over the Arno, and, shouting abuse against "the hypocrite Niccolò and his blessed Catherine," destroyed the houses of Niccolò and Tommaso

Soderini near the Ponte alla Carraia. At the instigation of their neighbours, the Mannelli, who had been admonished while Ristoro was a captain of the Party, they next looted and burnt the houses of Piero and Ristoro Canigiani near S. Felicità. The house of Donato Barbadori, who had no share in the misdeeds of the Parte Guelfa and was absent on the service of the State, shared the same fate. A horde of roughs broke open the prisons and released the prisoners, invaded the monastery of the Angeli where many of the citizens had placed their goods for safety, and sacked it, killing two lay-brothers. This, however, was more than the instigators of the riot had bargained for, and, seeing the work of vengeance accomplished and the mob proceeding to fresh excesses, they prevailed upon the Signoria to send soldiers with orders to hang the first five looters taken in each quarter, choosing Flemings or other foreigners by preference, as a warning to the rest.[1] This was done, and the tumult abated.

But, in the meanwhile, for one brief, ineffable moment, Catherine had tasted in anticipation the longed-for joys of martyrdom—only to be bitterly disillusioned. A band of armed rioters, probably at the instigation of the more embittered victims of the Parte Guelfa, rushed from the sack of the houses of the Canigiani, declaring that they would burn her alive or cut her into pieces. She was apparently alone with Neri, Barduccio, and Cristofano, and with her women, in the little house on the hillside of San Giorgio. Those who kept the house, fearing for their own safety, bade her and her followers leave them: "But she, conscious of her own innocence and suffering gladly for the cause of Holy Church, was in no wise moved from her wonted constancy; nay, smiling and encouraging her companions, imitating her Divine Bridegroom, she went to a place where there was a garden; and there, after some words of exhortation to them, she gave herself to prayer." Soon the men broke in, brandishing their weapons, and shouting: "Where is Catherine?" She went to

[1] For this "Tumulto degli Ammoniti," cf. Marchionne Stefani, Lib. X. rubr. 792–795; Ammirato, I. 2, pp. 717–721; Gino Capponi (the elder), *Tumulto de' Ciompi*, pp. 234–242; *Anonimo Fiorentino*, pp. 358–360.

meet them, and, with radiant countenance, falling on her knees before their leader, said: "I am Catherine; do to me whatever God will permit, but I charge you, in the name of the Almighty, to hurt none of these who are with me." The ruffian hesitated, and then bade her go away. "Why should I fly," she answered, "when I have found what I desired? I offer myself a living sacrifice to my eternal Bridegroom. If you are sent to kill me, act boldly; I shall not move from here; but harm none of my companions." At this the whole band went away in confusion; but when her companions gathered round her, rejoicing that she had escaped their hands, she wept bitterly, saying that she had thought that God was about to grant her the red rose of martyrdom, but now saw that her sins had deprived her of it. "I tell you," she wrote to Fra Raimondo, "that to-day I wish to begin anew, in order that my sins may not draw me back from the great bliss of giving my life for Christ crucified."

"My desire was not fulfilled of giving my life for the truth and for the sweet Spouse of Christ. But the eternal Bridegroom played a great trick upon me, as Cristofano will tell you fully by word of mouth. Needs must I weep, because so great has been the multitude of my iniquities that I did not merit that my blood should give life, nor illumine the blinded minds, nor pacify the son with the father, nor to build up a stone with my blood in the mystical body of Holy Church. Nay, it seemed that the hands were bound of him who wished to do it. And when I said: *I am she; take me and let this family be*; my words were knives that straightway pierced his heart. O my father, do you, too, feel wondrous joy, because never have I experienced in myself such mysteries with so great joy. Here was the sweetness of truth; here was the gladness of an upright and pure conscience; here was tasted the time of the new martyrs, as you know, foretold by the eternal Truth. No tongue would suffice to tell the greatness of the bliss my soul feels. For this I think myself so bound to my Creator that, if I were to give my body to burn, it seems not to me that I could make adequate return for so great a grace as I and my beloved sons and daughters have received.

St. Catherine in ecstasy.

Domenico Beccafumi — Accademia Siena

All this I tell you, not that you may receive bitterness, but that you may feel ineffable delight with sweetest gladness ; and that you and I may begin to bewail my imperfection, since so great bliss was prevented by my sins. Now how blessed would my soul have been, if, for the most sweet Spouse and for love of the blood and for the salvation of souls, I had given my blood ! I will say no more about this matter : I leave this and other things to Cristofano to say ; I would only tell you to beseech Christ on earth not to postpone the peace because of what has happened, but to conclude it the more promptly, in order that he may then carry out the other great deeds that he has on hand for the honour of God and for the reformation of Holy Church. There has been no change because of this ; on the contrary, the city for the present is pacified, most fittingly. Tell him to have pity and compassion upon these souls, who are in great darkness ; and tell him to deliver me speedily from prison ; for, unless peace is made, it seems that I cannot get out ; and I would fain come then to Rome to taste the blood of the martyrs, and to visit his Holiness, and to find myself again with you to narrate the admirable mysteries that God has wrought in these times, with gladness of mind and with joy of heart, with increase of hope, with the light of most holy faith."[1]

This was probably written on the day of the tumult, immediately after the Signoria had, for the present, put down the rising with practically no loss of life, save of those who had been executed by the law. "But, albeit that tumult had for the time ceased," writes Raimondo, "the holy virgin and her fellowship were by no means safe ; nay, such great fear had come upon all the inhabitants of the city that, even as in the time of the martyrs, there was no one who would receive her into his house. Her spiritual sons and daughters advised her to return to the city of Siena ; but she answered them that she could not depart from

[1] Letter 295 (96) ; in the Harleian and Casanatense MSS. Raimondo's account of the affair, *Legenda*, III. vi. 32, 33 (§ § 426, 427), is clearly based upon what Cristofano told him, slightly coloured, perhaps, by an unconscious desire to make it resemble the scene in the Garden of Olives in the fourth Gospel.

the Florentine territory until the peace was announced between the father and his children, for so, she said, she had as a command from the Lord. When they heard this, not daring to contradict her, they found a good man, one that feared God, who without any dread received her into his house, but secretly, on account of the fury of the people and of wicked men."[1] This good man was almost certainly the tailor, Francesco di Pippino, in whose little house, in the Piazza del Grano, Catherine thus found shelter for a few days. Her potent friends, the Canigiani, the Soderini, the Altoviti, had fled or were in hiding. On the day after the tumult, June 23, the official vengeance of the government completed the violence of the mob. All the laws in favour of the Parte Guelfa were annulled, and all those admonished by the captains of the Party since 1357 were declared eligible for office under certain conditions. The ordinances excluding magnates from all offices and councils, excepting those of the Parte Guelfa and the Council of the Podestà and Commune, were confirmed. Lapo da Castiglionchio was declared a rebel and put under ban, and various lighter sentences passed upon the others. Carlo Strozzi was banished from Florence for five years, and he and his descendants declared magnates. Tommaso Soderini was deprived of every office for life; Niccolò Soderini was put under bounds at thirty miles from Florence. Ristoro Canigiani was declared a magnate, while Piero Canigiani was excluded from office for ten years.

Nevertheless, the whole city was full of alarm. There was no festa or palio on the feast of St. John. And for the rest of the month the artisans and merchants did not open their shops, the citizens dared not lay down their arms, and strict guard was kept throughout Florence, night and day. The presence of Catherine seemed useless, and could only lead to fresh scandal. After a few days, she and her disciples left the city, and went to what Raimondo calls "a certain solitary place, outside the city, but not outside its territory, where hermits were wont to dwell." This is usually supposed to have been Vallombrosa, in the

[1] *Legenda*, III. vi. 34 (§ 428).

Casentino, where Giovanni dalle Celle and others were. It is stated, rather questionably, that Niccolò Soderini accompanied them thither.

The new Signoria, which entered office on July 1, with Luigi di Piero Guicciardini as Gonfaloniere of Justice, was judged by the people as composed of "peaceful and quiet men, who loved the repose of the city and their fellow-citizens." They entered upon their duties quietly, without the ringing of bells, the ceremony of installation being performed in the hall of council, instead of on the ringhiera. They at once ordered the citizens to lay down their arms, the contadini to leave the city on pain of death, the shops to be opened, the barricades pulled down, and every one to go about his business. "And the Signoria was obeyed in everything, and, in a very few days, it was all done. It seemed that there had never been any novelty in Florence, and every one commended the Signoria and the Colleges for the measures they had taken. The city passed every day from good to better, and it remained in repose and in quiet, without any murmuring, for ten days."[1] Under these circumstances, it seemed safe for Catherine and her company to return to Florence, where, says Fra Raimondo, she stayed at first secretly, "because of those who now held sway, who seemed to hate her exceedingly," but afterwards openly, waiting in ardent longing for the peace to be concluded between the Republic and the Church.

From Florence she now wrote her first letter to Pope Urban, whom, as we saw, she had known at Avignon, and with the harsher side of whose character she was probably already acquainted: "with desire of seeing you founded in true and perfect charity, in order that, like a good shepherd, you may lay down your life for your little sheep." She urges him to apply himself to the reformation of the Church. "Most holy Father, God has set you as shepherd over His little sheep of all the Christian religion; He has set you as the cellarer to deal out the blood of Christ crucified, whose vicar you are; and He has set you thus in a time in which iniquity abounds more than it

[1] Gino Capponi (the elder), *op. cit.*, pp. 245–247.

has done for ages, in your subjects, in the body of Holy Church, and throughout the whole of Christendom. And, therefore, you have the greatest need of being founded in perfect charity, with the pearl of justice. O sweetest father, the world can no more endure ; the vices so abound, and especially in those who are placed in the garden of Holy Church as sweet-smelling flowers to give the odour of virtue, that we see them so full of wickedness that they are polluting all the world. Alas! where is purity of heart and perfect chastity, whereby they should make the incontinent become continent by their virtue? Instead of this, the continent and the pure ofttimes taste impurity through their uncleanness. Alas! where is the largesse of charity and the care of souls, and the distributing to the poor, for the welfare of the Church and for their necessity? You know well that they do the contrary. Wretched that I am! With grief I tell you that the sons of the Church nourish themselves with the substance that they receive through the blood of Christ, and they are not ashamed to barter and gamble it with those most sacred hands that have been anointed by you, the vicar of Christ—not to speak of the other miseries which they commit. Alas! where is the profound humility with which they should confound their own sensual pride—the pride with which, with great avarice, they commit simony, buying benefices with presents or with flattery or with money, decked out in vain and dissolute fashion, not like ecclesiastics, but worse than laymen? Alas, sweet babbo mine, remedy this for us; comfort the agonized desires of the servants of God, who are dying with grief and cannot die. They are waiting with great desire for you, like a true pastor, to set hand to the correction, not only in word but in deed, letting the pearl of justice glow forth from you united with mercy, and, without any servile fear, to correct in truth those who are fed at the breast of this holy Spouse, those who are made ministers of the blood."

But, for this reformation of the Church, let him begin with the Sacred College itself, choosing a band of holy and fearless men for cardinals, who will aid him in his arduous task and correct the laity by the example of their own virtuous lives. And let him, without any delay, receive back the Florentines and their allies into the fold. Through the Divine Goodness, no great evil has resulted from the recent tumult. His children are pacified and asking him for mercy ; and, if they do not seem to be asking it in the way he would wish, let him grant it all the same, and they will prove more faithful than the others. "Alas, my babbo, I am fain to stay here no longer. Do with me afterwards what you will. Grant this grace and this mercy to me, miserable wretched woman, who am knocking at your door. My father, do not deny me the crumbs that I am asking for your children." [1]

Urban was no longer at Rome, but at Tivoli, alone with the four Italian cardinals : Corsini, Orsini, Brossano, and Tebaldeschi. Circumstances had made it imperative upon him to make peace with Florence on whatever terms could be obtained, and the ambassadors, especially Barbadori and Filippo Corsini, in spite of the treatment they had received, were doing their duty by the Republic. The new Signoria, no less than the Pope, was resolved to make peace without further delay, without haggling over the conditions.

In the meanwhile, a strange lull seemed to have fallen upon Florence. The priors, ardently pursuing their work of pacifying the city within and without, seem to have received no warning that anything was stirring beneath the surface. But the lowest dregs of the populace, still expecting to be punished for what they had done in the recent tumults, were holding secret meetings, taking fearful oaths, preparing to rise against the burgher government ; and those of the upper classes who had been admonished, not content with what they had achieved, were stirring them up. Not the slightest rumour of what was preparing had as yet reached the Signoria.[2]

[1] Letter 291 (15).

[2] Cf. Gino Capponi (the elder), *op. cit.*, pp. 251–255. In a passage, curiously suggestive of Catherine, he says : "Per lo peccato commesso contro a Santa Chiesa di Dio . . . . permise Iddio dare questa disciplina a questa nostra città, come appresso si dirà."

At last, on the afternoon of Sunday, July 18, a messenger rode into Florence through the Porta San Piero Gattolino, bearing a branch of olive in his hand, bringing letters from the Pope and the ambassadors, announcing that the terms of peace were arranged. The olive was fastened up at a window of the Palazzo Vecchio, and the great bell of the tower pealed out over the city, summoning the citizens to a parliament. "O dearest children," wrote Catherine to Sano di Maco and her other disciples at Siena, "God has heard the cry and the voice of His servants, that for so long a time have cried out in His sight, and the wailing that for so long they have raised over their children dead. Now are they risen again: from death are they come to life, and from blindness to light. O dearest children, the lame walk, and the deaf hear, the blind eye sees, and the dumb speak, crying with loudest voice: *peace, peace, peace;* with great gladness, seeing those children returning to the obedience and favour of their father, and their minds pacified. And, even as persons who now begin to see, they say: Thanks be to Thee, Lord, who hast reconciled us with our Holy Father. Now is the Lamb called holy, the sweet Christ on earth, where before he was called heretic and Patarin. Now do they accept him as father, where hitherto they rejected him. I wonder not thereat, for the cloud has passed away and the serene weather come. Rejoice, rejoice, dearest children, with a sweetest weeping of gratitude before the supreme and eternal Father; not calling yourselves contented with this, but praying Him soon to lift up the banner of the most holy Cross. Rejoice, exult in Christ sweet Jesus; let our hearts burst at the sight of the largesse of the infinite goodness of God. Now is made the peace, in spite of those who would fain have prevented it. Defeated is the infernal demon."[1]

The whole city was wild with joy. An exultant crowd filled the piazza, while the priors came out on to the ringhiera of the

[1] Letter 303 (246). Catherine is writing on Sunday, July 18. Another messenger of peace had arrived on the previous evening: "Sabato sera giunse l' ulivo a un' ora di notte; e oggi a vespero giunse l' altro." Cf. Gi Capponi, *op. cit.*, pp. 255, 256, and the *Anonimo Fiorentino*, pp. 365, 366.

palace, to the sound of music and salvos, and their notary read aloud the letters announcing the agreement that had been made between the Pope and the Republic. All Florence was illuminated, and the rejoicings were prolonged into the night. But on the next day, July 19, like a bolt from the blue, a rumour reached the Signoria that the whole State was on the brink of a precipice. Several arrests were made, and, at nightfall, one Simoncino, called Bugigatto, being examined under torture in the chapel of the palace, confessed that there was a plot for a general uprising of the lowest orders on the following morning. His cries were overheard by an artisan, who was mending the clock of the palace and was in the secret, and he gave the alarm. On the morning of Tuesday, July 20, the whole populace was up in arms, and the disastrous revolution of the *Ciompi*—the unskilled workers who, having no guild of their own, were deprived of political rights—burst, like a tidal wave, over Florence.

The chief question at issue was the right of association and combination, with which was connected a number of grievances especially on the part of those subjected to the consuls of the *Arte della Lana.*[1] But in the anarchy of the next few days, although the petition of the insurgents had been instantly accepted by the Signoria and passed through the Councils, all principle seemed confused in a carnival of outrage. Led by a huckster, Betto di Ciardo, carrying the great banner of Justice which they had taken from the palace of the Executor, one portion of the mob sacked and burned the houses of those of the wealthy citizens who were obnoxious to them, while another seized upon those whom they regarded as their friends, and, willingly or unwillingly, made them knights in the name of the People. Luigi Guicciardini, the Gonfaloniere, found himself included in both classes. The Eight of the War and Salvestro de' Medici were among those knighted, Buonaccorso di Lapo Giovanni one of those whose houses were destroyed. On the evening of the second day, July 21, the Podestà, Giovanni dei

[1] Cf. Rodolico, *op. cit.*, pp. 180 *et seq.*

Marchesi del Monte, surrendered the Palace of the Podestà, and the banners of the Guilds (the minor Arts having taken part with the populace) were hung out from its windows. On July 22, the Signoria pusillanimously abandoned the Palazzo Vecchio, and the mob swept in in triumph, while the bells of the tower pealed out in honour of the victory of the *popolo minuto*.

A wool-carder, Michele di Lando, who had served the Republic as a crossbowman in the wars, carried the banner of Justice into the palace. Him the populace acclaimed Gonfaloniere and Lord of Florence. It is needless to repeat the story of how this man, who had taken no part in the excesses of the mob, saved the State. Finding himself thus the sole ruler of the city, he instantly issued a proclamation that the ravages and brutalities of the insurgents must cease on pain of death, and summoned a parliament, where he was confirmed Gonfaloniere of Justice until the end of August. On the following day, July 23, he proposed the names of the new magistrates. Besides himself, four of the new Signoria represented the *popolo minuto*, two the minor Arts (including the shoemaker, Benedetto di Carlone, already mentioned), and two the greater Arts. They entered office with the usual formalities on July 25.

Nevertheless, the general panic did not abate. In spite of repeated proclamations from the Signoria, many citizens fled to their villas in the contado, taking their families and movable goods with them, while those that remained would not lay down their arms nor open their shops. The crossbowmen of the Republic were marched through the city, to restore confidence, without avail. There was a general attempt to reform the State; the admonitions of the Parte Guelfa were annulled, and admonished families readmitted to office; and, on the last day of July, all the papers in the ballot-boxes, from which the names of the magistrates were drawn, were burnt: "in order that all things might be reformed anew, and that good men and merchants might be put into office." On August 1, the priors went through the city in the morning, with trumpets and other instruments, which "mightily reassured those who wished to live in peace";

a thousand crossbowmen marched through in the afternoon, and it was proclaimed that every merchant could return in safety to carry on his business, with heavy penalties against any who should molest him. In the evening, the news came that the peace with the Pope had been signed, and that the absolution would soon arrive.[1]

It was an honourable and just peace that had been signed at Tivoli on July 28, the Pope on the following day giving leave to all the ecclesiastics of the Florentine dominion freely to celebrate Mass. The Florentines were to pay an indemnity of 250,000 florins in monthly instalments, to annul all ordinances against the Church within two months, to restore all confiscated goods to the churches, monasteries, and hospitals. The Pope on his side would absolve them fully from all censures. Perugia and Città di Castello were included, and the other colleagues and adherents of the Commune of Florence, who were subjects of the Church, on condition of sending ambassadors to the Pope to subscribe within two months; and, in the meanwhile, the Pope could not make war upon them. They were practically to retain their liberties, while acknowledging the papal suzerainty, paying an indemnity and their original tribute.[2] But Florence was too much harassed by internal dissensions to indulge in public rejoicing. Rumours of fresh trouble caused the citizens again to stand to arms on the following day, August 2, and for several days this state of siege continued, the city diligently guarded, and men hourly expecting a new rising.[3] Nevertheless, there was a short interval before the tumults began again.

With the conclusion of peace between Florence and the Holy See, Catherine's second great political work was done. In spite

[1] *Diario Compagnano*, in Corazzini, pp. 110–112.

[2] Gherardi, *op. cit.*, pp. 94–96, 221–223. The absolution was informally announced in Santo Spirito by Fra Agostino della Scarperia on August 10, but the actual bulls did not arrive until October. On October 23, the Bishop of Volterra and Fra Francesco of Orvieto solemnly absolved the city in the name of Pope Urban VI. Cf. *Anonimo Fiorentino*, pp. 373, 387, 388.

[3] *Diario Compagnano*, *loc. cit.*, p. 113.

of the great personal danger that she and her followers must have run from the blind hatred of the populace, she had remained in the city all through these tumultuous days of revolution and anarchy, until the news came that the treaty was actually signed. Then she gathered her followers round her, and announced her intention of returning instantly to Siena, now that she had fulfilled the command of Christ and His vicar.[1] Such was the excitement and alarm in the city that it was not thought safe for her even to have an audience with the Signoria. It was probably on August 2, in the midst of the renewed panic, that she looked her last upon Florence, and went quietly home, "back to her daily way divine."

There still exists, among the Strozzi manuscripts of the Biblioteca Nazionale of Florence, a fourteenth century copy of the letter which Catherine addressed on this occasion to the Gonfaloniere and Priors of the Republic. It is her farewell to Florence. "You have the desire," she says, "of reforming your city; but I tell you that this desire will never be fulfilled, unless you strive to throw to the ground the hatred and rancour of your hearts and your love of yourselves, that is, unless you think not of yourselves alone, but of the universal welfare of all the city." She suggests certain obvious reforms in the choice of magistrates, urges them to see that the conditions of the peace are properly carried out, and delicately hints that the exiles should be recalled. Then she speaks about herself:—

"Let the sorrow that I feel at seeing your city (which I regard as mine) in such great trouble be my excuse. I did not expect to have to write to you; but I thought, by word of mouth and face to face, to say these things to you, for the honour of God and your own utility. For my intention was to visit you, and to rejoice with you at the holy peace, for which peace I have laboured so long in all that I have been able, according to my possibility and my small power; if I had been able to do more, I would have done it. After rejoicing with you, and thanking the Divine Goodness and you, I would have departed and gone away

[1] Cf. *Legenda*, III. vi. 35 (§ 429).

to Siena. Now it seems that the demon has sowed so much, unjustly, in their hearts against me, that I have not wished that sin should be added to sin ; for thereby would the ruin be only increased. I have gone away, with the divine grace ; and I pray the supreme eternal Goodness to pacify and unite and bind your hearts together, one with the other, so in love of charity that neither demon nor creature can ever separate you. Whatever can be done by me for your welfare will I gladly do, even unto death, in spite of demons visible and invisible, who would impede every holy desire. I go away consoled, inasmuch as that is accomplished in me which I set before my heart when I entered this city, never to depart, though I should have to die for it, until I saw you, the children, reconciled with your father, seeing such peril and loss in souls and bodies ; I go away grieving and with sorrow, since I leave the city in such great bitterness. But may eternal God, who has consoled me in the one, console me in the other matter, so that I may see and hear that you are pacified in a good and firm and perfect state, that you may be able to render glory and praise to His name, and not stand under arms with such great affliction. I hope that the sweet clemency of God will turn the eye of His mercy, and fulfil the desire of His servants."[1]

[1] Unpublished. Appendix, Letter IV.

CHAPTER XII

THE BEGINNING OF THE SCHISM

"Multae disputationes factae sunt circa istam materiam, multi libelli editi pro utriusque partis defensione. Peritissimos viros in sacra pagina et iure canonico habuit toto tempore illo quo duravit id schisma utraque pars seu obedientia, ac etiam religiosissimos viros et (quod maius est) etiam miraculis fulgentes; nec unquam sic potuit quaestio illa decidi, quin semper remaneret apud plurimos dubia."—St. Antoninus, *Chronicorum*, III. tit. 22.

WE must now turn back to what had been passing at Rome and at Tivoli, while Catherine was thus engaged upon the work of her Divine Master at Florence.

Gregory had returned from Anagni in November, broken down in health and embittered in spirit. He found even the Romans turning against him. By lending ear to the suggestions of the nobles, especially the ambitious and intriguing Count of Fondi, Onorato Gaetani, he had alienated the friendship of the Bandaresi, the formidable representatives of the Roman People, who had the whole force of the Republic behind them. It was feared that they would endeavour to prevent the Pope from again leaving the city. The Cardinal of Marmoutier declares that Gregory told him that one of the Roman cardinals was plotting his death, in order himself to obtain the tiara.[1] One of the Pope's household told Alfonso da Vadaterra, who was then in Rome promoting the canonization of Birgitta, that Gregory intended to yield to the solicitations of the French cardinals and of his own family, and to return to Avignon. "I am absolutely certain," answered the hermit-bishop, "that he will never be able to do this; for I know that it is the will of God that our lord the Pope and his Curia should remain in Rome."[2] A few days after this conversation, Gregory's last

[1] Deposition of the Cardinal of Marmoutier, Gayet, doc. 39. Jacopo Orsini, the person meant, was already dead when the Cardinal made this statement.

[2] Raynaldus, vii. pp. 375, 376. Cf. Thomas de Acerno, *Rer. It. Script.*, iii. 2. coll. 715, 716.

illness came upon him. The Bandaresi forced their way to his bedside, to see for themselves if he were really dying. "The Pope cannot survive," one was heard to say to the other, as they passed out of the palace; "the time has come for us to be good Romans. Let us look to it that in this case the popedom shall remain with our nation."[1] From his deathbed, Gregory issued a bull empowering the cardinals to proceed immediately to the election of his successor without summoning or awaiting their absent colleagues, and ratifying the choice that should be made by the majority of two-thirds, even in the face of a hostile and obstinate minority. About the same time, he sent secretly after dark for Pierre Gandelin, the Provençal governor of the Castello Sant' Angelo, and committed to his care a large portion of the papal treasures, forbidding him to give up the keys of the fortress, chance what might, without an express order from the cardinals at Avignon.

This last French Pope recognized by the Church died on March 27, 1378, full of the gloomiest apprehensions; according to one account, regarding his death as a direct intervention of God to prevent his returning to Avignon; according to another, convinced that a fearful tempest was about to break upon the Church, for which he would be responsible for having lent faith to the visions of Birgitta and Catherine, and brought the papacy back to Rome. No sooner was the news of his death known, than preparations for the election of his successor began—both among the members of the Sacred College and those who, ostensibly, had no voice in the matter. There were mysterious meetings held by the Romans in the convent of Ara Caeli and in the Senator's palace on the Capitol. Deputations waited upon the cardinals to exhort them to choose a Roman, or at least an Italian Pope; the same counsel was shouted after them in the streets; and fierce threats were added. While the cardinals met each morning in Santa Maria Nuova, now Santa Francesca Romana, to celebrate a solemn requiem at the deceased pontiff's grave for the

[1] Declaration of Fra Luigi, Bishop of Assisi. *Archivio Vaticano*, LIV. 19, f. 183.

repose of his soul, the Bandaresi and other Romans who were present seized the opportunity to urge upon them the necessity of electing an Italian Pope and of maintaining the Apostolic Chair at Rome. The Romans took possession of the gates of the city, and seized upon the shipping in the Tiber. While the nobles, including Onorato Gaetani, Count of Fondi, and Niccolò Orsini, Count of Nola, high officials of the Church, upon whose protection the cardinals could have greatly relied, were expelled, bands of armed contadini and mountaineers from the Sabine and Alban hills came into the city, adding to the general confusion and alarm by their cries and uproar, hustling and threatening the French retainers and servants of the Sacred College. Clearly, the fathers were held in a trap.

Nevertheless, the cardinals did not apparently believe in the seriousness of the danger. They did not think it advisable to summon the Breton and Gascon mercenaries, some eight hundred of whom were within an easy march of Rome, nor necessary (though there was some difference of opinion among them on this point) to take shelter behind the battlements of Sant' Angelo. To the persistent supplications of the authorities of the city to choose a Roman or an Italian for Pope, they answered in general terms that they would elect one who would greatly please them and Italy and all Christendom. The four Italian cardinals, at the instance of the whole College, rebuked the Roman officials for their conduct; but without result.[1] The Senator of Rome, Guido de Pruinis, and the Bandaresi, in the name of the Republic, undertook the protection of the conclave and the guard of the Leonine city.[2] A proclamation was made, threatening all disturbers of the public order with

[1] Cf. Cardinal Corsini's statement, added to the declarations of his colleagues, Gayet, doc. 27.

[2] Fra Gonsalvo, a Dominican, then prior of Santa Sabina, says that they sent to the cardinals to offer a good and pacific guard for the freedom of the conclave, but at the same time to beseech them to console Rome and Italy in the election, and to warn them that, if their choice did not satisfy the Romans, there would be trouble with the people: they feared *ne forte aliquod non debitum populus faceret. Archivio Vaticano*, LIV. 15, f. 57*v*.

death; and a block, with the axe and other ghastly implements of the executioner's craft, was solemnly set up in the Piazza San Pietro. A general sense of alarm and expectancy pervaded the Eternal City.

There were sixteen cardinals then in Rome, of whom ten were French, four Italians, one an immediate subject of the Emperor, and one a Spaniard. They were divided into three parties: the Limousin, the French, and the Italian factions. The Limousin faction was composed of prelates connected by birth or other ties with the families of Clement VI, Innocent VI, and Gregory XI, and who desired to elect one of their own number to carry on the bad traditions that had put the ecclesiastics of their own race at the head of the clerical world. To it belonged the Cardinal of Limoges (Jean de Cros), the Cardinal of Poitiers (Guy de Malesset), the Cardinal of Marmoutier (Gérard du Puy), Cardinal Guillaume d'Aigrefeuille, Cardinal Pierre de Vergne, who were all Limousins, and the Cardinal of Viviers (Pierre de Sortenac), who was a Cahorsine. The Cardinals of Viviers and of Poitiers seem to have been the candidates most favoured by this group. Opposed to them was the so-called French faction, which included the Cardinal of Glandèves (Bertrand Lagier); the Cardinal of Sant' Eustachio (Pierre Flandrin); the Cardinal of Sant' Angelo (Guillaume de Noellet); the Cardinal of Brittany (Hugues de Montalais), an Angevin by birth, who had been chancellor of Brittany. To this latter faction also adhered the two strongest personalities of the Sacred College, though neither of them was a Frenchman: Cardinal Robert of Geneva, the butcher of the citizens of Cesena; and the Cardinal of Aragon, Pedro de Luna. Robert, younger son of Count Amédée III of Geneva, was connected by his grandmother, Agnes of Savoy, with the royal house of France, and held the Archbishopric of Cambray. The special aim of this faction was to free the Church from the domination of Limoges, even at the cost of electing an Italian Pope, though their choice would by preference have fallen upon the Cardinal of Sant' Eustachio or Cardinal de Noellet.

The leader of the four Italian cardinals was the dean of the cardinal bishops, Piero Corsini, the Cardinal of Florence, who (as we saw) had been raised to the cardinalate by Urban V in 1370. Gregory XI had made him Bishop of Porto, from which he is frequently styled the "Cardinal of Porto." He was a man of great ability and little moral courage. Francesco Tebaldeschi was a Roman of humble birth, who had been, like the aristocratic Corsini, one of the cardinals of Urban V; his title was of Santa Sabina, but he was always spoken of as the "Cardinal of St. Peter's," from his being archpriest of the basilica. He was an old man, broken down in health and tortured by gout. Jacopo Orsini, a member of the great Guelf house, was the only other Roman in the Sacred College. He was dean of the cardinal deacons, a comparatively young man of doubtful probity and of great ambition. While ostensibly leaning towards the French faction, he was secretly himself aiming at the tiara, counting upon the support of the Roman nobles and populace. The remaining member of this group was the Archbishop of Milan, Simone Brossano, a man learned in canon law, who had been promoted to the Sacred College by Gregory XI under the title of SS. Giovanni e Paolo on the Caelian Hill.

In addition to these sixteen cardinals, there were seven members of the Sacred College absent from Rome. Six of these, including the brother of Urban V, Anglico de Grimoard (the best of the French cardinals), were at Avignon. The seventh, Jean de la Grange, the Benedictine "Cardinal of Amiens," a wealthy and worldly monk, a subtle politician of great influence with the French King, had been the chief papal representative at the Congress of Sarzana, and was now at Pisa.

The one member of the Sacred College to whom Catherine, and all who looked for the salvation of Israel, turned was Pedro de Luna, who had ultimately supported the late Pope in restoring the See to Rome, where he apparently contemplated passing the rest of his life, as he had built himself a palace, was busily restoring his titular church of Santa Maria in Cosmedin, and had even chosen his place of burial in San Lorenzo. A man of blameless life, vast learning, great charity, and apparently sincere iety, insensible to moral or physical fear, there was, nevertheless, omething mysterious and inscrutable in his bearing and character. But of all the foreign cardinals he was the only one that the Romans loved and respected. He was intimate with Alfonso da Vadaterra, with whom, as also with Fra Raimondo and with Fra Gonsalvo, the Dominican prior of Santa Sabina, he discussed the situation with much apparent frankness. "In good sooth," he said one day to Fra Gonsalvo, in reference to the threats of the Romans, "I tell you that, even if I have to die for it, I shall choose no one for Pope save whom I wish. And why should I deem it an unworthy end, to die at the hands of this people and in this holy city where so many thousand saints have battled for the truth?"[1] Regarded by Catholic writers, in the light of his subsequent career, as an astute dissembler and designing hypocrite, it is, nevertheless, difficult for the impartial student of Church history not to recognize in Pedro de Luna a man of upright life and high ideals, zealously striving to find where the hidden jewel of truth lay concealed, and to follow where he deemed that the light led.

But there was another personage, not a member of the Sacred College, upon whom many eyes were turned in Rome at this crisis in the history of the Church. Bartolommeo Prignano was born at Naples, shortly before 1320, of a father who was by origin a native of Pisa, and of a Neapolitan mother. As Archbishop of Acerenza, and assistant to the Vice-Chancellor, he had resided at the court of Avignon, and was thoroughly conversant with the affairs and administration of the Church. As we saw, he had at first opposed Catherine, and had afterwards been impressed by her sanctity, though we do not know how far he had had any personal intercourse with her. He had come to Rome with Pope Gregory, by whom he had been promoted to the Archbishopric of Bari, and was now acting as Vice-Chancellor of

[1] Deposition of Fra Gonsalvo, *Archivio Vaticano*, LIV. 15, f. 58. The friar states (MS. *cit.*, f. 63 *v.*) that the Romans had such confidence in the Cardinal of Aragon that they would have been perfectly contented if he had been elected Pope.

the Holy See in the absence, at Avignon, of the Cardinal of Pamplona. In appearance, he was of short stature and thick-set, pallid and sallow in complexion. As to his character, Dietrich of Nieheim, afterwards one of his secretaries, assures us that he was "a man humble and devout, keeping his hands free from every gift, a foe and persecutor of simoniacs, a lover of chastity and justice, but one that relied too much on his own prudence, and over-readily gave credence to flatterers."[1] He lacked the suave and courteous manners of the Cardinal of Aragon, the air of a polished man of the world that distinguished the Cardinal of Geneva, the diplomatic astuteness and aristocratic dignity of the Cardinal of Florence; was brusque and impetuous, easily moved to anger, devoid of restraint and tact in word and in deed—albeit these traits had hitherto been kept in check by his comparatively inferior position.

The Archbishop had lately bought himself a house and a vineyard in Rome, in order to qualify as a Roman citizen. His enemies see a sinister purpose in all his movements during these days. He is said to have been incessant in secretly questioning the Pope's physician, Francesco Casini, during Gregory's last illness, as to the possibility of his recovery. During the nine days of requiem Masses for Gregory's soul at Santa Maria Nuova, he had seized the opportunity of asking Guido de Pruinis to present him to the Bandaresi and their colleagues; after which he appears frequently to have been present at their secret meetings on the Capitol. There is nothing in all this, however, in the least inconsistent with straightforward dealing, and the accusations made against him, of attempting to purchase the support of the Romans in his designs on the papacy, may be disregarded. It seems certain that he counselled them to be moderate and peaceable. Nardo di Giorgio, an apothecary who was then one of the Bandaresi, and seems to have made a very sinister impression upon the French prelates of the Curia, has left on record that one day he and other Romans requested the Archbishop to go to the cardinals to beseech them to give them

[1] T. de Nyem, *De Schismate*, I. 1.

a Roman or Italian Pope; to which Bartolommeo replied that they should not make any such supplication to the cardinals, but leave them to make their election freely, and, for his part, he believed that the cardinals would do well: "Then this witness and his companions were not well contented with his answer, and told him that they would seek another who would act more according to their wishes."[1]

Another prudent voice raised at these meetings was that of Fra Bonaventura Badoara of Padua, who had been elected general of the Augustinian hermits in the preceding year. It did not matter to the Romans, he said, that the Pope should be a Roman or an Italian, but only that he should remain upon Italian soil. They should content themselves with whatever Pope might be elected, whatever his origin; but, when once elected, they could supplicate his Holiness to take up his residence in Rome. Above all, he added, "let me urge you to do nothing, not even by signs, that can be taken as violence or pressure. For by these things the election can be rendered void."[2]

It is clear that there was no feeling of antagonism towards the Archbishop of Bari in the Sacred College. They regarded him as an experienced, eloquent and devout, and (as a subject of the Queen of Naples) politically neutral prelate; from his long residence in Avignon, the French looked upon him as almost one of themselves. Alfonso da Vadaterra had praised him highly to the Cardinal of Aragon, who, from personal knowledge of his qualities, regarded him as a suitable candidate for the papacy—but their testimonies differ on one important particular. The hermit-bishop's version is that Pedro de Luna told him that he had resolved to give his vote to the Archbishop of Bari, because the dissensions between the French and the Limousin factions made it impossible to elect an ultramontane member of the Sacred College. The Cardinal himself declares that he only

[1] Testimony of Nardo, *Archivio Vaticano*, LIV. 37, f. 142. I find the full name of this personage, *Nardus Georgii aliter dictus Lupus*, in an undated brief of Urban VI, *Cod. Vat. Lat.* 6330, f. 277.

[2] Baluze, I. coll. 1240, 1241.

intended to adopt this course in the event of the Romans compelling the fathers to choose a Roman or an Italian, and that he thinks that the majority of the Sacred College favoured the candidature of the Cardinal of Viviers.[1] But, a few days before the conclave, Tommaso Petra told Fra Raimondo that he saw that almost all the cardinals had agreed to elect the Archbishop of Bari.[2] This is questionable. There seems, however, little doubt that, in the event of their being unable, through internal dissensions or external pressure, to carry the election of their own candidate, the French and Limousin cardinals (and probably, though this is more uncertain, three of the four Italians) had contemplated the possibility of their agreeing upon the Archbishop of Bari. The Clementine position is that this course was only to be adopted in case the Sacred College was in danger and unable to proceed to a free election, while the Urbanists declare that the split between the two factions had secured his election before the conclave met.

The cardinals entered the conclave on the late afternoon of the Wednesday in Passion Week, April 7. Our knowledge of what happened all comes from the sworn testimonies and depositions of contemporaries and eye-witnesses, even of those who played leading parts in the events of that night and the following day. Nevertheless, it is impossible to find out the absolute truth of what brought about the temporary dissolution of the Catholic world. These testimonies and depositions were taken many months later, when the deadliest passions had been roused on either side, and the memories of the actors sharpened or distorted by the urgent need of proving their own party in the right. The clearest and fullest details by witnesses on the side of the Roman claimant are flatly contradicted by details, equally clear and full, by witnesses on behalf of Avignon.[3]

[1] Cf. Alfonso's testimony, in Raynaldus, vii. p. 377, with that of Cardinal de Luna, in A. Sorbelli, Appendix to St. Vincent Ferrer's *De Moderno Ecclesiae Schismate*, pp. 244, 245.

[2] Valois, I. pp. 30, 31.

[3] The depositions of Bishop Tommaso of Lucera, given by Muratori (*Rer.*

The historian to-day can merely strain after a *via media*, guided by the statements of the men who, for one cause or another, seem on either side the least open to suspicion of deliberate falsification.

A vast and clamorous crowd, partly armed, filled the piazza and surged round the Vatican, shouting: "Give us a Roman or at least an Italian Pope"; as the princes of the Church, one by one, made their way with difficulty into the palace, under the protection of the Senator. The rooms destined for the conclave were on the first floor, but a number of Romans seem to have pressed in after the cardinals and their attendants, and to have thronged the courtyard, probably continuing the threats that had been shouted in the square. The Romans had deputed Giovanni Cenci, chancellor of the city, Nardo di Giorgio, and others of their leaders, to guard the conclave; while, on the side of the cardinals, a similar function was assigned to Guillaume de la Voulte, Bishop of Marseilles, and the Bishops of Todi and Tivoli. Before the conclave was closed, the heads of the thirteen Rioni, with other Romans, came to the cardinals, and, respectfully at first, but afterwards with warnings of the consequences of a refusal, demanded that a Roman or an Italian should be elected to the papacy. The Cardinal of Florence, as dean of the cardinal bishops, answered that they would do what should be pleasing to God, useful for the Church, and honourable for the city. Aigrefeuille and Orsini, deans of the cardinal priests and cardinal deacons respectively, warned them that any interference would invalidate the election. All during the night, a great uproar continued in the piazza; according to the Urbanists, it was mere lighthearted singing and merry-making, with a wonderful absence of the slightest sinister element; according to the Clementines, it was the clamour of a furious mob,

It. Script., iii. 2), and of Bishop Niccolò of Viterbo, recently published by Pastor (*Acta Inedita*, document 3), on the one side, are as untrustworthy as the solemn testimonies of the cardinals themselves, so sedulously collected by the Abbé Gayet, on the other. M. Noël Valois, *La France et le Grand Schisme d'Occident*, I. pp. 35–83, is judicious and impartial.

threatening death to the cardinals if their will was not obeyed. It seems agreed by both parties that, about the middle of the night, a crowd composed mainly of rough peasants from the hills broke into the Vatican cellars, "volentes bibere de bono vino papale." At intervals, the cries of "Roman or Italian" rose up, within and without the palace, and reached the ears of the cardinals in their cells.

Early in the morning of Thursday, April 8, a band of Romans forced their way into the campanile of St. Peter's and rang the bells. They were answered by the tocsin of the Capitol, which clashed out *a stormo*, as though to call the populace to arms. The cardinals had entered the conclave and Corsini was about to address them, when the clamour was renewed, and the Bishop of Marseilles, with his colleagues, implored them not to elect a foreigner or they were all lost. Cenci and Nardo assured them that they could do nothing. Against his will, the Cardinal of Florence was led by Aigrefeuille and Orsini to the window, and the two latter addressed the armed and infuriated crowd below, promising that, if they would keep quiet and leave the cardinals to their deliberations, they should have a Roman or an Italian for Pope.

It is impossible to say with confidence whether this promise, manifestly extorted by fear and necessity, induced the cardinals to do what next they did, or whether their own dissensions had already impelled them to the choice they ultimately made. The Cardinals of Florence and Limoges first suggested that the election should be postponed; but it was feared that this might cause a general massacre of the Sacred College, which could only lead to complete anarchy in the Church. "I should be willing to lay down my life for the Faith," said Cardinal Lagier, "if God were to grant me such grace; but not for the nationality of a Pope." Then Orsini, who was bent at all costs upon keeping out the Archbishop of Bari, proposed that a friar minor should be dressed up in the papal robes and paraded as Pope, so that they could escape and hold a free election elsewhere. This plan was indignantly rejected by the Cardinal of Limoges and others, as leading the people to commit idolatry.[1] It was unanimously agreed to satisfy the people, or, at least, to take a course that would reconcile the interests of the Church with the demands of the Romans.[2] Pedro de Luna saw the time had come to carry out his plan, and informally suggested that the Archbishop of Bari should be elected; Orsini whispered to the Cardinal of Florence to propose Tebaldeschi; the Cardinal of Brittany named the Cardinal of Milan, who answered that he would not accept such an election, if they were to make him ten times Pope. "*Habemus pontificem*," cried the Cardinal of Geneva, perhaps ironically, seeing that Luna's candidate had the majority. The cardinals took their seats, and Aigrefeuille called on the Cardinal of Florence, as dean of the Sacred College, formally to propose a candidate. Corsini then named the Cardinal of St. Peter's, but added (so he tells us): "I should name an ultramontane member of the College, were it not for the promise we have made the Romans, and their bearing, and our fear of them."[3] The Cardinal of Limoges, whose turn was to speak next, said that St. Peter's was too old and his election would be too obviously a yielding to clamour; Florence and Milan were impossible, because of the hostility of their cities to the papal see; Orsini was too young and a Roman. He proposed the Lord Archbishop of Bari. All the rest concurred, with certain exceptions and reservations. The Cardinal of Sant' Angelo said that he agreed, although his vote could be of no avail, as he believed that the election was not valid. The Cardinals of Brittany and Milan said they yielded under protest, as the others were agreed. Cardinal Orsini declared that he would not give his vote to any one, under the circumstances, but would wait until he was at liberty. Several cardinals in voting for the Archbishop of Bari added the words: *ut sit verus papa;* evidently in repudiation of

[1] Testimony of the Bishop of Faenza, *Archivio Vaticano*, LIV. 40. Cf. *Rer. It. Script.*, iii. 2. coll. 680, 681. It is noteworthy that St. Antoninus (III. p. 389) ascribes a similar suggestion to Bartolommeo Prignano himself.

[2] Cf. Valois, I. p. 45.

[3] Depositions of the Italian cardinals, Gayet, doc. 27.

the suggestion that they should make a fictitious election. Cardinal de Luna's own account of the matter is that they did not wish to elect an Italian, but thought the Archbishop a sufficient man, and that if, when they were at liberty, the cardinals agreed, he would be re-elected ; if not, they assumed that he would abdicate. For his own part, he was not moved by fear ; but, seeing the cardinals agreed to satisfy the people, he proposed him and voted for him with the intention that, in any case, he would be content that he should be Pope.[1] It is evident that the cardinals thought that they had done their best, though they would probably have made a different choice under different circumstances. They had made a genuine attempt to satisfy the Romans, while not compromising the dignity of the Sacred College. It is questionable whether, at this moment, more than a small minority among them considered that the election was invalid, though the Cardinal of Glandèves seems to have protested from the outset that he had only acted from fear of death.

Either to gain time, or because the Archbishop had not yet accepted his election, the cardinals did not forthwith proclaim the new pontiff. The uproar in the piazza began again. Orsini, whose office it was to announce the election, advanced to the window, accompanied by the Cardinals of Florence and Geneva—the Bishop of Marseilles, who had completely lost his head with terror, incessantly imploring them to name a Roman. "O Romans," shouted Orsini to the crowd, "if you do not have a Pope you will like by the evening, you can cut me into pieces." A deafening roar of "Roman, Roman, we will have a Roman," was the answer—perhaps raised in part by the retainers of the Cardinal's own family in his interest. The Archbishop of Bari himself, who had been summoned to the palace together with Agapito Colonna and other Roman prelates, also appeared on the scene, apparently at another window, and exhorted the crowd to keep calm.[2] This done, the cardinals took a hasty meal, and

[1] His testimony in Sorbelli, *op. cit.*, pp. 251, 252.

[2] So at least the Bishop of Todi (Gayet, doc. 17), who adds that he thinks

returned to the chapel of the conclave, to arrange about publishing the election. Although by now aware of what had happened, Bartolommeo does not seem to have been present.

In the meanwhile, a rumour had spread through the crowd that they were being tricked, and the uproar was renewed. The cardinals, on the motion of Tebaldeschi, appear to have practically re-elected Bartolommeo. Orsini, who alone had continued in opposition, now went to the window, and told the people that the Pope was elected: "Go to San Pietro." He was understood as saying that the Cardinal of St. Peter's was Pope, and a rush was made to pillage Tebaldeschi's palace. "No, no," cried one of the French prelates of the Curia, "Bari, Bari!" A roar of execration burst from the crowd, who supposed that Jean de Bar, a hated Limousin prelate, kinsman to the late pontiff, was the person meant. Brandishing their swords and axes, the Romans burst into the conclave, shouting: "A Roman, a Roman, death to the traitor cardinals!" Hearing this fresh tempest sweeping upon them, ignorant of the misunderstanding that had arisen, the unfortunate cardinals could only suppose that the election of the Archbishop of Bari had failed to satisfy the Romans. Some vainly attempted to escape; the others, in spite of a vigorous protest from Cardinal de Luna, hastily resolved to present Tebaldeschi to the people as Pope. Notwithstanding the old Cardinal's protests, the conclavists took hold of him, dressed him in the papal robes, and seated him in the papal chair as Sovereign Pontiff, while the bells were rung and the *Te Deum* intoned. He attempted to resist, but was forcibly held down by the Cardinal of Marmoutier and the Cardinal of Brittany, while, in

that Bartolommeo did not then know of his election. Nardo, on the other hand, says that Orsini told him and the Bishop of Marseilles to tell the Romans from the cardinals that they would content them about a Roman or Italian Pope; he delivered the message himself, bidding them thank God and go away so that the Pope could freely come out: "And then some Romans, who were of the household of the said Lord Cardinal Orsini and of his kindred, hid their faces among the others, and shouted that they wanted a Roman only." *Archivio Vaticano*, LIV. 37, f. 142 *v*.

the deafening uproar when the Romans broke in, his feeble declaration that he was not the Pope was unheard, or taken merely as an expression of humility. They seized him and enthroned him on the altar. Prelates and people alike knelt to kiss his feet, and acclaimed him as vicar of Christ; and such was the press of unwelcome adorers, who added to the tortures that he was already suffering from the gout, that the poor old man began to rave wildly of antipopes and devils, and cursed the Romans who besought his apostolic benediction. After some hours, more dead than alive, he was carried in triumph to the papal apartments, and there left in peace.[1]

While this was in progress, the cardinals fled as best they could from the palace. Aigrefeuille, Pierre de Vergne, Viviers, Poitiers, and Limoges took refuge in the Castello Sant' Angelo, where they were joined later by the Cardinal of Brittany, whose house had been sacked and he himself roughly handled. The Cardinals of Florence, Milan, and Marmoutier got in safety to their own houses. Robert of Geneva, Noellet, Orsini, and Flandrin escaped from the city. The last to leave the chapel was Pedro de Luna, accompanied by his conclavist, the Dean of Tarascon, Fernando Perez, who states that, throughout all the disturbance, the Cardinal had rebuked and restrained the fury of the people. A number of Romans escorted them on their way, and, as they passed Sant' Angelo, the French supposed them prisoners, and attempted a rescue. Once over the bridge, the Cardinal was treated with all reverence by the populace.[2] Alfonso da Vadaterra, who visited him on his return from the

[1] The clearest account of this extraordinary affair is in Valois, I. pp. 52, 53. That given by Creighton, in his *History of the Papacy*, was written before the Vatican documents were made accessible. It is curious to notice that Catherine of Sweden, who was in Rome, supposes that the cardinals enthroned Tebaldeschi for fear lest the Romans should kill the real Pope because not a Roman. Cf. her testimony in Raynaldus, vii. pp. 380, 381. The Italian cardinals state that one of the others "told the people that the Lord of St. Peter's was elected but would not consent, and that they should induce him to consent." Gayet, doc. 27.

[2] Letter from the Dean of Tarascon, Rome, April 11, to the Precentor of Elne at Avignon. Gayet, doc. 22.

conclave, found him surrounded by the Romans who had accompanied him, "totus laetus et hilaris," and still (so he asserts) keeping up the fiction that Tebaldeschi was Pope. But, when left alone with Alfonso and Fernando Perez, he explained that, by his means, the Archbishop of Bari had been unanimously elected as true Pope, and that the Cardinal of St. Peter's had been enthroned simply for fear of the people.[1] He further told him that the new pontiff was in hiding for fear—which the Cardinal may well have believed, but which was by no means the case.

Bartolommeo Prignano had remained in the Vatican, with Cardinal Tebaldeschi and a few Italian prelates. He had had no official notification of his election, but Giovanni Cenci and the Bandaresi had already greeted him as Pope, and were busily calming the minds of the Romans. The storm had, indeed, completely subsided, and the following morning, Friday, April 9, found Rome at peace. Tommaso Petra tells us that, at daybreak, Alfonso da Vadaterra sent to him in the name of the Cardinal de Luna, asking him to go at once to Bartolommeo, to assure him from the Cardinal that he was as truly Pope as St. Peter, and that he had received a promise from influential persons of a place of safety and a sufficient force of armed men to bring him wherever he pleased. To this Bartolommeo answered that he was not afraid, and that there was no need of such an offer, for he wished to see his children freely and had no thought of leaving them, but he thanked the Cardinal for his solicitude.[2] The Cardinal had mistaken the situation ; the new Pope and the representatives of the Roman People were united against such intervention. Either freely or under pressure from Cenci and the Bandaresi, all the cardinals who had remained in the city came to the Vatican, followed (after some negotiation and attempted evasion) by the six who had taken refuge in Sant' Angelo. When Pedro de Luna arrived, Bartolommeo said that he did not mean to be deceived, and bade him tell him if he

[1] Raynaldus, vii. p. 378.

[2] Testimony of Tommaso Petra, *Archivio Vaticano*, LIV. 17, f. 80.

understood that he had been lawfully elected—to which the Cardinal answered in the affirmative. The cardinals retired into the chapel, and, almost immediately, summoned Bartolommeo, and informed him, by the mouth of the Cardinal of Florence, that they had elected him Pope. "I am not worthy," was the answer, "but I shall not contradict the Divine will; I accept."[1] He was at once robed in the papal vestments, and enthroned on the altar; the *Te Deum* was sung; the doors were thrown open for clergy and laity to pay their homage, while, in the absence of Orsini, Cardinal de Vergne from a window of the palace formally proclaimed to the people the election of Pope Urban VI.

"*By the goodness and industry of the Roman People*," wrote the Mantuan agent, Cristoforo da Piacenza, to his master, "the lord cardinals have elected the Lord Bartolommeo, Archbishop of Bari, for Pope, a man with whom the holy Church of God is certainly well provided." "I am certain that the holy Church of God will be well governed, and I dare to say that for more than a hundred years she has not had such a pastor. For he has no kindred, and is most friendly with the Queen, experienced in the affairs of the world, wise and prudent. All the Romans without distinction are supremely joyful for the sake of the city, which has gained back her Spouse."[2]

During Holy Week, the cardinals who had fled from Rome returned. On Easter Sunday, April 18, Urban was crowned by Cardinal Orsini in front of St. Peter's, "with the greatest solemnity and devotion," and went in procession with the cardinals, all riding on white horses, to take possession of the Lateran. The cardinals asked him for graces and favours, spiritual and temporal, for themselves and their relatives and friends, and in all respects treated him as lawful Pope. As such, they announced his election to the cardinals at Avignon, to the Emperor, and to the other princes of Christendom; but it seems

[1] Testimony of Cardinal de Luna, *loc. cit.*, pp. 259, 260.

[2] Despatches of April 9 and 12, 1378. Pastor, *Geschichte*, documents 10 and 11. The hermit-bishop, on the other hand (in the light of later events), tries to make out that the Romans misliked the election of a Neapolitan.

probable that this was done simply in obedience to Urban's commands, and they appear in several instances to have accompanied their letters with a secret message not to put implicit confidence in the official accounts of the election. The peculiar situation had alarmed the consciences of many in the city, but the Cardinal of Geneva and the Cardinal of Milan seem to have been the only members of the College who openly expressed any doubts as to Urban's title. When questioned, at least during Holy Week and Easter Week, the others seem invariably to have answered that Urban was as true a Pope as St. Peter, or words to a similar effect.[1] Francesco Casini, indeed, hinted to Cardinal Orsini that there were some who said that he was not Pope. "Get out of this, you devil," answered that emphatic prince of the Church; "whoso says this, lies in his throat. He is as much a Pope as you are a doctor of medicine."[2] Afterwards, the cardinals declared that they were still in fear of the Roman populace, surrounded by Urban's spies, and acting under compulsion; strange stories were told of ultramontane Carmelites and Augustinians who had fared badly at the hands of their Italian brethren for questioning the validity of the election.[3] Nevertheless, it is highly probable that, whether canonical or not, the cardinals would have accepted the situation, had it not been for Urban's own conduct.

Urban entered upon his pontificate with a sincere and uncompromising hatred of the corruption of the Curia and zeal for the reformation of the Church, but with a tactless vehemence that can only be explained on the assumption that his elevation had turned his head. Not content with enforcing regulations against simony and checking the luxury of the households of the cardinals, he

[1] Cf. especially the report of the Bishop of Viterbo, Pastor, *Acta Inedita*, doc. 3, in which, however, there is a manifest Urbanist exaggeration.

[2] Testimony of Francesco da Siena, *Archivio Vaticano*, LIV. 17, f. 76.

[3] Cf. Gayet, II. pp. 86, 92. One of the Bandaresi is said to have declared that, if any one ventured to call the validity of the election into question, "in veritate Romani quemcumque facientem dubium ponerent in peciis talibus, quod major pars esset auricula."

abused and insulted the individual members of the Sacred College, and announced that he would swamp them by the creation of new Italians and Romans. He stormed at them in public, calling one a fool, another a liar, bidding a third hold his tongue. He sprang from his seat to attack the Cardinal of Limoges, and there would have been a disgraceful brawl, if the Cardinal of Geneva had not intervened. On Low Sunday, April 25, the Cardinal of Amiens arrived in Rome, furious with his colleagues for electing an Italian, openly expressing his doubts as to the validity of the election. A violent scene took place in the papal palace. Urban declared that the Cardinal had destroyed the peace of the world by his treacherous diplomacy; the Cardinal retorted that, if his accuser were still the Archbishop of Bari, he would tell him that he lied in his throat. Such was Urban's bearing that even his salutary measures for reform, bidding cardinals repair and reside at their titular churches, bishops return to their sees, and the like, seemed to acquire the character of studied insults. Nor were the laity left untouched. Great nobles from Apulia and barons from the Campagna found themselves rebuked and their petitions denied them. Fra Gonsalvo, who had been absent from the city on business of his order during the conclave, tells us that at Gaeta he met Neapolitans returning from Rome, who were greatly scandalized at the conduct of the new pontiff, who drove people away from him with ignominy, "nobles and magnates and venerable clerics and religious." There was much discussion among the friars on the subject, but the prevalent opinion was that it made for righteousness and marked the beginning of a holy time, that men of bad life should be disturbed by the words of the Pope, for these persons "would not dare to go into the presence of Christ, the searcher of hearts."[1] Andrea di Piero Gambacorti, who had gone to congratulate him in his father's name, brought back a similar account of his proceedings to Pisa. "According to what he says," wrote the Prior of Gorgona to

[1] MS. *cit.*, ff. 58*v.*, 59. To the poor, however, Urban was gracious, granting them all the favours and graces they asked. Cf. Cristoforo da Piacenza in his despatch of June 24, Pastor, *Geschichte*, I. doc. 12.

Catherine, "this Holy Father of ours is a terrible man, and frightens people fearfully with his conduct and words. He seems to have a great trust in God, by reason of which he fears no man in the world, and he is manifestly striving to abolish the simony and great pomp that reigns in the Church of God."[1] But Urban did not reserve his wrath for evil-doers; the "servants of God" came in for their share, when they spoke unpalatable truths; we still possess Catherine's letter of apology for Fra Bartolommeo di Domenico, who, "by his fault of manner and his scrupulous conscience," had thus excited the ready anger of her "sweet Christ on earth."[2]

The presence of the Cardinal of Amiens in Rome seems to have brought things to a head. Led by him and Robert of Geneva, the cardinals resolved to use against Urban the weapon that the irregular nature of his election had put into their hands. Urban had mortally offended Onorato Gaetani, the Count of Fondi, by depriving him of the government of the Campagna, and refusing to repay a large loan which he had made to the Holy See. Amiens induced him to make common cause with the cardinals, and at the same time, together with the Cardinal of Geneva, he secretly encouraged Pierre Gandelin and Pierre Rostaing, who, in spite of promises from Urban and threats from the Romans, were still holding the Castello Sant' Angelo, not to surrender it to the Pope. This done, the ultramontane cardinals gradually left Rome, on plea of avoiding the heat, some with and some without Urban's leave, and made their way to Anagni (which the late Pope had fixed upon as the summer residence of the Curia), together with many other prelates of the court and the chamberlain, Pierre de Cros, who carried off the tiara of Gregory XI and most of the papal jewels. The first to go were the Cardinals of Aigrefeuille and Poitiers, who left on May 6; the last was Pedro de Luna, who stayed on in Rome until about June 24.

The position of the Cardinal of Aragon was a peculiar one. He could not but be aware that the election was regarded by most

[1] *Lettere dei discepoli*, 3. [2] Letter 302 (16).

spiritual persons as his work, and that they all looked to him to aid the Pope in reforming the Church. It is clear that he was most reluctant to break with Urban, or to take any steps against the unity of Christendom. When Fra Gonsalvo returned to Rome in June, he found him at Santa Maria in Cosmedin, his titular church, where he had taken up his residence in obedience to the papal decree. Alone with the Cardinal (whose confessor he was), the friar besought him to tell him the truth as to the reports that were spreading about Urban's election; to which he answered that they had elected him in good faith, but that his conduct since had been insupportable.[1] According to Alfonso da Vadaterra, he complained also of Urban's ingratitude. "The other ultramontane cardinals have all gone to Anagni," he said, as they walked together in his garden, "and why should I linger here with our lord, when he will grant me none of my requests?" At last, he decided to follow them, though Alfonso implored him not to go. "He told me," says the hermit-bishop, "that in his conscience he considered our lord the true Pope; but that, if he went to Anagni, he would do so to obviate the malice and sedition of the French cardinals, who had an utterly evil and vindictive intention against him; and that he thought to serve our lord the Pope better there than if he remained with him in Rome. And I believe certainly that he went with this good intention; he wished to catch others in Anagni, but, alas, was caught himself, which I cannot recall without heartfelt grief."[2]

Urban had at first no suspicion as to the intentions of the cardinals, and even talked of joining them at Anagni. He now took alarm, hearing that they were plotting against him and saying that he was not Pope, and summoned them to appear within a certain time in his presence at Tivoli, whither he went on June 27, accompanied by Cardinal Tebaldeschi. "I do not know what will happen," wrote Cristoforo da Piacenza, with cheerful optimism, to Lodovico Gonzaga, "but it is hoped that

[1] Deposition of Fra Gonsalvo, MS. *cit.*, f. 60.

[2] Raynaldus, vii. p. 379.

everything will be settled peaceably."[1] Urban had previously sent the three other Italians—Corsini, Brossano, and Orsini—to Anagni to assure the cardinals of his good intentions, "offering them many favours and advantages for themselves and their kin, and to do more for them than any Roman Pontiff had ever done." In public, the French cardinals professed themselves astonished that Urban should give credit to such reports about their intentions ; but, in private, they told their Italian colleagues that they regarded the Apostolic See as vacant, and urged them to stay with them. The three, however, returned to Urban, without having effected anything.[2] For a while, the cardinals continued to write to Urban as Pope and to treat him as such ; but this was only a device to gain time. At the summons of the chamberlain, Pierre de Cros, the Breton and Gascon mercenaries under Bernardon de la Salle marched up from Viterbo to Anagni for the defence of the Sacred College, passing within sight of Rome on their way. At the Ponte Salario, on July 16, the forces ot the Roman Republic attempted to dispute their passage, but were routed with loss of several hundreds killed. The infuriated Roman populace retaliated by a massacre of all the foreign priests and laymen who fell into their hands. The cardinals now openly declared that the election of Urban was null and void, because of the compulsion of the Romans, and, on July 20, summoned their Italian colleagues to join them at Anagni within five days. From Tivoli, on July 27, Marsile d'Inghen, who was representing the interests of the University of Paris at the papal court, wrote to the rector and heads of the University that a schism in the Church was imminent, and asked for instructions as to what he was to do under these circumstances.[3]

[1] Despatch of June 24. Pastor, *Geschichte*, I. doc. 12. The deposition of Pierre de Cros, Gayet, doc. 23, shows that the cardinals had hoped to entice Urban to Anagni in order to make him their prisoner.

[2] Cardinal Corsini's addition to the *casus* of the three Italian cardinals. Gayet, doc. 27. Cf. the report of the Bishop of Viterbo, Pastor, *Acta Inedita*, doc. 3.

[3] Du Boulay, IV. pp. 466, 467. Cf. Valois, I. p. 76 ; Gayet, II. p. 25. The letter from the foreign cardinals to the Italians is in Raynaldus, vii. p. 328.

The delay of the Sacred College in coming to a rupture with Urban had been in part due to the opposition of Pedro de Luna. "My lord of Geneva says that I am too conscientious," he said to Alvarez Martinez, a Spaniard attached to the Curia: "I certainly wish to see, and to see clearly, where the right lies; for I tell you that, if I were now to agree with them, and afterwards were in Avignon and found that by right this man was true Pope, I should go to him even barefoot, if I could not otherwise."[1] But at length, apparently sincerely converted by the arguments of his colleagues, he wrote to Fra Gonsalvo at Rome, asking him to come to him on important business. "I sent for you," he began, when the friar arrived, "that you might hear my confession, and that I might be comforted by your presence; but I must first ask you if you believe that the man at Tivoli is Pope, for, in that case, I think you cannot absolve me." "O holy Mother of God!" exclaimed the Dominican, "what is this? Do not flatter yourself, my lord Cardinal, that those words are written in water that you so often spoke to me in Rome to the contrary. What can you now answer to what you yourself then told me so frankly, as to your faithful son, your lover, your fellow-countryman?" The Cardinal, showing some embarrassment, admitted that he had come to Anagni with the intention of reconciling his colleagues with Urban, but declared himself now convinced that the latter was not Pope. To Gonsalvo's retort that the whole lot of them were being seduced by the devil, the Cardinal "answered right humbly that it was possible, for he was a mere man." He admitted that, if it had not been for Urban's behaviour, they would still have been with him, and professed his dread of schism, to avert which he asked Gonsalvo to exhort the Pope spontaneously to renounce the papacy, in order that they might proceed to a free election. Gonsalvo, "to escape from the snare into which I had fallen," accepted the commission, and the Cardinal paid his expenses back to Rome.[2]

[1] Baluze, I. col. 1182.

[2] Deposition of Fra Gonsalvo, MS. *cit.*, ff. 63*v.*–65.

Here he found Urban at S. Maria Maggiore, whither he had removed from Tivoli at the beginning of August, after having signed the peace with the Florentines. Tebaldeschi was the only cardinal in Rome—the other three Italians, at the end of July, having gone to Vicovaro and thence to Palestrina, where they were ostensibly negotiating with the Sacred College on Urban's behalf, in reality attempting to keep neutral. "I went to our lord the Pope," writes Gonsalvo, "and, after telling him my message concerning his abdication, I exhorted him, in the name of God, to dissipate the ambitious hosts of the devil which were mustering against him, and to take aid from God and all the Saints. But he, like a soldier who at length hears certain tidings that the longed-for war is decided upon, rejoiced, and answered me with joy: 'In God's own truth, I should reck little of laying down the papacy; but I will not resign to give place to the devil and make sinners exult. Nay, I will abide and beat them down in the name of the Lord our God.'"[1]

In the meanwhile, the Cardinals of Geneva, Poitiers, and Sant' Eustachio had been sent by their colleagues to Palestrina to induce the three Italians to come to Anagni; but without result. They now decided to proceed without them. On August 9, thirteen cardinals solemnly entered the cathedral of Anagni. After the Mass of the Holy Spirit had been sung, Jacopo d' Itri, Patriarch of Constantinople, preached from the text: *In te oculi respiciunt totius Israel, ut indices eis quis sedere debeat in solio tuo.*[2] The history of the usurpation of the kingdom by Adonijah the son of Haggith was, he declared, a figure of the present state of the Church. "Let us turn the eyes of our mind to our Queen, the glorious Virgin, that she may deign to plead our cause in the presence of the King her Son. The sheep of Christ's pasture are wandering through steep and devious ways, even as flocks that have no shepherd; he who usurpeth the name of shepherd, is not the shepherd, for he has not entered by the

[1] MS. *cit.*, f. 65*v*. (also in Raynaldus, vii. p. 318).

[2] "The eyes of all Israel are upon thee, that thou shouldest tell them who shall sit on the throne of my lord the king after him" (A.V., 1 Kings i. 20).

door into the sheepfold; he whose own the sheep are not, careth not to guard them from the invading wolves, from the roaring lions that are seeking to devour. Say, we beseech thee, O Queen, to the King: My only Son and my Lord, who didst lay down Thy life for all these, who didst redeem them by Thy precious blood, to place them on Thy right hand at the Day of Judgment; do Thou, the charioteer and the chariot of Israel, deliver them from the spoiler, and appoint a ruler and a shepherd over them. Instead of Adonijah who hath exalted himself in his pride, appoint unto them a meek and peaceful Solomon."[1] An encyclical letter signed by all the cardinals at Anagni was then read aloud, denouncing the intrusion into the papacy of the late Archbishop of Bari, declaring that they had only elected him to escape the peril of death, anathematizing him as an antipope, a deceiver and destroyer of Christians. They had previously addressed a letter to him in similar terms, exhorting him, "by the bowels of the mercy of Jesus Christ, whose Church and Spouse thou hast not blushed to invade," to lay down his usurped dignity, and strive to make amends by true penitence.[2] On August 27, for greater security, the Sacred College moved from Anagni to Fondi, to hold a fresh election under the protection of Onorato Gaetani.

The three Italian cardinals were now at Subiaco, where they kept in touch with both parties by letters and messengers, labouring, as they afterwards declared, "to deliver the Church from scandal and division, and to bring about her peace and union." At length, on September 4, they wrote to Urban from Suessa that they were about to take action, and were awaiting an answer from the other cardinals to know how to proceed. Shortly afterwards, they joined the Sacred College at Fondi; there is some evidence, from Clementine as well as Urbanist sources, that each of the three believed that he himself was to be the new Pope.[3]

[1] *Archivio Vaticano*, LIV. 31, ff. 4*v*.–7*v*. Many MSS. of this sermon have been preserved.

[2] Texts in Du Boulay, IV. pp. 467–478.

[3] Cf. Gayet, doc. 27; T. de Nyem, I. 10; Baluze, I. col. 1237.

In the meanwhile, Francesco Tebaldeschi, the last cardinal who adhered to Urban, died at Rome on September 6. A dying declaration, purporting to be his, was produced, to the effect that he died in the conviction that Urban VI was lawfully and canonically elected Pope. It seems certain that this was his belief, but by no means improbable that the document was forged in Urban's interests.[1] The Roman Pontiff was now left alone.

Queen Giovanna had received the first tidings of the elevation of her subject to the papacy with every manifestation of delight, and had sent a force of troops to Tivoli to guard his person, after the engagement at the Ponte Salario. But at the end of August, whether offended by Urban's treatment of her husband Otho, or seduced by her chancellor, Niccolò Spinelli, with whom the Pope had quarrelled, or really impressed by the declaration of the Sacred College, she turned against him, and sent the Count of Caserta with Niccolò Spinelli himself as her representatives to Fondi.[2] She was supported in this course, if, indeed, it had not first been suggested to her, by a letter from the King of France.

Early in April, the Cardinal of Amiens and Pierre de Cros had warned the King not to trust the official accounts of the election. In May, a month after the event, Urban had tardily notified his elevation to Charles by two envoys who arrived at Paris in June : Cecco Tortelli, a Neapolitan knight, and Pierre de Murles, a kinsman of Cardinal d'Aigrefeuille. The former was faithful to his countryman. The latter had secretly accepted a rival mission from the chamberlain and the French cardinals. While ostensibly acting as the envoy of the Pope and affirming Urban's lawful election, he privately warned the King that this was not the whole truth, and gave a vivid account of the violence to which the Sacred College had been subjected.[3] Not un-

[1] Cf. Raynaldus, vii. pp. 328, 329 ; Gayet, II. pp. 268–274 ; Valois, I. p. 72.

[2] Cf. T. de Nyem, I. 7, 8 ; Valois, I. pp. 77, 78. There was a report spread that Urban intended to give the kingdom of Naples to Louis of Hungary, and to send Giovanna to end her days in a convent.

[3] Valois, I. pp. 90–93. Cf. Relation of Jean le Fèvre in Du Boulay, IV. p. 523, and the deposition of Pierre de Cros in Gayet, doc. 23.

naturally, Charles declared that he must wait for more information before proceeding further in the recognition of the new Pope. At Avignon itself there was division ; two of the six cardinals, Anglico de Grimoard (as might have been expected from his past career) and the Cardinal of Pamplona, were unwilling to renounce allegiance to the man whom their colleagues at Rome had at first announced as Pope, and they even wrote to bid the custodians of Sant' Angelo surrender. But in August, a Franciscan friar, who had been confessor to the French Queen, came from Anagni with the formal declaration of the invalidity of Urban's election ; Charles accepted it, and wrote to the Queen of Naples assuring her of the applause of the world and of his own gratitude, if she would take the part of the cardinals and be the defender of the Church.[1] A little later, the Bishop of Farmagosta and Fra Niccolò da San Saturnino, the Dominican master of the Sacred Palace, arrived at Avignon on their way to Paris, with letters to the King, the Parliament, and the University. The six cardinals now definitely made common cause with their colleagues. At Paris, on September 13, the general assembly of the clergy of France decided that more information was needed, and advised the King not to commit himself. The latter, however, had already made up his mind ; he had offered his aid to the cardinals at Fondi ; and there can be little doubt that, although he did not at first publicly adhere to him, the second claimant to the papacy could fairly claim to have accepted the papal title with his full approval, *cum tuo suffragio*, as he wrote a few months later.[2]

The new conclave was held in the palace of the Count of Fondi, on September 20. The three Italians wished the election to be effected by way of compromise, the whole to be put into the hands of six cardinals, including themselves as three. This was negatived. Cardinal Corsini, as dean of the Sacred College, should have nominated a candidate, but he excused himself ; upon which the Cardinal of Limoges proposed the Cardinal of Geneva, who was unanimously elected. The three Italians abstained from

[1] Text of letter in Valois, I. p. 99 *n*.

[2] Valois, I. pp. 107, 108.

voting, but raised no objection. According to Pedro de Luna, they stated that they did this because of the danger that would otherwise involve their kindred and their goods, but he himself believed that they were discontented with the result.[1] On the following day, Robert of Geneva was proclaimed Pope as Clement VII, and, on October 31, he was solemnly crowned in the cathedral of Fondi.

The new Supreme Pontiff was proclaimed at Avignon on October 13; but the King of France still delayed taking the final step, until November 16, when, being so advised by a council assembled at Vincennes, he at length declared that he recognized Clement VII as lawful Pope.

But he had been anticipated throughout by his brother. Louis of Anjou, always dreaming of emulating the great Charles of his house who had conquered Naples, listened to the first appeal of the Sacred College, brought to him by Jean de Bar. He lent large sums of money to the cardinals, declared that the Count of Fondi was the anchor that Christ had provided for the salvation of the bark of Peter, acclaimed the election of Clement as the elevation of a personal friend,[2] and laid his sword and power at his feet—on the understanding, as was soon shown, that a very substantial reward should be his.

Queen Giovanna had already sent the Archbishop of Cosenza to congratulate Clement on his election, and an illustrious embassy of the noblest in her kingdom to assist at the coronation. It was not, however, until November 20 (four days after the King of France) that she made her solemn declaration in his favour. At the same time, she ordered the arrest of all Urbanist emissaries, and paid to Clement the 64,000 florins that she owed the Pope as her tribute to the Holy See.[3] The rest of Italy, with the exception of Savoy, Piedmont, and Monferrato, adhered to Urban, and Coluccio Salutati could freely, in the name of the Republic of Florence, pour forth the same torrents of fiery rhetoric upon the Clementine cardinals as he had previously employed against

[1] Gayet, doc. 31; Sorbelli, p. 268.

[2] See Valois, I. pp. 151 *n.*, 157 *n.*

[3] *Ibid.*, p. 160.

Urban's predecessor in the papacy. Only a few feudal nobles, like Francesco di Vico, the tyrant of Viterbo and titular prefect of Rome, openly opposed the Roman claimant—although Gian Galeazzo Visconti, who had succeeded his father Galeazzo as lord of Pavia in August, was married to a sister of the French King, and probably already contemplated the union of the whole Milanese dominion in his own person, secretly kept in touch with Louis of Anjou and the Clementine leaders.

From the outset, the Emperor Charles IV accepted Urban as lawful Pope, and vigorously supported his cause. Dying in November, 1378, he instructed his son and successor, Wenceslaus (whom Urban, after much delay, had recognized as King of the Romans at Tivoli, on July 26), to pursue the same course. But he did not carry all Germany with him. The Dukes of Bavaria, Luxemburg (the Emperor's own brother), and Lorraine, the Archbishop of Mayence, and, in general, the princes of the Empire most in touch with France, declared for Clement. Hostility to France led the counsellors of Richard II to adhere so fanatically to Urban that they refused to hear the other side; the Cardinal of Poitiers, appointed Clementine legate to England, was denied admission into the country; and those portions of France still subject to the English were compelled to adopt the faith of their rulers. Scotland acknowledged Clement, as also did Brittany, while Flanders was Urbanist. Louis of Hungary and Poland, then at the height of his power, after some delay, adhered to Urban. Charles the Bad of Navarre and Ferdinand of Portugal did not commit themselves. The Kings of Aragon and Castile, Pedro IV and Henry II, determined for the present to remain strictly neutral; and it is to the investigations of the ambassadors of Pedro and of Henry's successor, Juan I, that we owe the series of depositions and testimonies now preserved in the Vatican Archives upon which much of our knowledge of the details of the events that caused the Great Schism is ultimately based.

CHAPTER XIII

FROM SIENA TO ROME

"Prega la somma eterna Bontà di Dio, che ne faccia quello che sia suo onore e salute dell' anima; e specialmente ora, che sono per andare a Roma per compire la volontà di Cristo crocifisso e del vicario suo."—St. Catherine, Letter 316 (165).

AT the first rumour of a misunderstanding between the Sacred College and the Pope, Catherine had addressed an impassioned letter from Florence to Pedro de Luna : "with desire of seeing you a firm column, set in the garden of Holy Church, freed from that self-love which weakens every creature that has reason." "I seem to have heard," she wrote, "that discord is arising over there between Christ on earth and his disciples, from which I receive intolerable sorrow, for the mere dread that I have of heresy, which I fear greatly may come because of my sins. And, therefore, I beseech you, by that glorious and precious blood which was shed with such great fire of love, never to sever yourself from virtue and from your head. All other things—external war and other tribulations—would seem to us less than a straw or a shadow in comparison with this."[1]

Catherine had returned to Siena a few days before the solemn denunciation of Urban's usurpation of the papacy, at Anagni on August 9, announced the imminence of a schism in the Church. From her native city, she now beheld with unutterable anguish what men called the rending of the coat of Christ that was without seam. There can be no doubt that she heard only the extreme Urbanist version of what had happened, and she accepted it unreservedly with all the passionate fervour of her soul. "O men, not men, but rather demons visible," she cries, apostrophizing the cardinals, "how does the inordinate love that you have set on the dunghill of your own bodies, and on the

[1] Letter 293 (26). A better text is in the Palatine MS. 56, from which I quote.

delights and states of the world, blind you so, that, when the vicar of Christ, he whom you elected by a canonical election, wishes to correct your lives and that you should be sweet-smelling flowers in the garden of Holy Church, you now spread poison, and say he is not true Pope, but that you did it for fear, and for dread of the fury of the people? This is not the truth; and, if it had been, you were worthy of death for having elected the Pope with fear of men and not with fear of God. But this you cannot say, or, if you say it, cannot prove it; for what you did with fear, to appease the people, appeared manifestly to all when you put the mantle of St. Peter upon Messer di San Pietro, and said that you had chosen him Pope. This was seen not to be the truth; and it was found so, when the tumult ceased; and so he confessed, and you, too, that he was not Pope, but Messer Bartolommeo, Archbishop of Bari, was elected Pope. And what moved you, if the latter was not Pope, to re-elect him then afresh, with an orderly election, without any violence, and to crown him with such great solemnity, with all the order that is required for this function, as had not been done in the election of any of his predecessors? But I know what moves you to denounce him to the contrary: your self-love, which can brook no correction. For, before he began to bite you with words, and wished to draw the thorns out of the sweet garden, you confessed and announced to us, little sheep, that Pope Urban VI was true Pope. And so I confess, and do not deny him, that he is the vicar of Christ, who holds the keys of the blood in truth; which truth shall not be confounded by the liars and wicked men of the world, for the truth is the thing that sets us free. O wretches! you see not how you have fallen, because you have deprived yourselves of light. You have taken the poison for yourselves, but why do you give it to others? Have you no pity upon so many little sheep, who for this are leaving the fold?"[1]

And to the Count of Fondi, a few weeks before the election of Clement, she wrote that self-love and wicked anger had poisoned and corrupted him who should be a true worker in the

[1] Letter 312 (315), dated October 8, 1378, in the Harleian MS.

vineyard of the soul. "O dearest father, consider your position and look at your vineyard. In the secret of your heart, you hold that Pope Urban VI is the true Sovereign Pontiff; and whoso says otherwise is a heretic, rejected by God, no faithful Catholic, but a renegade Christian who denies his faith. We are bound to hold that he is the Pope, canonically elected, the vicar of Christ on earth, and we are bound to obey him even unto death. Even if he were so cruel a father as to hunt us with reproaches and with every torment from one end of the world to the other, we are still bound not to forget nor to persecute this truth. And if you said to me: 'On the contrary, I have been informed that Pope Urban VI is not in truth the Sovereign Pontiff'; I should answer that I know that God has given you so much light that, if you do not deprive yourself of it by the darkness of anger and resentment, you will know that whoso says this lies upon his own head. They make themselves liars, by retracting the truth that they delivered to us, and represent it as a lie. I know well that you know what has moved those who were set in the place of truth that they might spread the faith. Now they have contaminated the faith and denied the truth; they have raised such a schism in Holy Church that they are worthy of a thousand deaths. You will find that nought else has moved them save that passion which has moved you yourself, to wit, self-love which could not endure a harsh word or rebuke, nor to be deprived of territory, but conceived resentment and brought forth anger as child. By this they, and all who act against this truth, are depriving themselves of the goods of heaven. The evidence that can be seen of this truth is so plain and so clear and so manifest, that even the most unlearned person can see and understand it."[1]

Two of those for whose spiritual welfare she had been specially solicitous and upon whom she had based great hopes as possible champions of Christ and the Church—Duke Louis of Anjou and Queen Giovanna of Naples—were among the first to reject this truth, which to Catherine seemed so clear and manifest.

[1] Letter 313 (192), revised by the Harleian MS.

Pedro de Luna himself, the pious and charitable Cardinal of Aragon, had become one of the "incarnate demons." The prior-general of the Carthusians, Guillaume Rainaud, was preparing to lead his flock into the Clementine fold, and Catherine's appeal to him, written in her name by Stefano Maconi, passed unheeded.[1] She was doubtless to be spared the knowledge that a young Dominican, born three years after herself and just ordained priest by the hands of Pedro de Luna, of life as holy and of eloquence only less fervid than her own, destined to be raised to the altars of the Church as St. Vincent Ferrer, was throwing himself heart and soul into the conflict on behalf of Clement, and by his word and pen was soon to draw Spain from her attitude of neutrality to recognize the Pope of Avignon.[2] But she already saw the shining lights of the order passing into the enemy's camp; her zealous and devout master-general, Fra Elias of Toulouse, accepted Clement as Pope; the eloquence of the master of the Sacred Palace, Fra Niccolò da San Saturnino, had been employed on behalf of the cardinals at Anagni. The time has come, she writes to Suora Daniella of Orvieto, to take the food of souls, by offering up humble and continual prayers with impassioned desire to God, at the table of the Cross. "It is the time for this at all times; but neither thou nor any one else ever saw another time of greater necessity. Bethink thee, daughter mine, with sorrow and bitterness, of the darkness that has come into Holy Church. Human aid seems to be failing us; it befits thee and the other servants of God to invoke His aid. Look to it not to be negligent; it is time to watch and not to sleep. Thou knowest well that, if the guards and others of the city slept when the enemy were at the gates, there is no doubt that they would lose it. We are surrounded by many enemies; for thou knowest that the world and our own frailty

[1] Cf. Bartholomaeus Senensis, *op. cit.*, Lib. III. cap. 2. This letter, now lost, is not to be confused with Letter 55 (53), written to Dom Guillaume at an earlier date.

[2] His treatise, *De Moderno Ecclesiae Schismate*, was dedicated to the King of Aragon in 1380.

and the demon, with the many thoughts he brings, never sleep, but are always ready to see if we are sleeping, to be able to enter in, and like thieves plunder the city of the soul; and, even as our own soul, so, too, is the mystical body of Holy Church surrounded by many enemies. Thus thou seest that those who are set for columns and supporters of Holy Church have become her persecutors, with the darkness of heresy. We must not sleep, but defeat them with vigils, tears, sweat, with mournful and loving desires, with humble and continual prayer. Like a faithful daughter of Holy Church, pray and constrain the most high and sweet God to help us now in this need; and pray Him to strengthen the Holy Father and give him light. I speak of Pope Urban VI, truly Pope and vicar of Christ on earth. And so I confess, and we are bound to confess, before all the world; and on no account must we believe whoso should say or hold the contrary, but rather choose death."[1]

For more than three months, Catherine remained quietly at Siena, dictating to her secretaries her great mystical book, the *Dialogo*, which she finished in October, and her letters which she was despatching in all directions, while she awaited the summons to fight her last battle in the Eternal City.

The dates have been preserved in the manuscripts of an unusual number of the letters that she wrote or dictated during these months, beginning with one on August 27, to Madonna Lodovica di Granello Tolomei, on true and perfect charity.[2] We find her writing to Pope Urban himself, on September 18, urging him to reform the morals of the clergy, to appoint virtuous bishops, to surround himself with the servants of God and to lean upon their counsel.[3] On this very day, at Rome, Urban was creating a new College of cardinals to take the place of those who had deserted him, but six of the twenty-nine he had nominated (including the Bishop of Autun, who afterwards received it from Clement) refused to accept the hat from his hands. With the exception of Fra Bonaventura Badoara and the Archbishop of

[1] Letter 308 (164).

[2] Letter 304 (345).

[3] Letter 305 (17).

Pisa, the others were either men of small note or appointed for political reasons; they included Pileo da Prata, Archbishop of Ravenna, Agapito Colonna, and Philippe de Alençon, the Patriarch of Jerusalem, a kinsman of the King of France. The Bishop of London, William Courtenay, was among those who declined the papal offer. On October 4, Catherine wrote to Monna Agnese, the wife of the Florentine tailor, tenderly forbidding her to practise excessive and imprudent austerities;[1] and, on October 5, to Pope Urban again, the news of Clement's election having reached her: "with the desire of seeing you robed in the strong garment of most ardent charity, in order that the blows that are hurled at you by the wicked men of the world, lovers of themselves, may not be able to harm you." In the strength of this garment, let him fearlessly enter the battle against the Antichrist that the incarnate demons have raised up against him.[2] She wrote, on October 8, to the Queen of Naples, imploring her not to pervert the light into darkness by aiding the cardinals or acknowledging their Antipope; let her, at least, remain neutral until the truth is made manifest to her.[3] A letter to the tailor Francesco and his wife, a letter of spiritual comfort and exhortation, dated October 13, has a peculiarly interesting postscript: "I pray you to take at once to Giannozzo the letter that I send you with this, and do not fail to take it to him wherever he is."[4] Here we find Catherine in direct communication with Giannozzo Sacchetti, and, in the light of his tragic fate in the following year, it would have been of very great, even painful interest, to know what was the subject of the Saint's letter to him. A letter to a Florentine lady, on the patient reception of tribulations, with what seems a reference to the harsh judgments passed upon her own mission to Florence, is of October 20.[5] On October 23,

[1] Bibl. Nazionale di Firenze, MS. xxxviii. 130.

[2] Letter 306 (18).

[3] Letter 312 (315).

[4] Bibl. Nazionale di Firenze, MS. *cit.*

[5] Letter 307 (368). In several MSS. it is dated "a dì xx d'Octobre a Firenze, 1378," the address having got confused with the text. Catherine was at Siena and her correspondent at Florence.

she wrote to a certain Giovanni da Parma in Rome, whose conscience was disturbed by some unnamed book that he had been studying: God has given us a book, His Word, the Son of God, which was written on the Cross, not with ink but with blood, a book that the most unlettered and dull of apprehension can read; "and I am certain that, if you will read in this sweet book, your book, by which you seem to be so harassed, will not give you any trouble."[1] To Tora di Messer Piero Gambacorti, afterwards known in the history of the Dominican order as the Beata Chiara, who, after much opposition from her father, had just, by the intervention of Alfonso da Vadaterra, been allowed to take the veil, Catherine wrote, on October 26, warning her that the Divine Bridegroom whom she had chosen is very jealous, and urging her as soon as possible to become His true servant and bride.[2]

At last the summons came from Urban, who realized to the full what a weapon the venerated maiden of Siena would be in his hands, to come to Rome. Raimondo tells us that she at first pleaded that her constant journeys scandalized many in Siena, and some of her own sisters in religion; she required an express order from the Pope, that it might be quite clear that she was acting under holy obedience.[3] "By the great goodness of God, and by the command of the Holy Father," she wrote, on November 4, to the tailor Francesco, "I believe that I am going to Rome about the middle of this month, more or less, as shall please God, and we shall go by land; so I tell you this as I promised you. Pray God to make us fulfil His will. I pray you, Francesco, for the love of Christ crucified, to take the trouble of delivering the letters which I am sending you with this, quickly for the honour of God and to please me. Go to Monna Pavola and tell her, if she has not had what she wanted from court, to write to me, and I will do for her as for my

[1] Letter 309 (299).

[2] Letter 262 (322); the date (with some additional matter) is in the MS. xxxviii. 130 of the Bibl. Nazionale di Firenze.

[3] *Legenda*, III. i. 3 (§ 333).

mother. Tell her to pray, and to make all her daughters pray for us. Find Niccolò, the poor man of Romagna, and tell him that I am about to go to Rome, and that he must take heart and pray to God for us."[1] "Pray the supreme eternal goodness of God," she wrote to Suora Daniella, "that He may do with us what may be His honour and the salvation of souls; and especially now that I am to go to Rome to fulfil the will of Christ crucified and of His vicar. I do not know which way I shall take. Pray Christ sweet Jesus that He send us by that which is most to His honour, with peace and quiet to our souls."[2]

Catherine reached Rome on November 28, 1378, the first Sunday in Advent, *con molta pace*, as she wrote to Stefano Maconi, who was detained at Siena by family affairs.[3] A large band of men and women accompanied her, including Alessa, Cecca, Lisa, Giovanna di Capo, Neri di Landoccio, Barduccio Canigiani, Gabriele Piccolomini, Fra Bartolommeo di Domenico, Fra Santi, and Giovanni Tantucci. "Many more would have come," writes Raimondo, "if she had not forbidden it. Those who came committed themselves to the Divine Providence in voluntary poverty, choosing rather to go wandering and begging with the holy virgin, than, by staying in comfort in their own houses, to be deprived of such sweet and virtuous conversation."[4] Raimondo himself, who was still prior of the Minerva, met them in Rome, and Lapa seems to have joined them later. On November 30, Lando di Francesco, then in Rome as ambassador of Siena to obtain the restitution of Talamone, wrote to the Signoria: "Caterina di Monna Lapa has come here, and our lord the Pope has seen and heard her right gladly. It is not known what he

[1] See Appendix, Letter V. Monna Pavola, the head of a house of spiritual women in Fiesole, and Niccolò, a Romagnole beggar in Florence, were already among Catherine's correspondents.

[2] Letter 316 (165).

[3] Letter 319 (255). A portion of this letter, apparently in Barduccio's autograph, is preserved in the MS. T. iii. 3, at Siena. The statement of Barth. Senensis, *op. cit.*, Lib. I. cap. 10, that Stefano accompanied Catherine to Rome and wished to be sent as her ambassador to Naples, is manifestly erroneous.

[4] *Legenda*, III. i. 3 (§ 333).

has asked of her, but he was glad to see her. Castello Sant' Angelo is still holding out, and the Romans are bombarding it daily."[1]

Urban received Catherine in a public audience, surrounded by those of his new cardinals who were in Rome. At his bidding, she addressed them, urging them to constancy and faith in the Divine Providence. "This poor little woman puts us to shame by her courage," he said, when she had finished; "what need the vicar of Jesus Christ fear, although the whole world stand against him? Christ the Almighty is more powerful than the world, and He will never abandon His Church."[2]

The situation was full of peril. Francesco di Vico from Viterbo was ravaging the Patrimony, Giordano Orsini at Marino could threaten the very gates of Rome, Clement had armed galleys at the mouth of the Tiber to intercept Urban's communication with the sea, while in the Neapolitan territory and elsewhere troops were being collected, to decide the quarrel by force of arms. The Romans had taken the siege of Castello Sant' Angelo into their own hands, but could not prevail over the vigorous resistance of the two French captains, and Urban, unable to take up his residence in the Vatican, was compelled to remain at S. Maria in Trastevere. Here, on November 29, the day after Catherine's arrival, he issued a bull anathematizing the "nurslings of iniquity and sons of perdition": Clement himself, the ex-Cardinals of Amiens, Marmoutier, and Sant' Eustachio; the Count of Fondi; Pierre de Cros, the Patriarch of Constantinople, the Archbishop of Cosenza, and a number of other prelates; the Count of Caserta, Francesco di Vico, Niccolò Spinelli, and the three leaders of the Breton and Gascon mercenaries, Jean de Malestroit, Silvestre Budes, and Bernardon de la Salle.[3]

[1] *Lettere dei discepoli*, 10.

[2] *Legenda*, III. i. 4 (§ 334).

[3] Raynaldus, vii. pp. 362–366. Cf. Valois, I. p. 162. In December, Clement made Pierre de Cros, the Patriarch of Constantinople, the Archbishop of Cosenza, and Fra Niccolò da San Saturnino cardinals, together with the minister-general of the Friars Minor, Fra Leonardo de' Griffoni.

Urban's evident unwillingness to proceed against Pedro de Luna is noticeable, as also the fact that the bull still speaks of the three Italian cardinals, Corsini, Brossano, and Jacopo Orsini, who had retired to Tagliacozzo after the election of Clement, as "our venerable brother and our beloved sons." It is clear that he did not yet regard them as his enemies.

There is something heroic (tragically pathetic, even, in the light of his subsequent fall) in the figure of this coarse-grained, violent, and implacable man, firmly believing in the justice of his own claims to be the vicar of the Prince of Peace, surrounded by men who were prepared to turn against him when it should serve their purposes, thus setting out to battle against the world in what he deemed the cause of righteousness, with the pale, ecstatic figure of the stigmatized Bride of Christ by his side. His first impulse was to employ her for the conversion of the Queen of Naples, sending her and Catherine of Sweden together as his ambassadors to win her over to his side. Catherine of Siena accepted the mission with alacrity and enthusiasm; but Catherine of Sweden, who remembered with lively horror what she had seen of the court of Naples at the time of her brother's death, absolutely refused to go. Fra Raimondo, who also knew more of his sovereign and her ways than did his spiritual mistress, was so much impressed by the Swedish maiden's fears that he frankly opened his mind to Urban on the subject; and the latter, after some thought, decided that it was better that they should not go. Catherine, yearning like a mother over the Queen's soul, and longing herself for martyrdom, was bitterly disappointed. "If Agnes and Margaret had thought upon these things," she said, "they would never have won the crown of martyrdom. Is not our Bridegroom able to protect us? These are vain considerations, which proceed from lack of faith rather than from true prudence."[1] She had, for

[1] *Legenda*, III. i. 5 (§ 335). Cf. Comtesse de Flavigny, *Sainte Brigitte de Suède*, pp. 532–537, but I can find no evidence of any direct intercourse between the two Catherines.

the present, to content herself with sending another flaming letter to Giovanna, once more urging the Urbanist case upon her, threatening her with the divine vengeance and the rebellion of her own subjects as the result of her vacillations. "I beseech you," she wrote, "fulfil in yourself the will of God and the desire of my soul, with which I desire, with all my heart and with all the powers of my soul, your salvation. And, therefore, constrained by the Divine Goodness which loves you ineffably, I have set myself to write to you with great grief. I wrote to you once before about this matter. Have patience, if I burden you too much with words, and if I speak to you confidently, irreverently. The love that I bear you makes me speak with confidence; the sin that you have committed makes me depart from the reverence I owe you, and speak irreverently. Very much more am I fain to tell you the truth by word of mouth, for your salvation, and principally for the honour of God, than by writing."[1] For some while, Catherine continued to hope that she might still be able to go to Naples, and win the wayward soul of the Queen to what she deemed "the truth that we must know and love for our salvation."

Another and more grievous disappointment awaited Catherine. In November, Urban had decided to send a second embassy to France, and his choice had fallen upon Fra Raimondo as one of the ambassadors. The other was Jacopo di Ceva, "marshal of the Roman Curia," the same official who had acted as Pope Gregory's procurator in the process against the Florentines; and they were to be joined on their arrival by a third, Guillaume de la Voulte, whom Urban had transferred from the bishopric of Marseilles to that of Valence, and who had not yet joined the Clementines. The friar was charged with briefs to the King, to the University of Paris (which was divided on the question of the day, one strong party still favouring Urban, while another desired an appeal to a General Council), to the Duke of Anjou, to Cardinal de Grimoard,

[1] Letter 317 (316).

and various French bishops.[1] Early in December, Raimondo set out. After more than a year's separation, they had only passed a few days in each other's company, and Catherine, while urging him to go in the service of the Church, felt the separation most keenly. Instinctively, she knew that the long conversation they had together before he started was to be their last: "We shall never speak like this to each other again," she said. The ship lay waiting in the Tiber, that was to take him to Pisa. Catherine accompanied him to the bank; when the sailors began to row, she knelt awhile in prayer, and then, rising and weeping, made the sign of the Cross as the ship passed away. "She seemed to be saying," writes the friar: "thou, my son, wilt go in safety, for the sign of the holy Cross is protecting thee; but, in this life, thou shalt never see thy mother more."

Raimondo's ship, in spite of the Clementine galleys that were guarding the mouth of the Tiber and scouring all the Italian coast, reached Pisa in safety. Here he received a letter from Catherine, written "with desire of seeing you illumined with a true and most perfect light." "Do you know," she asks, "how much my soul desires this? As much as she desires herself to be delivered from darkness, and to be united and blended with the light. I beseech you, by the love of Christ crucified and of that sweet Mother Mary, that you strive, to the utmost of your power, to fulfil in yourself the will of God and my desire; for then will my soul be blessed. It is no longer time to sleep, but to wake up from the slumber of negligence and rise up from the blindness of ignorance, and royally espouse the truth with the ring of most holy faith, and proclaim that truth, never keeping it

[1] Cf. Denifle, *Chartularium Universitatis Parisiensis*, Tom. iii. pp. 663–665. The brief, giving the friar authority for preaching and acting against the election of Clement, is dated November 8, the others November 21 and 28; but it is clear from Raimondo's own words in the *Legenda* that he left Rome at least some days after Catherine's arrival, and her Letter 323 (54) shows that he had started by December 13.

lent for any fear; but be prepared boldly and generously ı give one's life, if need be, all inebriated with the blood of ıe humble and immaculate Lamb, drawing it from the breast ˆ His most sweet Spouse, Holy Church, which we see all ismembered."[1] The friar continued his journey by sea to enoa, and thence by land to Ventimiglia. Jacopo di Ceva as arrested at the frontier by the soldiers of the Count of eneva, Clement's brother. Raimondo himself received a arning that an ambush was set for him and that his death as certain, if he went any further; he returned to Genoa, ıd reported what had happened to Urban, who bade him stay here he was and preach the crusade against the Clementines.[2] 'he Pope appears to have been perfectly satisfied with his onduct; but to Catherine it seemed a betrayal of the truth, pusillanimous flight from martyrdom. "God has wished ou to know your own imperfection," she wrote, "showing ou that you are still a child that needs milk, and not a man ı live on bread; for if He had seen that you had teeth for , He would have given it to you, even as He did to your ompanions. You were not yet worthy to stay upon the field f battle, but you were driven back like a child; and you ed away willingly, and were glad at the grace that God ranted to your weakness. Naughty father mine, how blessed ould your soul and mine have been, if with your blood you ad built up a stone in Holy Church for love of the blood!"[3]

In the meanwhile, at Catherine's instigation, Urban had esolved to summon the "servants of God" to his aid, to fill ome with men of great repute for sanctity, and at least ecure that all the spiritual forces within the Church should e on his side. "In this horrible tempest that threatens the hurch with shipwreck," he wrote, on December 13, to the

[1] Letter 330 (99); in the Harleian and Casanatense MSS.

[2] *Legenda*, III. i. 6, 7 (§§ 336, 337).

[3] Letter 333 (100). Jacopo di Ceva was kept a prisoner until, like Guilıme de la Voulte, he passed over to the side of Clement. Cf. Denifle, *op. cit.*, om. iii. p. 557, and Valois, I. p. 125 *n.*

Prior of Gorgona, Don Bartolommeo Serafini, "we believe and hope to be divinely helped by the prayers and tears of the just, rather than by the arms of soldiers and by human prudence. Therefore, with Peter, who when he was sinking in the sea besought aid from the Lord, and straightway merited to be delivered by His loving hand, earnestly and with devotion of heart, we summon to our assistance the devout tears and assiduous prayers of the just children of the Church, that they may humbly and devoutly assail the ears of the Lord, and He may the sooner bend to have compassion upon us." The monk is to have special prayers and sacrifices offered, night and day, in all the congregations and hermitages of men and women in Tuscany and elsewhere, and to seek out certain representatives of the different religious orders, including Giovanni dalle Celle and William Flete, and with them present himself in Rome before the Pope by the second Sunday after the Epiphany.[1] A number of others, not named in this bull, seem also to have been summoned, including Frate Antonio da Nizza and Fra Paolino da Nola, of Lecceto, and three of the hermits of Monte Luco, above Spoleto.

Catherine herself forwarded the bull to the Prior of Gorgona. "Now is our time," she wrote, "in which it will be seen who is a lover of the truth. We must arise from slumber and place the blood of Christ before our eyes, in order that we may be more inspirited for the battle. Our sweet Holy Father, Pope Urban VI, true Supreme Pontiff, seems to mean to adopt that remedy which is necessary for the reformation of Holy Church; he wishes to have the servants of God by his side, and to guide himself and Holy Church by their counsels. For this reason he sends you this bull, in which is contained that you have to summon all those who are written there. Do it zealously and quickly, and without loss of time; for the Church of God has need of no delay. Set

[1] Bull published by Gigli, in notes to Catherine's letter to Don Bartolommeo. An earlier brief (of doubtful authenticity), dated September 6, 1378, is in Barth. Senensis, *op. cit.*, Lib. IV. cap. 5, and Tromby, *Storia del Patriarca S. Brunone*, etc., VII. App. I. doc. 38.

side every other thing, be it what it may, and urge on the others o be here soon. Do not delay, do not delay, for the love of God. Enter this garden to labour here ; Fra Raimondo has gone to labour over there, for the Holy Father has sent him to he King of France. Pray God for him, that He may make him true sower of the truth ; and that he may lay down his life for t, if there be need. The Holy Father bears himself well and oyally, like a man virile and just and zealous for the honour of God, as he is." [1] She wrote simultaneously to the hermits of Spoleto, Frate Andrea da Lucca and his companions ; to Giovanni lalle Celle ; to William Flete and Frate Antonio ; urging them to bey the call of the Pope and leave their cells. "I shall see," she vrote to the two of Lecceto, "if we have really conceived love or the reformation of Holy Church ; for, if it is so in sooth, you vill follow the will of God and of His vicar ; you will leave the vood, and come to enter the field of battle. But, if you do not lo it, *you will be disregarding the will of God*." [2] *And* to the ermits of Spoleto : "You need not fear delights or great conolations, for you come to endure and to find no pleasure save hat of the Cross." [3] "I pray you for another thing," she says t the end of the letter to Giovanni dalle Celle, "and urge you, n the name of Christ crucified, to go to Florence, and tell those vho are your friends, and who can do it, that they be pleased to elp their father and keep the promises they have made to him. Let them not show such great ingratitude for the graces they ave received from God and from his Holiness. You know well hat ingratitude dries up the fountain of piety, and how many races they have received. And what punishment have they eceived for the offences that they have committed ? None from im, but only favours. If they do not recognize this, they will eceive it from the Supreme Judge, which will be incomparably nore severe than any human chastisement. And, therefore, pray hem most earnestly to do their duty, and not let themselves

[1] Letter 323 (54). [2] Letter 326 (127).
[3] Letter 327 (135).

be deceived by the flatteries of that demon incarnate, the Antipope."[1]

The Prior of Gorgona and most of the others seem, sooner or later, to have obeyed the papal summons; but, to Catherine's indignation, William Flete flatly refused to leave his wood, declaring that this was a device of the devil to deprive the servants of God of their spiritual consolations. It was even whispered that Giovanni Tantucci had gone to Rome simply for advancement. Catherine was too much hurt to write to William himself on the matter. "The youth who is bringing you the present letter," she wrote to Frate Antonio, "told me that you would come before Easter, but now it seems from the letter that Friar William has sent me that neither he nor you are coming. I do not intend to answer that letter; but I am very sorry for his simplicity, because little honour of God or edification to his neighbour is the result of it. If he does not wish to come for humility or for fear of losing his peace, he ought to use that virtue of humility, that is, he should meekly and humbly crave leave from the vicar of Christ, beseeching his Holiness to be pleased to let him stay in the wood for his greater peace; resigning himself, nevertheless, to his will, like one truly obedient; and this would be more pleasing to God and profitable to his own soul. But it seems to me that he has done entirely the contrary, declaring that he who is bound to the divine obedience need not obey creatures. I should not care about the other creatures, but that he should include the vicar of Christ, this grieves me greatly, seeing him so at variance with the truth; for the divine obedience never draws us from obedience to him; nay, the more perfect our obedience to God, the more perfect is this other, and we are ever bound to be subject and obedient to his commands, even unto death. Even if the injunction he laid upon us should seem indiscreet, and deprive us of peace and consolation of mind, we should obey; and, if we did the contrary, I deem it to be a great

[1] Casanatense MS. 292. This passage is omitted in the printed versions of Letter 322 (71).

nperfection and a deceit of the demon. It seems, according to 'hat he writes, that two servants of God have had a great evelation that Christ on earth, and whoso has advised him to end for these servants of God, have been deceived, and that this ; a human thing and not divine, and has been an inspiration rom the devil rather than from God, to wish to draw His ervants from their peace and consolation ; saying that, if you and he others came, you would lose your fervour, and thus would ot be able to help with prayer, nor abide in spirit with the Holy 'ather. Too lightly is the spirit harnessed, if it is lost by change f place ! It seems that God is an accepter of places, and that Ie is to be found only in the wood, and not elsewhere in the ime of necessity. Then shall we say that, on the one hand, we lesire that the Church of God be reformed, that the thorns be lrawn out, and the sweet-smelling flowers of the servants of God e planted therein ; while, on the other side, we say that to send or them, and draw them from peace and quiet of mind, in order hat they may come to help this Bark, is a deception of the lemon ? He might at least speak for himself, and not speak of he other servants of God in general, since we need not bring the ervants of the world into it ! Not thus have acted Frate Andrea la Lucca, nor Frate Paolino, such great servants of God, although ld and in weak health, who had been so long a time in their eace ; nevertheless, at once, with labour and inconvenience to hemselves, they set out, and they have come and fulfilled their bedience ; and albeit the desire constrains them to return to heir cells, they would not therefore depart from the yoke ; but hey say : *let what I have said be as not said;* and drown their wn wills and their own consolations. Whoso comes, comes to ndure and not to be made a prelate, but for the dignity of many abours, with tears, vigils, and continual prayer. So one should lo. Now let us distress ourselves no more about this matter, or we should have too much to say ; but I am amazed at one hing, seeing that I know the contrary : that I should see it judged hat the Master, Giovanni, has come only to exalt himself. With ll my heart I feel intolerable grief at this, seeing, under the pretence of virtue, God so manifestly offended, for the intention of a creature neither can nor ought to be judged; even if we knew of some fault, which we saw by its result, we ought not to judge the intention, but with great compassion bear it in the sight of God; we do the contrary when deceived by our own opinions. May God in His infinite mercy send us in sincerity along the way of truth, and give us true and most perfect light, that we may never walk in darkness. I pray you and the Bachelor, and the other servants of God, to pray the humble Lamb that He may make me go by His way. I say no more. As for your coming and staying, and Friar William's, may the will of God be done. I hardly expected that he would come, and also I did not expect him to answer with such disregard of holy obedience, nor with such simplicity. Commend me to him and to all the others; I pray you and him to pardon me, if I have been the cause of scandalizing you and giving you trouble; I confess that I am a scandal to all the world, being so ignorant and full of defects as I am. Remain in the holy and sweet charity of God."[1]

Catherine seems soon to have forgiven her English disciple, who, for the rest, was working efficaciously for Urban in his solitude.[2] Those that came all stayed in the house that had apparently been assigned to Catherine by the Pope in the Rione della Colonna (not to be confused with the "Contrada di Piazza Colonna," where she afterwards took the house in which her chapel is still shown), and lived there as her guests. The number of persons who thus lived in her house was at the least twenty-four, sixteen men and eight women, and at times it increased to between thirty and forty. They lived entirely upon alms, partly begged in Rome itself, partly collected by her friends and disciples

[1] Casanatense MS. 292. The printed versions of this striking letter, 328 (130), omit a great part of this passage.

[2] He had a vision, while celebrating Mass, to the effect that Bartolommeo of Bari was truly Pope, and wrote to England upon the subject, with the result that his testimony was accepted by his countrymen as an argument for their adherence to the Roman claimant. Cf. the *Rationes Anglicorum*, in Raynaldus, vii. p. 338.

Lombardi

St. Catherine of Siena.

Andrea di Vanni — Church of San Domenico, Siena

in Siena and elsewhere. Most of them were fasting perpetually, and only ate one meal in the day. Each week one of the women in turn did the housekeeping, so that the others might be free for their devotions, or for whatever other matters had brought them to Rome. Raimondo tells us that one day Giovanna di Capo, whose turn it was, had forgotten to provide any bread or to tell Catherine that there was none in the house, but that, when the starving *servi di Dio* sat down to table, it was miraculously multiplied, so that an abundance was afterwards given to the poor.[1] Catherine herself frequently went through the streets to beg for what they needed, but, for the most part, she was absorbed in pressing her spiritual counsels upon Urban, in dictating letter after letter on his behalf, and in her usual apostolic work among the poor.

And, in the meanwhile, men's minds on both sides were growing more and more embittered, as the rent in the seamless coat widened, and the clash of temporal arms began to be heard above the thunders of ecclesiastical fulminations. "If Christ, who is our peace," wrote Luigi Marsili from Paris, to Guido dal Palagio, "He who out of diverse unbelieving nations has formed and united one Church in His own blood, does not intervene, I fear that this evil beginning will have a worse sequence and the worst end ; for men's wills are so discordant that they do not let their intellects freely consider the truth, and every day the one side gets further from the other. I am in a place where I can do nothing, save pray to God that He may make all those who are faithful to Him full of charity ; for, without that, we can have no perfect concord."[2] Vague prophecies of the approaching end of the world began to spread abroad, and there was a strange revival of the doctrines of the Abbot Joachim, that had been forgotten for more than a century. Even Giovanni dalle Celle was inclined to these opinions. We find him writing to Guido dal Palagio that, although Christ would not reveal the end of

[1] *Legenda*, II. xi. 4–6 (§§ 301–303).

[2] Letter dated December 6, 1378, included in *Lettere del B. Giovanni dalle Celle*, p. 18.

the world to His apostles, He had revealed it to the Abbot Joachim, in order that men might be ready for it, now that it was at hand. He interprets a prophecy ascribed to the Abbot as meaning that after Urban VI—"Papa Urbano che fa tanti miracoli"—will come a Gregory, who is to be the last Pope, after whom will come Antichrist, whom some say will be Pope: "Thou art young and wilt probably see all these things, if thou livest to the normal age." [1]

Nevertheless, the new year, 1379, opened well for the Urbanist cause. England had declared emphatically for the Roman claimant; the King of the Romans was treading in his father's steps; Louis of Hungary and Poland, the chief arbiter of war and peace in eastern Europe, gave hopes of armed intervention. On January 1, Catherine, who had already forgiven William Flete (perhaps in consideration of his letters to his own countrymen), wrote to Pietro di Giovanni Ventura and Stefano Maconi: "Through the sweet goodness of God, Holy Church and Pope Urban VI have in these days received the most satisfactory news that they have had for a long time. I send you with this a letter addressed to the Bachelor, in which you can see how God is beginning to pour out His grace upon His sweet Spouse. And so I hope in His mercy that He will continue, multiplying His gifts day by day. I know that His truth cannot lie; He has promised to reform her by much endurance on the part of His servants, and by means of their humble and continuous prayers, offered up with tears and travail." [2]

In Siena itself, the government and populace alike had unhesitatingly declared from the outset for Urban, who had sent Jacomo di Sozzino Tolomei, the Bishop of Narni, as his nuncio to the city. "As to the Holy Father," wrote Cristofano Guidini to Neri di Landoccio, "I do not believe that there is a single man in Siena who does not hold and believe that Pope Urban is the true pastor of Holy Church, and if any ambassadors of the

[1] *Lettere cit.*, 27. Cf. *Anonimo Fiorentino*, pp. 389, 390.

[2] Letter 332 (264).

Antipope come here, they will not be heard." [1] Stefano was still kept at Siena by his family affairs, which, in spite of Catherine's exhortations to cut and not wait to untie the knots that bound him to the world, he was unable to get off his hands. He kept up a constant correspondence with Neri di Landoccio, expressing the extreme delight with which he had heard of Urban's proceedings, and assuring him of the loyalty of the Sienese. "And, in proof of this, I tell thee further that when, a few days ago, it was first rumoured that an ambassador of that antidemon of Fondi was coming hither, who had already been to Pisa, and it was feared that he might be given audience here, many who desired the honour of God (among whom I will not exclude myself, however lukewarmly I may desire it) appealed to the Palace, and also to others outside who could prevent it; representing to them that this demon came to sow heresy and to contaminate our faith, adding that it would be greatly to the honour of God if he were burned. And Pietro and I in particular went at once to my lord of Narni, in order that he might go to the Signoria, offering ourselves as his servants to be the first to lay hands upon him; and I promise thee that we found the people so well disposed that thou wouldst have been greatly delighted; and especially those of the Palace, who at once gave orders that he should not be allowed to enter the gate. Besides this, they would have consented to his being stoned by the children; and I am certain that, if he had come, he would have lost his life, in one way or in another. I write thee this that thou mayest have some little pleasure at the good disposition that there now is in this unhappy city of ours, instead of the sorrow that in other times thou hast had, at seeing her hold against the obedience she owes to Holy Church. Do not forget me, sweet brother mine, but pray earnestly to God for me, for certainly I have very great need of it; praying Him especially that He grant me grace to know how to free myself from this corruption of the world, so that I may ever do His will in the way that is most pleasing to Him." [2]

[1] January 14, 1379. *Lettere dei discepoli*, 11.

[2] January 15, 1379. *Ibid.*, 12.

To Catherine it seemed that what Stefano needed was a more strenuous effort and more vigorous resolution to free himself. "Time is lost in waiting to untie," she wrote to him, "and thou art not sure of having it. It is better to cut decisively with a true and holy zeal. I would have thee, all manfully, set thyself free, and answer Mary who is calling thee with the greatest love, and the blood of these glorious martyrs, who with such great fire of love gave their blood for love of the blood, and their life for the love of life. It all boils, inviting thee and the others to come and endure, for the glory and praise of the name of God and Holy Church, and to put your virtue to the test. For into this holy city, of which God showed the dignity by calling it His garden, into this garden He has called His servants ; saying now is the time for them to come to test the gold of their virtues. Now let us not act as though we were deaf ; if our ears be stopped up by the cold, let us take the blood which is hot because mingled with fire, and let us wash them out, and all deafness will be taken away. Hide thyself in the wounds of Christ crucified ; fly from before the world, leave the house of thy parents, fly into the cavern of the side of Christ crucified, that thou mayest come to the land of promise. I say this same to Pietro, too. Place yourselves up at the table of the Cross, and there, all drunk with blood, take the food of souls, enduring pain, insults, mockery, and abuse, hunger, thirst, and nakedness, rejoicing with that sweet Paul, the Chosen Vessel, in persecution for Christ crucified. If thou wilt cut, as I have said, endurance will be thy glory ; otherwise, no, but it would be anguish to thee, and thy shadow would make thee afraid." [1]

Shortly before this, Stefano had been captured by a band of marauders in the Sienese contado, and released as soon as he called upon her name. Catherine took this as another sign to her disciple to free himself from the bonds that still bound him to the world, and give himself entirely to the service of God ; then, only, would he be delivered from the enemies of the soul

[1] Letter 329 (262). I quote from the original in the Biblioteca Comunale of Siena.

as he had thus been delivered from those of the body. Nevertheless, she does not bid him come to her, if his parents oppose it. "I do not bid thee come. I should, indeed, have been very glad if thou hadst come, and that thou shouldst come now, if thou canst without offence ; but, if it offends and distresses thy father and mother, no, as long as the offence is not necessary. Nay, I would have thee at this time avoid it, whenever thou canst. I am certain, if the Divine Goodness sees it to be best, that the offence will cease, so that thou canst come with peace. Come if thou canst."[1]

[1] Letter 365 (256). I quote from Barduccio's autograph in the possession of the Confraternity of Santa Lucia, the printed text being very corrupt in parts. But for what seems to be an explicit reference to the *Dialogo* at the end, I should have assigned this letter to a much earlier date than that generally accepted.

CHAPTER XIV

ON THE FIELD OF BATTLE

"State nel campo col gonfalone della santissima croce; pensate che il sangue di questi gloriosi martiri sempre grida nel cospetto di Dio, chiedendo sopra voi l'adiutorio suo. Pensate che questa terra è il giardino di Cristo benedetto, ed è 'l principio della nostra fede. E però ciascuno per sè medesimo ci debbe essere inanimato."—St. Catherine, Letter 347 (219).

NOTWITHSTANDING their having taken part in the conclave of Fondi, the three Italian cardinals at Tagliacozzo had not yet definitely committed themselves to either claimant to the papacy. Urban and Clement alike recognized them as members of the Sacred College and sought their alliance, and they themselves, while appealing to a General Council of the Church to decide the question, continued to write to both as lawful Sovereign Pontiff. In the latter part of January, 1379, they appear finally to have broken off negotiations with Urban, while still abstaining from formally and openly making common cause with Clement.[1] To them, from Rome, Catherine now sent one of the most fiery and eloquent of her letters: "with desire of seeing you return to true and most perfect light, and issue from the great darkness and blindness into which you have fallen." As is her wont, she begins by enunciating a universal doctrine of love and light, the light of truth and the love of God, which are obscured by love of self and of transitory things. Life, at its best, is but a flower that the Supreme Judge will pluck, when it pleases Him, with the hand of death. Fearful at that hour will be the reckoning exacted by God from those He has set in the highest places and who have failed in their duty. Through self-love, "the poison of self-love that has poisoned the world," they

[1] They were still writing to Urban as Pope on January 17; but, in private conversation, they spoke of him as "ille Romanus," and his rival as "Dominus Clemens." Cf. Gayet, II. pp. 279–281, and doc. 30; Raynaldus, vii. p. 370.

have turned their backs upon the truth that they themselves announced when they elected Urban. "O how mad you are, to have given the truth to us and preferred to taste the lie for yourselves!" In impassioned words, addressing them as "fools, worthy of a thousand deaths," she tells over again the whole story of the two elections, brushing away their supposed excuse that they did not actually vote for Clement. Had they not consented, they would not have been there, even if their lives had been the price of their refusal; for they could, at least, have protested, and did not do so. "On whatever side I turn, I find in you nothing save lies." Then, changing her tone, she implores them to return to the fold, and, at last, appeals to their national sentiment as Italians. "I have had the greatest sorrow for you three, and more wonder at your sin than at that of all the others who have committed it. For, if all had departed from their father, you ought to have been those sons who strengthened him, by manifesting the truth. Even if your father had given you nothing but reproaches, you ought not to play the part of Judas by denying his Holiness in every way.[1] Speaking merely naturally and in human fashion (for, according to virtue, we should all be equal), Christ on earth being an Italian and you Italians, I see no reason why patriotic passion could not move you, as it does the ultramontanes—save only love of self. Cast it henceforth to the ground, and do not await time (for time does not wait for you), but trample this affection under foot, with hate of vice and love of virtue. Return, return, and do not await the rod of justice; for we cannot escape from the hands of God. We are in His hands, either for justice or for mercy; better is it for us to acknowledge our faults, and to abide in the hands of mercy, than to remain in sin and in the hands of justice; for our faults will not pass unpunished, and especially those that are committed against Holy Church. But I will pledge myself to bear you in the sight of God, with tears and continual prayers,

[1] *Non dovevate però essere Giuda.* So the Harleian MS. The printed versions read: *non dovevate però essere guida.*

and to bear the penance together with you; if only you will return to the father, who, like a true father, is awaiting you with the opened wings of mercy. Alas, alas! do not fly or shun it; but receive it humbly, and do not believe the evil counsellors who have given you your death. Alas! sweet brothers (sweet brothers and fathers will you be to me, in as far as you abide in truth), resist no more the tears and sweat that the servants of God are shedding for you; for you could wash in them from head to foot. If you despised them, and the thirsting, sweet, and dolorous desires that are being offered up for you by them, you would receive a far severer condemnation. Fear God and His true judgment. I hope in His infinite goodness that He will fulfil in you the desire of His servants."[1]

Nevertheless, the three cardinals at Tagliacozzo continued to appeal to a Council as the only way of ending the Schism, until August, when Jacopo Orsini died. It was rumoured in Italy that, on his deathbed, he had professed his conviction that Urban alone was lawful Pope. This, however, was not the case. In his dying confession, signed and dated August 13, 1379, he declares that he acknowledges as Pope whoever shall be approved by the Church and the Council, and expresses his sorrow if, by written word or by work, he shall have ever done or said anything against him who shall thus be declared lawful Pope.[2] It was probably his hesitation that had hitherto prevented the Cardinals of Florence and Milan from declaring for Clement;

[1] Letter 310 (31), corrected by the Harleian MS.

[2] *Archivio Vaticano*, LIV. 40, printed in Raynaldus, vii. pp. 370, 371. On the other hand, Francesco Casini asserts that Orsini, shortly before his death, admitted to him that he was right in adoring Urban as the true Pope (*Archivio cit.*, LIV. 17, f. 76). The French King urged the two survivors to come to France, or at least some part of Piedmont near Dauphiné, to confer with him, while Clement assured them that their adherence to him would do more to restore peace to the Church than would the assembling of a Council. Valois, I. pp. 321–323. Both ultimately joined the Clementines. The dying profession of the Cardinal of Milan, that the election of Urban was under compulsion, and that Clement was lawful Pope, is dated September 12, 1381, in the *Archivio Vaticano*, LIV. 19, f. 141.

and it is curious to notice that, while Pedro de Luna, who had been the chief cause of Urban's election and had deserted him with the utmost reluctance, ultimately became the most strenuous and obstinate leader of the opposite faction, Jacopo Orsini, who had opposed the election from the outset, was the only member of the Sacred College who never entirely went over to the side of his enemies.

In the meanwhile, both Urban and Clement had appealed to the arms of mercenary soldiers, to make good their claims to be the vicar of the Prince of Peace. Castello Sant' Angelo still held out against the Roman People, and its defenders were reduced to the last extremities, those who fell into the hands of the besiegers being cruelly maimed and mutilated.[1] Clement had collected an army of Bretons and Gascons, including those whom he had urged to the slaughter of Cesena, and put them under the command of his nephew, Louis de Montjoie, with orders, in February, to march upon Rome; while Urban took into his pay the Compagnia di San Giorgio, a company of Italian mercenaries that had been raised by Alberigo da Barbiano, Count of Cunio in Romagna, a condottiere who bade fair to eclipse the fame of the foreign captains who had been the curse of Italy for the last half-century. Early in March, Clement, who was suffering from fever, moved from Fondi to Sperlonga, near Gaeta; from which, on April 17, 1379, he issued his famous bull to Louis of Anjou, conferring the kingdom of Adria upon him, which was to be a vassal kingdom of the Holy See, including Ferrara, Bologna, Ravenna, all Romagna, the Marches of Ancona, Perugia, Todi, Spoleto—the greater bulk, in fact, of the Papal States—with the provision that disputes between the new kingdom and that of Naples were to be decided by the Pope's arbitration, and that neither sovereign could succeed the other

Montjoie's army amounted to some six hundred lances—which, allowing three men to a lance, would mean about eighteen hundred soldiers. He set his headquarters at Marino, the

[1] Cf. Valois, I. p. 169 *n.*

stronghold of Giordano Orsini, from which he ravaged the country, without making any serious attempt to relieve the defenders of Sant' Angelo, who were compelled to accept an offer of mediation from Giovanni Cenci, and capitulated on April 27. With the solemn benediction of Urban, Alberigo da Barbiano marched out of Rome. Early on the morning of April 30, his company—which amounted to two hundred and forty lances, with a subsidiary force of Roman infantry—advanced from the neighbourhood of Tivoli towards Marino. Confident in his superior numbers, Montjoie moved to meet them, broke their first division under Galeazzo Pepoli, and drove them back upon the infantry—only to be in his turn crushed by the onslaught of Alberigo himself, who, pressing forward at the head of his main body, threw the three lines of the enemy into confusion and gained a complete victory. The Clementines lost more than a third of their army in killed and prisoners, the latter including Montjoie himself, Bernardon de la Salle, and Silvestre Budes.[1] The battle of Marino marks an epoch in the history of Italian wars ; for the first time, a purely Italian army had gained a conclusive victory over the foreign mercenaries, and the patriotic boast of Petrarca in his *Italia mia* had been justified : *Chè l' antiquo valore ne l' italici cor non è ancor morto.*

Castello Sant' Angelo had surrendered to the Roman People, and not to the Pope, whose demand that it should be given into his hands, to be guarded by him, was rejected by the Romans, who were keenly alive to the danger of his using it to command the city and curtail their liberties. After two days' fruitless negotiation, Urban was compelled to give way ; and on the morning of April 30, the morning of the battle of Marino, the Romans entered Sant' Angelo with their banners displayed, and began to

[1] See Luigi Fumi, *Notizie officiali sulla battaglia di Marino dell' anno* 1379, and *Un nuovo avviso della battaglia di Marino* (Studi e documenti di Storia e Diritto, anno VII. Rome, 1886) ; Canestrini, *op. cit.*, p. lxxi. ; Andrea Gattaro, in *Rer. It. Script.*, xvii. coll. 277, 278. The battle has been somewhat exaggerated by modern historians, on Gattaro's track.

raze it to the ground.[1] An expression in one of Catherine's letters, referring to the wonderful things that God had wrought four weeks before, *per mezzo di vile creatura*, has been taken as meaning that she had been instrumental in obtaining the capitulation of the fortress.[2] Of this, however, we know nothing. Swallowing his discomfiture with the best grace he could, Urban walked barefoot in procession from Santa Maria in Trastevere to St. Peter's, to offer solemn thanks to God for the double victory.

To the Bandaresi and their colleagues, "the maintainers of the Republic of Rome," whom she consistently treats as the temporal rulers of the Eternal City, Catherine addressed a letter on May 6, exhorting them to be grateful for the great benefits they had received from God. Let them show their gratitude by justice to their neighbours, by purity of life, by abstaining from rash judgment, by fidelity to the Church and the vicar of Christ. Nor is the letter without a touch of worldly wisdom : "Also I would have you grateful to this Company, who have been the instruments of Christ, helping them in all that is needed, especially with regard to these poor wounded. Bear yourselves charitably and peacefully with them, in order that you may preserve them to your aid, and not let them have any cause for turning against you. Thus it is meet you do, sweetest brothers, both because it is your duty and because it is urgently necessary." "It seems to me," she adds, "that a little ingratitude is being used towards Giovanni Cenci, who has laboured with such great zeal and fidelity, with an upright heart, only to please God and for our utility (and this I know to be the truth), abandoning everything else to deliver you from the scourge that Castello Sant' Angelo had become to you, and acting in the matter with so much prudence ; not only do they

[1] Letter of April 30, 1379, from Pietro Angeli da Montefiascone, one of the papal secretaries, to the Commune of Montefiascone. Fumi, *op. cit.*, doc. 2. Cf. Benvenuto da Imola, *Comentum*, II. p. 8.

[2] Letter 351 (20), which in the Harleian MS. is dated May 30, 1379. The MS., however, reads : *per mezzo di vili creature.*

now show him no sign of gratitude, not so much as thanking him, but the vice of envy and ingratitude is casting the poison of slander and much murmuring against him. I should not like him to be treated thus, nor any one else who served you; for it would be an offence to God and loss to yourselves. All the commonwealth needs wise, mature, and discreet men, and of a good conscience. Let it no more be so, for the love of Christ crucified. Adopt what remedy seems meet to your lordships, in order that the simplicity of the churlish may not interfere with your welfare. I say this for your own good, and not for any partiality of mine; for you know that I am a stranger, speaking to you for your own good estate, because I value you all, together with him, as much as my own soul. I know that, like wise and discreet men, you will consider the affection and the purity of heart with which I write to you, and so you will pardon my presumption in venturing to write. Be grateful, be grateful to God."[1]

She wrote at the same time to Count Alberigo and his *caporali*, who had not returned to Rome, but were still in the field, pressing on the campaign against the remnants of the Clementines in the Campagna, where Marino was being besieged by the Roman People. Perhaps she already knew that a portion of the Compagnia di San Giorgio was on the point of accepting money from Clement, when she wrote: "with desire of seeing you, you and all the rest of your company, faithful to Holy Mother Church and to the Holiness of Pope Urban VI, true Sovereign Pontiff, all combat royally and faithfully for the truth, that you may receive the fruit of your labours"; but, at least, the letter is nothing but a prose poem in honour of ideal Christian chivalry. Not otherwise might Dante have addressed his chosen warriors of God in the glowing red sphere of Mars. "O brother and dearest sons, you are knights who have entered the field to give your lives for love of life, and to give your blood for love of the blood of Christ crucified. Now is the time of the new martyrs. You are the first who have given blood. How great is the fruit that you will receive for it? It is life eternal, which is an

[1] Letter 349 (196), corrected by the Harleian MS.

infinite fruit. In this conflict you cannot but gain, whether you live or die. If you die, you gain life eternal, and are set in a place safe and not subject to change; and if you survive, you have made a sacrifice of yourselves voluntarily to God, and you will be able to keep what you possess with a good conscience." That last clause, alas, makes us realize that these new knights of Christ were, after all, mere soldiers of fortune; but Catherine goes on to exhort them always to keep the blood of the Lamb before their eyes, to fight for the truth that "the members of the devil" are denying, and enter upon the conflict with the highest intention alone, purifying their consciences by holy confession. Let the captain-general himself set the example. The holy soil of Rome, upon which they are fighting, should animate them to act manfully. "Keep in the field with the standard of the most holy Cross; think that the blood of these glorious martyrs is ever crying out in the sight of God, invoking His aid upon you. Think that this city is the garden of the blessed Christ and the very beginning of our faith, and, therefore, every one of his own accord should be filled with valour here. Be grateful, you and the others, be grateful for the benefit you have received, to God and to that glorious knight St. George, whose name you keep; may he defend you and be your guard, even unto death. Forgive me, if I have wearied you too much with words. Love of Holy Church and your salvation must excuse me, and my conscience which has been constrained by the sweet will of God. We will do like Moses; for the people fought, and Moses prayed; and whilst he prayed, the people conquered. So shall we do, if only our prayer be pleasing and acceptable to God."[1]

On this same day, May 6, Catherine wrote to the King of France and to the Queen of Naples, evidently thinking that the latter would have been moved by the victory of the Urbanists so near her own territories. She beseeches Giovanna to have pity upon her own soul, and again expresses her longing to come to

[1] Letter 347 (219). The authenticity of this letter has been occasionally called in question, but no student of the manuscripts can entertain the slightest doubt on the subject.

Naples, to plead with her face to face. She reminds her, "my mother and my daughter," of her old promise to aid the Crusade, and warns her that Urban, if she perseveres in opposing him, will pronounce sentence of deprivation against her as a heretic.[1] To Charles she writes at some length, with her usual conviction that it is self-love alone that is taking away from man the divine light and preventing him from discerning where the truth lies. She gives her usual statement of the Roman case, adding that he would find the "servants of God" unanimous for Urban, and that God certainly would not suffer His servants to walk in darkness. She implores the King to appeal to the theologians of the University of Paris, "for you have there the fountain of science, which I fear you will lose, if you continue this conduct," and not to be led away by his affection for his own country.[2] Nevertheless, in this same month, Charles practically ordered the University to declare for Clement, and obtained what professed to be an unanimous decision of all the faculties and all the nations composing it. In reality, the faculty of theology was divided, a large portion of the doctors, in spite of persecution, continuing in their adherence to Urban.[3]

Alarmed at the result of the battle of Marino, Clement decided to seek the protection of the Queen of Naples. On May 9, with Cardinal Lagier, Cardinal Flandrin, and his new Cardinal of Cosenza, he embarked at Gaeta, where the people received him with scarcely veiled hostility, and, with a fleet of six galleys and one galliot, he arrived at Naples on the following day. In spite of Giovanna and her court, the populace of Naples and not a few of the nobles believed in Urban; Bernard Rodhez, the

[1] Letter 348 (317).

[2] Letter 350 (187). An unmistakable "servant of God," Friar Peter of Aragon, had just sent Charles what he claimed to be a direct revelation from the Lord on behalf of Urban, but which, to a large extent, contradicted Catherine's contention that the tumult of the people had not influenced his election. In Du Boulay, IV. p. 581, and Raynaldus, vii. p. 398. For an Urbanist proposal, in 1381, to transfer the University of Paris to Prague, see Denifle, *op. cit.*, Tom. iii. doc. 1642.

[3] Cf. Valois, I. pp. 137–140.

Provençal archbishop, having joined Clement at Fondi, Urban had appointed a Neapolitan, Lodovico Bozzuto, to replace him; but the latter had not dared to take possession of his see, for fear of the Queen. Giovanna gave Clement a magnificent reception, and all her courtiers flocked to pay him reverence. But, while she was entertaining him in the Castello dell' Ovo, the populace began to gather together, murmuring against her for having received this "Carnival Pope," and the partisans of the Urbanist archbishop fanned the flames. A carpenter was denouncing the Queen in one of the piazze, when a gentleman of the city, Messer Andrea Ravignano, chanced to pass: "How now, fellow? Darest thou speak against thy liege lady?" A volley of Neapolitan abuse was the answer, to which Messer Andrea retaliated by a blow which destroyed the sight of one of the carpenter's eyes. At once the whole Neapolitan populace rose in fury, shouting: "Viva Papa Urbano," "Muoia Papa Clemente," "Muoia l'Anticristo!" While one band rushed to sack the Archbishop's palace and the houses of the Clementine prelates, the rest swept down to the shore towards the Castello dell' Ovo, shouting death to the Queen herself, if she defended her Antipope. The Urbanist archbishop was put in possession of the see, and the populace illuminated the whole city at nightfall. Pope and Queen were alike terrified. On May 13, Clement, with his three cardinals, his six galleys and one galliot, left Naples, and returned to Sperlonga; while Giovanna, on May 18, the vigil of the Ascension, published a decree declaring that she held Urban as lawful Pope, and that he was to be obeyed as such throughout her kingdom. She despatched the Count of Nola, Messer Ugo da San Severino, the Prior of the Certosa, and others to Rome as her ambassadors, to make complete submission to the Holy See.[1] Catherine wrote exultantly to three Neapolitan ladies, at the news of the shining out of the light upon their city: "The heart of Pharaoh is broken, that of the Queen, I mean, who has shown so much obstinacy up

[1] *Cronicon Siculum* (ed. J. de Blasiis), pp. 35–37; *Diurnali detti del Duca di Monteleone*, pp. 15, 16; *Anonimo Fiorentino*, p. 396. Cf. Fumi, *op. cit.*, docs. 4 and 5.

to now, by departing from her head, Christ on earth, and adhering to Antichrist, member of the demon ; she has persecuted the truth and exalted the lie. Thanks, thanks be to our Saviour, who has illumined her heart, whether by force or by love, and has shown His wonderful works in her."[1]

On May 22, Clement embarked for Provence, leaving his Cardinal Jacopo d'Itri, the former Patriarch of Constantinople, as his legate in Italy. After much trouble on the way, he finally, on June 20, reached the papal palace of Avignon.

At Whitsuntide, Urban took up his residence in the Vatican. "Most holy Father," wrote Catherine, "may the Holy Spirit overshadow your soul and heart and affection with the fire of divine charity, and infuse a supernatural light into your understanding, in such wise that in your light we little sheep may see light, and that no deception that the devil might wish to practise upon you with his malice may be hidden from your Holiness. I desire, most holy Father, to see fulfilled in you all the other things that the sweet will of God demands of you, of which I know that you have very great desire. I hope that this sweet fire of the Holy Spirit will work in your heart and soul, as it did in those holy disciples, when it gave them strength and power against the visible demons and against the invisible. In its virtue they beat down the tyrants of the world, and by endurance they spread the faith. It gave them light and wisdom to know the truth and the doctrine that Truth itself had left, whereby the affection, which follows the understanding, robed them with the fire of His charity, so that they lost all servile fear and human pleasure, and only attended to the honour of God, and to draw souls from the hands of the demons ; and they were fain to offer to every creature the truth with which they found themselves illumined. But it was only after much vigil, humble and continual prayer, and the great mental labour in which they spent those ten days, that they were filled with this strength of the Holy Spirit ; the

[1] Letter 353 (337). In Letter 362 (318), Catherine states that Giovanna herself wrote to her, confessing that Urban was true Pope and declaring her intention of being obedient to him.

labour and holy exercise came first. O most holy Father, it seems that they are teaching us and are exhorting your Holiness to-day, and that they are showing us in what way we can receive the Holy Spirit. What is this way? That we should keep in the house of knowledge of ourselves, in which knowledge the soul is always humble, neither running to excess in gladness nor yielding to impatience in adversity." "I rejoice that this sweet Mother Mary and sweet Peter, the Prince of the Apostles, have restored you to your own place. Now the eternal Truth wishes you to make in your garden a garden of the servants of God, and to nourish them therein with temporal substance, as they will you with spiritual; so that they will have nought else to do, save cry in the sight of God for the good estate of Holy Church and for your Holiness. These will be the soldiers who will give you perfect victory."[1] At the beginning of June, Marino surrendered to the Romans; Rocca di Papa and other *castelli* followed; Giordano Orsini submitted to the Pope. On June 12, Urban issued a triumphant brief to all the Catholic world, "giving thanks to the Most High with ineffable joy of mind." "He who knoweth all things is our witness that, if we thought that we had not entered the sheepfold by the door, we should not have dared to sit in the chair of Peter for an hour." Convinced that God by the Holy Spirit has chosen his weakness to sustain the burden of the universal Church, and that He will never desert her, he is prepared to encounter all dangers and persecutions. Already the storms are abating; the mercenaries have been defeated; Sant' Angelo, *non sine miraculo*, has surrendered; his beloved Neapolitan children have driven the Antipope from Naples; Giovanna has abjured her errors, has acknowledged him as true vicar of Christ and successor of the bearer of the keys, and from day to day he is expecting her ambassadors.[2]

These ambassadors never came. Giovanna's conversion had only lasted a few weeks. Her envoys were intercepted by a

[1] Letter 351 (20), which the Harleian MS. dates May 30 (Whit Monday), 1379.

[2] Raynaldus, vii. pp. 386, 387.

Clementine galley (possibly at her own instigation), and, when released, she recalled them to Naples, and began vigorously to persecute the Urbanists, especially the Archbishop Bozzuto, whom she regarded as responsible for the tumult. Unable to get him personally into her hands, she destroyed his house and wasted his possessions in the country.[1] Apparently, her conversion, induced by a momentary fit of terror, was forgotten as soon as she heard that her husband Otho was at hand, with fresh troops for her support. A few days later, her niece Margherita, whom she had treated as a most beloved daughter, left Naples, to join her husband, Charles of Durazzo, to whom Urban had already offered the crown in the event of Giovanna proving obstinate.

Urban had decided to make a fresh attempt to win the King of France from his Clementine faith, and again chose Fra Raimondo as his ambassador. This time, he wished the friar to attempt the journey by way of Barcelona, for which purpose, on May 9, he had addressed a brief to the King of Aragon, commending Raimondo to him, in the hope that a Spanish safe-conduct might at length enable him to enter France in safety. Raimondo's instructions are still preserved in the Archives of the Vatican. He is to tell over again the official Roman version of Urban's election, enthronement, and coronation, to lay stress upon the way the cardinals obtained (and used) spiritual and temporal favours from him, announced his election, and treated him for three months as Pope. He is to call the King's attention to the voluntary coming of the Cardinal of Amiens to Rome, the acceptance of the Bishopric of Ostia by the Cardinal of Glandèves, the dying declaration of the Cardinal of St. Peter's, the adherence of the greater part of the Universities. Also, "the Lord Charles, the last Roman Emperor of blessed memory, fully informed of the truth, held him for true Pope as long as he lived"; the King of the Romans and Bohemia, the Kings of Hungary, Aragon, Castile, England, Portugal, Cyprus, and Navarre (Urban apparently interpreting the neutrality of several of these powers in his own favour), and many other princes in

[1] Valois, I. p. 177*n.*; *Diurnali cit.*, p. 16.

Italy and elsewhere, hold him as true Pope canonically elected, and he is obeyed as true vicar of Christ and legitimate successor of St. Peter throughout their dominions. Following in the footsteps of St. Peter, he has fixed his residence in Rome; but, although an Italian by birth, he always was, and still is, a Frenchman in will, and is prepared to satisfy the King in all his just and reasonable demands. Already his cause has begun to triumph, as shown by the unanimous decision of the King of the Romans and the electors of the Empire in his favour, and the surrender of Castello Sant' Angelo. The sudden death of the Cardinal Gilles Aycelin de Montaigu, who had opposed him in Avignon, and the incurable illness that has overtaken "the former Cardinal of Geneva, now Antipope," upon whose face a mark of infamy appeared as soon as he deserted him, are to be used as serious arguments on his behalf. Let the King note well how everywhere, even in France, women and children and almost all the lower orders, by the inspiration of the Holy Spirit alone, acclaim Urban as true Pope, even as it is written by the Prophet: *Out of the mouths of babes and sucklings thou hast perfected praise.* In so arduous a business, as touching Catholic Faith, let the King listen and give credit to the wise, and not be deceived by flatterers and false counsellors, which would be contrary to his honour and the salvation of his soul, and bring disgrace upon his royal blood and lineage.[1] Once more Raimondo failed. In spite of Urban's protests, Pedro de Luna, who was now as vigorous in the Clementine cause as he had been reluctant to adhere to it, had been honourably received by the King of Aragon at the beginning of the year as legate of Clement, and had secured the imprisonment of Urban's former ambassadors, Perfetto Malatesta, Abbot of

[1] I quote direct from the *Archivio Vaticano*, LIV. 33, ff. 132–135. These instructions, which are headed: *Sequuntur ea que Domino Regi Francie sunt exponenda per . . . pro parte domini nostri domini Urbani pape sexti:* were first identified by Valois, I. pp. 313–315*n*. For the sudden death of Cardinal Aycelin, which the Urbanists regarded as a divine judgment, cf. St. Antoninus, III. p. 390. The triviality of the personalities against Clement is quite matched by the arguments used against Urban by Jean le Fèvre and other French ambassadors to the Count of Flanders.

Sassoferrato, and Fra Menendo, who had been nominated Urbanist Bishop of Cordova.[1] Raimondo had been his personal friend, but, nevertheless, through the Cardinal's influence, the entry into France was now as closed to him on the Spanish side as it had been before from Provence.

Raimondo remained at Genoa, preaching an Urbanist crusade, and acting as provincial of the province of Lombardy. He wrote to Catherine, pleading with her not to judge him by her own standard, and imploring her not to love him less because he had failed her again. The Saint answers as though she herself had fallen short in love and faith, and been an instrument to spoil God's work by lack of confidence in Him. As to the special love and special faith that binds us to a most dear friend, we must never believe or imagine that such a friend wills aught save our good ; and nothing whatever, "neither word of creatures, nor illusion of the devil, nor change of place," must diminish this pure trust which comes from love. Therefore, Raimondo's fears, "lest the affection and charity I bear you be diminished in me," come from his own imperfection in love and faith ; but she does not conceal her bitter disappointment that he has found means of casting to earth the burden laid upon him : "If you had been faithful, you would not have had all this hesitation, nor yielded to doubts about God and about me, wretched woman ; but, like a faithful son, ready for obedience, you would have gone, and done what had been possible. And if you had not been able to go upright, you would have gone crawling ; if you could not go as a friar, you would have gone as a pilgrim ; if you had no money, you would have gone on alms. This faithful obedience would have wrought more in the sight of God, and in the hearts of men, than all human prudence would do. My sins have prevented me from seeing this in you, but I am quite certain that, in spite of natural shrinking, you, nevertheless, had and have a good, holy intention, and the desire better to fulfil the will of God and that of Christ on earth, Pope Urban VI." "I wish by all means that you had gone ; nevertheless, I

[1] Cf. Sorbelli, *op. cit.*, pp. 18, 19.

abide in peace, because I am certain that nothing happens without mystery.'

"I tell you, sweetest father, that, whether we will or no, the present time invites us to die. Then remain no longer alive; end all pains in pain, and increase the delight of holy desire in pain, so that our life may only pass with crucified desire, and we may voluntarily give our bodies to the beasts to devour, that is, voluntarily, for love of the truth, cast ourselves into the tongues and hands of men like unto beasts, even as have done the others who, like dead men, have laboured in this sweet garden, and watered it with their blood, but first with tears and sweat. But I (unhappy is my life!), because I have not put this water to it, have refused to shed my blood therein. I will no more thus; but let our life be renewed, and the fire of desire increase. You ask me to pray the Divine Goodness that He may give you some of the fire of Vincent, of Lawrence, of sweet Paul, and of that loving John; then, you say, you will do great deeds. Surely, you speak the truth, for, without this fire, you would do nothing, neither little thing nor great; nor should I rejoice in you. You commend our order to me, and I commend it to you, for, perceiving how things stand, my heart is bursting in my body thereat. Our province in general still shows itself obedient to Pope Urban and to the vicar of the order, which vicar, I tell you, bears himself right well for the truth; in most prudent fashion, according to the present state of things, does he bear himself in the order and against those who wickedly contradict the truth. And if any one said the contrary, according to what little I know about it, no truth is in his mouth. The most holy Father has given him commands and full authority to absolve all those provincials who are rebels against his truth. It is no time to sleep, but with great solicitude to pray our sweet Spaniard [1] to look down upon his order, which order used ever to work for the exaltation of the faith, and now has become its contaminator. I am sorrowful thereat, even unto death, but can do no more, save offer up my life in tears and in very great affliction. As to

[1] St. Dominic.

what you write me, that Antichrist and his members are seeking diligently to have you in their hands, do not fear ; for God is strong enough to take light and power from them, so that they may not accomplish their desires. And you should also think that you are not worthy of so great a good, and, therefore, need not be afraid. Have confidence ; for sweet Mary and the Truth will be always with you. I, a vile slave, who am set on the field where blood has been shed for love of the blood (and you have left me here, and are gone away in God's name), will never cease working for you. I beseech you to act so that you give me no matter for tears, nor for being ashamed in the sight of God. As you are a man in promising to do and to bear for the honour of God, do not be now a woman when we come to the point ; for I should appeal from you to Christ crucified and to Mary. Beware lest He deal with you as He did with the Abbot of Sant' Antimo, who, for fear and under colour of not tempting God, left Siena and came to Rome, thinking to have escaped prison and to be safe ; and he was put in prison, with the penalty that you know. Thus are pusillanimous hearts served. Then be utterly manly, so that death may come to you. Know that I should not be here now, if it had been possible to go safely; but it was impossible, by sea or by land ; for it was decided that I should go to Naples. Pray, and bid others pray to God and Mary, that He may make us do what is His honour. Fra Bartolommeo, the Master, Fra Matteo, and the others are ready to do whatever needs, for the honour of God and the utility of Holy Church, and to do violence to their own weakness. They and all the others commend themselves to you ; the *Nonna* blesses you ; and I ask your blessing, and beseech you to pardon me, if I have said anything contrary to the honour of God and the reverence I owe you. Let my love excuse me."[1]

The reference to the imprisonment of Fra Giovanni di Gano shows that yet another of Catherine's disciples had disappointed

[1] Letter 344 (101), with unpublished passages from the Casanatense MS. 292. A reference to the state of Naples, and the papal mission to the King of Hungary, shows this letter was not written before the latter part of June, 1379.

her expectations. Nothing is known of the matter, but it is likely that he had shrunk from doing one of Urban's missions to Siena. Relations had again grown strained between Catherine's native city and the Holy See, in consequence of the refusal of the Sienese to assist Urban with men and money, to which they were pledged by the terms of the peace between the league and the Church, as also by the conditions of the restitution of Talamone. Francesco Casini, who was now Urban's physician as he had been Gregory's, had vainly attempted to smooth things over in the papal court. "Do not think," he wrote to the Defenders, "that I can interpose on behalf of the Commune or of the citizens, while you behave thus; rather, while you act in this way, would I wish the Pope to think I was a Scotsman."[1] We have two letters of Catherine herself to them on the subject, urging them to assist the Pope as they had promised, especially now that he was not demanding their aid to recover the temporalities of the Church, but simply for the defence of the faith, reminding them that they had found no difficulty in giving similar support to the Florentines against the Holy See, and assuring them that Urban loved them cordially as sons.[2] She wrote at the same time to the prior and brethren of the *Disciplinati* of the Madonna, urging them to put all the moral pressure they could upon the Signoria, and to Stefano Maconi, bidding him be fervent and not tepid in this work: "If you will be what you ought to be, you will set all Italy aflame, not merely your own city."[3] But, with the mercenaries of Hawkwood and Lucio di Lando demanding money, and scattered bands of Bretons threatening the contado, the Sienese were probably really unable to fulfil their pledges to Urban's satisfaction; and, though Stefano urged the Signoria to pawn the goods of the Commune, and send a force to Rome, however small, as proof of their good will, nothing was done. "In all spiritual things," he wrote to Neri

[1] Letter of June 5, 1379. Fumi, *op. cit.*, doc. 5.

[2] Letters 311 (203) and 367 (204).

[3] Letters 321 (144) and 368 (261). The full text of the letter to the *Disciplinati* is in the Casanatense MS. 292.

di Landoccio, "he would be obeyed as true pastor; but, in temporal matters, they plead their great poverty and the misery into which they are come. I am grieved to the heart at seeing that the Holy Father has not had full satisfaction from this city; and I promise you that I have so much spoken about it, and especially while Maestro Francesco was here, that I was several times told that I talked more than befitted me on the subject. But I should reck little of this, if only I saw done what is the honour of God."[1]

There were similar difficulties elsewhere. The Florentines fully acknowledged Urban's election, and turned a deaf ear to the appeals of Louis of Anjou against him; but they were exceedingly slow in carrying out their part of the treaty, and already behind hand with the payment of the indemnity. It is probable that, in the continual state of alarm and anarchy into which the Republic had sunk after the tumult of the Ciompi, this was inevitable; the Pope himself ultimately recognized the fact; but Catherine wrote to the Priors and Gonfaloniere, reproaching them for their ingratitude: "Let us not deceive ourselves, my sweet brothers. Many are the offences and iniquities which we have committed against God, against our neighbour, against the vicar of Christ, and against Holy Church; you cannot cloak this iniquity by the sins of the pastors and ministers of the Church, for it does not pertain to you to punish them, but to the Supreme Judge and to His vicar. Now, notwithstanding these sins of yours, which have merited great punishment, you have received so much mercy; you have been restored with great benignity to the breast of Holy Church, made capable of receiving the fruit of the blood, if you will, by Pope Urban VI, true Supreme Pontiff and vicar of Christ on earth, who has pardoned you and absolved you with such great charity, giving you what you have asked, treating you not like children who had offended and rebelled against their father, but as though you had never offended him. Now you see him in such great

[1] June 22, 1379. *Lettere dei discepoli*, 13.

need; and not only do you not help him, but you do not even keep what you have promised. Thereby you show signs of great ingratitude; for which I fear that, if you are not truly grateful, God will permit you to inflict the punishment upon yourselves, even as you have done in the past."[1] The Republic of Perugia had concluded a final and complete peace with Urban at the beginning of the year, 1379, but was no less tardy in paying the tribute, though the Pope was sorely in need of every soldo. Catherine sent Neri with a letter to the Priors of the People and Commune: "with desire of seeing you succour your father and yourselves, in his need and yours; for to aid him is to contribute to your own safety, spiritually and temporally"; urging them to show their gratitude and secure their own liberty by giving him all the aid in their power.[2] But it is notable that none of the Italian communes, however dissatisfied with Urban, showed any disposition to desert him for Clement. When, a few months later, a quarrel broke out between the Roman Pontiff and the Bolognese, and Clement sent a bishop to offer to grant the vicariate of Bologna to the Commune on their own terms, if they would recognize him as Pope, the Bolognese answered that, at the bidding of the cardinals, they had acknowledged Urban, and that they intended to obey whoever should ultimately be decided by the Church to be the true successor of Peter.[3]

In Catherine's letter to the Perugians, we find this remarkable passage: "You see these times prepared for great burdens, and our country doomed to the coming of princes; and we are fragile like glass, because of our many sins and great dissensions. If, therefore, we desert our father and do not help him, we shall be in danger; for, being severed from our strength, we shall be too weak." And again: "Keep united, for Christ crucified, and then do not fear any tyrant; for the aid of God, for the love

[1] Letter 337 (199). Cf. Gherardi, *op. cit.*, pp. 94–96.

[2] Letter 339 (205). Cf. Pellini, I. pp. 1237–1242. Stefano's letter of June 22 shows that Neri had gone to Perugia before that date.

[3] Cf. Raynaldus, vii. p. 389; *Cronica di Bologna*, col. 522.

of whom you will succour His Spouse, will deliver you."[1] While Clement was urging Louis of Anjou to invade Italy for the phantasmal kingdom of Adria, Urban was appealing to Louis of Hungary and Charles of Durazzo, his cousin, to succour the Roman Church and deprive Giovanna of the Neapolitan throne. In the January of this year, 1379, ambassadors from the King had been in Florence, announcing that their master was coming with an army to Italy after Easter, and demanding assistance from the Commune.[2] But, for the present, Louis was engaged in helping Francesco da Carrara and the Genoese in their war against Venice, the famous War of Chioggia, which was taken by their allied forces on August 15; and, at the end of the month, Charles arrived with ten thousand Hungarians in the Trevisano, where the Lord of Padua was pressing on the siege of Treviso itself.

It is heartrending to find Catherine involved in this deplorable affair; but it is clear from her letters that she was merely Urban's tool, acting in good faith, without the slightest realization of the extent to which he and Charles were prepared to carry out their scheme. Nothing can palliate the infamy of Charles's conduct towards his kinswoman and benefactress, but some slight excuse for Urban may be found in the fact that Clement had been the first to summon the foreigner into Italy. In her long letter to the King of Hungary, urging him, as he had always been the champion of the faith against the infidels, to be now the defender of the Church, Catherine sets before his eyes the "true and most perfect charity that seeketh not her own," and bids him make peace with his other enemies and come speedily. "Will you endure that Antichrist, member of the demon, and a woman should cast all our faith into ruin and darkness and confusion?" "Much good will result from your coming. Perhaps, this truth will be made clear without human power, and this poor little woman, the Queen, will be delivered from her obstinacy either by

[1] Letter 339 (205). Similarly, to the Sienese, in Letter 311 (203): "Noi vediamo il tempo ad avvenimento de' signori" (Harleian MS.).

[2] *Anonimo Fiorentino*, p. 391.

fear or by love. You see how long Christ on earth has borne with her, in not having deprived her in fact of what she has lawfully forfeited, only because he waited for her amendment and for love of you. If now he were to do it, he would be acting justly, and stand excused in God's sight and in yours." [1] And to Charles of Durazzo she wrote : " with desire of seeing you a virile knight, fighting manfully for the glory and praise of the name of God, and for the exaltation and reformation of Holy Church " ; bidding him come swiftly to Urban's succour, since God has chosen him to be a column in the Church, an instrument to extirpate heresy and exalt the truth, but first overcome the enemies of his own soul, by purifying his heart and amending his life.[2] She had shortly before sent Neri and another of her followers, the Abate Lisolo, to Naples, with a last appeal to Giovanna herself, imploring her as her *dolcissima madre*, *carissima madre*, for her own salvation, for the sake of her people whom she was plunging into civil war, to return to the truth before it should be too late. " Alas, how can your heart endure without bursting that your subjects should be divided because of you, and that one should hold the white rose, another the red ; the one cling to the truth, the other to the lie ? See you not that they are all created by that most spotless rose of the eternal will of God, and recreated by grace in that most ardent crimson rose of the blood of Christ ?" [3] Catherine's letter, together with Urban's summons, was probably delivered to Charles at Padua at the beginning of November, and he at once returned to Hungary, to concert measures with the King.

Connected with Charles's presence at Treviso is one of the saddest episodes of Catherine's life. In Florence, after the

[1] Letter 357 (188). A slightly better text is in the Harleian MS.

[2] Letter 372 (189).

[3] Letter 362 (318). A letter to Neri from Fra Bartolommeo di Domenico, dated Rome, September 1 (*Lettere dei discepoli*, 16), shows that the former had gone to Naples shortly before that date, and that Catherine had at length been compelled to abandon the idea of going thither in person, as the Pope refused his consent.

overthrow of the Ciompi, mainly through the strange desertion of their cause by Michele di Lando,[1] the chief share in the government had remained with the artisans of the minor Arts; many of the noblest and most influential of the burghers were in exile or under bounds, no less than the lowest plebeians who had taken part in the tumults; plots within and without the city, for the restoration of the exiles and the overthrow of the new régime, were incessant; while Cante de' Gabrielli of Gubbio (a descendant of that Messer Cante who, as Podestà, had passed sentence against Dante three-quarters of a century before), as Captain of the People for both six months of 1379, did fearful deeds of justice or injustice, beheading or hanging real or supposed traitors, torturing suspected persons to extort denunciations of their fellow-citizens. The exiles looked to the advent of Charles of Durazzo much as Dante had done to that of Henry of Luxemburg, and the prince himself was ready to lend the aid of his soldiers to restore the adherents of the Parte Guelfa to Florence.

Apparently in April, Giannozzo Sacchetti had been arrested (for debt, according to Marchionne Stefani), and cast into the prison known as the Stinche. "I understand," wrote Catherine, on May 8, to Bartolo Usimbardi and Francesco di Pippino, "that Giannozzo has been taken; I know not how long he will stay there. I am pleased at what you, Francesco, write to me about it, that you will never abandon him, and so I command you, in the name of Jesus Christ, to visit him very often, to comfort and help him in all that you can; think that God demands nought else of us, save that we should show upon our neighbour the love that we have for Him. I commend him earnestly to you, and tell him from me to be a good knight, now that God has put him on the field, and that his fighting must be true patience, by bowing his head with humility to the sweet will of God. Comfort him much in my name and in that of all this family,

[1] Cf. Rodolico, *op. cit.*, pp. 199–206, whose researches reveal Michele's conduct in a most sinister aspect, instead of the halo of legendary glory with which he had previously been surrounded.

who all have great compassion for him."[1] Shortly afterwards, Giannozzo was set at liberty; Marchionne Stefani, who pursues him with relentless partisan hate in his chronicle and spares no effort to blacken his name, declares that he deceived his creditors by his edifying conduct in prison, and robbed a fellow-prisoner of his jewels, by the sale of which he escaped into Lombardy. This is certainly a calumny; but it seems clear that Giannozzo joined the Florentine rebels in the Paduan district, and, in September, he was with the Hungarian army at the siege of Treviso, where (in understanding with Lapo da Castiglionchio) Benedetto Peruzzi persuaded him to join a conspiracy for the restoration of the Guelf exiles to Florence, with the aid of Charles of Durazzo.

Giannozzo returned to Tuscany with letters from the prince, to raise money to hire four hundred lances for this purpose from the Compagnia di San Giorgio, which was now in Charles's pay. In the Florentine contado, he visited Guido della Foresta, Piero Canigiani, Antonio da Uzzano, Donato Strada, and Bonifazio Peruzzi, all of whom professed themselves favourable to the undertaking. But the Florentine ambassadors who were with Charles, attempting to arrange peace between Genoa and Venice, had warned the Signoria; and, on October 12, Giannozzo and Bonifazio Peruzzi were arrested in a villa at Marignolle, and handed over to Cante de' Gabrielli. Examined under torture on the following evening, Giannozzo confessed the whole plot, denounced Piero Canigiani and his other accomplices, and (so it was said) even accused himself of having forged the letters he had brought from Charles of Durazzo. His own brother, Franco Sacchetti, was the first to propose, in the Council of the Captain, that he should be put to death as a traitor to his native land. On October 15, Giannozzo was brought in a cart through the city to the place of execution, and there beheaded. The other conspirators were condemned to a fine of two thousand florins; Bonifazio Peruzzi and Antonio da Uzzano paid; but Piero Canigiani and the others, being unable to find the amount

[1] Unpublished. Appendix, Letter VI.

within a month, were put under ban, and their goods forfeited to the Commune. The King of Hungary and Charles of Durazzo denied all knowledge of the matter, the latter even declaring that the death of such a traitor had been too merciful. But it was afterwards admitted that the letters were authentic, and that Giannozzo's confession of forgery, if really made, had been extorted from him by torture, in order to avoid political complications.[1] A similar conspiracy came to light in December, Marchionne Stefani being then one of the priors, when, to appease the clamour of the populace led by the demagogues Tommaso Strozzi and Giorgio Scali, several of the noblest Florentine citizens were beheaded. Among them was Donato Barbadori, who had ever served the Republic with such fearless fidelity, and who died calmly and emphatically protesting his innocence.

[1] Cf. Marchionne Stefani, Lib. X. rubr. 821, 827, 905 ; Manni's *Cronichetta d' Incerto*, p. 217 ; *Anonimo Fiorentino*, pp. 402–404, and Gherardi's preface, pp. 260–262 ; Palermo, *op. cit.*, pp. ciii.–cxxx. ; Rodolico, *op. cit.*, pp. 331–336.

CHAPTER XV

THE PASSAGE FROM THE WORLD

"Al cielo è ritornata
La Sposa al suo Sposo,
L' amorosa a l' amoroso,
Et a l' amante l' amata."
Neri di Landoccio, *In Laude della Serafica Vergine.*

All this while, Catherine's life was being slowly consumed in the burning fire of her love for the Church; in her, indeed, had the word of the Psalmist been fulfilled to the letter: *The zeal of thine house hath eaten me up; and the reproaches of them that reproached thee are fallen upon me.* These months in Rome had been for her a time of intense agony, physical and mental, of impassioned labour by word and deed, while her bodily infirmities increased continually, until she seemed no longer to resemble a living being.

Towards the close of 1379, Catherine had moved with her spiritual family from the Rione della Colonna, and hoped soon to return to Siena. "We have taken a house near San Biagio," she wrote, on December 4, to Neri di Landoccio, who was still at Naples, "between the Campo de' Fiori and Sant' Eustachio, and we think to return before Easter, by the grace of God." [1] This was the house near the Minerva, in the present Via S. Chiara, where her cell is now venerated as a chapel, and it was here that her last mysterious illness came upon her. Here she endured that prolonged torment of soul and body, offering up herself as a willing victim to her Divine Bridegroom. To those that loved her, and stood by her side during these months from January 30, the Monday after Sexagesima Sunday, when her last agony began, until April 29, the Sunday before the

[1] Letter in the Casanatense MS. 2422. "Di frate Raimondo abiamo buone novelle, che egli sta bene, et lavora molto forte per la santa Chiesa."

feast of the Ascension, when she passed away, it seemed a new, unheard-of spiritual martyrdom, the death for which she had so often besought the Lord, for the renovation of the Church and the expiation of the sins of the world.

Two of the letters have been preserved that Barduccio wrote to Urban at her dictation at this time; for it is clear that she was frequently prevented from speaking to him face to face. In one, she bewails the fact that the new cardinals and prelates whom he has made, far from setting an example of virtue and abnegation, are simply following in the steps of their predecessors: "who had grown old in vice, in much pride, impurity, and avarice, committing the greatest simony." Already Urban had wearied of his first reforming zeal, and there would soon be little to choose between him and the man whom Catherine deemed the Antipope; but the Saint was never to realize this. "Pardon my presumption, most holy Father," she writes, "that I have ventured to write confidently to you, constrained by the Divine Goodness, and by the need that is manifest, and by the love I bear you. I should have come, instead of writing, but did not wish to weary you by coming so often. Have patience with me; for I shall never cease from urging you, by prayer, and by word of mouth or letter, as long as I live, until I see in you and in Holy Church what I desire, for which I know you desire, much more than I, to give your life."[1] In the other, she exhorts him to follow the example of St. Gregory the Great and govern the Church with prudence, especially in his dealings with the Roman Republic, whose ambassadors have just received an insulting reply from the rebellious Prefect, Francesco di Vico: "I have heard, most holy Father, of the reply that the impious Prefect has made you; verily, full of anger and of irreverence towards the Roman ambassadors. About this reply, it seems that they will call a general council, after which the heads of the Rioni and certain other good men will come to you. I beseech you, most holy Father, as you have begun, so to continue to confer often with them, and, with prudence, bind them with the bond of love. And

[1] Letter 364 (21).

so I beseech you now, as to what they will say to you after the council has been held, to receive them with all the sweetness that you can, pointing out to them what is necessary, according as shall seem fit to your Holiness. Pardon me ; for love makes me say what, perchance, need not be said. For I know that you must know the nature of your Roman children, how they are led and bound more by gentleness than by any other force or by harshness of words ; and you know, too, the great necessity that there is for you and Holy Church to preserve this people in obedience and reverence to your Holiness ; because here is the head and the beginning of our faith. And I humbly beseech you to strive with prudence always to promise only what you see to be possible for you completely to fulfil, in order that harm, shame, and confusion may not follow afterwards. Pardon me, sweetest and holiest Father, for saying these words to you. I trust that your humility and kindness is content that they should be said to you, and that you will not despise or scorn them because they come from the mouth of a very vile woman ; for a humble man does not consider who speaks to him, but looks to the honour of God, and to the truth, and to his salvation." Let the Pope remember "the ruin that came upon all Italy, because no check was put upon those evil rulers, who governed in such wise that they have been the cause of the spoliation of the Church of God." [1]

This letter to Urban was Catherine's last political testament. It was written on the evening of Monday, January 30, the Monday after Sexagesima Sunday.[2] She had barely finished dictating it, when her agony came upon her, the repetition of a

[1] Letter 370 (22), corrected by the Harleian MS., with which I read: "della risposta che v' ha fatta l' empio prefetto, drittamente empiuto d' ira," etc. Further on, Catherine refers to an insult to the Sienese ambassador. The Sienese had attempted to make peace between the Pope and the Prefect. Cf. *Cronica Sanese*, col. 265. Augusta Drane (II. pp. 235, 236) has curiously misunderstood and mistranslated the Saint's reference to the Roman council.

[2] That is, if Fra Tommaso Caffarini is right in identifying it with the one mentioned by Catherine herself in Letter 373 (102), of which he does not seem certain. *Supplementum*, III. i. (Casanatense MS. 2360), ff. 132–134.

stroke she had had on the previous night. "After we had written a letter," wrote Barduccio to Suor Caterina Petriboni, a nun in the Florentine convent of S. Piero a Monticelli, "she had another stroke, so much more terrible that we all mourned for her as dead, and she remained for a long space of time in such a state that no sign of life appeared in her; then, after several hours, she rose up, and it did not seem that she was herself."

A few days later, the rancour that, since the destruction of Sant' Angelo, had been steadily increasing between Urban and the Romans came to a head. To Catherine's spiritual eyes, the whole city seemed full of demons, urging the populace to rise in tumult and take the Pontiff's life. Fra Raimondo pictures her to us, wrestling in spirit with the Lord, beseeching Him, for honour of His name and for the sake of the Church, to inflict upon her body all the chastisements that the Roman People had merited for the innumerable sins committed in the Eternal City, and so restore harmony between them and the Pope. It is said that the populace assailed the Vatican in arms, and that Urban ordered the gates of the palace to be thrown open, received the insurgents seated upon his papal throne, and succeeded in appeasing their fury.[1] We do not know what part Catherine played in this affair, but the reconciliation was attributed to her prayers, and not improbably was due to her direct influence upon Giovanni Cenci, the democratic leader of the Roman republicans. In that case, this was her last political work, and surely not the least noble of her achievements.

"Then," writes Barduccio Canigiani, "began new pains and

[1] Cf. *Legenda*, III. ii. 2–4 (§§ 345, 346); Gobelinus Persona, *Cosmodromium*, cap. 76. The accounts of this affair given by Raynaldus, vii. p. 389, and Maimbourg, I. pp. 147, 148, are simply taken from Gobelinus, that of St. Antoninus, III. pp. 714, 715, being based upon the *Legenda*. Raynaldus and Maimbourg ascribe it to the latter part of 1379, but Catherine, Letter 373 (102), seems to imply that it took place on February 2, 1380. We read in the *Anonimo Fiorentino*, pp. 401, 402, under October 10, 1379, of an earlier tumult, where it is stated that the Roman People had made Giovanni Cenci tribune of Rome: "E 'l Papa ebbe gran paura. Onde la cosa si riposò in questo tribuno." In 1380, Giovanni Cenci was appointed Senator of Rome.

cruel torments to increase in her body every day. And, we being now come to Lent, she began, notwithstanding her weakness, to be so zealous in prayer that it was a wondrous thing, with those humble sighs and dolorous laments that drew our hearts from us. I think you know that her prayers were of such intensity, that one hour of prayer more consumed that poor little body than two days upon the rack would have done another.[1] Therefore, every morning with tears we lifted her up after Communion, in such a state that whoso saw her deemed her dead, and carried her to her couch. And, after an hour or two, she would rise up, and we went to San Pietro, which is a long mile from us, and then she set herself to prayer, and she remained there until nearly vespers, after which she returned home, so exhausted that she seemed a dead woman ; and acting thus she continued, every day in the same way, until the third Sunday of Lent."

These are things of which it is impossible for us to speak in the language of modern life. We have Catherine's own words, in the two wonderful letters written to Fra Raimondo on February 15, 1380, the Wednesday after the first Sunday in Lent, in which she takes leave of him and of the world. Never was the psychology of saintliness so marvellously revealed by one who had penetrated its depths, no less securely than she had scaled its heights.

"In the name of Jesus Christ crucified and of sweet Mary.

"Dearest and sweetest father in Christ sweet Jesus. I, Catherine, servant and slave of the servants of Jesus Christ, write to you in His precious blood, with desire of seeing you a column newly founded in the garden of Holy Church, like a faithful bridegroom of the Truth, as you ought to be ; and then shall I deem my soul blessed. I would not have you look back because of any adversity or persecution, but I would have you glory in adversity ; for in enduring we manifest our love and constancy, and render glory to God's name ; in other wise, no. Now is the

[1] *Stando in su la corda due giorni*, more literally, "two days of the strappado," the mediaeval Italian method of examining prisoners. I quote the original vernacular of this letter, appended to the early Venetian editions of the *Dialogo*.

time, dearest father, to lose oneself utterly, and to think nothing about self; even as did the glorious labourers, who, with such great love and desire, offered up the life of their body and watered this garden with blood, with humble and continual prayers, and by enduring even unto death. Look to it that I do not see you timid, so that your own shadow frighten you, but a virile warrior; and never depart from that yoke of obedience that the Sovereign Pontiff has laid upon you; and, also, in the order carry out what you see to be the honour of God; for the great goodness of God demands this of us, and He has set us there for nought else. Consider how great is the need that we see in Holy Church; for we see her utterly left alone. And thus the Truth made manifest, as I write to you in the other letter; and even as the Spouse is left alone, so is her bridegroom left alone. O sweetest father, I will not conceal the great mysteries of God from you; but I will recount them as briefly as can be, according as the weak tongue can narrate. And, also, I will tell you what I would have you do. But receive what I tell you without pain; for I know not what the Divine Goodness will do with me, whether He will make me remain or summon me to Himself.

"Father, father and sweetest son, wonderful mysteries has God wrought from the day of the Circumcision until now; so much that the tongue would not be sufficient to be able to narrate them. But let us let all that time go, and come to the Sunday of Sexagesima, on which day there were, as in brief I am writing you in the other letter, those mysteries which you shall hear; for it seemed to me that never had I borne the like. For so great was the pain in my heart, that my habit was rent, as much of it as I could grasp, as I went round the chapel like a person in agony. Whoso had restrained me, would have verily taken my life. When the evening of Monday came, I was constrained to write to Christ on earth and to three cardinals; I had myself helped, and went into the study; and when I had written to Christ on earth, I could write no more; so great were the pains that increased in my body. And, after a little while, the terror of the demons began, in such wise that they made me utterly stupefied, mad with rage against me, as if I, worm, had been the cause of taking from their hands what they had long time possessed in Holy Church. So great was the terror, with the bodily pain, that I wished to fly from the study, and to go into the chapel; as though the study had been the cause of my pains. I raised myself up; and, not being able to walk, I leaned upon my son Barduccio. But at once I was hurled down; and, being hurled down, it seemed to me as though the soul had been severed from the body; not in that way as when she passed away from it, for then my soul tasted the bliss of the immortals, receiving that sovereign good together with them;[1] but now she seemed like a thing reserved; for I did not seem to myself to be in the body, but I saw my body as though it had been another. And my soul, seeing the pain of him who was with me, turned to know if I had aught to do with the body, to say to him: 'Son, do not fear'; and I saw that I could not move the tongue nor any other member, any more than a body separated from life. Then I left the body as it was, and my understanding kept fixed upon the abyss of the Trinity. My memory was full of the recollection of the necessity of Holy Church and of all the Christian people. I cried out in God's sight, and with confidence besought the divine aid, offering Him my desires, and constraining Him by the blood of the Lamb, and by the pains that had been borne; and so earnestly was it besought, that it seemed to me certain that He would not deny that petition. Then I besought Him for all of you, praying Him to fulfil in you His will and my desires. Then I besought Him to deliver me from eternal damnation. While I remained thus for a very long while, so long that the family mourned for me as dead, all the terror of the demons had passed away. Then came the presence of the humble Lamb before my soul, saying: 'Fear not; for I will fulfil thy desires and those of My other servants. I would have thee see that I am the good craftsman, and do as the potter, who mars and makes again as seems good to him. Thus do I with these My vessels; I can mar them and make them again; and, therefore, I take the

[1] She refers to her trance, or mystical death, in 1370. Cf. chapter v.

vessel of thy body and make it again in the garden of Holy Church, in other wise than in the time passed.' And, that sweet Truth clasping me round with most winning ways and words which I pass over, my body began to breathe a little, and to show that the soul had returned to her vessel. I was full of wonder, and such great anguish remained in my heart that I still have it there. Every joy, every consolation, and all bodily food were taken from me; when I was then brought back into the place above, the room seemed to me full of demons; and they began to give me another battle, the most terrible that I ever endured, striving to make me believe and see that I was not she who was in the body, but, as it were, an unclean spirit. I called upon the divine aid with a sweet tenderness, not, indeed, refusing labour, albeit I said: 'O God, come to my assistance; O Lord, make haste to help me. Thou hast allowed me to be alone in this battle, without the consolation of the father of my soul, of which I am deprived through my own ingratitude.'

"Two nights and two days passed with these tempests. True is it that the mind and desire received no injury, but the understanding remained ever fixed upon its object, and the body seemed, as it were, to have died. Afterwards, the day of the Purification of Mary, I wished to hear Mass. Then were all the mysteries renewed; and God showed the great need that was, and is, as afterwards appeared; for Rome has been all on the point of revolting, traducing miserably and with great irreverence. But God has laid the ointment upon their hearts, and I believe that the affair will have a good conclusion. Then God imposed upon me this obedience, that, all this time of holy Lent, I should have the desires of all the family sacrificed and offered up in His sight, with this sole intention, namely, for Holy Church; and that I should hear a Mass every morning at dawn; which, you know, is an impossible thing for me, but, in obedience to Him, everything has become possible. So much has this desire become a part of me, that the memory retains nought else; the understanding can see nought else, and the will can desire nought else. And not merely does she reject the things of this world for this, but, though she holds converse with the true citizens, the soul neither can nor will rejoice in their joy, but only in the hunger which they have, and had while they were pilgrims and wanderers in this life.

"In this and in many other ways, which I cannot narrate, my life is being distilled and consumed in this sweet Spouse; I in this fashion, and the glorious martyrs with their blood. I pray the Divine Goodness soon to let me behold the redemption of His people. When it is the hour of tierce, I rise up from Mass, and you would see a dead woman going to San Pietro; and I enter anew to labour in the little bark of Holy Church. There I stay thus until nearly the hour of vespers; and from that place I would fain never go, nor day nor night, until I see this people a little settled and established with their father. This body keeps without any food, even without a drop of water; with such great and sweet bodily torments as I never endured at any time, so that my life hangs upon a thread. Now I know not what the Divine Goodness will please to do with me; as far as I feel, I do not say that I perceive His will and intention with regard to me; but, as to bodily sensation, it seems to me that I am to consume it at this time with a new martyrdom in the sweetness of my soul, that is, in Holy Church. Then He will, perhaps, make me rise again with Him; He will put an end and bound both to my miseries and to my crucified desires; or He will keep His wonted ways in circling round my body with His power. I have prayed, and am praying His infinite mercy to accomplish His will in me, and not to leave you or the others orphans, but ever to direct you along the way of the doctrine of truth, with true and most perfect light. I am certain that He will do it.

"Now I pray and urge you, father and son given me by that sweet Mother Mary, if you hear that God is turning the eyes of His mercy upon me, to begin your life anew; and, like one dead to all feeling of sense, cast yourself into this little bark of Holy Church. And be always cautious in speaking with others. You will seldom be able to have an actual cell; but I would have you always dwell in the cell of the heart, and always bear it with you.

For, as you know, when we are locked into that, our enemies cannot offend us. Then, every exercise that you do will be directed and ordained according to God. Also, I pray you to ripen your heart with a holy and true prudence, and to let your life be an example in the eyes of the laity, by never conforming yourself with the customs of the world. And let that generosity towards the poor and voluntary poverty, which you have always had, be renewed and refreshed in you, with true and perfect humility ; and do not let it ever grow lax, because of any state or exaltation that God gives you ; but plunge yourself down more deeply into the valley of that humility, finding delight in taking the food of souls at the table of the Cross, embracing humble, faithful and continual prayer as a mother, with holy watchfulness, celebrating Mass every day, unless by chance it should be necessary to abstain from it. Shun unnecessary and light speech, but be and show yourself mature in what you say, and in all you do. Cast away all tenderness for yourself and all servile fear ; for the sweet Church has no need of such folk, but of cruel persons, cruel to themselves and pitiful to her. These are the things which I pray you to strive to observe. Also, I pray you to get into your hands the Book and all my writings which you can find, you and Fra Bartolommeo and Fra Tommaso and the Master ; and do with them what you see to be most to the honour of God, together with Messer Tommaso ;[1] in them I found some recreation. I pray you further, as far as you will be able, to be the pastor and ruler of this family, even as a father, to preserve them in love of charity and in perfect union ; so that they may not be left scattered, like sheep without a shepherd. And I think to do more for them, and for you, after my death than in life. I will pray the eternal Truth to pour out over you all the fulness of grace and gifts that He has given to my soul, in order that you may be shining lights set on a candlestick. And I pray you to pray to the eternal Bridegroom that He may make me fulfil manfully the obedience that He has laid upon me, and may forgive me the multitude of my iniquities. Also, I pray you to pardon me all

[1] Tommaso Petra, then one of the papal secretaries.

ne disobedience, irreverence, and ingratitude that I have com- nitted towards you, and all the pain and sorrow that I have caused ou, and the little solicitude that I have had for your salvation. ask your benediction.

"Pray earnestly to God for me, and have prayers offered, for he love of Christ crucified. Forgive me for having written vords of bitterness to you; I do not write them to you to listress you, but because I am in doubt, and know not what the goodness of God will do with me. I want to have done my duty. And do not make yourself unhappy, because with bodily presence am far away from you, and you from me; for, although your presence would be a very great consolation to me, I have greater onsolation and gladness at seeing the fruit that you are producing n Holy Church. Now I beseech you to labour more zealously, or never had she such great need. And Christ on earth and Messer Tommaso are sending you the instruments with which rou will be able to work well.[1] And never, because of any per- secution, depart without leave of our lord the Pope. Take comfort, take comfort in Christ sweet Jesus, without any bitter- ness. I say no more to you. Remain in the holy and sweet charity of God. Sweet Jesus, Jesus Love."[2]

The letter, or rather revelation, which accompanied this, and which Fra Tommaso Caffarini declares that Catherine wrote with ner own hand, is entitled: "To the aforesaid Maestro Raimondo, signifying to him certain things and new mysteries that God had wrought in her soul on the Sunday of Sexagesima":—

"In the name of Jesus Christ crucified and of sweet Mary.

"I was panting with sorrow, through the crucified desire which was newly conceived in the sight of God; for the light of the understanding had mirrored itself in the eternal Trinity, and in that abyss was seen the beauty and dignity of the rational creature, and the misery into which the soul falls by the fault of

[1] *i.e.* the papal briefs, several of which, addressed to Raimondo at Genoa, are n the *Archivio Vaticano*, Reg. 310.

[2] Letter 373 (102). I quote throughout from the fuller and more accurate ext of the Casanatense MS. 292.

mortal sin, and the necessity of Holy Church which God manifested in His breast; and how no one can attain to taste the beauty of God in the abyss of the Trinity, save by the means of this sweet Spouse, because we must all pass through the gate of Christ crucified, and this gate is not found elsewhere than in Holy Church. I saw that this Spouse offered life, for she holds life in herself in such wise that there is no one who can slay her, and that she gave strength and light, for there is no one who can weaken her nor give her darkness, as far as concerns her very self. And I saw that her fruit never fails, but ever increases.

"Then said God eternal: 'All this dignity, which thy understanding could not comprehend, is given to man by My goodness. Look with grief and bitter sorrow, and thou shalt see that none go to this Spouse save for her external raiment, that is, for her temporal substance. But thou seest her destitute of those who take or seek what is within this Spouse, to wit, the fruit of the blood. Whoso does not bring the price of charity with true humility, and with the light of the most holy faith, shall not partake of this fruit to life, but to death; he would act like the thief, who takes what is not his; for the fruit of the blood belongs to those who bring the price of love, because she is founded in love and is love itself. And for love I would have every man give to her, according as I, God eternal, give to My servants to administer in diverse ways, even as they have received. But I am grieved that I find no one to minister to her. Nay, it seems that every one has abandoned her. But I will find the remedy.'

"The sorrow and the fire of desire waxing stronger, I cried out in the sight of God, saying: 'What can I do, O inestimable Fire?' And His benignity replied: 'Thou canst offer up thy life anew, and never give thyself rest. To this exercise have I set and am setting thee, thee and all those who follow and shall follow thee. Take heed, then, never to slacken, but ever to increase your desires; for I, with affection of love, shall surely succour you with My grace for soul and for body. And, in order that your minds may not be occupied in other things, I have made provision by giving an impulse to her whom I have set to govern you, and with mysteries and new ways I have drawn her and put her to this exercise; whereby she with her substance serves my Church, and you with continual, humble, and faithful prayers, and with those exercises that shall be necessary.[1] These will be assigned to thee and to them by My goodness, to each one according to his degree. Devote, then, thy life and thy heart and thy affection solely to this Spouse, for Me, without thyself. Gaze upon Me, and behold the bridegroom of this Spouse, to wit, the Sovereign Pontiff, and see his good and holy intention, which intention is without moderation; and thou seest that, even as the Spouse is alone, so is he alone. I permit that, with the methods he uses without moderation, and with the fear that he gives his subjects, he should sweep out My Church. But another shall come who with love shall bear him company, and fill her again.[2] It will fare with this Spouse as fares with the soul; for, first, fear enters her, and afterwards, when she is stripped of vices, love fills her again and reclothes her with virtues. All this shall be by sweet enduring, which is and shall be sweet to those who, in very truth, are nourished and shall be nourished at her breast. But do thou bid My vicar reconcile himself with every person, according to his power, and give peace to every one who will receive it. And to the columns of Holy Church say that, if they wish to repair her great ruin, they must do thus: they must unite together to be a garment to cover up the conduct that appears faulty in their father. Let them live ordered lives, and keep at their sides persons who fear and love Me. Let them meet together, casting

[1] This passage, in the plural, is addressed to Catherine's followers in general, *tutti quelli che ti seguitano e seguiteranno*, the *quella ch' io ho posta che vi governi* being Catherine herself. The change from *thee* to *you*, and back from *you* to *thee*, is thus clear.

[2] *Ma altri verrà che con amore l' accompagnerà e la riempirà.* That Catherine's contemporary disciples understood the sentence thus, seems clear from Fra Tommaso Caffarini's translation: *Sed alius veniet qui cum amore eum associabit et replebit Ecclesiam;* but the Italian might equally mean: "Another shall come who shall bear *her* company in love, and fill her again." Cf. Dante, *Purg.* vi. 114. In any case, it is simply the common mediaeval prophecy of the ideal Pope, the *papa angelico,* who is to reform and renovate the Church.

themselves to earth; and, when they do so, I who am Light will give them that light which shall be necessary to Holy Church. And, when they have seen among themselves what should be done, let them report it to My vicar, with true unity, promptly, boldly, and with great deliberation, and he will be constrained not to resist their good wills, because he has a holy and good intention.'[1]

"My tongue is not sufficient to narrate such great mysteries, nor what the understanding saw and the affection conceived. The day passed, full of wonder, and the evening came. And feeling my heart so drawn by affection of love that I could make no resistance to it, but must needs go to the place of prayer, and feeling that disposition come which I had at the time of death,[2] I knelt down with very great self-reproach, because I served the Spouse of Christ with great ignorance and negligence, and was the cause through which others did the same. Rising up, with the impression before the eye of my understanding of what I have said, God placed me before Himself, albeit I am always present to Him, because He contains all things in Himself; but in a new way, as though memory, understanding, and will had nought to do with my body. And with such great light did it contemplate this Truth, that in this abyss were then renewed the mysteries of Holy Church, and all the graces past and present received in my life, and the day on which my soul was espoused in faith.[3] All these things passed away from my mind, through the fire that had waxed stronger; and I attended only to what could be done to make a sacrifice of myself to God for Holy Church, and to remove the neglect and ignorance of those whom God had put into my hands. Then the demons cried out terribly against me, looking by the dread they inspired to impede and slacken my free and flaming desire. They struck against the outward body; but

[1] This was evidently to be the subject of the letter to three cardinals, which she found herself unable to write.

[2] *i.e.* in 1370.

[3] *E il dì che in fede fu sposata l' anima mia.* So the Casanatense MS., with which Fra Tommaso's Latin version corresponds.

the desire was the more enkindled, and I cried out: 'O God eternal, receive the sacrifice of my life in this mystical body of Holy Church. I have nought to give, save what Thou hast given me. Take my heart, and press it out over the face of this Spouse.' Then eternal God, turning the eye of His clemency, plucked out my heart, and pressed it out into Holy Church. And with such force had He drawn it to Himself that if, not wishing that the vessel of my body should be shattered, He had not straightway circled it round with His strength, my life would have departed. Then the demons cried out much more, as though they had felt intolerable pain; and they strove to fill me with terror, threatening to deal with me in such wise that I should be unable to do this exercise. But because Hell cannot resist the virtue of humility joined to the light of most holy faith, my mind drew itself together the more, and worked with weapons of fire, hearing such winning words in the sight of the Divine Majesty, and promises that gave joy. And, in truth, I was thus in so great a mystery that the tongue henceforth is no longer sufficient to speak of it.

"Now I say: thanks, thanks be to the most high, eternal God, who has placed us on the field of battle, like knights, to combat for His Spouse with the shield of most holy faith. The field is left free for us, by that virtue and power with which was defeated the demon who possessed the human race, and who was defeated, not in virtue of the humanity of Christ, but in virtue of His Godhead. With this will he now be defeated; that is, the demon will not be defeated by the mere suffering of our bodies, but in virtue of the fire of the divine, most ardent, and inestimable Charity. Thanks be to God, Amen. Sweet Jesus, Jesus Love."[1]

In this mystical agony, Catherine passed the next ten days, between her house and St. Peter's, until the third Sunday in Lent, when, as she prayed in the basilica before Giotto's mosaic of the

[1] Letter 371 (103), corrected and supplemented by the Casanatense MS. 292. A Latin version by Fra Tommaso Caffarini is in his *Supplementum*, III. 1 (Casanatense MS. 2360), ff. 123–126 *v*.

Navicella, it seemed to her that the bark of the Church was placed upon her shoulders, and that it crushed her to death with its weight. Her disciples carried her back, in a dying state, and laid her upon her couch, from which she never rose again save once. "She lay in this way for eight weeks," writes Barduccio, "without raising her head, full of such intolerable torments from head to foot, that she ofttimes said: 'These are not bodily or natural pains, but it seems that I have given leave to the demons to torment this body at their pleasure.' And, verily, it seemed surely that it was so; for she endured the most grievous pains that were ever heard, and it would seem to me a profanation to tell you of her patience; but this much will I tell you, that, when a new agony came, she raised her eyes with joy to God, and said: 'Thanks be to Thee, eternal Bridegroom, who every day dost newly grant such gifts and such graces to me, wretched woman, and Thy unworthy servant.'"

Tommaso Petra tells us how, hearing of her condition, he went to visit her, and found her lying upon the hard boards that formed her bed, in the room that had been transformed already into an oratory. He urged her to make her last will and testament, by prescribing a rule of life for all her disciples, that each might know what he or she should do after her death. "Leave us," he said, "all rich in divine love by this last will and testament, for I am certain that this injunction that I lay upon you will be most pleasing to the Lord."[1] At his bidding, she summoned all her spiritual sons and daughters who were then in Rome, and delivered to them "a devout, notable, and fruitful discourse," of which one of those present has left an account in writing. It is, as it were, a summary of what, all through her life, she had striven to teach them by word and by deed:—

"In the first place, she said that, in the beginning of her spiritual life, she recognized that, in order to give herself entirely to God and to possess Him fully, it was first necessary to strip her heart and affection of every sensitive love of every creature and

[1] Tommaso Petra's letter to Fra Bartolommeo, with some slight variations, is included in both the *Supplementum* and the *Processus*.

of every created thing outside of God ; because the heart cannot be given completely to God, unless it be free, open, pure, and single ; and that she had chiefly striven to do this, with great solicitude, being desirous to seek God by the way of suffering.

"She said, further, that she kept the eye of her understanding steadfast in a light of living faith, holding for certain that whatever happened to her or to others proceeded from God, through the great love that He bears His creatures, and not through hate. And thence she acquired and conceived a love and a readiness for holy obedience to the commands of God and those of her superiors, thinking that all their commands proceeded from God, either for the necessity of her salvation or for the increase of virtue in her soul. And she added : 'This I say, in the sight of my sweet Creator : I have never in the least degree sinned against obedience, through His goodness.

"Next, she said that God had made her see that she could never come to perfection, nor acquire in herself any true virtue, without the means of humble, faithful, and continuous prayer ; saying : 'This is the mother which conceives and nourishes all virtues in the soul ; and without her they all grow weak and fail.' Very much did she exhort us to be zealous in prayer, defining two kinds of prayers, vocal and mental. To vocal prayer, she said, we should apply ourselves at fixed hours ; but to mental prayer, continuously ; ever striving to know ourselves and the great goodness of God towards us. She said, also, that, in order to attain to purity of mind, it was necessary to abstain utterly from every judgment of our neighbour and from every empty talk about his doings, but always to consider the will of God in His creature ; adding, with great emphasis : 'On no account must we judge the will of a creature ; even if we see a thing to be a manifest sin, we must not pass judgment upon it, but, in holy and true compassion, offer it up to God with humble and devout prayer.' And on another occasion, speaking upon this point, she declared to the father of her soul that never, for any persecution, murmuring, detraction, injury, or insult, that had been said or in any way done to her, had anything ever entered into her mind save that whoso did, or spoke thus to her, was impelled by charity or by zeal for the salvation of her soul. And for this she thanked the inestimable goodness of God, who with this light had saved her, through His grace, from the danger of judging her neighbour.

"Lastly, she said that she had set very great hope and confidence in the Divine Providence ; and to this she invited and exhorted us all. She told us that she had found and tasted its wondrous greatness from her childhood. And she added : 'You, too, have experienced and seen it so great and so bountiful that, if our hearts had been harder than stone, our hardness and coldness must needs have been dissolved. Be enamoured, then, children, of this sweet Providence, for it will never fail whoso hopeth in it, and especially you.'

"Exhorting us and humbly inciting us to these and many other things, she besought us for what our Saviour left as testament to His holy disciples, that we should love one another. And, speaking with enkindled speech, she often said : 'Love one another, my children, love one another, for by this shall you show that you have had me and own me for mother, and I shall hold you to be my most beloved children ; for, by being virtuous, you will be my glory and my crown. And I will pray the Divine Goodness to pour out upon you all the abundance of gifts and graces which it has pleased Him to infuse into my soul.'

"Also, she laid this command upon us all : 'My children, do not let your desires slacken, touching the reformation and good state of Holy Church. But, ever more enkindled, offer tears with humble and continual prayer in the sight of God for this sweet Spouse, and for the vicar of Christ, Pope Urban VI' ; saying of herself : 'Long while have I borne this desire ; but especially, now more than seven years ago, it seemed that God put this exercise and enflamed desire into my soul. And, from then until now, no time has ever passed without my offering it up before the Divine Goodness, with mournful and painful and sweet desires ; and it has pleased His goodness for this to lay upon this weak body and make it bear many diverse and varied infirmities and sufferings. But, especially at the present time, it seems that my sweet Creator, as He did with Job, has given leave to the demons to torment and smite it as they please. Never do I remember at any time to have borne so many sweet sufferings and torments as now I bear. Thanks be to His infinite goodness, which makes me worthy to endure for glory and praise of His name in this sweet Spouse. And now, at the last, it seems to me that my most sweet Bridegroom, after so much enflamed and panting desire, so many sufferings and bodily infirmities, wills that my soul should utterly leave this dark prison and return to her source. I speak not as though I saw the certainty of His will in this, but it seems to me so.'

"And then, speaking emphatically, she added: 'Hold for certain, sweetest and dearest children, that, in departing from the body, I in truth have consumed and given my life in the Church and for the Church; which thing is a most special grace for me.' And, to comfort us all, who were weeping bitterly round her, she said: 'My children, you ought not to be grieved at this, but to have singular joy and gladness thereat; considering that I am leaving a place of such great sufferings and shall go to rest in the pacific sea, God eternal, and to be united, without any mean, to my most sweet Bridegroom. And I promise you that I shall be more perfectly with you, and shall be able to help you more there than I have been able to do here, inasmuch as I shall be delivered from darkness and united with the true and eternal light. Nevertheless, I commit both life and death to the will of my Creator; for, if He sees that I can be of any use to any one here, I would not shun labour, nor torment, nor any pain; but I am ready, for His honour and for the salvation of my neighbour, to give my life a thousand times a day, and each time with greater suffering than the other, if it were possible.'

"Her discourse being ended, she called us each one by name, and enjoined upon each one what she wished him to do after her life, if it was God's pleasure that it should now be ended; and each one, with humility and reverence, received her obedience. Then she besought us all humbly, to pardon her if she had not given us a virtuous example by her teaching and her life, nor helped us with her prayers before God as much as she could and ought, and if she had not satisfied our needs as she was bound, and for every pain, trouble, and sorrow of which she had been the cause to us, saying: 'Every failing has been through my want of knowledge. But I verily confess in the sight of God that I have always had, and have, a continuous and inflamed desire of your perfection and salvation; and if you, my most beloved children, follow this, you will be, as I said, my crown and my glory.' And at the end, while we all wept, she blessed each individually, in her usual way, in Christ."[1]

On the evening of Holy Saturday, March 24, Fra Bartolommeo di Domenico arrived in Rome. He was then prior of San Domenico at Siena, and had been sent by his provincial on business of the order. Not knowing of Catherine's illness, he at once went to the house, and was aghast at her altered aspect. Only by bending down his ear to her mouth, and then with difficulty, could he hear her whisper that it was well with her by the grace of our sweet Saviour. The next morning, it being Easter Day, he celebrated Mass in her room; when, to the great wonder and consolation of all, she rose from her couch unaided, and, together with her other spiritual children, received the Blessed Sacrament from his hands. Afterwards, she relapsed into her motionless condition, but had recovered her speech sufficiently to talk freely with him during the few days that he remained in Rome. At length, Bartolommeo's duty calling him back, she bade him return to Siena, laying upon him as her last command that he should make himself the constant companion of Fra Raimondo, who would shortly be elected master-general of the order. The friar then implored her, if it was the will of God that he should go, to obtain from Him as a sign that he might see her restored to health first. Accordingly, on the following

[1] This was first published by Gigli, apparently from a contemporary MS., as an appendix to the *Dialogo*. Cf. *Legenda*, III. iv. 1–5 (§§ 360–364). It is clear from Barduccio's letter to Suor Caterina that this took place many days before the end, before either Fra Bartolommeo or Stefano Maconi came to Rome.

day, he found her as merry and joyous as she had been of old when enduring the pains in her side. She stretched out her arms, tenderly embraced him, and again bade him depart. "But I, if I may speak with the Prophet, *deceived by the Lord*, decided to set out. I departed therefore; but, after I had reached my convent at Siena, I was informed by a letter from one of her sons that, on that very day, not long after my departure, she had returned to the same state of inability to move body and limbs in which she had been before. Then, after a few days, as the *Legenda* telleth, she blissfully passed from this dying life and valley of tears to the long-desired, sweet embraces of her Bridegroom." [1]

A few days after Bartolommeo had left, Stefano Maconi at last arrived in Rome. Catherine's last letter to him, half playfully bidding him come or she would get him no more indulgences, nor do anything else for him, and seeming surprised, perhaps a little hurt, at a report that he intended to become a monk (of which he had told her nothing), had given no hint of her approaching end; [2] but he had heard of her plight from the others, and, while praying at night in great sorrow in the vaults under the Spedale, had heard a voice: "Go to Rome, for the time of thy dear mother's departure is at hand." It was now his office to write what seems to have been the last letter written in her name: "Write, my son Stefano," she said, "to Siena to Fra Bartolommeo, that the Lord is exercising His mercy upon me, and therefore let him, and all his companions in San Domenico, beseech the Bridegroom Jesus to suffer me to offer up my life, even to the shedding my blood for His glory, to illumine the face of the Church." [3]

The end came on April 29, the Sunday before the Ascension, after prolonged and continual suffering. A few hours before the dawn, all the spiritual family were summoned, and Giovanni Tantucci gave her the absolution, *a culpa et a poena*, for the

[1] *Processus*, coll. 1358–1361.

[2] Letter 369 (263).

[3] Barth. Senensis, *op. cit.*, Lib. I. cap. 11, 12. Cf. Augusta Drane, II. pp. 258–260.

reception of the indulgence granted by the Pope at the hour of death. When day came, extreme unction was administered by the Abbot of Sant' Antimo, whose fall had already been forgiven him.

Catherine lay as though she were unconscious ; but, shortly after receiving the unction, she began to change utterly, and to move her face and arms as though enduring a last and most terrible assault from evil spirits. This lasted nearly two hours. She said, again and again : "*Peccavi, Domine, miserere mei*" ; and : "*Credo, credo*" ; and once, after having been silent for a little, as though hearing an accusation brought against her, she answered with a joyous countenance : "Never vainglory, but always the true glory and praise of Jesus Christ crucified." Then, as though a victory had been won, her face was suddenly all transfigured, her eyes grew radiant, "and it seemed that she had come forth from a great abyss." They helped her to sit up ; and, while leaning upon Monna Alessa in whose arms she had been lying, keeping her eyes fixed upon the Crucifix, she began to speak of the goodness of God, and to make a general confession, accusing herself in particular of negligence in seeking the salvation of souls and the reformation of the Church, and of ingratitude for the divine gifts. "I have not reverenced the innumerable gifts and graces of so many sweet torments and sufferings as has pleased Thee to lay upon this weak body, and, therefore, I have not borne them with that inflamed desire and love with which Thou hast given them to me." Then she asked again for the indulgence *a culpa et a poena*, saying that it had been granted to her by both Pope Gregory and Pope Urban. "She spoke," writes Barduccio, "like one that was starving for the blood of Christ." Turning to those of her spiritual children who had not been present at the discourse which she had uttered "many days before," she now told each (as she had done the others) what she would have him do after her life. Pointing to Stefano with her finger, she said : "And thee, in virtue of holy obedience, I command in the name of God to go by all means to the Carthusian order, for God has called and chosen thee to that." She asked pardon of all with great humility, for the little solicitude that it seemed to her she had had for their salvation, said some words to a Roman disciple named Lucio, and lastly to Barduccio, and then returned to her prayers. Let Barduccio tell the rest :—

"O that you had seen with what reverence and humility she received many times the blessing of her sorrowful mother ; verily, I tell you it was a sweet sorrow. O what a holy thing it was to see that disconsolate mother commend herself to her blessed daughter, and ask and receive her blessing ; verily, they moved our hearts ; and, in particular, the mother besought the daughter to obtain grace for her from God, that she might not offend Him in her great sorrow. All these things did not distract her from her prayers ; but, speaking continuously of God, she prayed on ; and, as she drew near her end, she offered special prayers for Holy Church, for which she repeated that she was giving her life, and prayed for Pope Urban VI, whom she emphatically confessed was true Sovereign Pontiff, exhorting her children to lay down their lives for this truth. Then she prayed with great fervour for all her beloved children whom God had given her to love, using many of those words that our Saviour used, when He prayed to His Father for His disciples, praying so fervently that not only our hearts, but the stones should have broken. Making the sign of the Cross, she blessed us all ; and thus she approached her longed-for end, persevering continuously in prayer, and saying : 'Lord, Thou dost summon me to Thyself, and I am coming to Thee, not by my own merits, but solely through Thy mercy, which mercy I crave from Thee in virtue of Thy blood.' And, at the last, she cried out many times : *Sangue*, *Sangue*. Finally, after the example of our Saviour, she said : 'Father, into Thy hands I commend my soul and my spirit' ; and thus sweetly, with her face like an Angel's, bowing down her head, she gave up the ghost." [1]

It was about midday, "the sixth hour, that is to say, the culmination of the day," as Dante has it, when Catherine thus

[1] *Lettera cit., di Barduccio di Piero Canigiani a suor Caterina Petriboni ; Leggenda minore*, pp. 163 et seq. ; *Legenda*, III. iv. 6 (§ 365) ; *Epist. Domni Stephani*, § 7.

passed to the embraces of her Divine Bridegroom. Stefano carried the body to the church of the Minerva, where it lay until the evening of Tuesday, May 1, exposed to the veneration of the people, working innumerable miracles, as men deemed, upon the souls and bodies of those that approached it. Thinking still more to enkindle their devotion, Giovanni Tantucci went up into the pulpit, and attempted to address the crowd ; but such was the noise of the throng that he could not get a hearing. He cried out in a loud voice : "I had meant to say somewhat in praise of this holy virgin, but it is manifest to all that she has no need of our sermons, for her eternal Bridegroom is Himself declaring her merits, and honouring her in His own fashion" ; and came down to join them. Urban himself had the funeral carried out with all ecclesiastical pomp, and Giovanni Cenci, the Senator of Rome, had another requiem offered in the name of the Roman People, with equal solemnity. Thus, for one brief moment, did the Papacy and the Republic of Rome seem to meet in harmony and union by the side of Catherine's tomb.

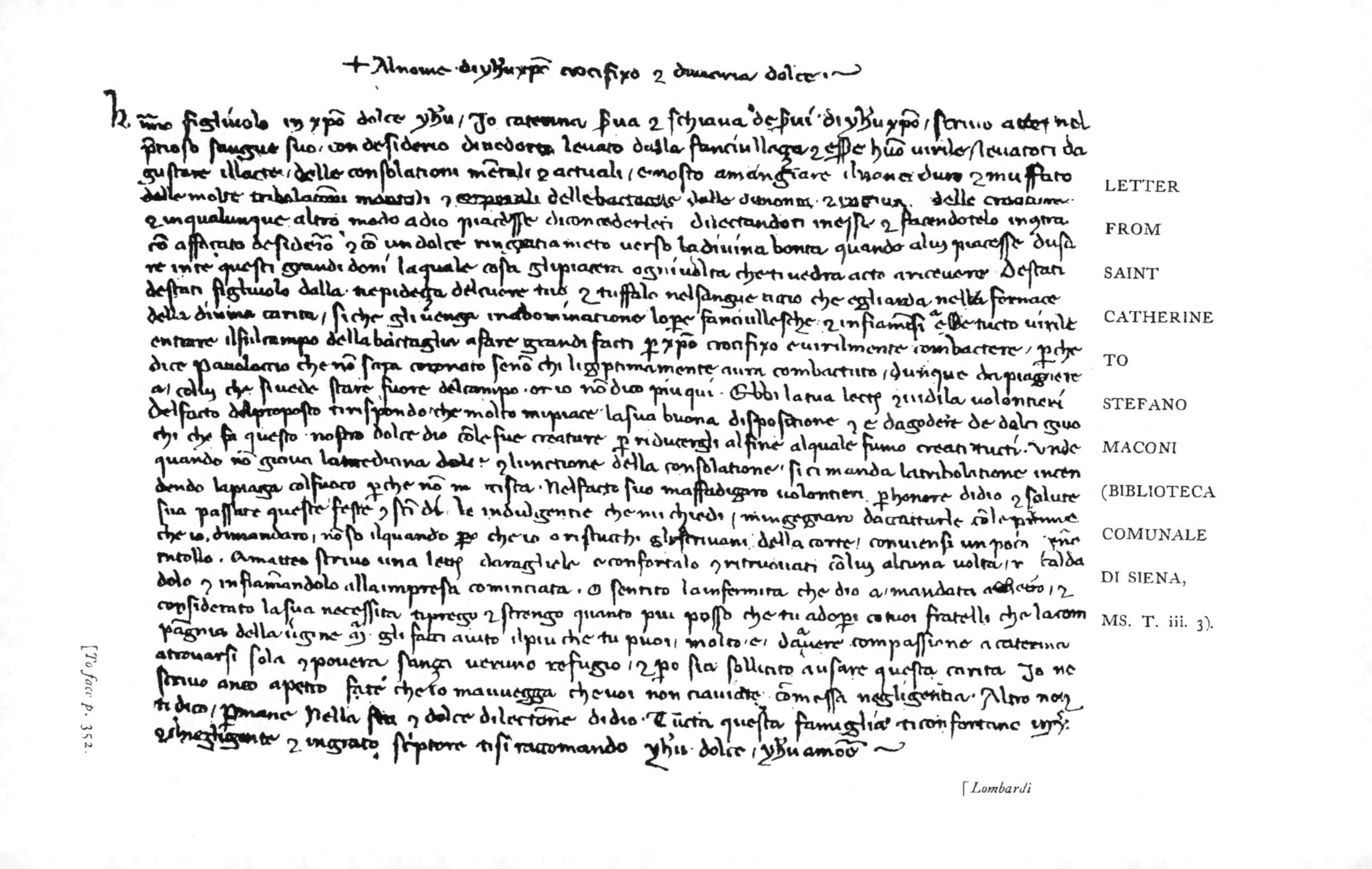

LETTER FROM SAINT CATHERINE TO STEFANO MACONI (BIBLIOTECA COMUNALE DI SIENA, MS. T. iii. 3).

[*Lombardi*

[*To face p.* 352.

CHAPTER XVI

CATHERINE'S LITERARY WORK

"Anco vi prego che il Libro e ogni scrittura la quale trovaste di me, voi e frate Bartolomeo e frate Tomaso e il Maestro, ve le rechiate per le mani; e fatene quello che vedete che sia più onore di Dio, con missere Tomaso insieme: nel quale io trovava alcuna recreazione."—St. Catherine to Fra Raimondo, Letter 373 (102).

At the end of her life, Catherine took thought for the written word that she was leaving behind her, still to speak with her voice after she had passed away. We have seen her, in her last letter, commend her works to Fra Raimondo and her other literary executors: *il Libro e ogni scrittura la quale trovaste di me*. The literary value of these remains is probably the last thing of which the Saint, "this blessed virgin and mother of thousands of souls," as Barduccio calls her, would have thought; she was not, in any normal sense of the words, a "woman of letters"; but, nevertheless, her spiritual and mystical writings rank among the classics of the language of her beloved native land, and hold, indeed, a position of unique importance in the literature of the fourteenth century.

It was in the brief interval between her leaving Florence and her going to Rome, a few months of comparative peace which she passed at Siena in the late summer and early autumn of 1378, that Catherine had completed her wonderful book: the *Dialogo*, or *Trattato della Divina Provvidenza*, also known as the *Libro della Divina Dottrina*.

"When the peace had been announced," writes Fra Raimondo, "she returned to her own home, and set herself with fresh diligence to the composition of a certain book, which, inspired by the supreme Spirit, she dictated in her vernacular. She had besought her secretaries (who were wont to write the letters which she despatched in all directions) attentively to observe everything when, according to her custom, she was rapt out of her corporeal senses, and carefully to write down whatever she then dictated. This they did heedfully, and compiled a book full of high and most salutary doctrines, which had been revealed to her by the Lord and were dictated by her, by word of mouth, in the vernacular speech."[1] In her last letter, Catherine simply refers to it as *il libro nel quale io trovava alcuna recreazione*, "the book in which I found some recreation"; and, although her friends and disciples thus describe her as dictating it to her secretaries while "rapt in singular excess and abstraction of mind," it is not clear that she herself would have made any claims of supernatural authority for it, or have regarded it as anything more than the pious meditations of a spirit "athirst with very great desire for the honour of God and the salvation of souls," one who (in her own characteristic phrase) "was dwelling in the cell of knowledge of self, in order better to know the goodness of God."

The book is concerned with the whole spiritual life of man, in the form of a prolonged dialogue, or series of dialogues, between the eternal Father and the impassioned human soul, who is here clearly Catherine herself. It seems to be properly divided into six treatises or *Trattati*: an Introduction (cap. 1 to cap. 8), the *Trattato della Discrezione* (cap. 9 to cap. 64), the *Trattato dell' Orazione* (cap. 65 to cap. 86), the *Trattato delle Lagrime* (cap. 87 to cap. 134), the *Trattato della Divina Provvidenza* (cap. 135 to cap. 153), and the *Trattato dell' Obbedienza* (cap. 154 to cap. 167).[2] It opens with a striking passage on what we may call the essence of mysticism, the possibility of the union of the soul with God in love:—

"When a soul lifts herself up, athirst with very great desire for the honour of God and the salvation of souls, she exercises

[1] *Legenda*, III. i. 2 (§ 332). Cf. III. iii. 1 (§§ 349, 350). In the Vatican MS., *Cod. Barb. Lat.* 4063, the book is entitled simply: "Il libro facto per divina revelacione de la venerabile et admirabile vergine beata Katherina da Siena."

[2] The arrangement I adopt is a compromise between that of the manuscripts and early editions of the Italian text and that given by Fra Raimondo in his Latin version—a compromise which, as far as making the *Trattato delle Lagrime* a separate treatise, seems justified by Catherine's own reference to it in Letter 154 (63), as well as by internal evidence.

erself for a while in habitual virtue, and dwells in the cell of nowledge of self, in order better to know the goodness of God ; or love follows knowledge, and, when she loves, she seeks to ollow and to clothe herself with the truth. But in no way does the reature taste and become illumined by this truth as much as by neans of humble and continuous prayer, based on knowledge of elf and of God ; for prayer, exercising the soul in this way, unites er to God, as she follows the steps of Christ crucified ; and thus, y desire and affection and union of love, she is transformed into Him. This it seems that Christ meant when He said : *If a man ove Me, he will keep My words ;* and again : *He that loveth Me hall be loved of My Father, and I will love him and will manifest Myself to him, and he will be one with Me and I with him.* And in nany places we find similar words, by which we can see that it is rue that, by affection of love, the soul becomes another He." [1]

The rest of the book is practically an expansion of the evelation that Catherine had in a vision, after receiving Holy Communion on a feast of the Blessed Virgin, in the autumn of he previous year ; a revelation which, in a more partial form, she ad already set forth in a letter to Fra Raimondo.[2] It is, as it were, a gathering together of the spiritual teachings scattered hrough her letters. On the whole, it reads somewhat less ecstatically, as though written with more deliberation than the etters, and is in parts drawn out to considerable length, and sometimes moves slowly. The effect is that of a mysterious voice from the cloud, talking on in a great silence ; and the result s monotonous, because the listener's attention becomes over-strained. Here and there, it is almost a relief when the Divine Voice ceases, and Catherine herself takes up the word. At other times, however, we feel that we have almost passed behind the veil that shields the Holy of Holies, and that we are, in very truth, hearing Catherine's rendering into finite words of the neffable things which she has learned by intuition in that half nour during which there is silence in Heaven. The importance of

[1] Cap. I. [2] Letter 272 (90).

the *Dialogo* in the history of Italian literature has never been fully realized. In a language which is singularly poor in mystical works (though so rich in almost every other field of thought), it stands with the *Divina Commedia* as one of the two supreme attempts to express the eternal in the symbolism of a day, to paint the union of the soul with the suprasensible while still imprisoned in the flesh. The whole of Catherine's life is the realization of the end of Dante's poem : " to remove those living in this life from the state of misery, and to lead them to the state of felicity " ; and the mysticism of Catherine's book is as practical and altruistic as that of Dante's, when he declares to Can Grande that the whole *Commedia* " was undertaken not for speculation, but for work. For albeit in some parts or passages it is treated in speculative fashion, this is not for the sake of speculation, but for the sake of work."[1] Thus Catherine, in the preliminary chapters of the *Dialogo*, " wishing more virilely to know and follow the truth," makes her first petition to the eternal Father for herself, only because " the soul cannot perform any true service to her neighbour by teaching, example, or prayer, unless she first serves herself by acquiring and possessing virtue." By the infinite desire that proceeds from love, the soul can make reparation to God for her neighbour's sins, as well as for her own. Even as charity gives life to all the virtues, so all the vices have their root in self-love, and both are realized in action by means of others. " There can be no perfect virtue, none that bears fruit, unless it be exercised by means of our neighbour." [2]

For virtue to be perfect, it must be exercised with discretion, " which discretion is nought else than a true knowledge that the soul should have of herself and of Me, and in this knowledge it has its root." Discretion, which springs from charity and is nurtured in the soil of humility, should be the lamp of the whole spiritual life, directing all the powers of the soul to serve God and to love her neighbour, offering up the life of the body for the salvation of his soul, and her temporal substance for the

[1] *Epist.* X. 16.

[2] *Dialogo*, cap. 1–cap. 8, cap. 11. Cf. Letters 311 (203), 282 (39).

'elfare of his body. The face of the Church, the Spouse of 'hrist, has grown like that of one smitten with leprosy, through ıe impurity, the self-love, the pride and avarice of her ministers, those who feed at her breasts"; but by the prayers, desires, ꜫars, and labours of God's servants, her beauty will be restored ɔ her, for the humanity of the Word still stands as the bridge etween earth and Heaven.

This figure of the Word as the bridge from time to eternity, ıe road to which has been broken by the fall of Adam, is worked ut at length, Catherine laying stress upon the doctrine that "the ternal Truth has created us without ourselves, but will not save s without ourselves." The bridge has three steps or grades: he Feet that were nailed to the Cross; the Side, that was pierced ɔ reveal the ineffable love of the Heart; the Mouth, where the itterness of gall and vinegar is turned to peace. On the bridge Catherine's imagery suddenly changing form) is the garden of he Church, to minister the bread of life and the blood that is rink, in order that the pilgrims may not faint by the way. 'hese three steps also represent the three powers of the soul: 'ill, memory, and understanding; as likewise the three states of he soul in God's service, by which she passes from servile fear nd mercenary obedience to true fidelity and friendship, and, ıstly, to perfect filial love.

"I require of you that you love Me with that love wherewith love you. This you cannot do to Me, because I loved you 'ithout being loved. All love that you bear Me you owe Me as debt, and not as a free gift, because you are bound to give it Ле; and I love you freely, not in duty bound. You cannot, hen, render to Me the love that I require of you; and, therefore, ave I set you in the midst of others, in order that you may do to hem what you cannot do to Me; that is, love them freely and 'ithout reserve, and without expecting any return from it; and ıen I consider done to Me whatever you do to them. So this ɔve must be flawless, and you must love them with the love 'herewith you love Me. And knowest thou how he who loves 'ith spiritual love perceives that he is not perfect? If he feels pain and affliction when it does not seem to him that the creature whom he loves corresponds to his love, and he deems that he is not loved as much as he thinks he loves; or when he is deprived of the consolation of familiar intercourse with that creature, or sees another loved more than himself. In this, and in many other things, he will be able to perceive that this love towards Me and his neighbour is still imperfect, and that he has drunk from this vessel outside the fountain-head, albeit he first drew this love from Me. But because his love for Me is still imperfect, therefore he shows it imperfect towards the one whom he loves with spiritual love. All comes from the root of spiritual self-love not being entirely plucked out from his heart. And thus I often permit a soul to love in this wise, in order that she may know herself and her own imperfection. I withdraw Me from her in feeling, in order that she may enclose herself in the cell of self-knowledge, where she may acquire all perfectness; and then I return to her with more light and more knowledge of My truth, so that she may deem it a grace to be able to slay her own will for My sake, and never cease from watering her vineyard, and plucking out the thorns of evil thoughts, and setting therein the stones of virtues established in the blood of Christ crucified, which she has found in going across the bridge of My only-begotten Son." [1]

To this state of perfection in love, the soul comes by perseverance in holy prayer, offered up continually in the house of knowledge of self and of God, inebriated with the blood, clad in the fire of divine charity, fed on the sacramental food. Vocal prayer is but the preparation for mental prayer, in which God visits the soul, and the affection of charity is in itself a perpetual prayer. Souls that love God less for His own sake than for the consolation that they find in Him are easily deceived. When that consolation fails them, they think they offend God; and, for fear of losing their own peace, they do not succour their neighbour in his need, not realizing that "every vocal or mental exercise is ordained by Me, that the soul may practise it to come to perfect

[1] Cap. 64.

charity towards Me and towards her neighbour, and to preserve her in that charity."[1] Such souls are deluded by spiritual self-love, and are easily deceived by false visions that come from the devil. But the soul who has attained to perfect love, and who truly knows herself, does not consider the gifts and graces of her divine Friend, but the charity with which He gives them. Without leaving the cell of self-knowledge, she goes forth in God's name, prepared to endure sufferings, and to put into practice for the service of her neighbour the virtues that she has conceived in her mystical habitation. Thus the soul attains a fourth state, of perfect union in God : "for there is no love of Me without love of man, and no love of man without love of Me, for the one love cannot be separated from the other."[2]

In this state of perfect union, the Saints receive such strength that they not merely bear with patience, but long with panting desire to endure suffering for the glory of God's name. With St. Paul, such as these bear in their bodies the marks of Christ : "that is, the crucified love that they have glows out in their bodies, and they reveal it by despising themselves, and by delighting in insults, enduring troubles and pains from whatever side and in whatever way I concede them." Perfectly dead to their own will, they are never deprived of the presence of God even in feeling : "I continually reside by grace and by feeling in their souls ; and whenever they wish to unite their mind with Me through affection of love, they can do so ; for their desire has attained to such complete union, through love's affection, that nothing can separate them from Me."[3] But although such souls ever possess God by grace, and realize His presence in feeling, they cannot be uninterruptedly united to Him as long as they are fettered to the body : "For, when such souls rise up with panting desire, they run with virtue along the bridge of the doctrine of Christ crucified, and reach the gate ; lifting up their minds to Me, bathed and inebriated with blood, inflamed with the fire of love, they taste in Me the eternal Godhead, which is to them a sea of peace, with which the soul becomes so united

[1] Cap. 69. [2] Cap. 74. [3] Cap. 78.

that the mind has no other movement save in Me. Although mortal, she tastes the bliss of the immortals, and, although still with the weight of the body, she receives the joy of the spirit; whereby ofttimes the body is lifted up from the earth through the perfect union that the soul has made in Me, as though the heavy body had become light. It is not that its weight is taken from it; but, because the union which the soul has made in Me is more perfect than that between her and the body, therefore the strength of the spirit united to Me raises the weight of the body from the earth, and the body remains motionless, all fordone by the affection of the soul, so that (as thou mayest remember to have heard from some creatures) it would not be possible to live, unless My goodness girded it round with strength. Therefore, I would have thee know that it is a greater miracle to see the soul not leave the body in this union, than to see many dead bodies raised up again. And for this, I, for a while, withdraw this union, making her return to the vessel of her body; that is, the bodily sense, which was totally alienated through the affection of the soul, return to consciousness; because it is not that the soul departs from the body, for this she does not, save by means of death, but the faculties depart because of the affection of the soul which is united to Me by love. Then is the memory found full of nought but Me; the understanding uplifted to contemplate My truth as object; the will, that follows the understanding, loves and unites itself to what the eye of the understanding sees. All these powers being gathered and united together, immersed and drowned in Me, the body loses its feeling; the eye, seeing, sees not; the ear, hearing, hears not; the tongue, speaking, speaks not, save as sometimes I permit to relieve the abundance of the heart, and for the glory and praise of My name; the hand, touching, does not touch; the feet, going, do not go. All the members are bound and occupied by the bond and by the consciousness of love. By this bond they are subjected to reason and united with the affection of the soul, and, as it were against their own nature, all cry together to Me, the eternal Father, that they would fain be separated from the soul and the soul from the body; and, therefore, they cry out before Me, with the glorious Paul: *O wretched man that I am! Who shall deliver me from the body of this death?*"[1]

Such souls yearn to be delivered from the body, but are perfectly resigned to the will of God, rejoicing in being allowed to suffer for His honour. Their union with Him, thus temporarily interrupted, is ever renewed with increased intimacy: "I ever return with increase of grace and with more perfect union, ever revealing Myself to them anew, with a more lofty knowledge of My truth."[2] It is for such souls as these, with their prayers and sweat and tears, to wash the face of Christ's Spouse, the Church: "for which reason I showed her to thee in the guise of a damosel, whose face was all made filthy, as though of one smitten with leprosy, by the sins of her ministers and of all the Christian community who feed at her breast."

A frightful picture of the corruption of the clergy follows, in the *Trattato delle Lagrime*, after Catherine has touched at some length upon "the infinite variety of tears," and the way of coming to perfect purity. The dignity of the priesthood, and the ineffable mystery of the Sacrament which they have to administer, require a greater purity in the ministers of the Church than in any other creature. They are God's anointed, His Christs, with power over the Lord's sacramental body that even the Angels have not, and He considers all injuries done to them as inflicted upon Himself, as persecution of His blood. But, in contrast with Peter himself, Sylvester, Gregory, Augustine, Jerome, Thomas Aquinas, and the other holy ecclesiastics of olden time, we are shown the modern priests and prelates, whose lives are founded in self-love, and who perform the office of devils. Avarice, lust, and pride are the masters that they serve. The table of the Cross is deserted for the sake of the tavern; the

[1] Cap. 79. In his Latin version, Fra Raimondo glosses: "Nota quod iste status est ille, in quo erat ista benedicta virgo Catharina de Senis: ut oculi nostri viderunt apertissime."

[2] This is worked out in cap. 83, cap. 84, of which the modern printed editions and translations contain only a mutilated version of what we find in the MSS. and in Fra Raimondo's Latin.

poor are left destitute, while the substance of the Church is squandered upon harlots. Nay, more, the leprosy of unnatural vice, the sin from which even the devils flee in horror because of their angelical nature, has contaminated their minds and bodies. The priests celebrate Mass after a night of sin, and often their mistresses and children join the congregation; others use the Blessed Sacrament of the altar to make love-charms to seduce the little sheep of their flock, or persuade them to commit fornication under pretext of delivering them from diabolical possession. Some priests, realizing their own sinful state sufficiently to fear God's judgments, only pretend to consecrate when they say Mass, and thereby lead the people into idolatry by making them worship as the body of Christ what is no more than a piece of bread. The prelates connive at infamous monks corrupting the nuns in the monasteries under their charge. Ministers of the Church have become usurers; benefices and prelacies are bought and sold, while the poor are left to die of hunger. Spiritual things are abandoned, while the rulers of the Church usurp temporal power and secular government.[1] It is only possible here to touch very slightly upon the contents of these terrible chapters; but the student of the religious life of the fourteenth century is compelled to face the fact that in them we have the testimony of Boccaccio's *Decameron* confirmed by the burning words of a great saint, who does not shrink from putting them into the mouth of God Himself.

From this Catherine turns to the contemplation of the Divine Providence, shown in the creation of man in God's image and likeness, with memory, understanding, and will, for the Beatific Vision; in his redemption by means of the Incarnation; and in the institution of the Blessed Sacrament for his spiritual sustenance. As an instance of this Providence, in a particular case, we have a somewhat mysterious allusion to one whose soul was saved by a

[1] Cap. 121–cap. 130. Cf. Caesarius Heisterbacensis, *Dialogus miraculorum* (ed. Strange, Cologne, 1851), dist. IX. cap. 6; *Revelationes S. Birgittae*, I. 49, IV. 133. An equally appalling picture is given, some years later, by Nicolas de Clémanges, in his *De ruina Ecclesiae*, cap. 15–cap. 23 (*Opera*, Leyden, 1613).

violent death. "I would have thee know that, to save him from the eternal damnation which thou seest he had incurred, I allowed this to happen, in order that by his blood he might have life in the blood of My only-begotten Son. For I had not forgotten the reverence and love which he bore to Mary, the most sweet Mother of My only-begotten Son, to whom it is given by My goodness, for reverence of the Word, that whoso holds her in due reverence, be he a just man or a sinner, shall never be taken or devoured by the infernal demon. She is as a bait set by My goodness to take all rational creatures."[1] Catherine's own miraculous communions, when her Divine Bridegroom intervened to give her the food of Angels which the priests would fain have denied her, show God's providential dealings with souls that hunger for the sweet Sacrament.[2] There are three states of the human soul: those of mortal sin, imperfect love, and perfect charity; and in each God's Providence acts in diverse ways to draw her to Himself.

One of the means He uses to draw the imperfect from their imperfection is an absorbing devotion for a fellow-creature, the *amor amicitiae* of which the Angelical Doctor writes, the kind of love of which Dante had given the supreme exposition in the *Vita Nuova*. By such a love, the soul is exercised in virtue and raised above herself; the heart is stripped of all sensitive passion and disordered affection. By the perfection of this love can be measured the perfection of the soul's love of God. When one who loves in this way sees himself deprived of the delight he used to have in familiar intercourse with the person loved, and sees that person now more intimately associated with another than with himself, the very pain that he feels will teach him to know himself, and will spur him on to hatred of his own selfishness and to love of virtue. He will humbly repute himself unworthy of the desired consolation, and will be assured that the virtue, for which

[1] Cap. 139. Cf. the salvation of Buonconte da Montefeltro, *Purg.* v. 100–107. Catherine alludes to this case in similar words in Letter 272 (90). Probably, either Niccolò di Toldo or Trincio Trinci is the person meant.

[2] Cap. 142. Cf. *Legenda*, II. xii. 4–14 (§§ 316–324).

he should chiefly love that person, is not diminished in his regard. This love will have taught him to desire to bear all suffering for the glory of God.[1] For tribulation is the test of true charity, and, with those who have come to the perfect state, God uses the means of suffering and persecution to preserve and augment their perfection. Goaded on by their hunger for the salvation of souls, forgetting themselves, they knock, night and day, at the gate of Divine Mercy. For the more man loses himself, the more he finds God. This truth they read in the sweet and glorious book of the Word, and bring forth the fruit of patience. Although, with St. Paul, they have received the doctrine of truth in the abyss of the Godhead, they have likewise received the thorn in the flesh, to keep them in self-knowledge and humility, and to make them compassionate towards the weaknesses and frailty of others. The anguish that they endure, in seeing the sins that are done against God, purges them from all personal sorrows; and God suffers Himself to be constrained by their panting desires, to have mercy upon the world, and by their endurance to reform His Church: "Verily, such as these can be called another Christ crucified, My only-begotten Son; for they have taken upon themselves the office of Him who came as mediator to end the war, and to reconcile man with Me in peace, by much endurance even unto the shameful death of the Cross." [2]

The whole being of such a saint is attuned to mystical music, and has become one sweet harmony, in which all the powers of the soul and all the members of the body play their parts. This spiritual melody was first heard from the Cross, and those that followed have learnt it from that Master. "My infinite Providence has given them the instruments, and has shown them the way in which to play upon them. And whatever I give and permit in this life is to enable them to increase the power of these instruments; if they will only know it, and not obscure the light by which they see, with the cloud of self-love and their own pleasure and opinion." [3] Inebriated with trust in the Divine Providence, these souls embrace the doctrine of voluntary poverty,

[1] Cap. 144. [2] Cap. 145, cap. 146. [3] Cap. 147.

choosing Lady Poverty, the Queen, as their bride, with whom they become mistresses of all spiritual wealth :—

"Then that soul, as though inebriated and enamoured of true and holy Poverty, passing out of herself into the supreme eternal Greatness, and transformed in the abyss of the sovereign inestimable Providence (in such wise that, while still in the vessel of the body, she saw herself out of the body by the overshadowing and rapture of the fire of Its charity), kept the eye of her understanding fixed upon the Divine Majesty, saying to the supreme and eternal Father : 'O eternal Father, O fire and abyss of Charity, O eternal Beauty, O eternal Goodness, O eternal Clemency, O hope and refuge of sinners, O inestimable Bounty, O eternal and infinite Bliss ! Thou that art mad with love, hast Thou any need of Thy creature ? Yea, it seemeth to me that Thou dost act as though Thou couldst not live without her, albeit Thou art the life from which all things have life and without which nothing lives. Why, then, art Thou thus mad ? Thou art mad, because Thou art enamoured of what Thou hast made. Within Thyself Thou didst take delight in her, and, as drunk with desire of her salvation, Thou dost seek her when she flies from Thee ; she shuns Thee, and Thou drawest near her. Nearer to her Thou couldst not come than to clothe Thyself with her humanity. What then shall I say ? I will do as one that is tongue-tied, and say : *Ah, Ah ;* for there is nought else I can say, since finite speech cannot express the affection of the soul which desires Thee infinitely. Methinks I can say with Paul : *Eye hath not seen, nor ear heard, neither have entered into the heart of man*, the things which I have beheld. I have seen the hidden things of God. My soul, thou hast tasted and seen the abyss of the sovereign and eternal Providence.'"[1]

Obedience is the special virtue that ruled Catherine's spiritual life, even as poverty had informed that of St. Francis and the realization of justice had been the inspiration of that of Dante.

[1] Cap. 153. Catherine's treatment of holy Poverty, cap. 151, is thoroughly Franciscan. It is curious to notice how loosely she often quotes the Scriptures ; Fra Raimondo usually corrects her in his Latin version.

She treats it as the key which the Father put into the hand of the Word to unlock the gate of eternal life, and which the Word left with His vicar at the Ascension. All the faith is founded upon it. Each soul receives it into her hand at baptism, and must fasten it, with the cord of detachment, to the girdle of resignation to the will of God. Like poverty, obedience is a bride of souls, a queen enthroned above the tempests of the world. Besides the general obedience to which all are bound, there is the special obedience of the religious life, shown in its perfection in the ideals with which Benedict, Francis, and Dominic founded their orders. The chapter dealing with the Franciscans and Dominicans, the sublime ideals of their two patriarchs who based their rules on poverty and learning, respectively, and the degeneration of their followers, is thoroughly Dantesque in spirit and in expression. Catherine has, however, worse things to record against the friars of her own order than those which the divine poet puts upon the lips of the Angelical Doctor ; even the vow of chastity is continually broken, and the light of science perverted by them to darkness. The days of Thomas Aquinas, whom Catherine ever names with profound admiration and marked personal love (he was one of the saints with whom she used to speak in her visions), and of Peter Martyr, whose career appealed to the sterner side of her character, have passed away.[1] The resemblance at times between Catherine's phraseology, as well as her thought, in the *Dialogo* as in the Letters, with that of Dante, is not likely to be entirely fortuitous. Although she never mentions the poet, and assuredly had never read the *Divina Commedia*, she must frequently have heard his lines quoted by her followers. Neri di Landoccio, at least, appears to have

[1] Cap. 158. Cf. Dante, *Par.* xi., xii., and xxii. 73–93. The encyclical letters issued by Fra Elias of Toulouse, as master-general of the order, in 1368, 1370, and 1376, strikingly confirm Catherine's testimony as to the corruption and degeneracy of the Dominicans at this time. "We have come to such a pass," he had written in 1376, "that whoso cares for the ceremonies of the Church is pointed out with the finger, and whoso keeps the rules of the order is reckoned by the others as of singular life." See *Monumenta ordinis Fratrum Praedicatorum historica*, tom. v. pp. 306–312.

been a Dante student.[1] It would be pleasant to think of such passages as the mystical espousals of St. Francis with Poverty, the praises of St. Dominic, or St. Bernard's invocation to the Blessed Virgin, being read aloud in Catherine's circle, and Saint and secretaries alike being fired by the music of him who had fought the same battle for righteousness more than half a century before.

From the consideration of her own order, Catherine turns to the religious life in general, the excellence of its ideals, the disastrous results when these are corrupted or neglected. The perfect religious, *il vero obbediente*, he who has humbled himself like a little child to enter into the kingdom of Heaven, is contrasted with the unfaithful and disobedient monk or friar, "who stays in the bark of his order with such great pain to himself and to others, that in this life he tastes the pledge of hell." Midway between the two types is that of the average religious, neither perfect nor corrupt, but lukewarm in his profession, ever in danger of falling, but still with the power of joining the truly obedient in their holy race. After a glowing eulogy of the virtue of obedience, illustrated by the miracles that the saints of old have wrought by its power, and a recapitulation of the whole book, Catherine ends with the impassioned eloquence of what may be called her universal prayer :—

"Thanks, thanks be to Thee, eternal Father, for Thou hast not despised me, Thy creature, nor turned Thy face from me, nor contemned my desires. Thou that art light, hast not considered my darkness ; Thou that art life, hast not considered my death ; nor hast Thou, the physician, turned from my grievous maladies. Thou art eternal purity, and I am full of the mire of many miseries ; Thou art infinite, and I am finite ; Thou art wisdom, and I am foolishness ; for all these and other infinite evils and defects that are in me, Thy wisdom, Thy goodness, Thy clemency, and Thy infinite blessedness has not despised me ; but in Thy light Thou hast given me light, in Thy wisdom I have known the truth, in Thy clemency I have found Thy charity and the

[1] Cf. *Lettere dei discepoli*, 18. But Capecelatro, pp. 343, 344, following Ignazio Cantù, much overstates Catherine's possible knowledge of Dante.

love of my neighbour. Who has constrained Thee to this? Not my virtues, but Thy charity alone. May this same love constrain Thee to illumine the eye of my understanding in the light of faith, in order that I may know and comprehend the truth Thou hast revealed to me. Grant that my memory may be capable of retaining Thy benefits, that my will may burn in the fire of Thy charity, and that fire make my body pour forth blood ; so that with that blood, given for love of the blood, and with the key of obedience, I may unlock the gate of Heaven. This same grace I crave of Thee for every rational creature, in general and in particular, and for the mystical body of Holy Church. I confess and do not deny that Thou didst love me before I was, and that Thou dost love me ineffably, as mad with love for Thy creature.

"O eternal Trinity, O Godhead, Thou that, by Thy divine nature, didst make the price of the blood of Thy Son avail! Thou, eternal Trinity, art a sea so deep, that the more I enter therein, the more I find, and, the more I find, the more I seek of Thee. Thou art the food that never satiates ; for, when the soul is satiated in Thine abyss, it is not satiated, but it ever continues to hunger and thirst for Thee, eternal Trinity, desiring to behold Thee with the light of Thy light. *As the hart panteth after the water brooks*, so does my soul desire to issue from the prison of the darksome body, and behold Thee in truth. O how long shall Thy face be hidden from my eyes? O eternal Trinity, fire and abyss of charity, dissolve henceforth the cloud of my body ; the knowledge that Thou hast given me of Thyself, in Thy truth, constrains me to desire to leave the heaviness of my body, and to give my life for the glory and praise of Thy name ; because I have tasted and seen, with the light of the understanding in Thy light, Thy abyss, eternal Trinity, and the beauty of Thy creature. Contemplating myself in Thee, I see that I am Thy image ; Thou, eternal Father, hast given me of Thy power, and of Thy wisdom in the understanding, which wisdom is assigned to Thy only-begotten Son ; the Holy Spirit, which proceeds from Thee and from Thy Son, has given me the will, whereby I am made able to love. Thou, eternal Trinity, art the Maker, and I the work of Thy hands; I have known, by Thy recreation of me in the blood of Thy Son, that Thou art enamoured of the beauty of what Thou hast made.

"O abyss, O eternal Godhead, O deep sea! And what more couldest Thou give me, than give Thyself? Thou art fire that ever burnest and art not consumed; Thou art fire that consumest all self-love in the soul by Thy heat; Thou art fire that destroyest all coldness; Thou dost illumine, and by Thy light Thou hast made me know Thy truth. Thou art that light above all light, with which light Thou givest supernatural light to the eye of the understanding, in such abundance and perfection that Thou dost clarify the light of faith; in which faith I see that my soul has life, and in this light she receives Thee, the Light. In the light of faith, I acquire wisdom, in the wisdom of the Word, Thy Son. In the light of faith, I am strong, constant, and persevering. In the light of faith, I hope; it will not let me faint on the road. This light teaches me the way, and, without this light, I should walk in darkness; and, therefore, I besought Thee, eternal Father, to illumine me with the light of most holy faith. Verily, this light is a sea, for it nourishes the soul in Thee, sea of peace, eternal Trinity; the water of this sea is never stormy, and, therefore, the soul has no fear, because she knows the truth; it is ever clear and reveals things hidden; and thus, where the most abundant light of Thy faith abounds, it, as it were, makes the soul certain about what she believes. It is a mirror, as Thou, eternal Trinity, dost make me know; for, gazing into this mirror, holding it with the hand of love, it shows me myself in Thee, who am Thy creature, and Thee in me, by the union which Thou didst make of the Godhead with our humanity. In this light it reveals Thee to me, and I know Thee, supreme and infinite Good, good above all good, blissful good, incomprehensible good, inestimable good; Beauty above all beauty; Wisdom above all wisdom. Yea, Thou art very Wisdom; Thou, the food of Angels, hast given Thyself to men with fire of love; Thou, the raiment that coverest up my nakedness, dost feed the famished in Thy sweetness; sweet Thou art, without any bitterness.

"O eternal Trinity, in Thy light which Thou didst give me, receiving it with the light of most holy faith, I have known (for Thou makest it plain to me by many and wondrous revelations) the way of great perfection, in order that I may serve Thee with light and not with darkness; that I may be a mirror of good and holy life, and thus rise up from my own miserable life; for, through my sins, I have ever served Thee in darkness; I have not known Thy truth, and, therefore, have not loved it. Why did I not know Thee? Because I did not see Thee with the glorious light of most holy faith, for the cloud of self-love darkened the eye of my understanding; and Thou, eternal Trinity, with Thy light didst dissolve that darkness. And who shall reach Thy height, to render Thee thanks for so measureless a gift, and such great benefits as Thou hast granted me, the doctrine of truth which Thou hast given me, which is a special grace beyond the general grace which Thou dost give to other creatures! Thou wishest to condescend to my necessity, and to that of other creatures who will look into it as into a mirror. Do Thou, Lord, answer for me; Thou Thyself hast given, do Thou Thyself answer and make satisfaction, infusing a light of grace into me, in order that with that light I may give Thee thanks. Robe, robe me with Thyself, eternal Truth, so that I may run this mortal life with true obedience and with the light of most holy faith, with which light it seemeth that Thou dost inebriate my soul anew."[1]

At the end of one of her longest letters to Fra Raimondo, the letter that reads almost like a first sketch of the *Dialogo*, and contains the vision which was to be the starting-point of that book, Catherine claims to have learnt to write by a miracle, the power having suddenly come to her by a kind of spiritual intuition, while staying at the Rocca d' Orcia in the autumn of 1377. "This letter," she says, "and another that I sent you, I have

[1] Cap. 167, corrected by the Vatican MS., *Cod. Barb. Lat.* 4063, with which Fra Raimondo substantially agrees.

written with my own hand on the Isola della Rocca, with many sighs and abundance of tears, so that the eye, though seeing, saw not; but I was full of wonder at myself and at the goodness of God, considering His mercy towards the creatures that possess reason, and His providence, which so abounded towards me that, for my refreshment, since I was deprived of this consolation which through my ignorance I did not possess, He had given me and prepared me to receive the faculty of writing; in order that, descending from the height, I might have somewhat wherewith to relieve my heart, that it might not burst, since He does not wish to draw me yet from this darksome life. In a wondrous way, He set it for me in my mind, even as the master does to the child when he gives him the copy. Thus, as soon as you had left me, with the glorious evangelist John and Thomas of Aquino, I began to learn in my sleep. Forgive me for writing too much, for my hands and my tongue are in tune with my heart."[1]

This, however, was not the first letter that Catherine thus wrote. We learn from Fra Tommaso Caffarini that, when she "rose from prayer with the desire of writing," she wrote a letter to Stefano Maconi with her own hand, at the end of which she said: "Know, my dearest son, that this is the first letter that I have ever written." He adds, on Stefano's authority, that she afterwards often wrote her own letters, as also certain pages of the *Dialogo*, and tells us elsewhere that the two wonderful epistles to Fra Raimondo at the end of her life, in which she takes leave of him and of the world, were also written by her own hand.[2] But, as already stated, at the present day, with six exceptions, we possess only copies; and even these six originals were evidently

[1] Letter 272 (90). Cf. Letter 119 (178), to Alessa. It is uncertain whether the other letter to which Catherine refers is that numbered 267 (91), as seems most probable, if it is one of those preserved to us; Augusta Drane, by some inexplicable error, identifies it with Letter 226 (89), which was obviously written to Raimondo at Avignon in the previous year.

[2] *Supplementum*, Pars I. tract. i. ad finem (ff. 9–10 in the Casanatense MS.), Pars III. tract. i. (f. 122); *Processus*, col. 1279. Unless this passage is one of the lost postscripts to the letters we possess, the letter to Stefano Maconi has not been preserved.

written at the Saint's dictation by one of her secretaries. Not a single word written by Catherine's own hand has been preserved.

Catherine's earliest letters were written for her by her women companions, Alessa, Cecca, and occasionally Giovanna Pazzi ; as also were probably the more purely domestic of her later ones, and those addressed particularly to women. Afterwards, Cristofano Guidini and Gherardo Buonconti seem occasionally to have written at her dictation ; but, during the greater part of her political activity, she had three regular secretaries, the three young nobles whom we have already so often met : Neri di Landoccio Pagliaresi, Stefano di Corrado Maconi, and Francesco di Messer Vanni Malavolti. Francesco Malavolti has left us a delightful picture of Catherine's method of composition at this time. We see her dictating simultaneously to these three young men, three letters : one to Pope Gregory, another to Bernabo Visconti, the third to a certain great nobleman whose name Francesco does not remember. She dictates now to one, now to another ; at times with her face covered by her hands or veil, as though absorbed in thought, at others with clasped hands and head raised up to Heaven ; at intervals she seems rapt in ecstasy, but, nevertheless, goes on continuously speaking. Then, suddenly, all three stop writing, look puzzled, and appeal to her for aid. They have all taken down the same sentence, but for which of them was it meant ? Catherine smilingly assures them that there is no cause for concern : " Dearest sons, do not trouble, for you have done this by the work of the Holy Spirit ; when the letters are finished, we shall see how these words fit in with our intention, and then arrange what had best be done." And, of course, Francesco tells us that, though the three letters were to such different people and included various matters, the words in dispute were found to prove essential to all the three.[1] Fra Raimondo tells us that on these occasions she dictated the letters rapidly and continuously,

[1] *Contestatio Francisci de Malavoltis*, cap. vii. (Casanatense MS., pp. 460, 461). It is impossible now to identify these letters, as that to Bernabo Visconti is clearly not the one still preserved to us, which contains no passage common to any of Catherine's letters to Gregory.

without even the smallest pause for thought, as though she were reading all she said from a book placed in front of her.[1] To these three was added, in 1378, the young Florentine, Barduccio di Piero Canigiani, who accompanied her back from Florence to Siena, and never left her until the end. During the last months of her life, while they were in Rome, he seems to have been her only regular secretary. At least five of the six letters of which the originals still exist were written by his hand.

Nearly four hundred of Catherine's letters have been preserved to us. It is easier to speak of their literary importance and their historical interest than of their spiritual fragrance, as of lilies of the valley plucked in some shaded world-forsaken garden, imbued with an unearthly, mystical beauty, as grown under suns that rose from a suprasensible orient. They are written to men and women in every condition of life and every grade of society. Her correspondents include a Romagnole mendicant in Florence, a Jewish usurer in Padua, no less than two Sovereign Pontiffs and three Kings. Leaders of armies, rulers of Italian republics, receive her burning words and bow to her inspired will, no less than private citizens seeking her counsel in the spiritual life, or simple monks and hermits in their cells striving to find the way of perfection. She can warn a Queen: "instead of a woman, you have become the servant and slave of nothingness, making yourself the subject of lies and of the demon who is their father";[2] while she bids the wife of a tailor: "Clothe yourself in the royal virtues."[3] Her wonderful, all-embracing and intuitive sympathy knows no barriers, but penetrates into the house of shame as well as into the monastery. While she writes to Suora Eugenia, her niece in Santa Agnese at Montepulciano, "with desire of seeing thee taste the food of Angels," the mystical food, which is "the desire of God, whom the desire that is in the soul's affection draws to herself, so that the two become one";[4] to the Abbess and nuns of San Piero a Monticelli, "with desire of seeing you true servants and brides of Christ

[1] *Legenda*, Prologue I. (§ 7).
[2] Letter 317 (316).
[3] Letter 251 (362).
[4] Letter 26 (159).

crucified," a letter full of the same spiritual poetry that impregnates the story of Piccarda in Dante's *Paradiso*;[1] or to the Dominican nun of Orvieto, Suora Daniella, "who, not being able to continue her great works of penance, had come into great affliction," on the holy virtue of discretion;[2] she can address to a harlot in Perugia, "with desire of seeing thee partake of the blood of the Son of God," a letter as outspoken as tender in expression, beginning and ending in the name of *Maria dolce Madre*.[3]

Some of these letters are purely mystical, ecstatic outpourings of Catherine's heart, the translation into ordinary speech of the conversation of Angels, overheard in suprasensible regions. Such are pre-eminently the letters to Fra Raimondo, and, in a lesser degree, that to Suora Bartolommea della Seta, a nun of Pisa.[4] Others are a nearer approach to familiar domestic correspondence, in which the daily needs of life become ennobled, and even the innocent japery of her friends and followers is not neglected. Among these are the letters to Stefano Maconi; but even more delightful examples are to be found in those sent to Francesco di Pippino and Monna Agnese, so sadly curtailed and mutilated in all the printed editions, letters as full of high spirituality as of homely common-sense.[5] Some are written as guides to men and women through all the snares of the world or the trials of the religious vocation. Conspicuous among the latter are the numerous letters Catherine addressed to Carthusians and monks of Monte Oliveto, towards which orders, next to her own beloved Dominicans, she evidently felt the greatest affection.[6] Among the former, we have those to Andrea di Vanni, the

[1] Letter 79 (149). [2] Letter 213 (163).

[3] Letter 276 (373). For another instance of Catherine's large-hearted outlook upon questions of this kind, see Letter 8 (82), on the admission of a youth of illegitimate birth into the Olivetan order.

[4] Letter 221 (152).

[5] See Appendix, Letters V. and VI., which, however, are in a different key.

[6] For Catherine's relations with the Olivetani, cf. Placido M. Lugano, *Origine e Primordi dell' Ordine di Montoliveto*, pp. 157–164.

painter, in his capacity of Captain of the People, and to Lorenzo del Pino, the learned decretalist of Bologna; [1] and, above all, the letters to her Florentine friends and associates, the Soderini and the Canigiani, who had suffered so heavily in what she deemed the cause of righteousness. "It seems to me," she wrote to Niccolò Soderini, when a new sentence of banishment fell upon him, "that the divine sweet goodness of God has now anew shown you a most special love, in having made you follow the teaching and the lives of the saints; He has made you worthy to endure for the glory and praise of His name, in order to render you the fruit in life eternal, instead of in this life." [2] Two of Catherine's letters to Piero Canigiani have been preserved, one of them hitherto unpublished. The first, written "with desire of seeing you founded in true and most perfect love, in order that you may be robed in the bridal garment of perfect charity," contrasts the love of self with the divine love: "that true and most perfect love, which is so full of delight and sweetness that no misfortune can take that sweetness from it nor disturb it; but misfortune only the more strengthens the mind, because it brings the soul nearer to her Creator." [3] The second extols the "glorious virtue of perseverance," and urges the Guelf politician to beware of getting involved in the toils of faction, but, like a true pilgrim, turn from the affairs of the world to seek his true home.[4] Those to Messer Ristoro, five in number, must be read in their entirety. As Augusta Drane truly observes, they "form a series by themselves, and contain a body of instructions for the sanctification of persons living in the world, which for their prudence and practical wisdom have never been surpassed."

There are other letters, again, as we have seen, especially those to the Popes and great prelates, which confront the most

[1] Letters 358 (212), 363 (213), 193 (224).

[2] Letter 297 (218). Cf. Letter 314 (343), to Costanza Soderini. Niccolò was put under bounds at Treviso, on August 27, 1378. Cf. *Anonimo Fiorentino*, p. 376.

[3] Letter 96 (233).

[4] Appendix, Letter VII.

arduous problems of Church and State, assailing the corruption of the times with a fervour and a fearlessness that Savonarola himself was not to surpass. One of Catherine's latest letters to a high ecclesiastical dignitary has peculiar interest, as connecting her with the subsequent development of the Schism; it is addressed to Angelo Correr, newly appointed by Urban to the Castello bishopric of Venice, "with desire of seeing you illumined with a true and most perfect light," urging upon him the work of reformation; for, otherwise, "you would be verily a demon, because you would be abandoning the will of God, and conforming yourself with that of the devil."[1] How Angelo Correr followed this light was soon to be seen.

Catherine thus stands with Petrarca as the second great letter-writer of the fourteenth century. It is noteworthy that, although the dates of their correspondence overlap (it seems to me most probable that the Saint began writing letters in 1370, the year of her entry into public life, although the majority of those that have been preserved date from 1376 to 1379), and they were to some extent battling in the same cause, they had, with the exception of Charles V of France, only two correspondents in common: the physician, Francesco di Bartolommeo Casini, and the Augustinian friar, Bonaventura Badoara, the "Cardinal of Padua."[2] In Petrarca's epistles to Urban V, we find something of the same spirit that inspired Catherine in writing to Gregory XI and Urban VI; but, as a rule, their epistolary styles are poles asunder. Catherine's language is the purest Tuscan of the

[1] Letter 341 (34).

[2] Petrarca, *Rer. Sen.*, Lib. XVI. ep. 2, 3, Lib. XI. ep. 14; Catherine, Letters 244 (227), 334 (30). Fra Bonaventura had pronounced Petrarca's funeral oration at Arquà, in 1374. Catherine's letter to him as cardinal (of which there are better texts, with additional matter, in the Casanatense MS. 292 and the Palatine MS. 57) was sent to him when at Florence, in the spring of 1379. Cf. *Anonimo Fiorentino*, pp. 393–395. He was instrumental in the restoration of Talamone to Siena. On June 10, 1385, he was murdered on the Ponte Sant' Angelo at Rome. The Bartolommeo della Pace and Giovanni da Parma, to whom Petrarca addressed letters (*Ep. varie*, 50, 54, 61), are evidently not Catherine's correspondents of those names.

golden age of the Italian vernacular, as far as possible removed from Petrarca's would-be Ciceronian Latin; her eloquence is spontaneous and unsought; at times, in her letters as in the *Dialogo*, the richness of the writer's ideas is such that the rapidity and ardour of her thought outleaps the bounds of speech, metaphor follows close upon metaphor, one image has hardly been formed when another takes its place, until logic and grammar are swept away in the flood and torrent of impassioned words.

The simple, but profound philosophy underlying all Catherine's writings is the same that, put into practice, armed her to pass unsubdued and unshaken through the great game of the world.

Love is the one supreme and all-important, all-embracing, all-enduring, limitless and boundless thing. In a famous passage of the *Purgatorio*, Dante had shown how Creator and every creature is moved by love; how, in rational beings, love is the seed of every virtue and of every vice, because love's natural tendency to good is the material upon which Free Will works for bliss or bane.[1] But Catherine goes a step further than this. Not only God, but man, in a sense, is love. "Think," she writes, "that the first raiment that we had was love; for we are created to the image and likeness of God only by love, and, therefore, man cannot be without love, for he is made of nought else than very love; for all that he has, according to the soul and according to the body, he has by love. The father and mother have given being to their child, that is, of the substance of their flesh (by means of the grace of God), only by love."[2] And in another place: "The soul cannot live without love, but must always love something, because she was created through love. Affection moves the understanding, as it were saying: I want to love, for the food wherewith I am fed is love. Then the understanding, feeling itself awakened by affection, rises as though it said: If thou wouldst love, I will give thee what thou canst love."[3] Love nurtures the virtues like children at its breast; it robes the

[1] *Purg.* xvii. and xviii.

[2] Appendix, Letter I. Cf. Letter 196 (4).

[3] *Dialogo*, cap. 51.

soul with its own beauty, because it transforms the beloved and makes her one with the lover.[1] "Love harmonizes the three powers of our soul, and binds them together. The will moves the understanding to see, when it wishes to love; when the understanding perceives that the will would fain love, if it is a rational will, it places before it as object the ineffable love of the eternal Father, who has given us the Word, His own Son, and the obedience and humility of the Son, who endured torments, injuries, mockeries, and insults with meekness and with such great love. And thus the will, with ineffable love, follows what the eye of the understanding has beheld; and, with its strong hand, it stores up in the memory the treasure that it draws from this love."[2]

Then, since the supreme act of Divine Love is seen in the Sacrifice of Calvary, and again in the mystical outpouring of Pentecost, Love's symbols for Catherine are blood and fire—but, above all, blood, and sometimes this finds startling expression. She calls her letters written in blood. Those to whom they are addressed are bidden drink blood, clothe themselves in blood, be transformed and set on fire with blood; they are inebriated with blood; their will, their understanding, and their memory are filled with blood; they are drowned beneath the tide of blood. "Drown yourself in the blood of Christ crucified," she writes to Fra Raimondo, "and bathe yourself in the blood; inebriate yourself with the blood, satiate yourself with the blood, and clothe yourself with the blood. If you have been unfaithful, baptise yourself again in the blood; if the demon has darkened the eye of your understanding, wash it with the blood; if you have fallen into ingratitude for gifts which you have not acknowledged, be grateful in the blood; if you have been an unworthy pastor, and without the rod of justice tempered with prudence and mercy, draw it from the blood; with the eye of understanding, see it in the blood, and take it with the hand of love, and grasp it with panting desire. Dissolve your tepidity in the heat of the blood, and cast off your darkness in the light of the blood.

[1] Letter 108 (172). [2] Letter 95 (308).

I wish to robe myself anew in blood, and to strip myself of every raiment which I have worn up to now. I crave for blood; in the blood have I satisfied and shall satisfy my soul. I was deceived when I sought her among creatures; so am I fain, in time of solicitude, to meet companions in the blood. Thus shall I find the blood and creatures, and I shall drink their affection and love in the blood." [1]

And Catherine carries this into actual life; the blood that splashes the streets and palaces of the Italian cities in the fierce faction-fights, the blood that is poured out upon the scaffold at the Sienese place of execution, fires her imagination and seems shed by Love itself. The sight and smell of blood have no horror for her. We find the fullest realization of this in one of the most beautiful and famous of her letters, that to Fra Raimondo describing the end of the young noble of Perugia, Niccolò di Toldo, unjustly doomed to die by the government of Siena:—

"I went to visit him of whom you know, whereby he received such great comfort and consolation that he confessed, and disposed himself right well; and he made me promise by the love of God that, when the time of execution came, I would be with him; and so I promised and did. Then in the morning, before the bell tolled, I went to him, and he received great consolation; I brought him to hear Mass, and he received the holy Communion, which he had never received since the first. That will of his was harmonized with and subjected to the will of God, and there only remained a fear of not being strong at the last moment; but the measureless and inflamed goodness of God forestalled him, endowing him with so much affection and love in the desire of God, that he could not stay without Him, and he said to me: 'Stay with me, and do not abandon me, so shall I fare not otherwise than well, and I shall die content'; and he leaned his head upon my breast. Then I exulted, and seemed to smell his blood, and mine too, which I desire to shed for the sweet Spouse Jesus, and, as the desire increased in my soul and I felt his fear, I said: 'Take heart, sweet brother mine, for soon shall we come to the

[1] Letter 102 (93).

nuptials ; thou wilt fare thither bathed in the sweet blood of the Son of God, with the sweet name of Jesus, which I wish may never leave thy memory, and I shall be waiting for thee at the place of execution.' Now think, father and son, how his heart lost all fear, and his face was transformed from sadness to joy, and he rejoiced, exulted, and said : 'Whence comes such grace to me, that the sweetness of my soul should await me at the holy place of execution ?' See, he had reached such light that he called the place of execution *holy*, and he said : 'I shall go all joyous and strong, and it will seem to me a thousand years till I come thither, when I think that you are awaiting me there' ; and he spoke so sweetly of God's goodness, that one might scarce sustain it. I awaited him, then, at the place of execution ; and I stayed there, waiting, with continual prayer, in the presence of Mary and of Catherine, Virgin and Martyr. But, before he arrived, I placed myself down, and stretched out my neck on the block ; but nothing was done to me, for I was full of love of myself ; then I prayed and insisted, and said to Mary that I wished for this grace, that she would give him true light and peace of heart at that moment, and then that I might see him return to his end. Then was my soul so full that, albeit a multitude of the people was there, I could not see a creature, by reason of the sweet promise made me. Then he came, like a meek lamb, and, seeing me, he began to laugh, and he would have me make the sign of the Cross over him ; and, when he had received the sign, I said : 'Down ! to the nuptials, sweet brother mine, for soon shalt thou be in eternal life.' He placed himself down with great meekness, and I stretched out his neck, and bent down over him, and reminded him of the blood of the Lamb. His mouth said nought save *Jesus* and *Catherine ;* and, as he spoke thus, I received his head into my hands, closing my eyes in the Divine Goodness, and saying : *I will.*"

Then to her ecstatic gaze the heavens seemed to open, and she saw the God made Man, in brightness like the sun, receive the victim's blood into His own open wounds, his desire into the fire of His divine charity, blood into blood, flame into flame, and the soul herself pass into His side, "bathed in his own blood, which availed as though it were the blood of the Son of God." But, as the soul thus entered and began to taste the divine sweetness, "she turned to me, even as the bride, when she has come to her bridegroom's door, turns back her eyes and her head to salute those who have accompanied her, and thereby to show signs of thanks. Then did my soul repose in peace and quiet, in such great odour of blood that I could not bear to free myself from the blood that had come upon me from him. Alas, miserable and wretched woman that I am, I will say no more ; I remained on earth with the greatest envy." [1]

Ordina quest' amore, O tu che m' ami, sang Jacopone da Todi : "Set this love in order, O thou that lovest Me." Following out this Franciscan line, Dante had based his *Purgatorio* (which symbolizes the whole life of man) upon the need of ordering love rightly. And it is the same with Catherine. "The soul," she says, "that loves disordinately becomes insupportable to herself." Only the Creator may be loved for Himself alone and without any measure. Too readily may a spiritual love for a creature become entirely sensual, if the eye is not kept fixed on the blood of Christ crucified.[2] And this love disordered grows up into the monster of self-love, *amore proprio*, which plays the same part in Catherine's doctrine as did the *Lupa*, the she-wolf of Avarice, in the *Divina Commedia*. "Self-love," she writes, "which takes away charity and love of our neighbour, is the source and foundation of every evil. All scandals, and hatred, and cruelty, and everything that is untoward, proceed from this perverse root of self-love ; it has poisoned the entire world, and brought disease into the mystical body of Holy Church and the universal body of the Christian religion." [3] And she makes magnificent use of

[1] Letter 273 (97), corrected by the Harleian MS.

[2] Letter 76. Cf. the curiously interesting Letter 245 (122), "to a Genoese of the third order of St. Francis, who had engaged in a spiritual friendship with a woman, whereby he endured much travail." I find in the Casanatense MS. 292 that this tertiary was a certain Fra Gasparo.

[3] *Dialogo*, cap. 7.

this doctrine in addressing the democratic rulers of the Italian republics. "You see, dearest brothers and lords," she writes to the Anziani and Consuls and Gonfalonieri of Bologna, "that self-love is what lays waste the city of the soul, and ravages and overturns earthly cities. I would have you know that nothing has wrought this division in the world save self-love, from which has risen and rises all injustice."[1] Through self-love, she tells the Signoria of Florence, the virtue of justice has died out in monarchies and republics alike: "The legitimate sovereigns have become tyrants. The subjects of the Commune do not feed at its breast with justice nor fraternal charity; but each one, with falseness and lies, looks to his own private advantage, and not to the general weal. Each one is seeking the lordship for himself, and not the good state and administration of the city."[2] Similarly, it is to self-love alone that Catherine ascribed the war between the Tuscan communes and the Holy See, no less than the Great Schism itself; self-love had transformed Gregory's legates to ravening wolves, and Urban's cardinals to incarnate demons.

Man, therefore, must draw out the two-edged sword of love and hate, and slay this worm of sensuality with the hand of Free Will. He must utterly cast off servile fear. "Servile fear takes away all power from the soul. I think not that man has any cause to fear, for God has made him strong against every adversary."[3] "No operation of the soul that fears with servile fear is perfect. In whatever state she be, in small things and in great, she falls short, and does not bring to perfection what she has begun. O how perilous is this fear! It cuts off the arms of holy desire; it blinds man, for it does not let him know or see the truth. This fear proceeds from the blindness of self-love; for, as soon as the rational creature loves itself with sensitive self-love, it straightway fears. And this is the cause for which it fears; it has set its love and hope upon a weak thing, that has no firmness in itself, nor any stability, but passes like the wind."[4]

[1] Letter 268 (200). [2] Letter 337 (199). [3] Appendix, Letter I.

[4] Letter 242 (37), to the Bishop of Florence, Angelo Ricasoli, when he left

Whether he be in the cloister or in the world, man must enter the cell of self-knowledge, *la cella del cognoscimento di noi*, and abide therein. At its door he must set the watch-dog, conscience, to rouse the understanding with its voice: the dog whose food and drink are blood and fire.[1] Within that cell, he will know God and man; he will understand God's love, possess His truth, and freely let himself be guided by His will. The cell of self-knowledge is the stable in which the traveller through time to eternity must be born again. "Thou dost see this sweet and loving Word born in a stable, while Mary was journeying; to show to you, who are travellers, that you must ever be born again in the stable of knowledge of yourselves, where you will find Me born by grace within your souls."[2]

In addition to the book and the letters, a certain number of prayers, twenty-six in all, have been preserved, which Catherine uttered on various occasions. One, the shortest, is said to be the first thing that she wrote with her own hand:—

"O holy Spirit, come into my heart; by Thy power draw it to Thee, its God, and grant me love with fear. Guard me, Christ, from every evil thought; warm me and reinflame me with Thy most sweet love, so that every pain may seem light to me. My holy Father and my sweet Master, help me now in all my ministry. Christ Love, Christ Love, Amen."[3]

The others are mystical outpourings, which were taken down at the time by the Saint's disciples, and repeat in similar or slightly varied forms the aspirations that breathe from her other writings. We have the same "sweet enragement of celestial love," the same impassioned contemplation of the sovereign mysteries of the faith, the same devotion to the Blessed Virgin, the same

the city to observe the interdict. Catherine had previously used the same words to Cardinal Pierre d'Estaing, Letter 11 (24).

[1] Cf. Letters 2 (50) and 114 (267).

[2] *Dialogo*, cap. 151. Cf. Botticelli's allegorical picture of the Nativity in the National Gallery.

[3] *Orat.* IV. A slightly different version of this prayer, in Latin, is given by Fra Tommaso Caffarini in the *Processus*, col. 1279, and in the *Supplementum*, MS. *cit.*, f. 9.

desire of offering up her own life for the salvation of souls and the reformation of the Church. It is, indeed, piteous to watch this exquisitely tender and angelical woman besieging Heaven with prayers for that grim and ruthless man whom she called her "sweet Christ on earth," imploring God to look upon his good will, to hide him under the wings of His mercy so that his enemies, the *iniqui superbi*, may not be able to injure him, to robe him with the purity of the faith, to give him light that all the world may follow him, to temper his "virile heart" with holy humility. In the striking prayer composed on the feast of the Circumcision, probably that of 1380, when those "admirable mysteries" began to work within her that finally delivered her from the world, we find Catherine including not only Urban, but those very schismatics whom she had addressed as incarnate demons, men worthy of a thousand deaths; now her only thought is for the salvation of their souls, and she beseeches the God of sovereign clemency to punish their sins upon her own body. The last of the series consists of the words she uttered when she regained consciousness on the Monday after Sexagesima, when her household were weeping for her as dead. It strikes the key-note of her passion, and seems, as it were, to sum up the aspirations of those weeks of prolonged suffering:—

"O eternal God, O divine Craftsman, who hast made and formed the vessel of the body of Thy creature of the dust of the ground! O most sweet Love, Thou hast formed it of so vile a thing, and hast put therein so great a treasure as is the soul, which bears the image of Thee, eternal God. Thou, good Craftsman, my sweet Love, Thou art the potter who dost mar and make again; Thou dost shatter and mend this vessel, as pleases Thy goodness. To Thee, eternal Father, I, wretched woman, offer anew my life for Thy sweet Spouse, that, as often as pleaseth Thy goodness, Thou mayest draw me from the body and restore me to the body, each time with greater pain than the other; if only I may see the reformation of this sweet Spouse, Thy holy Church. I demand this Spouse of Thee, eternal God. Also, I commend to Thee my most beloved children, and I beseech Thee, supreme ıd eternal Father, if it should please Thy mercy and goodness) draw me out of this vessel and make me no more return, not) leave them orphans, but visit them with Thy grace, and make ıem live as dead, with true and most perfect light; bind them)gether in the sweet bond of charity, that they may die of ardent esire in this sweet Spouse. And I beseech Thee, eternal Father, ıat not one of them may be taken out of my hands. Forgive s all our iniquities, and forgive me my great ignorance, and ıe great negligence that I have committed in Thy Church, in ot having done what I might and should have done. I have ınned, Lord, be merciful unto me. I offer and commend my ıost beloved children to Thee, because they are my soul. And it please Thy goodness to make me still stay in this vessel, do hou, sovereign Physician, heal and sustain it, for it is all torn nd rent. Grant, eternal Father, grant us Thy sweet benediction. ımen."

CHAPTER XVII

THE DISSOLUTION OF THE FELLOWSHIP

"In toto hoc tam gravi scismate, ipsa Christi ecclesia continue et indesinenter regitur et semper regetur a spiritu sancto."—St. Vincent Ferrer, *De Moderno Ecclesiae Schismate*, III. 4.

"Sono molti che dicono: Io credo in Dio, ma non credo nè a papa, nè a antipapa."—Franco Sacchetti, *Sermone* II.

NOT in the written word alone did the spirit of Catherine of Siena live on after her bodily death. She had left behind her more than her mystical writings: a devoted company of men and women, trained by her in the cell of self-knowledge, pledged to consecrate their lives to righteousness, to labour to the end for the conversion of souls, for the unity and reformation of the Church.

With her last breath, she had deputed Monna Alessa to succeed her as head of the *famiglia*, while all in general were to look to Fra Raimondo for spiritual direction. William Flete and Messer Matteo Cenni were to preside over the continuation of her work in Siena itself. But, although the correspondence between the various members shows how for years they kept closely associated, *nella santa memoria della Mamma* (as Stefano Maconi puts it), the actual fellowship was inevitably broken up, and each one went on the way that Catherine had pointed out to him. Alessa herself did not long survive her beloved friend and spiritual mistress, but died shortly afterwards in Rome.

Fra Raimondo was at Genoa when Catherine died, preparing to go by sea to Pisa on the way to Bologna, where a general chapter was to be held of that portion of the Dominican order that still adhered to Urban, in opposition to the chapter-general under the Clementine obedience that Fra Elias of Toulouse had summoned for Whitsunday at Lausanne. The friar tells us that he was full of apprehension, both because of the storm that was raging at sea and because he feared the Clementines were lying n wait, to take vengeance upon him for having preached the :rusade against them. He had been singing the high Mass of 5t. Peter Martyr, and was going up to the dormitory to prepare 'or the journey, when, as he paused to say the *Regina caeli* before he Madonna's statue, a voice spoke in his heart: "Fear not; am here for thee; I am in heaven for thee; I will protect and lefend thee; be assured and fear nothing; I am here for thee." t was the hour of Catherine's death, though he knew it not.[1] At Bologna, he was elected master-general in May, in opposition o Fra Elias, and the schism in the Dominican order was now :omplete.[2]

A similar disruption had taken place in the other orders in the previous year. The general chapter of the Carthusians held at Grenoble under Dom Guillaume Rainaud had declared for Clement, upon which, in December, Urban had appointed a general apostolic visitor of the houses faithful to him.[3] At Naples, in October, the general chapter of the Franciscans, under Cardinal Leonardo de' Griffoni, had likewise decided to adhere to Clement. The Olivetani, on the other hand, being a mainly talian order, were for the most part Urbanist.

Raimondo's task as master-general of the Dominicans was one that would have tried all the powers of a much stronger nan. He found the whole order rent by the Schism, the ndividual convents either practically deserted, or else corrupt and ebellious. The utmost he could do was to induce the chapter-general to decree that, in every province under his obedience, here should be at least one convent of the regular observance, ontaining at least twelve friars, in which the original rule of St. Dominic should be maintained in all its pristine severity. Under is auspices, this reform was begun in Germany by Conrad of Prussia in 1389, and in Venice, in 1391, by Fra Giovanni Dominici, a young Florentine friar of great fervour and eloquence,

[1] *Legenda*, III. iv. 9, 10 (§§ 368, 369).

[2] Cf. *Chronica ordinis Praedicatorum*, ed. Reichert, pp. 26, 27 (*Monumenta . F. P. historica*, tom. vii.).

[3] Cf. Tromby, VII. pp. 45–51.

who had seen Catherine in his boyhood, and believed himself to have been miraculously delivered from an impediment in his speech by her intercession. In this work he found devoted and indefatigable assistants in Bartolommeo di Domenico and Tommaso Caffarini; but the results were only local and temporary, though several of the houses that were thus founded, for men and women, remain to this day. And, in the meanwhile, at the chapter-general of the Clementine obedience held under Elias at Avignon on the feast of Pentecost, 1386, Raimondo and his fellow-labourers were denounced as *scelerati ac reprobi fratres*, and threatened with condign punishment under the constitutions of the order.[1] Even the friars of the Roman obedience murmured against the reform; and, in 1395, Raimondo issued an encyclical letter, denying that he was dividing the order and disorganizing convents, by inducing friars to emigrate to houses of the strict observance, and scandalizing people by the spectacle of two Dominican communities in the same town with different rules; those who divide the order are the men who do not observe the constitutions. At the same time, he was worn out by illness, and distracted by the political missions undertaken on behalf of Urban and his successor, in Sicily and elsewhere.[2] He was of too gentle a nature to adopt severe measures, which, for the rest, could only have resulted in driving the Italian friars into the Clementine obedience. In 1396, he went to Germany, to urge on the work of reform there, and never returned. "Although it would be a joy for me to see thee," he wrote to Giovanni Dominici from Cologne, "nevertheless, it is not really necessary for thee to come personally here to bring me back to Italy; especially because I know that thy presence in the city of Venice is both useful and necessary. But, to speak familiarly with thee, it would avail more for my return if thou, with the superior

[1] *Monumenta O. F. P. historica*, tom. viii. pp. 22–24.

[2] For Raimondo's work as reformer, cf. *Chronica ordinis praed.*, pp. 26–29; Fra Tommaso Caffarini, *Historia disciplinae regularis instauratae in coenobiis Venetis O. P.*; J. Luchaire, in *Revue Historique*, tom. 74 (Paris, 1900); *Analecta Bollandiana*, xx. p. 113.

and other sons, wouldst procure some *viaticum* for me, with which, by God's aid, I may be able to come back to you; for I have spent both what I had and what I have not yet got, and have incurred debts, which I do not think I can satisfy without a large sum of money. So do anything you can to help me, for, as I deem, you will accomplish a useful act of charity and one pleasing to God. For, on account of the long illness which has detained me, I shall need many things, if God lets me return to you, which I did not need when I came to these parts. Nevertheless, I commit all to the eternal providence of our Saviour, in whom I desire with my whole heart that thou and the family committed to thee may fare ever better."[1] He died at Nuremberg, on October 5, 1399, leaving a memory of much sweet charity and personal holiness. But the Acts of the chapter held in that city in 1405, under his successor, Tommaso da Fermo, show unmistakably that his work as a reformer had been ineffectual. After the schism had been ended, Fra Leonardo da Firenze, in his encyclical letter of 1421, paints a deplorable picture of the corruption in the Dominican order: *in nostro ordine, ubi, proh dolor, nullus est ordo.*[2]

In Raimondo's last letter to Giovanni Dominici, he mentions the zeal for the reform of the order that is being shown in Pisa by Suor Chiara de' Gambacorti. This is the daughter of Messer Piero Gambacorti, Monna Tora, whom we have met among Catherine's correspondents, and who had at length become a Dominican nun. In October, 1392, the rule of the Gambacorti had been overthrown in Pisa, by a conspiracy organized by Jacopo d' Appiano, Piero's secretary; Messer Piero himself and two of his sons, Benedetto and Lorenzo (Tora's half-brothers), were brutally murdered; and it is said that Tora, in order to preserve the *clausura*, refused to give shelter to Lorenzo, when wounded and flying from his enemies. More edifying than this appalling example of "detachment" is it to read that, when a

[1] Letter of December 18, 1398, in Fra Tommaso Caffarini, *op. cit.*, pp. 231–233.

[2] *Monumenta O. F. P. historica*, tom. viii. pp. 112–133, 162.

fresh revolution broke out, and the family of Jacopo d' Appiano were in their turn pursued by the populace, Tora sheltered the wife and daughters of her father's murderer in the cloistered retreat that she had closed against her brother.

To Barduccio Canigiani, Don Giovanni dalle Celle had written a beautiful letter of spiritual consolation on Catherine's death, tenderly inviting him to come to Vallombrosa and be once more one of his sons in religion. "Come, most beloved son, to him who of old was thy father; come to thy brethren, who are expecting thee with such great desire that they will think they are receiving an Angel of God, if thou dost come."[1] But Catherine had disposed otherwise. "When the holy virgin was departing from this world," writes Fra Raimondo, "she bade him join me and lead his life according to my direction; which I think she did because she knew that he would linger in the body but a short while. For, after the virgin's death, Barduccio contracted the malady which the physicians call consumption, and, albeit he sometimes seemed to grow better, he, nevertheless, finally died of it. Wherefore, I, fearing lest the air of Rome would harm him, sent him to Siena, where, after a brief time, he passed away to Christ. Those who were present at his death bear witness that, whilst he was at his last breath, gazing on high with a glad countenance, he began to laugh, and so, with a laugh of joy, he gave up the ghost, in such wise that the signs of that joyous laugh still appeared in his dead body. This thing, I think, befell because in his passing he beheld her, whom in life he had loved with true charity of heart, robed in splendour, coming with gladness to meet him."[2] Barduccio died in December, 1382, at Siena. His father and brother were already dead; Messer Ristoro had died at Lucca, in December, 1380; Piero Canigiani himself, persecuted and put under bounds by the Republic, passed away in exile at Sarzana, in August, 1381.[3] Of the once power-

[1] *Lettere del B. Giovanni dalle Celle*, 26.

[2] *Legenda*, III. i. 11 (§ 341).

[3] *Anonimo Fiorentino*, pp. 422, 428. Niccolò Soderini died at Lucca on March 20, 1381. *Ibid.*, p. 423. In the reaction of 1382, Carlo Strozzi and Tommaso Soderini were recalled to Florence.

ful Florentine politicians who had listened to Catherine's words, Buonaccorso di Lapo Giovanni alone remained. Highly trusted by the State, and employed in many embassies, he was accused on his return from a mission to Milan, in November, 1388, of having accepted a bribe from Gian Galeazzo Visconti. He appealed to be heard in his own defence, upon which Franco Sacchetti, speaking for the College of Gonfalonieri, proposed that he should be heard in secret and at night. Having thus obtained three days' grace, Buonaccorso fled from Florentine territory, and was declared a traitor and a rebel.[1] There was one faithful disciple of Catherine's still left in Florence; untouched by the winds of faction that smote these *più alte cime*, the tailor, Francesco di Pippino, still continued to work in her sweet memory, making his humble home a centre for all that looked for righteousness in those stormy times. "When thou dost wish to write to me," wrote Giovanni dalle Celle to Guido dal Palagio, "give the letters to Francesco, the tailor, a man faithful and loyal even unto death."[2]

The great friendship that bound Neri di Landoccio to Stefano Maconi remained unbroken until the former's death. In obedience to Catherine's dying charge, to join the Carthusians, and in spite of much opposition from his own family, Stefano entered the Certosa of S. Pietro di Pontignano in the spring of 1381. "I tell thee, dearest brother," he wrote, on May 30, to Neri, "with heartfelt gladness, that our benign God, through His inestimable goodness and not for my own merits, has turned the eye of His mercy towards me, wretched man, unworthy of any grace, and has vouchsafed to let me receive the holy habit here. I write this to thee, albeit very briefly, in order that thou mayest partake with me of the sweet joy and gladness that my soul feels. I do not tell thee how and why it came to pass, because the time is too short and the story too long; but this, at least, I will not conceal from thee, that our holy Mamma has amply shown me by the results what she promised so emphatically

[1] *Anonimo Fiorentino*, p. 480; Gherardi's introduction, p. 280.

[2] June 1, 1392. *Lettere cit.*, 23.

at her most blessed end, to help us more afterwards than before."[1] In the following year, to his great dismay, he was made prior of Pontignano. "My sweet brother," he wrote to Neri, "I invite thee to have compassion upon me, and also to aid me with holy prayer, beseeching God to give me grace to correct my life and to be His true servant even unto the end, and that He may grant me to bear the weight that He has deigned to lay upon my shoulders, as shall be to His honour and my salvation. When I took the holy habit, I thanked God, and thought to sing with the Psalmist: *Lo, then, I would wander far off and remain in the wilderness;* but Obedience, the bride that our holy Mamma gave me, wishes me, for my greater weal, to sing: *I was as a beast before Thee.* Therefore am I fain to begin again to glory in the Cross of Christ crucified, and to rejoice in the Cross, and to abide nowhere else save there."[2] In 1389, at the instance of Gian Galeazzo Visconti, Stefano was transferred to Milan, and made prior of the Carthusian convent of Our Lady and St. Ambrose. Here he was influential in keeping the Milanese despot faithful to the Urbanist obedience, and in furthering the interests of the Commune of Siena at his court. He was much concerned, too, in the founding of the great Certosa of Pavia, which Gian Galeazzo was erecting with such lavish magnificence, and of which Don Bartolommeo Serafini, the former prior of Gorgona, was the first superior.[3] It is pleasant to fancy that we may see idealized portraits of Stefano and Bartolommeo among the white-robed Carthusians who are bearing their crosses after Christ in Ambrogio Borgognone's picture.

From Pavia, we find Stefano on one occasion coming on business of his order to Genoa, and there, *con santi ragionamenti di*

[1] *Lettere dei discepoli*, 21. Cf. Tromby, VII. p. 54; Barth. Senensis, *op. cit.*, Lib. II. cap. 2. Stefano had previously been taken prisoner by a band of Breton mercenaries, and set free, without payment of ransom, by the intervention of Hawkwood—the second occasion upon which he had been delivered by calling upon Catherine's name.

[2] *Ibid.*, 25.

[3] Barth. Senensis, *op. cit.*, Lib. II. cap. 13. Cf. Stefano's letter to Matteo Cenni, of July 27, 1391, *Lettere dei discepoli*, 33.

Anderson

The Monks of the Certosa.

Ambrogio Borgognone — Accademia, Parma

olci materie, having much happy intercourse with Fra Raimondo, ra Tommaso Caffarini, Madonna Orietta Scotti, Francesco Ialavolti, and others who still had Catherine's name in their earts and on their lips.[1] In 1398, in the chapter-general held ear Cilli in Styria, he was elected prior-general of the whole arthusian order under the Roman obedience, in opposition to he aged Dom Guillaume Rainaud, who, from the mother-house f Grenoble, still ruled the rest of the Carthusians who adhered o the Popes of Avignon. A pleasant letter to Fra Tommaso has een preserved to us, in which Stefano informs him of his election, nplores his prayers and commends himself to those of Fra aimondo, and, now that he will no longer reside in Italy, ommits the book of Catherine's letters (the famous manuscript f the Certosa of Pavia) and her other relics to his correspondent's are.[2]

Neri di Landoccio, in the meanwhile, had fulfilled Catherine's bedience by becoming a hermit, first at Agromaggio near lorence, where one of her Florentine friends, Leonardo di Iiccolò Frescobaldi, had founded a hermitage, and afterwards t another *romitorio* outside the Porta Nuova of Siena. Here, e kept closely in touch with the surviving members of the ellowship, gathered disciples round him, and lived a life of ustere holiness. He died on March 12, 1406, and was buried t the convent of the Olivetani outside Porta Tufi.[3]

Catherine's other secretary, Francesco Malavolti, remained in he world for some years after her death. His wife and children aving died, an uncle, Niccoluccio Malavolti, seeing the pleasure hat he took in horses and arms, advised him, if he did not marry gain, to become a knight of St. John. Francesco tells us how e resolved to do this, was accepted by the chapter-general of the rder at Genoa, and returned to Siena to prepare the armour,

[1] *Lettere dei discepoli*, 34.

[2] Letter of October 17, 1398, in Fra Tommaso Caffarini, *op. cit.*, pp. 230, 31

[3] Cf. the touching letter from Luca di Benvenuto, one of Neri's disciples, to er Jacomo, in *Lettere dei discepoli*, 46.

weapons, and horses that were needed. But, in the night before the day upon which he was to be made a knight and receive the habit, Catherine herself appeared to him in a vision, rebuking him for still clinging to the vanities of the world, and bade him rise, seek out Neri di Landoccio, and go with him to the convent of Monte Oliveto Maggiore, where he would be received without any opposition: "Dost thou not remember how I told thee that, when thou shouldst think I was furthest from thee, I should then be most near thee, and that I should lay such a yoke upon thy neck that thou wilt never be able to shake it off?" Francesco was at once seized with such a desire to take the Olivetan habit, that it seemed the night would never end. He rose at dawn, and hastened to find Neri in his hermitage, who likewise had seen Catherine in the night and been prepared for his coming. They went together to Monte Oliveto, where, the abbot-general being absent, the prior agreed to receive Francesco into the order. He returned to Siena, sold his armour, weapons, horses, and distributed the proceeds to the poor, and then, going back to the convent, received the habit on the same evening, the vigil of St. Lucy.[1] This was in 1388. But Francesco's instability pursued him even into the cloister. After filling various offices, sometimes that of master of novices, but more frequently cellarer, at different convents of the order, he left the Olivetani in 1410, and became a black monk of St. Benedict. We find him, in 1413, a Benedictine in the abbey of San Miliano near Sassoferrato, sending his recollections of Catherine to Fra Tommaso Caffarini, as his *Contestatio*, to form part of the Venetian Process; "concerning those wondrous things," he says in the accompanying letter, "which I saw the Lord work in His creatures by means of the glorious and holy virgin, Catherine of Siena, our most sweet mother, what time I bore her company in the city of Siena and without. And albeit I do not narrate a hundredth part of what I saw, I nevertheless ratify and confirm all that is said in the Legend of the Virgin by Master Raimondo

[1] *Contestatio Francisci de Malavoltis*, cap. i., MS. *cit.*, pp. 433-436.

of venerable memory, and bear witness that all the things recounted in it are most true."[1]

With Catherine's death, all thoughts of reformation seem to have died out of Urban's heart, and he began to tread the path upon which the Popes of the Renaissance were to follow. He had already, in April, 1380, formally deprived Queen Giovanna of her kingdom and all her fiefs, and released her subjects from their allegiance under pain of excommunication. To defend herself from him and her Hungarian cousins, Giovanna, with the approval of Clement, adopted Louis of Anjou as her heir, and appealed for French protection. In the autumn, Charles of Durazzo entered Italy with a Hungarian army, and, at the beginning of June, 1381, was crowned in Rome by Urban, as King of Naples and Jerusalem, under the title of Charles III. The price of the ceremony was the confirmation of the Neapolitan fiefs that Urban had granted to his own infamous nephew, Francesco Prignano, which included the principality of Capua, the duchy of Amalfi, and the counties of Caserta and Fondi —a transaction in which the exiled Florentine, Lapo da Castiglionchio, acted as Charles's legal adviser. Giovanna's despairing appeal to Louis of Anjou, practically offering him immediate possession of the kingdom, came at an inauspicious moment—the Duke being fully occupied in the regency of France for the young King, Charles VI. Charles advanced upon Naples, and, on July 16, occupied the city, the Queen taking refuge in the Castello Nuovo. Her husband Otho made a valiant attempt to break through and rescue her, but was defeated and taken prisoner; and, on September 2, Giovanna surrendered. She was imprisoned in Castello dell' Ovo, while the populace shouted for Urban, whose legate, Cardinal Gentile di Sangro, proceeded

[1] Letter of April 12, 1413, prefixed to his *Contestatio*, pp. 427–429 in the Casanatense MS., ff. 157*v*.–158 in the MS. at Siena. Cf. Placido M. Lugano, *op. cit.*, p. 163 *n*. An earlier letter of Francesco's, written from the Olivetan convent of S. Girolamo di Quarto outside Genoa (which Alfonso da Vadaterra had founded and where he was buried in 1388), to Neri di Landoccio, is in *Lettere dei discepoli*, 40.

to take vengeance upon the Clementines. Two cardinals, Leonardo de' Griffoni and Jacopo d' Itri, had been captured with the Queen ; the former denied his allegiance to Clement and burned his red hat ; the latter was publicly degraded, and then imprisoned. The Archbishop of Salerno, Giovanni d' Acquaviva, is said to have been burned alive.

Tardily, in June, 1382, Louis of Anjou started to rescue the imprisoned Queen and win the royal crown from Charles of Durazzo. His approach was Giovanna's death-warrant. She had been previously sent to the Castello di Muro in the interior of the country, and thence, on the last day of July, what purported to be her dead body was brought to Naples and laid out in state in Santa Chiara, where a solemn requiem was sung. The actual manner of her death is as uncertain as its precise date, but there can be little doubt that she had been murdered at the command of her successor ; according to one version, she was strangled by two of his Hungarian soldiers, while she knelt in prayer. For more than a year, Louis abstained from assuming the royal title, professing to believe that Giovanna still lived.

We are not concerned with the ensuing struggle between Charles and Louis, nor with the miserable deaths of both competitors—Louis dying of the plague at Bari in September, 1384, and Charles by the hands of assassins at Visegrád in February, 1386, the fruit of his perfidious usurpation of the crown of Hungary after the death of the great King Louis.

In the previous year, Charles had definitely broken with Urban, had been solemnly excommunicated by him, and had sent his army under Alberigo da Barbiano, whom he had made Constable of Naples, to besiege him in Nocera. It was on this occasion that Urban committed one of the most appalling crimes of the age. His overbearing conduct, and crazy partiality for his abominable nephew, had passed the bounds of endurance. At Nocera, in January, 1385, just before the siege, he discovered what was probably nothing more than a design on the part of certain members of the Curia to put him under restraint for the good of the Church, but which his suspicious mind magnified into a plot against his life. The Bishop of Aquila and six cardinals, including the English Benedictine, Adam Easton, were promptly arrested, and subjected to prolonged tortures under the superintendence of one Basil, a Levantine pirate of Genoese origin, noted for his hatred of the clergy; while Urban himself walked in the garden, reading his breviary aloud, and glutting his ears with their cries. When released from Nocera by Raimondello Orsini and Tommaso da San Severino at the head of a band of foreign mercenaries, the remnants of the army of Louis of Anjou, Urban dragged his prisoners with him. He had the Bishop of Aquila, who was too maimed by torture to follow, butchered by the way, but was compelled to set the English Cardinal at liberty through the intervention of Richard II. The other five he took with him to Genoa in September, and imprisoned them in his house. None of these unfortunate men were ever seen again. When the Pope left Genoa in December, 1386, they were either thrown into the sea, or strangled and buried in quicklime under the stables of the house.[1] The rest of the Sacred College shrank from him in horror, save a few insignificant Neapolitans whom he had recently raised to the purple, but only two, one of whom was the Cardinal of Ravenna already mentioned, actually went over to his rival.

The tragedy of Urban's pontificate ended with his death in the Vatican on October 15, 1389. He who had set out as a strenuous reformer of the Church, and a friend of the servants of God, thus ended his days in the worst corruption and in sacrilegious bloodshed, detested by all, his authority set at nought even by the Italian powers which acknowledged him as Pope. Creighton puts it to his credit that he refused to purchase the allegiance of Aragon by unworthy means. Madness seems the only possible explanation of the terrible fall of the man in whom Catherine had so passionately believed. One

[1] Dietrich of Nieheim, *De Schismate*, I. 50–52, 56, 57, 60, gives a full account of these horrors, which he himself witnessed.

of the few who remained faithful to him to the last was Messer Tommaso Petra, the steadfast friend of all her spiritual fellowship.

Ignoring the claims of the rival College at Avignon, fourteen cardinals at Rome, on November 2, elected a successor to Urban in the person of the Cardinal of Naples, Pietro Tomacelli, a prudent and virtuous man, who took the name of Boniface IX. Five years later, on September 16, 1394, Clement VII died at Avignon. On September 28, Pedro de Luna, through whose influence, supported by the eloquence of Vincent Ferrer, Aragon, Castile, and Navarre had been drawn from their neutrality to embrace the Clementine faith, was elected his successor, and assumed the title of Benedict XIII. He had previously taken an oath that he would abdicate, if the majority of the Sacred College should deem this the way to restore unity to the Church. Once elected, however, all the efforts of the French court and the vehement assaults of the University of Paris failed to make him carry out this pledge. An united embassy from England, France, and Castile, in the summer of 1397, drew from him nothing but an evasive answer. Deserted by his own cardinals, and besieged in the papal palace of Avignon in 1398, he was no more moved to surrender his claims to be the sole vicar of Christ than he was to take any vengeance upon his enemies, or to exult in his triumph, when, in 1403, his cardinals returned and the kingdom of France once more acknowledged him as Pope. Always gracious and magnanimous, never yielding to excess of anger or exhibiting vindictive feelings, still, to all appearances, as devout and edifying a man as when he had attracted the sympathy of Catherine and her "servants of God," Benedict remained unshaken in his resolution not to resign the Papacy, save in his own way and at his own time. On the other side, Boniface was no less irreconcilable ; his answer to the united embassies of the three Kings had been equally evasive and unsatisfactory ; and, for the rest, he was occupied in restoring the temporal power of the Papacy, which, to a large extent, he effected by destroying the liberties of the

.oman Republic in 1398, rebuilding Castello Sant' Angelo as fortress to overawe the city, and, in 1399, crushing the Count f Fondi, Onorato Gaetani, whose fiefs were now absorbed into ıe Papal States.

As prior-general of the Carthusians of the Roman bedience, Stefano Maconi laboured zealously to bring the chism to an end. Himself a strong supporter of the claims f Boniface, from whom he had received special faculties and postolic authority for his work, his most ardent efforts were irected to healing first the breach in his own order. In 1402, :om the Styrian charterhouse of St. John, he addressed a long :tter to the fathers of the Grande Chartreuse, urging them ɔ be one body and one spirit with their brethren in the :hurch, offering to lay down his own office for the sake of ınity. In eloquent and impassioned words, he tells again the tory of the heroic labours of his seraphic mother, Catherine, ɔr the Church, reminding them, and especially Dom Guillaume, f the letter he had written to them at her dictation, when he first heard that they were about to follow the party of the chismatics, appealing to them to bear witness to the truth that he had then announced to them. "Come, then, to our ommon Mother, my brethren; fulfil my joy, for I have ıothing more at heart than your salvation, to serve the Divine ;lory together with you, and to behold the unity of the :hristian Republic under its lawful head and ruler, the Roman 'ontiff. Although I am ignorant and unskilled in all things, nd overladen with grievous errors, yet will I become for ·ou the first example of our humiliation, and be the beginning ·f our longed-for union. Now by these letters do I cast nyself upon the earth, and lie utterly prostrate at your feet. :ome and trample upon me at your will. I am prepared to uffer all things, to endure all things. My mind is ready to ındergo whatever you will think my confusion, but to me /ill seem glory, if only I may see the unity of our universal Mother, the Church, and of our order; if only the cloud /ith which the Lord has covered the daughter of Zion in

His anger may be dispelled, and your brightness shine forth upon us as of old; and the wandering stars in the firmament of the Church shine out in their places for ever, according to the word of the prophet: *And the stars have given light in their watches, and rejoiced; they were called, and they said: Here we are; and with cheerfulness they have shined forth to Him that made them.*"[1]

The younger monks were greatly moved by Stefano's letter, and would probably have answered in the same spirit, had it not been for the strenuous opposition of their old and venerated head, Dom Guillaume. But, in the June of this same year, 1402, the latter died, and was succeeded as prior of the Grande Chartreuse, and prior-general of the whole order under the obedience of Benedict XIII, by Boniface Ferrer, the brother of St. Vincent. Stefano had not long to wait for a more favourable opportunity to renew his appeal.

After the short and stormy pontificate of Innocent VII (Cosma Meliorati of Sulmona, who succeeded Boniface IX in 1404), Angelo Correr, then Patriarch of Constantinople, who had been closely associated with Catherine's surviving followers in Venice, was elected Pope by the cardinals of the Roman obedience, in November, 1406, and took the name of Gregory XII. He had previously taken an oath to abdicate, as soon as his rival should abdicate or die, and to make no new cardinals. An old man, of high repute for holiness, the cardinals had elected him, as they declared, less as Pope than as a commissioner for the restoration of unity. He at once expressed his eagerness to meet and confer with Benedict, declaring that he would go in a fishing-boat, if no galley were available, or on foot with his staff, if he could not get a horse. And Benedict, on his part, professed himself no less ready and eager for an interview.

Thus two men now faced each other, both of whom had received Catherine's words while she yet lived; for in each of them she had seen a possible reformer of the Church. And it is

[1] Barth. Senensis, *op. cit.*, Lib. III. cap. 2.

only too clear that neither of the two really intended to keep the pledge he had made on accepting election. Gregory always bore on his person one of Catherine's teeth, which he treasured as a relic; he sent for Stefano Maconi, to confer with him about her canonization and the peace of the Church; but he had fallen into the hands of his own kindred, especially Antonio Correr, one of his nephews, an intriguing and luxurious prelate, who were resolved not to let the loaves and fishes of the Papacy go out of their family; and, in political matters, he had become a mere tool of the ambitious and warlike young King Ladislaus of Naples, the son of Charles of Durazzo. Benedict, on his part, in spite of his protestations, had not altered his attitude by a jot. After much negotiation, each claimant being desirous that the meeting should take place in a city subject to his own obedience, Gregory, in April, 1407, consented to the choice of Savona, a city that acknowledged Benedict, who actually went there in November. Gregory, on the other hand, moved to Lucca, where, in May, 1408, in flagrant violation of his pledges, he created four new cardinals, including two of his own nephews (Antonio Correr and Gabriele Condulmer), and Fra Giovanni Dominici. Upon this, his former cardinals renounced their allegiance and fled to Livorno. In the meanwhile, King Ladislaus had marched upon Rome, and, on April 25, perhaps in understanding with Gregory, he occupied it with his army.[1]

The patience of the Catholic world was now exhausted. In this same May, 1408, France withdrew her allegiance from Benedict, who fled to Perpignan. The cardinals of the Roman obedience met those that had deserted Benedict at Livorno, from which, on July 14, the united Colleges summoned the bishops of Christendom to a Council. In spite of threatened armed intervention from Ladislaus, who still adhered to Gregory, the Council met at Pisa on March 25, 1409. Of those princes of the Church who had shared in the conclave

[1] Cf. Creighton, I. pp. 225–227, where a suggestive characterization of the rival claimants to the Papacy is given.

that elected Urban, and who alone knew how the Schism had really arisen, only two were still alive: Benedict himself, under the protection of King Martin of Aragon at Perpignan, and the aged Cardinal of Poitiers, Guy de Malesset, who now presided over the deliberations of the assembly. On June 5, the Council deposed both Gregory and Benedict as heretics and schismatics; the *Te Deum* rose up from the cathedral of Pisa to thank God for the deliverance of His Church; the bells rang out, and were caught up by the campanili of village after village, until the news in this way reached Florence. On June 26, twenty-four cardinals, fourteen of whom had previously acknowledged Gregory and ten Benedict, elected the Cardinal Archbishop of Milan, Peter Philargis, a friar minor of Greek origin, who assumed the title of Pope Alexander V.

We are not here concerned with the legality of these proceedings. Catholic historians assure us that the cardinals had no right either to summon the Council or to depose the Pope, whichever of the two claimants we regard as legitimate. As neither Gregory nor Benedict would resign their claims, the result was that the Church had now to witness the spectacle of three rival Popes instead of two. But, were we to apply Catherine's test of the adherence of the "servants of God,"[1] we should be compelled to accept Alexander. This time, however, her own followers were divided. Assailed by the foulest lampoons, denounced as an ally of Mahomet and Simon Magus, Giovanni Dominici not only kept faithful to Gregory, but used all the powers of his eloquence to prevent him from abdicating; although his own master-general, Fra Tommaso da Fermo, had taken part in the Council, and the Dominican order as a whole acknowledged Alexander as Pope in the most emphatic language.[2] It seems uncertain whether Stefano Maconi was actually present at the Council, but it is quite clear that, notwithstanding his personal friendship with Gregory, he now

[1] Letter 350 (187).

[2] Cf. *Monumenta O. F. P. historica*, tom. viii. pp. 138–143.

leclared unhesitatingly for Alexander. He had already written gain to the fathers of the Grande Chartreuse, declaring that he Council was lawful and canonical, that the cardinals were nspired by the Holy Ghost in summoning it, and whoever hey elected Pope would undoubtedly be the true vicar of Christ.[1] He now went in person to the general chapter of he Carthusians of both obediences, held at the Grande Chartreuse in the following year, 1410, where the whole order olemnly recognized Alexander as Pope; and there, in the presence of the assembled fathers, he resigned his generalship. Boniface Ferrer, who (like his brother St. Vincent) still dhered to Benedict, did not attend the chapter, but tendered his resignation by letter.

The Carthusians being thus reunited by his efforts, Stefano returned to his beloved Siena, as once more prior of Pontignano. Cristofano Guidini and the other surviving members of Catherine's fellowship received him with joy. Ser Cristofano had lost his wife and six children in the pestilence of 1390, the one surviving daughter, Nadda, having become a nun. He had then devoted his whole life to the service of the poor and the infirm in the hospitals, and, before the end of this year, 1410, he breathed his last in Stefano's arms. In the following year, Stefano was again transferred from Siena, and made prior of the Certosa of Pavia. At Siena, he had doubtless seen and heard a young Franciscan friar, born in the year of Catherine's death, whom we now call San Bernardino; we find him a little later, in a letter written to Fra Angelo Salvetti from Pavia, vividly expressing the great joy with which he has heard of the abundant fruit that Fra Bernardino Albizzeschi is producing in the Church of God.[2]

From Pavia, Stefano witnessed the pontificate of Alexander's successor, the infamous Baldassare Cossa, John XXIII, which must have caused much searching of heart among the "servants of God" who had so gladly welcomed the result of the Council

[1] Barth. Senensis, *op. cit.*, Lib. III. cap. 8.

[2] *Ibid.*, Lib. IV. cap. 9.

of Pisa. He was still there when the Council of Constance met in 1415—the final movement for unity coming not from the rival claimants to the Papacy nor from their cardinals, but from the new King of the Romans, Sigismund of Hungary. Giovanni Dominici, now known as the Cardinal of Ragusa, having been allowed to convoke the Council anew as legate of Gregory XII, the fathers, on July 4, accepted Gregory's abdication. They had previously, on May 29, deposed John. But, at Perpignan, the indomitable old Benedict still held out. The personal intervention of King Sigismund himself proved fruitless; Benedict would only abdicate on his own impossible terms. In November, he fled, and took refuge in Peñiscola, a strong castle securely placed over the Mediterranean. Aragon, Castile, and Navarre now withdrew their obedience from him, St. Vincent Ferrer publicly declaring that, although Benedict was the lawful Pope, the three Kings were thus offering an Epiphany gift to God and the Church for unity and peace. To all appeals, Benedict had one inflexible reply: "Here is the ark of Noah." On July 26, 1417, the Council condemned him as a perjurer, an incorrigible schismatic, and a heretic; and, on November 11, Ottone Colonna, the son of the Cardinal Agapito already mentioned, was elected Pope, and took the title of Martin V.

The Schism was now officially at an end, and the Church practically pledged to the cause for which Catherine had battled to the death—the validity of the claims of Urban and his successors in the Roman obedience. But, from his refuge at Peñiscola, Pedro de Luna (as we will now again call Benedict) still asserted his prerogatives, anathematizing the new Pope and his cardinals, protesting that he alone was the vicar of Christ. He grew hard and embittered, even putting two priests to the torture to obtain evidence of a plot against his life. Nor was he without adherents. In September, 1419, complaints were made that the majority of the inhabitants of Languedoc and Guyenne still acknowledged him, and he was still being obeyed in some parts of Scotland in 1420. He had also the powerful support of the Counts of Armagnac. At length, either on November 29, 1422, or May 23, 1423 (the uncertainty being, perhaps, due to an intentional mystification on the part of his followers), he died.[1] Strange, mysterious being to the last, it is most probable that he was not the mere perjurer and hypocrite of Catholic tradition; it may well be that he really believed in his own claims, and held that, in the confusion and turmoil of the world, the truth abided in him alone; in himself, a gracious and loveable personality, until, rejected and assailed by all, the fierce Spanish blood flared up in his old age. His strenuous refusal to abdicate at the bidding of kings and universities had borne fruit in the liberation of the Church from the oppressive yoke of France. Unwittingly, Pedro de Luna had destroyed the power of the Giant, whom Dante had seen in the Earthly Paradise, dragging the transformed chariot of the Spouse from the Tree to which the mystical Griffin had bound it. Let us leave him thus, the man to whom Catherine had twice written in the precious blood as her "dearest father in Christ sweet Jesus," and ignore the deplorable sequel in which his followers strove to perpetuate the Schism after his death.

The prolonged struggle in which Catherine and he had borne their parts being now concluded, Stefano's one desire was to be free to give himself entirely to divine contemplation. At length, in 1421, "at his earnest entreaties, because of his old age, his infirmities, and many labours undertaken for the order," he was allowed to resign his office of prior of the Certosa of Pavia, it being decreed that all honour should be paid him in whatever convent he chose for residence. In spite of invitations from Pontignano, he chose to remain in the Certosa of Pavia, and there, on August 7, 1424, he passed away, with the names of Mary and Catherine upon his lips.[2]

When Tommaso Caffarini died in 1434, the last of Catherine's spiritual family had joined her again. But, already, the movement that she had initiated had come to an end, to be renewed half a century later, in another form and without success, by Fra

[1] Valois, IV. pp. 450–454.

[2] Barth. Senensis, *op. cit.*, Lib. V. cap. 6.

Girolamo Savonarola on the one hand, and, on the other, in the mystical sacrifice of those women, clad in the habit she had worn and bearing the same marks of Christ's passion on their members, Lucia of Narni, Osanna of Mantua, Colomba of Rieti, who attempted to imitate her work among the corrupt courts of the Renaissance. Ostensibly, Catherine's labour had failed. A century after her death, the state of her beloved Italy was more deplorable than when she had departed from it, the Papacy immeasurably more corrupt than it had been in the darkest days of the Schism, and a far greater division and more permanent in the Church was about to open. But the true value of the work to which the whole power of a human soul has been dedicated, cannot, any more than the lasting result of any great or small religious movement, thus be measured, for, by its very nature, it is not manifested in outward and visible effects; its most perfect flowers and fruits throughout the ages are in the invisible garden of the spirit, grown to be gathered only by Him who feedeth among the lilies.

APPENDIX

UNPUBLISHED LETTERS OF SAINT CATHERINE

"In quibus litteris cernere erat divinae virginis prope animatam imaginem verissimis expressam sanctitatis lineamentis."—Stefano Maconi (Barth. Senensis, Lib. III, cap. 2).

I

A Misser Bartolomeo della Pace [1]

Al nome di Jesù Christo crucifixo et di Maria dolce.

Carissimo et reverendo padre in Christo dolce Jesù : io Katerina, serva et schiava de' servi di Jesù Christo, scrivo a voi nel pretioso sangue suo ; con desiderio di vedervi cavaliere virile et non timoroso, considerando io che il timore servile toglie la forza dell' anima et non può piacere al suo Creatore. Conviensi adunque al tucto torre questo timore. Non mi pare che l' uomo abbi cagione di temere ; però che Dio l' à facto forte contra ogni aversario. Che può il dimonio contra noi ? Egli è facto infermo ; perduto à la potentia per la morte del Figliuolo di Dio. Che può la carne, che è infermata per gli flagelli et battiture di Christo crucifixo ? Cioè, che l' anima che raguarda il suo Creatore, Dio et Huomo svenato in sul legno della sanctissima croce, pone freno di subito a ogni movimento carnale et sensuale. Che potrà il mondo colla superbia et stolte delitie sue ? Sconficto l' à colla profonda humilità, sostenendo obrobrio et vituperio. Debbasi confondere l' umana superbia d' insuperbire dove Dio è humiliato. Così diceva il nostro Salvatore, invitandoci a non temere di timore servile, dicendo : Rallegratevi, ch' io ò vinto il mondo. Sì che i nimici sono sconficti, et l' uomo è forte,

[1] Bartolommeo di Smeduccio, Lord of San Severino in the Marches, styled himself "Bartolommeo della Vittoria," after his victory over Rodolfo Varano and the papal forces in 1377 ; he probably acquired the title "della Pace" in 1385, when appointed captain-general of the army of the allied Italian communes against the foreign mercenaries, upon which occasion he was presented with a banner inscribed PAX. Cf. L. Passerini, *Smeducci di San Severino*, in Litta, *Famiglie celebri italiane*, disp. 160, and Sozomeno, *Rer. It. Script.*, xvi. col. 1129. Bartolommeo was deprived of his lordship by his nephews in 1388, and died in 1399. The heading of the letter is an addition of the copyists.

et di tanta forteza che da veruno può essere volto,[1] se egli non vorrà. Questo dolce Dio ci à data la forteza della voluntà, che è la roccha dell' anima, che nè dimonio nè creatura me la può torre. Adunque bene potiamo stare sicuri et non timorosi. La sicurtà vostra voglio che sia in Christo dolce Jesù. Egli ci à vestiti del più forte vestimento che sia, dell' amore affibbiato colla maglia del libero arbitrio, che il puoi sciogliere et legare secondo che vuogli. Se questo vestimento della carità egli il vuole gittare, egli può, et se egli il vuole tenere, ancho può. Pensate, carissimo padre, che il vestimento primo che noi avessimo fu l' amore: però che fummo creati alla ymagine et similitudine di Dio solo per amore, et però l' uomo non può stare sanza amore, che non è facto d'altro che d' esso amore, chè ciò che egli à secondo l' anima et secondo il corpo à per amore; perchè à il padre et la madre dato l' essere al figliuolo, cioè, della substantia della carne sua, mediante la gratia di Dio, solo per amore. Però che è tanto obligato il figliuolo al padre, et etiandio per l' amore che egli gli à, che ve lo inchina la natura, non può sostenere niente del padre d' ingiuria che gli sia facta,[2] s' egli è vero figliuolo. Guarda già che per uno amore proprio di sè egli fussi venuto a odio con lui. Costui non seguita la natura sua, ma per la sua cechità n' è uscito fuori.

Veramente così è, caro padre in Christo dolce Jesù, che l' anima naturalmente in sè medesima dee amare et seguitare il suo padre Creatore, Dio eterno, chè, vedendo che Dio l' à creata solo per amore, sentesi trarre verso di lui, et non può sostenere le ingiurie che gli sieno facte. Vuolne fare la vendecta per l' amore ch' egli à al padre; et questa è la ragione[3] perchè l' anima vuole sempre fare vendecta contra la parte sensitiva, che è suo nimico mortale; però che colui che va dricto a essa sensualità, egli rimane morto di morte eternale, crucifigge Christo un altra volta, chè voi sapete che solo per lo peccato egli morì. Sì che l' anima inamorata di Dio, sommo eterno Padre, vuole seguitare la natura sua; l' amore gli fa perdere, et l' amore fa vendecta di sè medesimo, percotendo la falsa passione sensitiva, el dimonio, el mondo, et la carne, percotendo col coltello dell' odio et dell' amore, odio et dispiacimento del peccato, amore delle virtù, dilectandosi di quello che Dio amò, odiando quello che egli odiò. Allora rende l' anima il debito suo al padre, seguita la sua natura, già mai none escie. Guarda già che non ci mettessi il veleno dell' amore proprio di sè medesimo, d' amarsi fuori di Dio, ponendo lo studio suo nelle delitie, stati, et dilecti del mondo, fare della

[1] So the Harleian MS. and the Palat. MS. 57; the Palat. MS. 60 reads *vinto.*

[2] The Palat. MS. 60 has: *neuna ingiuria che al padre sia facta.*

[3] So the Harleian MS. and Palat. MS. 57; the Palat. MS. 60 reads *cagione.*

carne sua uno dio, tenendola con disordinato dilecto et dilicatezze. Questo tale non tanto che facci vendecta del nimico che gli à morto il padre, ma esso medesimo l' uccide.

Or non voglio che sia in voi; ma voglio che seguitiate l' anima gentile vostra, che Dio v' à data, con amore et libero arbitrio. Vi strignete et vi legate in questo vestimento, che non sarà dimonio nè creatura che vel possa torre. Così vestito et armato delle virtù, col coltello dell' odio et dell' amore, perderete il timore servile; possederete la città dell' anima vostra; none schiferete mai i colpi di veruna tribulatione o pena che poteste sostenere, nè volgerete il capo adrieto, cioè, cominciando a entrare nella via delle virtù et poi rivolgiervi il capo adrieto a ripigliare il vomito de' peccati mortali. Non voglio così, ma con una vera perseverantia infino all' ultimo: però che il cominciare non è coronato nè degno di gloria; ma solamente il perseverare. Grande viltà è dell' uomo di cominciare una cosa buona et non trarla a fine. O di quanta confusione sarebbe degno quel cavaliere che si truova nel campo della battaglia, et volgiessi le spalle adrieto, avendo quasi vinto!

Su, padre carissimo, non più negligentia, nè volgete più il capo adrieto a raguardare le stolte miserie del mondo; chè passano e' dilecti suoi come il vento, sanza veruna fermeza o stabilità. Non vi fidate della gioventudine del corpo vostro, nè delle signorie del mondo: testè l' uomo è vivo, testè è morto; testè è sano, testè infermo; testè signore, testè è facto servo. Adunque quanto è stolto l' uomo che ci pone l' affecto disordinato; fidasi di quello che non si può fidare, aspecta quello[1] che non si può avere, et fugge quello ch' egli può avere et tenere per suo, cioè, la gratia che la può avere quantunche e' vuole et quando egli vuole; non per sè, ma per essa gratia, dono di Spirito Sancto, che gli à dato il libero arbitrio. O inextimabile dolcissima carità, chi t' à mosso? Solamente l' amore. O dolcissimo amore Jesù, per fare più forte questa anima, et torle la debolezza nella quale era caduta per lo peccato, tu l' ài murata atorno atorno, intrisa la calcina coll' abondantia del sangue tuo, il quale sangue fa unire et conformare[2] l' anima nella divina dolce voluntà et carità di Dio! Chè come in mezo tra pietra et pietra per conformarsi insieme in forteza, vi si mette la calcina intrisa coll' acqua, così Dio à messo in mezo fra la creatura et sè il sangue dell' unigenito suo Figliuolo, intriso colla calcina viva del fuoco dell' ardentissima carità; però che non è sangue sanza fuoco, nè fuoco sanza sangue. Sparto fu il sangue col fuoco dell' amore che Dio all' umana generatione ebbe. Per questo muro è facto l' anima tanto forte, che veruno vento contrario el

[1] So the Palat. MS. 60; the others read *quel tempo.*

[2] So the Palat. MS. 60; the others, *confermare.*

potrà dare a terra, se non vorrà smurarlo sè medesimo, dandovi col piccone del peccato mortale.

Quale sarà quel cuore tanto duro et ostinato, che non si muova a raguardare tanto infinito amore, et la grande sua dignità, dove egli è posto per gratia di Dio et non per debito? Non sarà veruno che raguardandolo et ponendoselo per obiecto, che non trapassi ogni sensualità, et non disolva ogni duritia et ignorantia, et riceverà perfectissimo lume et cognoscimento di sè; vedendo et cognoscendo sè non essere et la bontà di Dio in sè, che gli à dato l' essere et ogni gratia che è fondata sopra l' essere. Accendasi il cuore et l' anima vostra in Christo dolce Jesù, con amore et desiderio a renderli cambio a tanto amore, a renderli vita per vita. Egli à dato la vita per voi, et voi vogliate dare la vita per lui, sangue per sangue. Et io v' invito, da parte di Christo crucifixo, a dare il sangue vostro per lo sangue suo, quando verrà il tempo aspectato da' servi di Dio, d' andare a racquistare quello che ci è tolto; cioè, il luogo sancto del sepolcro di Christo, et sì l' anime degli infedeli che sono nostri fratelli, ricomperati del sangue di Christo come noi: el luogo trarre delle mani loro, et l' anime loro delle mani delle dimonia et della loro infedeltà. Invitovi a non essere negligente nè tardare quando sarete invitato, quando il padre sancto rizerà il gonfalone della sanctissima Croce, ordinando il sancto et dolce passaggio. Non mi pare che sia veruno che se ne debba ritrarre nè fuggirlo, ch' egli non corra. Per timore di morte non tema. Et però dissi ch' io desideravo di vedervi cavaliere virile et non timoroso; il sangue vi farà inanimare, et fortificheravi; torravi ogni timore. Priegovi, per l' amore di Christo crucifixo, che con letitia et desiderio attenete la 'nvitata di queste dolci et gloriose noze, che sono noze piene di letitia, di dolceza, et d' ogni suavità. A queste noze si lascia la inmonditia, et si libera della colpa et della pena; pascegli alla mensa dell' Agnello, che è cibo in essa et servitore. Vedete che il Padre ci è mensa che tiene in sè ogni cosa che è, excepto che il peccato, che non è in lui. El Verbo del Figliuolo di Dio ci è facto cibo, arrostito al fuoco dell' ardentissima carità. Lo Spirito Sancto ci è servitore, essa carità che per le sue mani ci à donato et dona Dio. Ogni gratia et dono spirituale et temporale egli ce la ministra continuamente. Bene saresti semplice, voi et chi il facessi, che si dilungassi da tanto dilecto. Parmi che ogniuno, se non potessi andare ricto, vi vada carponi, acciò che potiamo mostrare segno d' amore allui, dandogli la vita per amore della vita, scontiare i difecti et i peccati nostri collo strumento del corpo, sì come collo strumento del corpo abbiamo offeso.

Questa sarà la sancta et dolce vendecta che noi faremo di noi medesimi. Essendo vinta questa parte sensitiva et fragile corpo nostro, rimarremo vincitori. La ragione et l' anima nostra rimarrà libera et donna; possederà Dio, che è sommo eterno bene. Non indugiamo più tempo, padre carissimo; seguitate le vestigie di Christo crucifixo; bagnatevi nel sangue di Christo crucifixo, nascondetevi nelle piaghe di Christo crucifixo, ponetevi per obiecto dinanzi a gli occhi dell' anima vostra Christo crucifixo, acciò che rimaniate in amore et in timore filiale, temendo la colpa et non la pena. Non dico più. Perdonate alla mia ignorantia; l' amore et il desiderio mi scusi, et il dolore di vederci correre ostinati et accechati nelle miserie del peccato mortale. Permanete nella sancta et dolce dilectione di Dio. Jesù dolce, Jesù amore.[1]

II

Sine Titulo

Al nome di Jesù Christo chrocifisso et di Maria dolce.

Charissimo figluolo in Christo dolce Jesù: io Katerina, serva et schiava de' servi di Jesù Christo, schrivo ad voi nel prezioso sangue suo; con desiderio di vedervi piena la memoria del sangue di Christo, dolce Jesù chrocifisso, et aperto l' occhio dello intelletto ad riguardare il fuoco della divina charità, la quale v' è manifesta in esso sangue di Christo Jesù dolce. Allora la volontà et l' affetto s' empierà et sazierà d' amore, però che l' affetto ama quello che lo intelletto à veduto, et così vedrò adcordate et conghreghate le tre potenzie dell' anima nostra, et sarà adempiuta quella parola che disse el nostro Salvatore: Quando saranno due o tre conghreghati nel nome [mio], Io sarò in mezzo di loro; et veramente così è. Et questo parve che il nostro Salvatore volesse dire: che conghreghate le tre potenzie dell' anima, chella memoria s' empia del sangue et de' benifici d' Iddio, l' occhio dello intelletto veggia, ponendosi per obbietto l' amore ineffabile che Iddio gl' à, nella volontà ami.[2] Seghuita che, conghreghate queste tre penitenzie [*potenzie*], tutte l' operazioni che l' uomo fa adopera,[3] tutte sono conghreghate nel nome d' Iddio, perchè per lui è fatto ogni cosa. Allora l' anima nostra ghode, chessi vede avere Iddio in mezzo di sè per grazia et per effetto dolce d' amore. Adunque io voglo che siate sollecito ad andare alla fonte del sangue, et empietene il vasello della memoria vostra. Altro non dico.

[1] Harleian MS. 3480; Biblioteca Nazionale di Firenze, MSS. Palatini, 57, 58, and 60. In the Palat. MS. 60, the letter is headed: *Al Re Carlo della Pace;* an obvious error of the copyist.

[2] Perhaps we should read: *che* [or *et*] *la volontà ami.*

[3] Probably a slip for: *sa adoperare;* or: *fa et adopera.*

Priegovi per l' amore di Christo chrocifisso etc. Permanete nella santa et dolce dilezione di Dio. Dolce Jesù, dolce Jesù, Amen.[1]

III

Sine Titulo

Al nome di Jesù Christo chrocifisso et di Maria dolce.

Ad voi, charissimo figluolo in Christo dolce Jesù: io Chaterina, serva et schiava de' servi di Jesù Christo, ischrivo ad voi nel prezioso sanghue suo; con desiderio di vedervi vestito di Christo dolce Jesù, et spoglato dello antico vecchio peccato, el quale procede dallo amore propio sensitivo chel l' uomo à assè medesimo. O me, egli è quello amore che acciegha l' anima, togle la vita, et dagli la morte, togle la ricchezza della virtù, et dagli la povertà. Egli iscondante del prossimo suo.[2] S' egli è subito [*subdito*], non ubbidisce, perchè è fondato in superbia. S' egli è parlato [*prelato*] o signore, non corregge, per timore di non perdere la signoria. S' egli è giudice, non giudica giustamente secondo coscienzia, ma secondo le volontà et piaceri degl' uomini. Tutto questo procede dalla perversità dell' amore propio, chè se l' uomo non amasse sè per sè, ma amasse sè per Dio, non farebbe così; col timore suo farebbe ciò che avesse affare, tenendo Iddio dinanzi ad gl' occhi dello intelletto suo, et perde l' amore sensitivo, et adquista uno amore ineffabile del suo Chreatore; spogla sè dell' uomo vecchio, et veste sè dell' uomo nuovo, chè vestendosi d' amore d' affetto di carità si truova vestito di Christo chrocifisso; cioè, che non cercha nè Iddio nè virtù sanza faticha, ma per la via della Chroce, seguitando le vestigie della prima dolce Verità. Questo fa l' anima inamorata d' Iddio, che poi che [à] aperto l'occhio dello intelletto ad riguardare l' amore inistimabile che Iddio gl' à, che per amore gl' à dato il Verbo dell' unigenito suo Figluolo, et il Figluolo à dimostrato l' amore con pena, sostenendo infine alla obbrobiosa morte della Chroce, allora concepe tanto amore in sè che in tutto egli vuole seghuitare in pena et in chroce, sostenendo fame et sete, persechuzione, molestie, dal mondo, dal dimonio, et da sè medesimo; con tutti resiste et combatte, per amore della virtù. Egli ama quello che Iddio ama, odia quello che Iddio hodia, perchè Christo benedetto amò la virtù et avea in hodio il peccato, et però ne volle morire et punirlo sopra il corpo

[1] Biblioteca Riccardiana, MS. 1303. In transcribing these letters, I reproduce faithfully the orthography of the writer of the manuscript in each case, with its variations. The text of this and the following letter is manifestly corrupt.

[2] i. e. *Egli è scordante del prossimo suo.*

suo. Costui il volle seghuitare, per sì fatto modo n' è fatto amatore delle pene, che se fussi possibile avere virtù sanza faticha, non la vuole, per unirsi con Christo chrocifisso. Costui fa il contrario che colui che è nello amore propio. Egli à il cuore largo et liberale d' amare Iddio et il prossimo suo chome sè medesimo, hubbidiente et humile sanza superbia, giusto giudice che rende ad ciaschuno il debito suo ; non è ciecho nè ingnorante ; anzi è illuminato, et [con] vera sapienzia discerne et vede quello che à affare, perchè egli à tratto da sè l' amore propio che l' accechava ; riceve l' aiuto della grazia, collo amore divino et lume della fede, mediante il sangue del Figluolo d' Iddio ; di questo si sazia, et sì se ne inebbria di fuoco d' amore. Veste sè dell' uomo nuovo, che ripara a' colpi delle ricchezze et delle adversità del mondo et agli inganni del dimonio, et in tutti è forte ; per Christo chrocifisso se reputa fare ogni cosa. Nelle pene si diletta, ne' diletti temporali si contrista, per hodio et dispiacimento della parte sensitiva, che è istata et è ribella al suo Chriatore. Ad questo modo si spoglia dell' amore di sè, et vestesi dello amore d' Iddio. Vedete quanto è necessario ad essere vestito di sì glorioso vestimento. Essendo noi posti in questo campo della battalgla, per gli colpi checci sono dati, verremo meno. Però dissi io che io desideravo di vedervi vestito, considerando me che altro modo non c' era ad potere ghustare et avere Iddio per grazia in questa vita. Priegovi che siate sollecito et non nighrigente, cercando le vie et modi el quale vel faccino avere. Ischrivestimi se mi parea il meglio lo stare di qua, perchè avete desiderio per più pace et salute vostra, del venire. Figluolo mio dolce, io non so bene discernere quale sia il meglio ; ma voi avete provato di qua et di costà ; dove voi trovate più pace et più quiete et meno pericolo dell' anima vostra, quello pigliate, secondo chello Spirito Santo v' amaestra. Et io ò preghato et pregherrò lui che vi spiri, o qui o costì o a Roma, di farne quello chessia più honore suo et bene di voi. Altro non vi dico. Permanete nella santa et dolce dilezione d' Iddio. Jesù dolce, Jesù amore.[1]

IV

A' Signori Priori dell' Arti et il Gonfaloniere della Giustitia della Città di Firenze

Al nome di Jesù Christo crocifixo et di Maria dolcie.

Karissimi fratelli et signori miei in Christo dolcie Jesù : io Caterina, serva et schiava de' servi di Jesù Christo, scrivo a voi nel prezioso sangue suo ; con desiderio di vedervi legati et uniti nel legame della carità, el quale

[1] Biblioteca Riccardiana, MS. 1303.

legame è di tanta fortezza che nè dimonio nè creatura il può tagliare, et di tanta unione che niuno può separare l' anima che [è] unita in questa perfetta carità. Nolla può separare il mondo co' suoi inganni, nè colle sue frode, nè colle sue mormorationi et infamie, nè il dimonio colla sua astutia, nè con diversi et sottili inganni suoi, che spesse volte con inganni si pone in sulla lingua della creatura, facendoli dire parole di rimproverio al proximo suo. Questo fa solo per privarlo dell' unione della carità. Nè la propria sensualità colla fragile carne la può separare, ma con lume della ragione le dispregia, con dispiacimento della propria colpa sua; questi conbatte virilmente col mondo, et non è mai vinto, ma sempre vince, perchè Dio, che è somma et etterna fortezza, è dentro nell' anima sua per gratia; et in qualunque stato la persona è, vive virilmente et con affetto di virtù, quando è legato in sì dolcie legame et unito nella dilectione et carità dolce del proximo suo. Se elli è subdito secolare, elli è sempre obediente alla leggie divina, osservando i dolci comandamenti di Dio, et alla legge civile, non trapassando le costutioni et comandamento del signore suo; se elli è religioso, è osservatore dell' ordine infino alla morte; et se viene a stato di signoria, in lui riluce la margarita della santa giustitia, tenendo ragione et giustitia al piccolo come al grande, et al povaro come a richo; et non la guasta questa virtù della giustitia, nè per piacere alli huomini, nè per rivenderia di pecunia, nè per amore che elli abbi al suo bene particulare; però che non atende al suo bene proprio, ma al bene universale di tutta la città, et però apre l' ochio dello intelletto non passionato per alcuna ingiuria che elli abbi ricevuta, ma al bene comune. Questa è quella dolcie virtù che pacifica la creatura col suo Creatore, et l' uno cittadino coll' altro, perchè ella escie della fontana della carità et vincolo d' amore et unione perfetta, la quale à fatta in Dio et nel proximo suo. Onde considerando me ch' ella v' è tanto di necessità, et singularmente in questo tempo, dixi che io desideravo di vedervi legati et uniti nel legame della carità, però che in altro modo non verreste in effetto di quello che desiderate.

Voi avete desiderio di riformare la vostra città, ma io vi dicho che questo desiderio non s' adempirà mai, se voi non vi ingegniate di gittare a terra l'odio et il rancore del cuore et l' amore proprio di voi medesimi, cioè, che voi non atendiate solamente a voi, ma al bene universale di tutta la città. Unde io vi priego per l' amore di Christo crocifixo, che per l' utilità vostra voi non miriate a mettere governatori nella città più uno che un altro, ma huomini virtuosi, savi et discreti, e' quali col lume della ragione diano quello ordine che è di necessità, per la pace dentro et per confermatione di quella di fuori, la quale Idio ci à conceduta per la infinita sua misericordia, d' avere pacificati i figliuoli col padre, et rimesse noi pecorelle nell' ovile della santa Chiesa. Et però fate che voi non siate ingrati a tanto benefitio, el quale avete ricevuto da Dio, col mezzo delle lagrime et della continua oratione de' servi suoi, non per le nostre virtù, ma solo in virtù della focata carità di Dio, el quale non dispregia l' oratione et il desiderio de' servi suoi. Dicovi che, se non sarete grati et conoscenti al vostro Creatore, si secharebbe verso di noi la fonte della pietà; unde io vi priego che giusto al vostro potere voi vi studiate di mostrare questa gratitudine, d' ordinare che voi tosto abiate le messe et l' asolutione ordinata, acciò che si possa dire l' officio con voce di laude dinanzi a Dio, et una processione ordinata con debita devotione, acciò che le dimonia, che per li nostri peccati anno accopata [*sic*] la città et tolto il lume et il conoscimento alli huomini, si caccino, legandole con questo dolcie legame della carità, et così non ci potranno nuocere, ma più tosto noi noceremo alloro. Per questo modo compierete el vostro et el mio desiderio, cioè, di riformare la città vostra in buono stato, et terretela in vera et perfetta pace. Ma se ogniuno volesse tirare a suo parere con poco senno di ragione, nol fareste mai; però che la cosa che non è unita, non può tenere pur la casa sua, non tanto che una città così fatta. Vogliono essere huomini maturi, esperti, et non fanciulli, et così vi priego che facciate; et ingegnatevi di tenere i cittadini vostri dentro et non di fuore, però che usciti non fece mai buona città, la quale reputo mia; et il dolore ch' io ò di vederla in tanta fadiga mene scusi. Non credetti scrivarvi, ma a bocha con voce viva vi credetti dire queste simili parole, per honore di Dio et vostra utilità; chè mia intentione era di visitarvi, et fare festa con voi della santa pace, per la quale pace io tanto tempo mi son afadigata, in ciò che io ò potuto secondo la mia possibilità et la mia pocha virtù: se più virtù avessi avuta, più virtù avrei adoperato. Fatta festa et ringratiato la divina bontà et voi, mi volevo partire, et andarmene a Siena. Ora pare che 'l dimonio abbia tanto seminato ingiustamente ne' cuori loro verso di me, che io non ò voluto che si agiunghino più offesa sopra offesa, però che quanto più se n' agiugnesse, più cresciarebbe ruina. Sommi partita colla divina gratia, et priego la somma etterna Bontà che pacifichi et unisca et leghi e' cuori vostri, l' uno coll' altro, sì in affetto di carità, che nè dimonio nè creatura vi possa mai separare. Ciò che per me per la salute vostra si potrà adoperare, infino alla morte adoperrò volentieri, a malgrado de' dimoni visibili et invisibili, che vogliono impedire ogni santo desiderio. Vommene consolata, perchè [è] compiuto in me quello che io mi puosi in cuore quando entrai in questa città, di mai non partirmi, se io ne dovessi morire, infino che io non vedessi pacificati voi figliuoli col vostro padre, vedendo tanto pericolo et danno nell' anime et ne' corpi; dolorosa et con tristitia mi parto, lassando la città in tanta amaritudine; ma Dio etterno che m' à consolata dell' una mi consoli dell' altra, che io vi vegha et senta pacificare in buono et fermo et perfetto stato, acciò che potiate atendere a rendere gloria et loda al nome suo, et non con tanta aflitione stare sotto l' arme. Spero che la clementia dolcie di Dio vollerà l' ochio della sua misericordia, et compirà il desiderio de' servi suoi. Altro non vi dico. Permanete nella santa et dolcie dilectione di Dio. Jesù dolce, Jesù amore.[1]

V

A Francesco di Pippino sarto in Firenze

Al nome di Jesù Christo crucifixo et di Maria dolce.

Carissimi figliuoli in Christo dolce Jesù:[2] io Caterina, serva et schiava de' servi di Jesù Christo, scrivo a voi nel pretioso sangue suo; con desiderio di vedervi constanti et perseveranti ne la virtù, acciò che riceviate la corona de la gloria, la quale non si dà a chi solo comincia, ma a chi persevera infine a la morte. Unde io voglio che perseveriate et cresciate in virtù, et non sia veruna tribulatione nè battaglia dal demonio nè da le creature che vi faccia vollere el capo adietro. Bagnatevi nel sangue di Christo, annegando et uccidendo ogni propria volontà et passione sensitiva, et allora sarete facti forti, che neuna cosa vi potrà muovere, però che sarete fondati sopra la viva pietra, Christo dolce Jesù, et così sarete constanti et perseveranti infine a la morte, et ricevarete el premio de le vostre fadighe. Non dico più qui.

Per la grande bontà di Dio, et per comandamento del santo padre, mi credo andare a Roma per di qui a mezzo questo mese, più et meno come piacerà a Dio, et faremo la via per terra; sì che io vel fo sapere, come io vi promissi. Pregate Dio che ci faccia compire la sua voluntà. Prego voi, Francesco, per l' amore di Christo crucifixo, che duriate fadiga di dare le lettere che io vi mando con questa, prestamente, per honore di Dio et piacere di me. Andate infine a Monna Pavola, et ditele, se ella non àe avuto di corte quello che ella voleva, che me lo scriva, et io farò per lei come per madre. Ditele che preghi, et faccia pregare le figliuole tutte per

[1] Biblioteca Nazionale di Firenze, Strozzi MS., xxxv. 199. This important letter was written between August 2, 1378, when Catherine left Florence, and October 23, when the absolution was formally pronounced.

[2] In the plural because addressed to Monna Agnese as well, though only Francesco's name appears in the title.

noi. Ritrovate Nicolò povero di Romagna, et ditegli come io so per andare a Roma, et che si conforti et preghi Dio per noi. Sopra tutto vi prego che la lettera di Leonardo Frescubaldi voi la diate in sua mano el più tosto che potete, et così quella di frate Leonardo; non vi sia grave di portarglili, se elli non fusse costì. Barduccio vi prega che diate una sua lettera al padre et a' fratelli, et dite loro che vi diano se egli vogliono mandare cavelle, et fate di mandarci o recarci quello che vi daranno, se voi venite qua. Permanete ne la santa et dolce dilectione di Dio. Jesù dolce, Jesù amore. Fatta adì IIII di Novembre, 1378, in Siena.[1]

VI

A Bartalo Usimbardi et Francesco di Pippino

Al nome di Jesù Christo crucifixo et di Maria dolce.

Carissimi figliuoli in Christo dolce Jesù: io Caterina, serva et schiava de' servi di Jesù Christo, scrivo a voi nel pretioso sangue suo; con desiderio di vedervi grati et cognoscenti de' beneficii ricevuti dal vostro Creatore, acciò che in voi si notrichi la fonte della pietà. Questa gratitudine vi farà solliciti ad exercitarvi alla virtù; però che, come la ingratitudine fa l' anima pigra et negligente, così questa dolce gratitudine le dà fame del tempo, in tanto che non passa ora nè punto, che ella non lavori. Da questa gratitudine procede ogni vera virtù. Chi ci dà carità? Chi ci fa umili et patienti? Solo la gratitudine. Et perchè vede el grande debito che à con Dio, s' ingegna di vivere virtuosamente; però che cognosce che Dio non ci richiede altro. Et però, figliuoli miei dolci, recatevi con grande sollicitudine a memoria e' molti beneficii ricevuti da lui, ad ciò che perfectamente acquistiate questa madre de le virtù.

Ebbi in questi dì le vostre lettere, cioè, una da Bartalo, una da Francesco, et una da Monna Agnesa, le quali viddi volontieri. Rispondovi de la spesa del privilegio, che ogni cosa à pagato el sangue di Christo crucifixo, et però neuno denaio ci bisogna, ma voglio che vi costi lagrime cordiali et oratione per la santa Chiesa et per Christo in terra, et che voi preghiate ogni dì strettamente Dio per lui. Et bene confesso che se noi dessimo el nostro corpo ad ardere, non potremmo satisfare a tanta gratia quanta Dio ci à facta; chè in questa vita aviamo la certezza de la nostra salute, se noi avremo viva fede, et saremo grati et cognoscenti. Ma el nostro dolce Dio non ci richiede più che noi potiamo fare. Siatemi virtuosi, et brigate di

[1] Biblioteca Nazionale di Firenze, MS. xxxviii. 130. Cf. Letter 289 (292).

crescere per modo che io me n' avegga. Mandovi per frate Jacomo Manni, portatore di questa lettera, el privilegio con la bolla papale, in sul quale è Monna Pavola del monasterio da Santo Giorgio, et Monna Andrea sua serva, et setevi su voi quattro, cioè, Bartalo et Monna Orsa, et Francesco et Monna Agnesa. Et però quando l' avete ricevuto, fatene levare i vostri nomi per carta al vescovado come bisogna, et il privilegio darete a Monna Pavola quando sarà tornata, che ora è qua. Ò inteso come Giannozzo è preso; non so quanto vi starà. Piacemi quello che voi, Francesco, me ne scrivete, cioè, di non abandonarlo mai, et così vi comando, per parte di Christo crucifixo, che molto spesso el visitiate, confortiate, et soveniate in ciò che v' è possibile; pensate che Dio non ci richiede altro, se non che sopra el proximo nostro manifestiamo l' amore che aviamo allui. Io vel racomando strettamente, et diteli per mia parte che sia buono cavaliere, ora che Dio l' à messo in campo, et il suo combattere sia la vera patientia, chinando per humilità el capo a la dolce voluntà di Dio. Molto el confortate per mia parte et di tutta questa fameglia, i quali tutti gli anno grande compassione. Quando Dio el permettarà, gli scriverò una lettera. Diteli che faccia ciò che può per spacciarsi tosto, et non miri perchè non abbi apieno sua intentione. Altro non vi dico. Permanete ne la santa et dolce dilectione di Dio. Benedicete i fanciulli. Jesù dolce, Jesù amore. Facta a dì VIII di Maggio in Roma.[1]

VII

A Piero Canigiani da Fiorenze[2]

Al nome di Jesù Christo crocifixo et di Maria dolce.

Karissimo padre et figluolo in Christo dolce Jesù: io Katerina, schiava de' servi di Jesù Christo, scrivo a voi nel pretioso sangue suo; con desiderio di vedere in voi quella gloriosa virtù della perseverantia, la quale è quella virtù che è coronata. Et che modo terremo ad acquistare et conservare in noi questa virtù? Il modo è questo. Voi sapete che ogni virtù s' acquista col lume, et sanza esso niuna virtù si può acquistare, perchè ogni virtù à vita dalla carità, la quale carità è uno amore; chè l' anima col lume della fede, il quale è nell' occhio dell' intellecto, vede l' amore ineffabile che Dio l' à; vedendolo, cognosce la inextimabile bontà di Dio et sè essere

[1] *i.e.* 1379. Biblioteca Nazionale di Firenze, MS. xxxviii. 130. Cf. Letter 89 (290).

[2] *patri meo secundum carnem*, adds the scribe, Barduccio Canigiani.

amata da lui prima che ella fosse; unde concipe uno amore, perchè col lume vide che Dio è degno d' essere amato, et che ella è obligata ad amarlo per debito. Questo così facto amore incatena et lega tucte l' altre virtù, per sì facto modo che una non se ne può avere perfectamente che tucte l' altre non s' abbino. Adunque col lume s' acquisterà questa reale virtù della perseverantia. Questo lume la conserva, et questo lume l' accresce: anco, tanto cresce o menoma, quanto il lume crescesse o menomasse; però che esso facto che l' anima si truova sanza il lume, è sanza questa virtù della perseverantia, et subito volta il capo adietro. Bene dobiamo dunque studiare che questo lume non ci sia tolto dalla nuvola dell' amore proprio, cioè, d' amare sè et le cose del mondo et lo stato sensitivamente; chè, per lo libero arbitrio che l' uomo à, si può voltare ad ogni mano. Unde se l' occhio dell' intellecto è mosso dall' appetito sensitivo, subito si pone a vedere et a volere cognoscere queste cose transitorie, le quali passano come il vento, et in esse si vuole dilectare; ma perchè ciecamente vede, non cognosce che in esse non è perfecto dilecto nè riposo; anco, v' è tanta inperfectione et inquiete, che l' anima che disordinatamente l' ama è incomportabile a sè medesima; ma se l' affecto ordinato muove l' intellecto, egli si pone a vedere et cognoscere la verità, la quale il fa fermo et stabile, et però abraccia et seguita la doctrina di Christo crocifixo, che è essa verità, dove ella truova compito dilecto, unde ella spregia sè medesima, cioè, quella perversa legge che impugna contra lo spirito. Et perchè à cognosciuta la verità, odia quello che prima amava, et ama quello che odiava. Per questo modo fugge et schifa la colpa, però che la colpa nostra non sta in altro se non in odiare quello che Christo amò, et amare quello che egli odiò. Tanto gli dispiacque la colpa, che egli la volse punire sopra al corpo suo. Anco, ne fece una ancudine, sopra la quale fabricò le nostre iniquità; et tanto amò l' onore del padre et la salute nostra, che per rendere allui l' onore et a noi la vita della gratia, la quale avamo perduta per la colpa d' Adam, et acciò che la virtù et la buona et santa vita ci valesse ad vita eterna, corse all' obrobriosa morte della santissima Croce. Per questa via conserveremo questa virtù: satollianci d' obrobrii; aviliamo noi medesimi; facianci piccoli per vera humilità, se noi voliamo essere grandi nel conspecto di Dio. Lassiamo ogimai i morti sotterrare a' morti, et noi seguitiamo la vita di Christo dolce Jesù, perseverando infino alla morte nelle vere et reali virtù. Ad questo voglio che attendiate, et non ci mectete indugio di tempo, ma con perseverantia, però che 'l tempo nostro è breve, tanto che non potiamo più che con grande desiderio spogliarci di questa vita mortale et dirizzarci verso il nostro fine. Raguardate bene che egli è così; et niuno è, giovane [nè] vecchio, ricco nè povero, sano nè infermo, nè signore nè subdito, che si possa fidare o pigliare speranza d' avere pure un' ora di tempo. Matto sarebbe chi la pigliasse, però che noi vediamo che ella viene vota manifestamente, che quelli che si credono bene stare subito vengono meno. Voglio dunque che raguardiate la brevità del tempo vostro, acciò che, con amore et con santo timore di Dio, l' affecto vostro sempre vadi inanzi et mai non torni adietro, crescendo continuamente. Troppo sarebbe peggio et maggiore ruina dell' anima et del corpo, dopo il cognoscimento et buona voluntà che l' uomo avesse ricevuto da Dio, il tornare adietro che l' offese dinanzi, et di maggiore riprensione è degno nel conspecto di Dio et degli huomini. Tucto dì vediamo questo, che non pare che mai bene gli pigli, se non ritorna già nello stato virtuoso suo. Non vorrei che l' amore proprio di voi o de' figluoli, colorato col colore della giustitia con parervi fare meglio, vi facesse rattaccare a questi affanni miseri degli stati del mondo. So che non bisogna dire molte parole. Io voglio che attendiate alla vostra salute in cognoscere i beni immortali et mectervi socto i piedi i beni mortali. Lassate la conversatione de' servi del mondo, et dilectatevi di quella de' servi di Dio.

Guardate, guardate quanto avete cara l' anima vostra, et anco per vostro bene secondo il mondo, che voi non v' impacciate di queste frasche. Fatemi come il vero peregrino, chè così dobiamo fare, perchè tucti siamo peregrini et viandanti in questa vita. Il peregrino non attende ad altro se non di giugnere al termine suo. Pigliasi la vita [*via*] sua, et più no. Et con buona providentia mira di lassare le vie dubiose et passare per le sicure. Se egli truova luoghi pacifichi et dilectevoli, non si rista però, ma va pure per li facti suoi. Et se gli truova in guerra o malagevoli, nè più nè meno; se già egli non vedesse che sanza suo danno, o impedimento del cammino et termine suo, potesse fare alloro utilità; per altro modo, no; sì che nè pace nè guerra possono mai impedire il buono peregrino.

Così voglio che facciate voi. Su dunque, peregrino, destatevi dal sonno, chè non è ora da dormire, ma è tempo di vigilia. Gittate a terra il carico de' pensieri et affanni del mondo, et tollete il bordone della croce, acciò che abiate con che difendervi da' nimici che trovaste tra via. Empite il vasello del cuore vostro di sangue, il quale è il vostro conforto, acciò che per debilezza non veniste meno nel tempo delle fatighe. Ponetevi dinanzi a l' occhio dell' intellecto vostro Dio, il quale è il vostro fine et termine, et corrite con fame et desiderio delle virtù; chè avendone desiderio, desiderrete di giugnere al fine vostro. Necessario v' è di corrire con l' affecto del desiderio, con la memoria di Dio, sì come sempre corriamo verso il termine della morte, chè mai per niuna cosa rista questo corso. Dormendo, mangiando, parlando, et in ogni altra cosa, sempre corriamo verso la morte. Così dobiamo noi fare, et faremo se in ogni nostra operatione ci porremo Dio dinanzi; però che allora sempre staremo col suo santo timore. Così sarà lunga et crescerà questa virtù della perseverantia in noi; unde nella fine riceveremo il fructo delle nostre fatighe et la corona della gloria, riposandoci nel termine di vita eterna. In altro modo, no. Et perchè altro modo io non ci veggo, dixi che io desiderava di vedere in voi questa gloriosa virtù della perseverantia, la quale s'acquista, conservasi, et cresce per lo modo che decto abiamo. Voglio adunque che con grande diligentia et sollicitudine v' ingegniate d' acquistare in voi questi modi, acciò che si compi in voi la voluntà di Dio et il desiderio dell' anima mia, perchè cerco la salute vostra quanto la mia propria. Spero nella infinita dolce bontà di Dio, che vi darà gratia di farlo. Altro non vi dico. Permanete nella santa et dolce dilectione di Dio. Jesù dolce, Jesù amore.[1]

VIII

Alla Priora et Monache di Santa Agnesa da Monte Pulciano

Al nome di Jesù Christo crocifixo et di Maria dolce.

Karissime madre et figluole in Christo dolce Jesù: io Katerina, schiava de' servi di Jesù Christo, scrivo a voi nel pretioso sangue suo; con desiderio di vedervi annegate nel sangue dello svenato Agnello, il quale vi mostra l' amore ineffabile del vostro Creatore, che per trarci della servitudine del dimonio ci donò questo Verbo del suo Figluolo, acciò che col mezo della morte ci tollesse la morte et rendesseci la vita della gratia. In questo sangue conciperete amore a l' honore di Dio et alla salute dell' anime, seguitando questo humile Agnello che, per honore del padre et salute nostra et di tucto il mondo, sostenne tante pene, stratii, obrobrii, et villanie, et nell' ultimo la vituperosa morte della Croce. In questo glorioso sangue sarete fortificate; diventarete patienti, che di niuna cosa vi turberete, perchè avrete veduto col lume della fede che Dio non vuole altro che la nostra santificatione, et per questo fine ci dà et permecte ciò che ci dà in questa vita. Et ancora per desiderio che avrete di conformarvi col vostro Sposo, Christo dolce Jesù, unde d' ogni cosa vi rallegrarete, così della tribolatione come della consolatione, et così della sanità come della infermità; però che l' anima che

[1] Casanatense MS. 292. This letter was evidently written from Rome in the latter part of 1379.

è annegata in questo dolce sangue perde in tutto sè, et non cerca tempo nè luogo a modo suo, ma a modo di Dio. Ogni cosa à in debita reverentia, perchè tucto vede che l' è conceduto dal suo Creatore per amore. Niuna cosa le dà pena, se non l' offesa di Dio et la dannatione dell' anime, la qual pena non affligge nè disecca l' anima, anco la 'ngrassa, perchè è fondata nell' affecto della carità. Adunque bene è da inebriarsi di questo pretioso sangue per continua memoria, poi che tanta utilità ne seguita; et a questo v' invito. Godete et exultate, madre et figluole mie dolci in Christo, che ora avete di nuovo ricevuto del sangue di Christo in grande abondantia; però che il santo padre, Papa Urbano sexto, m' à conceduta la indulgentia di colpa et pena nella extremità della morte per tucta cotesta famiglia, cioè, a quelle che non l' anno, et anco m' à conceduto uno certo perdono a cotesto luogo: non è ancora dichiarato quanto nè quando, etc. Destatevi, destatevi, karissime, a ricognoscere sì smisurata largezza di carità, con uno dolce ringratiamento verso la divina Bontà. Guardate che non foste ingrate, per l' amore di Christo crocifixo; ora vi conviene levare da ogni negligentia, et con una sollicitudine et fame exercitarvi all' oratione santa, et studiarvi d' acquistare le vere virtù. Non cessate d' orare con molta vigilia, lagrime et sudori, per la reformatione della dolce Sposa di Christo, la quale vediamo in tanta aversità che già non pare che possa più; et per lo santo padre, il quale è giusto huomo, virile, et zelante de l' honore di Dio. Strignete lo Sposo vostro, che infonda in lui uno lume di gratia, col quale egli confonda la tenebre, divella i vitii, et pianti le virtù. Et per noi pregate, che ci dia gratia di compire la voluntà sua, et che noi diamo la vita per lo suo honore et per amore della verità. Altro non vi dico. Permanete nella santa et dolce dilectione di Dio. Jesù dolce, Jesù amore.[1]

[1] Casanatense MS. 292, which also contains a fuller text of the other letter, 336 (157), addressed to the same prioress and nuns.

BIBLIOGRAPHY

A. PRIMAL SOURCES FOR CATHERINE'S LIFE AND HER WORKS

(1) The Legend.

S. Catharinae Senensis Vita. Auctore Fr. Raimundo Capuano [*Legenda*]. Acta Sanctorum, Aprilis, Tom. III. Antwerp, 1675. New edition, Paris and Rome, 1866.

Legenda dell' amirabile vergine beata Chaterina da Siena suora della penitentia di Santo Domenicho. Printed by Fra Domenico da Pistoia and Fra Piero da Pisa, Florence, at the monastery of San Jacopo di Ripoli, 1477.

La perfecta et consummata hystoria e vita de sancta Catherina Senese virgine admirabile et desponsata da Christo Jesù. Printed by Johannes Antonius de Honate, Milan, 1489.

La Vita della Serafica Sposa di Gesù Cristo S. Caterina da Siena. Translated from the Latin Legend of Fra Raimondo by Bernardino Pecci, as vol. I. of Girolamo Gigli, *L' opere della Serafica Santa Caterina da Siena*, Siena, 1707. Reprinted, Rome, 1866.

(2) The Process.

Processus quorundam dictorum et attestationum super celebritate memoriae ac virtutibus, vita et doctrina beatae Catharinae de Senis. Biblioteca Comunale di Siena, MS. T. i. 3 ; Biblioteca Casanatense (Rome), MS. 2668.

Processus contestationum super sanctitate et doctrina beatae Catharinae de Senis. Edmundus Martène et Ursinus Durand, *Veterum Scriptorum et Monumentorum, etc., Amplissima Collectio.* Tom. vi. Paris, 1729.

(3) The Supplement.

Libellus de Supplemento legendae prolixae Virginis Beatae Catharinae de Senis. By Fra Tommaso Caffarini. Biblioteca Comunale di Siena, MS. T. i. 2 ; Biblioteca Casanatense (Rome), MS. 2360.

Supplemento alla vulgata leggenda di S. Caterina da Siena. Translated from the Latin of Fra Tommaso by P. Ambrogio Ansano Tantucci, as vol. V. of Gigli's edition of the *Opere*, Lucca, 1754. Reprinted, Rome, 1866.[1]

(4) The Minor Legend.

Epitome vitae beatae Caterinae de Senis, per fratrem Thomam eiusdem civitatis et ordinis praedicatorum. In the *Sanctuarium* of Boninus Mombritius, vol. I., Milan, 1479.

La admirabile legenda de la seraphica vergine et del sposo eterno Jesù benigno

[1] The references in the text of the present volume are to the Roman reprint of 1866.

peculiarmente dilecta sposa, Sancta Catherina da Siena. End of fifteenth century; probably Milan. A copy in the British Museum.

Leggenda minore di S. Caterina da Siena e lettere dei suoi discepoli. Edited by F. Grottanelli. Bologna, 1868.

(5) The Letters.

Lettere manoscritte di S. Caterina da Siena e di altri Beati, raccolte dall' abate Luigi de Angelis. Biblioteca Comunale di Siena, MS. T. iii. 3.

Other manuscripts.[1] Rome: Biblioteca Casanatense, MSS. 292 and 2422; Biblioteca Vaticana, *Cod. Vat. Lat.* 939; Biblioteca Nazionale Vittorio Emanuele, MS. 102 (MS. S. Pant. 9). Florence: Biblioteca Nazionale, MSS. Palatini, 56–60; cl. viii. MSS. 1270 and 1380, cl. xxxv. MSS. 187 and 199, cl. xxxviii. MS. 130; Biblioteca Riccardiana, MSS. 1303, 1345, 1678. British Museum: Harleian MS. 3480.

Epistole utili e divote de la beata e seraphica vergine Sancta Chaterina da Siena del sancto ordine de la penitentia de miser sancto Domenico, sposa singulare del salvatore nostro miser Jesù Christo. Printed by Giovanni Jacomo Fontanesi. Bologna, 1492.

Epistole devotissime de Sancta Catharina da Siena. Collected by Fra Bartolomeo da Alzano da Bergamo. Printed by Aldo Manuzio, Venice, 1500.

Epistole et orationi della seraphica vergine santa Catharina da Siena. Venice, Federico Toresano, 1548.

Lettere devotissime della beata vergine santa Caterina da Siena, nuovamente con tutta la diligentia che si ha potuto ristampate. Venice, "al segno della Speranza," 1562.

Lettere etc. [same title]. Venice, Domenico Farri, 1584.

L' Epistole della Serafica Vergine S. Caterina da Siena. With the annotations of Padre Federigo Burlamacchi. Vols. II. and III. of Gigli, *L' opere della Serafica Santa Caterina da Siena.* Lucca, 1721, and Siena, 1713.

Le Lettere di S. Caterina da Siena. Edited by Niccolò Tommaseo. 4 vols. Florence, 1860.

(6) The Dialogue.

Il Libro facto per divina revelacione de la venerabile et admirabile vergine beata Katerina da Siena. Biblioteca Vaticana, *Cod. Barb. Lat.* 4063 (formerly Barberini, xlvi. 5).

Il Libro detto Dialogo della venerabile vergine et sposa di Jesù Cristo, Sancta Caterina da Siena. Biblioteca Riccardiana, MS. 1267.

Libro de la divina providentia composto in vulgare da la seraphica vergine santa Chaterina da Siena. [Bologna, Baldassare Azzoguidi, 1472.]

El libro de la divina doctrina revellata a quella gloriosa et sanctissima vergine sancta Caterina da Siena. Naples, Karl Bonebach, 1478.

[1] This is not intended as a complete list of MSS. of the *Letters*, but simply of those used for the present work. The same applies to the MSS. cited of the *Dialogo*.

BIBLIOGRAPHY

Dialogo de la seraphica virgine sancta Catherina da Siena de la divina providentia. Venice, Matteo Capcasa, 1494.

Dialogus Seraphice ac Dive Catharine de Senis cum nonnullis aliis orationibus. Brescia, Bernardinus de Misintis, 1496.

Dialogo de la seraphica vergine sancta Catharina da Siena, el qual profondissimamente tracta de la divina providentia. Venice, Cesare Arrivabeno, 1517.

D. Catharinae Senensis virginis sanctissimae Dialogi, a D. Raymundo à Vineis Capuano ex Italico in Latinum conversi. Cologne, 1601.

Il Dialogo della Serafica Santa Caterina da Siena, composto in volgare dalla medesima, essendo Lei, mentre dettava ai suoi Scrittori, rapita in singolare eccesso ed astrazione di mente. Vol. IV. of Gigli, *L' opere*, Siena, 1707. Reprinted, Rome, 1866.

B. SELECTED GENERAL BIBLIOGRAPHY

Ammirato, Scipione. *Istorie Fiorentine.* Part I. tom. ii. Florence, 1647.

Anonimo Fiorentino. See *Diario.*

Antoninus, St. *Chronicorum Tertia Pars.* Lyons, 1586.

Baluze, E. *Vitae Paparum Avenionensium.* 2 vols. Paris, 1693.

Bartholomaeus Senensis. *Vita Beati Petri Petroni.* Siena, 1619.

Bartholomaeus Senensis. *De Vita et moribus Beati Stephani Senensis Cartusiani.* Siena, 1626.

Belcari, Feo. *La Vita del Beato Giovanni Colombini da Siena, fondatore dell' ordine de' poveri Giesuati.* Siena, 1541.

Benvenuto da Imola. *Comentum super Dantis Aldigherii Comoediam.* Ed. W. W. Vernon and J. P. Lacaita. 5 vols. Florence, 1887.

Bianco, El. *Laudi spirituali del Bianco da Siena.* Ed. T. Bini. Lucca, 1851.

Boulay (Du), C. E. *Historia Universitatis Parisiensis.* Tom. iv. (1300–1400). Paris, 1668.

Bridget, St. *Revelationes caelestes seraphicae matris S. Birgittae Suecae Sponsae Christi.* Munich, 1680.

Caffarini, Tommaso [and Bartolommeo di Domenico]. *Tractatus super informatione originis et processus ac plenariae approbationis et confirmationis Fratrum et Sororum ordinis de Poenitentia S. Dominici.* And : *Historia disciplinae regularis instauratae in coenobiis Venetis ordinis Praedicatorum.* In Flaminio Cornaro, *Ecclesiae Venetae antiquis monumentis illustratae*, vol. VII. Venice, 1749.

Canestrini, G. *Documenti per servire alla storia della Milizia Italiana dal XIII. secolo al XVI.* (Archivio Storico Italiano, series I., vol. xv.). Florence, 1851.

Capecelatro, Alfonso. *Storia di S. Caterina da Siena e del Papato del suo tempo.* 4th edition. Siena, 1878.

Capponi, Gino (the elder). *Il Tumulto de' Ciompi.* Ed. G. Tortoli. Florence, 1858.

BIBLIOGRAPHY

Capponi, Gino. *Storia della Repubblica di Firenze.* Vols. I. and II. Florence, 1888.

Cardella, L. *Memorie storiche de' Cardinali.* Vol. II. Rome, 1793.

Carpellini, D. C. F. *Gli Assempri di Fra Filippo da Siena.* Siena, 1864.

Chronicles. *Cronica di Bologna*, by Fra Bartolommeo della Pugliola ; *Cronica Sanese*, by Agnolo di Tura and Neri di Donato ; *Cronica di Pisa ;* in Muratori, *Rer. It. Script.*, vols. xviii. and xv., Milan, 1731, 1729. *Cronicon Siculum incerti authoris*, ed. J. de Blasiis (Società Napoletana di Storia Patria), Naples, 1887.

Colombini, Giovanni. See *Lettere.*

Corazzini, G. O. *I Ciompi : cronache e documenti.* Florence, 1887.

Creighton, M. *A History of the Papacy from the Great Schism to the Sack of Rome.* Vol. I. London, 1897.

Denifle, H. S. *Chartularium Universitatis Parisiensis.* Tom. iii. Paris, 1894.

Diario d' Anonimo Fiorentino dall' anno 1358 *al* 1389. Edited by Alessandro Gherardi. (Documenti di Storia Italiana pubblicati a cura della R. Deputazione di Storia Patria per le provincie di Toscana, dell' Umbria, e delle Marche, vol. VI.) Florence, 1876.

Diurnali detti del Duca di Monteleone. Ed. N. F. Faraglia. (Società Napoletana di Storia Patria.) Naples, 1895.

Douglas, R. Langton. *A History of Siena.* London, 1902.

Drane, Augusta Theodosia. *The History of St. Catherine of Siena and her Companions.* 2nd edition. 2 vols. London, 1887.

Ferrero, E. *Di un codice delle Lettere di Santa Caterina da Siena.* (Atti della R. Accademia delle Scienze di Torino, vol. XV.) Turin, 1880.

Flavigny, Comtesse de. *Sainte Brigitte de Suède : sa Vie, ses Révélations et son Œuvre.* Paris, 1892.

Frigerio, Paolo. *Vita di S. Caterina da Siena.* Rome, 1656.

Gayet, Louis. *Le Grand Schisme d'Occident d'après les documents contemporains. Les Origines.* 2 vols. Florence and Berlin, 1889.

Gigli, Girolamo. *Vocabolario Cateriniano.* Lucca, 1760.

Gobelinus Persona. *Cosmodromium, hoc est, Chronicon Universale usque ad annum Christi* 1418. Frankfort, 1599.

Gherardi, Alessandro. *La Guerra dei Fiorentini con Papa Gregorio XI detta la Guerra degli Otto Santi.* Florence, 1868.

Graziani. *Cronaca della città di Perugia dal* 1309 *al* 1491 *nota col nome di Diario del Graziani.* Ed. A. Fabretti. (Arch. Stor. It., Series I., vol. xvi.) Florence, 1850.

Guidini, Cristofano. *Memorie di Ser Cristofano di Galgano Guidini da Siena scritte da lui medesimo nel secolo XIV.* Ed. C. Milanesi. (Arch. Stor. It., Series I., vol. iv.) Florence, 1843.

Heywood, William. *The Ensamples of Fra Filippo. A Study of Mediæval Siena.* Siena, 1901.

BIBLIOGRAPHY

Heywood, William. *Palio and Ponte.* London, 1904.

Landucci, Ambrogio. *Sacra Leccetana Selva.* Rome, 1657.

Lettere del B. Giovanni Colombini da Siena. Ed. A. Bartoli. Lucca, 1856.

Lettere del B. Don Giovanni dalle Celle e d' altri. Ed. P. Bartolommeo Sorio. Rome, 1845.

Lettere dei discepoli di S. Caterina. See A (4).

Lettere di Santi e Beati Fiorentini. Ed. A. M. Biscioni. Florence, 1736.

Lombardelli, Gregorio. *Sommario della disputa a difesa delle Sacre Stimate di Santa Caterina da Siena.* Siena, 1601.

Lugano, Placido M. *Origine e Primordi dell' Ordine di Montoliveto.* Florence, 1903.

Magnan, J. B. *Histoire d'Urbain V et de son siècle.* Paris, 1862.

Maimbourg, L. *Histoire du Grand Schisme d'Occident.* 2 vols. Paris, 1678–80.

Malavolti, Orlando. *Historia de' fatti e guerre de' Sanesi.* Venice, 1599.

Manni, D. M. *Cronichette antiche di vari scrittori del buon secolo della lingua toscana.* Florence, 1733.

Monaldi, Guido. *Diario del Monaldi* (1340–1381). *Istorie Pistolesi.* Prato, 1835.

Monumenta ordinis Fratrum Praedicatorum historica. Ed. Reichert, tom. iv, v, vii, viii. Rome, 1899, 1900, 1904.

Nieheim. *Theoderici de Nyem De Schismate.* Ed. G. Erler. Leipsic, 1890.

Osio, L. *Documenti diplomatici tratti dagli Archivi Milanesi.* Vol. I. Milan, 1864.

Palermo, F. *Rime di Dante e di Giannozzo Sacchetti.* Florence, 1857.

Pardi, Giovanni. *Della Vita e degli Scritti di Giovanni Colombini.* (Bullettino Senese di Storia Patria, Anno II.) Siena, 1895.

Pastor, L. *Geschichte der Päpste im Zeitalter der Renaissance.* 2nd edition. Vol. I. Freiburg im Breisgau, 1891.

Pastor, L. *Acta Inedita Historiam Pontificum Romanorum Illustrantia.* Vol. I. Freiburg im Breisgau, 1904.

Pellini, Pompeo. *Historia di Perugia.* Part I. Venice, 1664.

Petrarca. *Libri et Epistolae Francisci Petrarchae.* Venice, 1501.

Pinus, Joannes. *Divae Catharinae Senensis Vita.* Bologna, 1505.

Professione, A. *Siena e le compagnie di ventura.* Siena, 1898.

Politi, Ambrosio Catarino. *Vita Miracolosa della serafica S. Catherina da Siena.* Venice, 1591.

Raynaldus, O. *Annales ecclesiastici ubi desinit Cardinalis Baronius.* Tom. vii. (1356–1396). Lucca, 1752.

Rodolico, N. *La Democrazia Fiorentina nel suo tramonto* (1378–1382). Bologna, 1905.

Scudder, Vida D. *Saint Catherine of Siena as seen in her Letters.* London, 1905.

BIBLIOGRAPHY

Sercambi, G. *Le Croniche di Giovanni Sercambi Lucchese.* Ed. S. Bongi. Vol. I. Rome, 1892.

Stefani, Marchionne di Coppo. *Istoria Fiorentina.* Ed. F. Ildefonso di San Luigi. Libri VIII–XI. Florence, 1780–1783.

Thorold, Algar. *The Dialogue of the Seraphic Virgin Catherine of Siena.* London, 1896.

Tocco, Felice. *I Fraticelli.* (Arch. Stor. It., Series V., vol. xxxv.) Florence, 1905.

Tromby, B. *Storia del Patriarca S. Brunone e del suo Ordine Cartusiano.* Tom. vii. Naples, 1777.

Valois, Noël. *La France et le Grand Schisme d'Occident.* 4 vols. Paris, 1896–1902.

Villani, Matteo. *Historie Fiorentine.* (Muratori, *Rer. It. Script.*, vol. xiv.) Milan, 1729.

Vincent Ferrer, St. *De Moderno Ecclesiae Schismate: trattato di Vincenzo Ferrer.* Ed. A. Sorbelli. Rome, 1900.

Archivio Segreto della Santa Sede. De Schismate. Arm. LIV, vols. 14–41.

Ibid., Regesta Gregorii XI et Urbani VI.

Formularium Urbani VI, Biblioteca Vaticana, *Cod. Vat. Lat.* 6330.

INDEX

INDEX

INDEX

INDEX

INDEX

28

INDEX

INDEX

INDEX

INDEX

INDEX

INDEX

INDEX

Richard Clay & Sons, Limited, London and Bungay.

Made in the USA
Middletown, DE
29 July 2016